"IF YOU FAIL YOU WILL DIE. GOOD LUCK OR GOOD-BYE."

All I could do was stand and stare at the place where he'd been. *This* was the test, and if I didn't pass it I would die? But what was there in this room to harm me?

That was when I heard the rumble and felt the vibration, and looked around to see that the walls to my left and right had begun to move inward. Each wall had ten feet to cross, and then they would meet in the middle of the room. Panic flared as I looked wildly from one moving wall to the other.

The walls rumbled steadily toward me. A terror screamed at me to *do* something. I put my hands to my mouth to keep from screaming aloud, the words of defeat ringing in my mind: *There's nothing to do! Nothing to do! Nothing to do!*

THE BLENDING
by Sharon Green

THE BLENDING ENTHRONED

CONVERGENCE

Book One of THE BLENDING

SHARON GREEN

An Imprint of HarperCollins*Publishers*

This is a work of fiction. Names, characters, places, and incidents are products of the author's imagination or are used fictitiously and are not to be construed as real. Any resemblance to actual events, locales, organizations, or persons, living or dead, is entirely coincidental.

EOS
An Imprint of HarperCollins*Publishers*
10 East 53rd Street
New York, New York 10022-5299

Copyright © 1996 by Sharon Green
Cover art by Tom Canty
Library of Congress Catalog Card Number: 96-96418
ISBN: 0-380-78414-9
www.eosbooks.com

First Eos printing: February 2000
First AvoNova printing: November 1996

Eos Trademark Reg. U.S. Pat. Off. and in Other Countries, Marca Registrada, Hecho en U.S.A.
HarperCollins® is a trademark of HarperCollins Publishers Inc.

Printed in the U.S.A.

10 9 8 7 6 5

For Ruth Dawn Lewallen—
who made it possible for me to write this
book . . . and to live . . . and to eat . . .

"Friend" is too weak a word; only a real, live
saint could have put up with me for so long,
and I'll never forget you despite your terrible
taste in printers.

HISTORY AND PROPHECY

. . . and so the major error of the past was discovered. In order to have full control of the world around us, there must be a Blending not only of Air, Water, Fire, and Earth, but of Spirit as well. That fifth aspect, so important and yet overlooked for so long, completed the magic necessary for dominance, which in human terms meant rule.

When the first Fivefold Blending, comprised of Elmin Ofgin, Azelin Rays, Widia Almoy, Summia Kamb, and Failin Jarl, came together to defeat the tyrannical Four, our Empire was saved from the dark time of oppression that seemed destined to continue on forever. The Four were each High-level practitioners, and had they Blended with one of Spirit—but they did not, and so met their downfall.

When the Five took their place as the rulers of our Empire, they were first to speak of the Prophecy and then they announced the laws made necessary thereby. Where the Prophecy came from is unclear, but none doubted when it was first spoken of three hundred years ago, and none doubt it today. The Four will attempt to return to reestablish their tyranny, and should we stray from the laws laid down for our protection, they may very well succeed.

For this reason the competitions are held every twenty-five years, and the strongest of the new Blendings takes over our rule and protection for the next quarter century. No Blending is permitted to compete a second time after having won the first, and no Blending may simply be appointed without having competed and won. During each rule comes a crisis, which cannot be bested without the laws having been followed to the letter. What causes these crises to arise is another question which seems without answer, and yet most believe them linked directly to the Prophecy.

The crisis faced by the Second Five . . .

. . . mentioned in the Prophecies. There will be Signs to show that the Chosen Blending has arrived in our midst, but nowhere are the signs detailed. It has been promised that they will spring from all corners of the land, that their might will be seen clearly by all those about them, that they will blend as well in their ordinary lives as they do in the the Blending of their aspects. There will also be "subtle happenings" surrounding them as well as "obvious signs," but many of the more obvious signs are to appear "out of the sight of the Five's enemies." Who those can be is not clear, as the only enemy of the promised, Chosen Five is the Dreaded Four. Therefore . . .

It was the time the Prophecy spoke of, but naturally none of us was aware of it. No one in the whole Empire knew, and if they had, what could they have done about it? But such questions are futile, I'm told, and now isn't the time to dispute that. My purpose is to speak of what happened, as though I had been everywhere at once. I find the idea extremely foolish, but the others insist that only I can do the narrative justice. A more likely guess is that they don't want to be bothered themselves, and so put it onto me.

Well, the choice is made, so I suppose I'd better get on with this great "honor." You must know the people who comprised the two Blendings which came into ultimate conflict not once but twice, but you have no need to meet them all at once. I'll first introduce the members of the Blending I, Tamrissa Domon, became a part of, and the way in which we "happened" to come together. The others will need to wait their turn, until the narrative advances a bit farther. Too bad for them.

We've discovered that the first of our Blending to begin the journey was Lorand Coll, who was born in the aspect of Earth magic. His birthplace was the bucolic environs of Widdertown, located almost atop the western border of the Empire. Widdertown is surrounded by farms and ranches, which supply many of the western duchies with delicacies their own farms are unable to produce. Some of those delicacies have even found their way, suitably protected by preservation methods, to the capitol, but there I get ahead of myself. This is meant to be Lorand's story.

ONE

LORAND COLL—EARTH MAGIC

Lorand stood in the farmyard just at dawn, watching the su rise like the great ball of Fire magic that it was. The rooster had already crowed and the birds were still calling out thei morning welcome, the air was clean and fresh, and life wa beginning anew. Lorand, tall and husky with blond hair an mild brown eyes, could remember a time when the renewa of the day had renewed him as well, but that time no seemed long past.

"Up already, Lorand?" his mother called from the house glancing out at him from behind the mild spell of screenin that kept insects from entering. "Your Pa'll be pleased t'se ya so eager t'start the day's work."

Lorand made no effort to answer her, but that wa perfectly all right. Every time she found him standin outside in the morning she said the very same thing, the continued on her way to begin breakfast. Not once had sh even commented on how often he'd been out there of late doing nothing but staring at the sunrise. Or apparentl staring at the sunrise.

"Out there agin, Lor?" his father's voice came next after moment or two, not as wearily uncaring as his mother's ha been. "Somethin' botherin' you, boy?"

Lorand watched one of the barn cats jump up to fencepost before beginning its bath, the cat being too fastidi ous to sit in the dirt of the yard like lesser animals. In strange way Lorand knew exactly how it felt, and the tim had come to speak to his father about it.

"Pa, have you ever wondered which practitioner of Fir magic was strong enough to create the sun?" he aske without turning. "Or what the world would be like if mos people *couldn't* do magic? How would we live and get thing accomplished?"

Lorand heard his father's heavy footsteps leave the hous

and approach the place where he stood, so he finally turned to look at the older man. Camil Coll wasn't quite as tall as his son, but was just as husky and had the same light hair and dark eyes. He, too, had been born under the aspect of Earth magic, as had the woman he had married. Neither of them were High or even Middle practitioners, which made them suited only for farmwork. Camil's weathered face usually wore an expression of satisfaction that said the condition suited him, a state his second-born son found it impossible to agree with.

"Boy, who created th' sun is somethin' we ain't meant t'know," he told Lorand shortly, making no more effort to speak properly than he ever did. "What th' world would be like if'n most folk couldn't do magic's a foolishness question, an' I ain't got no time f'r fantasy. *You* ain't got th' time neither, since tomorra's when you'll be helpin' y'r brothers an' me Encourage thet field a corn our workers planted last week. Th' day after we'll be Encouragin' the rice bog, but t'day we gotta try our hands at that new crop a fancy furrin beans. Let's us have breakfast, an' then we c'n get started."

His father began to turn back to the house, but Lorand couldn't afford to let the moment pass. He *had* to say what was needed, and he had to say it now.

"Pa, I won't be helping with the beans, because I'm leaving today." His words stopped his father short, so Lorand hurried to get it *all* said. "Last week when I went into Widdertown, the guild man told me that I qualified as a Middle practitioner."

His father hesitated for a long moment, then turned back to him with what the older man obviously thought was a smile.

"You know I don't b'lieve in all thet nonsense, but I ain't too mean t'give ya congratulations," he said, offering a large, blunt-fingered hand. "If'n y'mean t' go back t'town t'celebrate alone, there's no need. Soon's we see t'th' beans, y'r brothers 'n me'll go with ya."

"Pa, I'm not going for a celebration," Lorand said slowly after deliberately taking his father's hand. "I'm going to Gan Garee to test for High practitioner."

"T' th' *capitol?*" his father demanded, his thick fingers closing uncomfortably tight around Lorand's own. "Whut they been tellin' ya, boy? Thet y'all pass th' test real easy?

Thet th' Empire's short a High practitioners, so they'll give ya welcome an' make ya one of 'em? Din't I allus tell ya it don't work thet way? Onct they get ya t' th' capitol ya'll be all alone, easy pickin's fer—"

"For those who take advantage of honest countryfolk," Lorand interrupted wearily, freeing his hand with one sharp pull. "Yes, Pa, you *have* always said that, but what you never said was how you knew it was true. Give me the names of people around here who had that happen to *them,* and I'll ignore the law and go right now and talk to them."

"You sayin' my word alone ain't good enough, boy?" his father returned in a growl, broad face darkening with anger. "Don't give a damn 'bout thet there law. Whut I wanna know is, you really think y'r big 'nough t'say *thet* t'*me?*"

"In other words, there *isn't* anyone around who had that done to them," Lorand answered evenly, refusing to be drawn off into a different argument. "What you've said has been nothing but opinion. I know you love this farm, Pa, but I don't and that's why I'm leaving. Will you wish me good luck?"

The older man stood stiffly, glaring at Lorand as if trying to change his son's mind through sheer willpower. Lorand could feel the vibration of anger-magic rumbling through the ground under his feet, but that wasn't unexpected. Almost automatically, he calmed the rumbling with his own talent. He'd hoped the effort would also calm his father, but that would probably have been beyond even an Adept's ability.

"Never shoulda let ya go t'thet there school," his father growled, and the ground vibrated again with this new subject causing anger-magic. "Shoulda spit on th' law an' kept ya here, an' none a this woulda happened. Filled y'r head with mindless dreams an' barefaced lies, they did, an' you swallered it all right down. Well, if'n y'r thet much of a damn fool, go on, then. Who needs ya here? Get out an' stay out an' don't never come back."

"Pa, I haven't said goodbye to Ma or my brothers," Lorand called after the broad back stomping away from him toward the house. "It will only take a minute or two—"

"Ya don' *have* a Ma 'r brothers no more," his father shouted without stopping. "All y'got's th' clothes on y'r back so get 'em outa here b'fore I claim *them* along with th' rest If'n I paid fer it, I get t' keep it. Now, get off 'n my land!"

And then the door slammed, closing painfully and finally

on the only life Lorand had so far known. Lorand felt as if somebody had taken a stick to his insides, although nothing had happened that hadn't been expected. Camil Coll had never been an understanding man, and didn't take kindly to being balked. And he never changed his mind once he made it up, so there was no sense in standing there hoping that this time it would be different.

Lorand went to the barn and through it, pausing just short of the doors on the far side to reach behind the bales of hay stacked there. He'd worked on the farm for years without more than token—and minimal—payment, so last night he'd packed the clothes and possessions that were his by right of having earned them. He'd hoped the precaution would be unnecessary, but—

"Lor." Lorand turned fast at the sound of his name, but it was only his older brother Mildon. The two of them were very much alike to most people's eyes, but that was only on the outside. Inside they were so different that they barely knew each other.

"Lor, I can't believe you're really going," Mildon said now, his soft, dark eyes deeply troubled. "Pa didn't mean what he said, he was only feeling hurt. He has such big plans for all of us, and now you've disappointed him . . ."

"And what big plans are those, Mil?" Lorand asked bluntly when his brother's voice trailed off the way it usually did. "To be treated like field workers on this farm until he dies? We do exactly as much work as he does, but how much of a share of the profits have *you* gotten? Don't you ever want to marry and have a family and place of your own?"

"But *this* place will be mine, Lor," Mildon answered with an unaccustomed frown. "I know that, and so do you. And as far as a family goes, I'm still too young to need to worry about that."

"Mil, you're almost twenty-five," Lorand said slowly and clearly, for the first time trying to get through to his brother. "Most of the people you went to school with are already married with their families started, and even most of the girls *I* went to school with are spoken for. When are you going to stop repeating what he says, and start thinking for yourself?"

"That's my Pa you're talking about, and yours as well," Mildon pointed out with mild reproof. "He only wants what's best for us, Lor, and he even agrees about the girls I've

been considering. Allia is my first choice, along with Vadra
and maybe even Suso. As soon as I'm ready to take a
wife . . ."

"Mil, wake up!" Lorand interrupted sharply, more upset
than he cared to think about. "Allia was married six months
ago, and Vadra even before that. You never liked Suso and
she couldn't stand *you,* but even she's promised. The only
ones who might be left are Widdertown girls, and most of
them would rather live with their *mothers* than out on a
farm. If you keep listening to *him* you won't ever have a wife
and you'll have *this* place as your own in about forty or fifty
years, when he finally gets around to dying. But if you don't
already know that, you probably never will. Say goodbye to
Ma and the boys for me."

"How can you go anywhere without coin, Lor?" Mildon
asked as Lorand reached behind the bales for the case he'd
packed. His voice was somewhat uneven, as if part of him
wanted to think about what his younger brother had said,
but he obviously still had his orders. "I know you can't have
more than a few coppers, so how do you expect to live? If
you were hoping Pa would help out . . ."

"Tell Pa that's something else he was wrong about,"
Lorand interrupted again, slinging the full leather case under
his left arm. "They don't *charge* you to test for High
practitioner, they pay your way because testing for High is
something all Middles are required to do by law. And they
give you fifty silver dins to live on, which should last a while
even in Gan Garee. If I happen to run short, I can always
hire out to Encourage someone's garden or litter of pets.
There aren't that many who can work with animals, I'm
told . . ."

Lorand let it trail off when Mildon looked away. They
were supposed to have pretended that Mildon had come out
to talk to his younger brother on his own, but that had *never*
happened. Mildon didn't seem capable of doing anything
but echoing their father, reinforcing whatever the eldest Col
said by apparently agreeing with him. Lorand had still been
very young when he'd first understood that, and it was
almost as if the realization had caused Mildon's death. After
that Lorand no longer had an older brother to look up to,
and at times he still felt the pain of that loss.

"Look, Mil . . . let's just say goodbye," Lorand offered
after a long and awkward moment. "If you're comfortable

and happy as you are, I have no business telling you you're wrong. I'd just like you to understand that I can't do it your way, and don't even want to. If I wasn't leaving to test for High, I'd be going for another reason. Take care of yourself."

Mildon hesitated before taking the hand Lorand offered, as though he felt he might be betraying their father by doing it. But he still took the hand, shook it soberly, then turned and walked away. Going back to report, Lorand thought with a sigh as he went on his own way.

The farm road leading to the main road was maintained in good repair, but Lorand felt strange walking it rather than riding. He hadn't walked any real distance since boyhood, not with horses available, but luckily he also hadn't bonded with any of his mounts. He watched the dirt of the road as he scuffed along, knowing it would have been impossible to leave behind a horse that loved him, picturing his father using a charge of horse-stealing to get the horse—and him—back. Or trying to. He'd already bid farewell to the scenes of his childhood, and had the strongest conviction that he'd never be back. He wanted to turn for a final look at the farm, but something kept him from doing even that little. As though some Wild magic had taken over his destiny, and now swept him along before its undeniable strength. . . .

The idea was silly, and Lorand dismissed it with a headshake just as he spotted Hat Riven and his father Phor waiting for him down where the roads met. Phor drove a small farm wagon to take his son Hattial into Widdertown, an act that made Lorand both jealous and angry. Phor Riven didn't want Hat to leave any more than Lorand's father wanted *him* to go, but the elder Riven had insisted on seeing his son off. Why couldn't his own father have been like that . . . ?

Some questions aren't meant to have satisfying answers, and Lorand knew that was one of them. The question might come back to him again and again on dark and lonely nights, but right now it was early morning and people were waiting for him. He picked up his pace a little, suddenly very anxious to be in Widdertown and *really* on his way.

"Morning, Lor," Hat called as soon as Lorand got close enough. "Looks like we got the nice day we were hoping for."

"Sure does, Hat," Lorand agreed. "Morning, Mr. Riven. I really appreciate your stopping for me like this."

"Won't mince words, Lorand," Phor Riven answered, his long, thin face cold with disapproval. "No man enjoys seein' his son go off on his own, not with th' world bein' the way it is. But a real man sees that son off with love an' support, lettin' him know he'll be missed. One who don't ain't worth thinkin' about, not by others and not even by his blood. You climb on up here, and we'll get along t' town."

Lorand nodded and put his case in the wagon, then climbed up to the seat. Hat looked almost as angry as his father, and Lorand felt warmed—but also bleak. Sometimes it helps to think you might be wrong, that there might be reasons for someone doing something painful that you just haven't seen. Now . . .

The ride into Widdertown was silent, and by the time they got there things had already begun to come awake. People stood outside of the shops sweeping their brand new wooden walks, proud that the growth of the town now demanded such big city additions. There was talk of cobblestoning the main streets to make them more passable during the spring rains, but so far it was no more than just talk. Laying the stones would require the hiring of strong Middle practitioners of Earth magic, and probably even the services of a Middle in Spirit magic to smooth it all out. The town wasn't quite ready for an expense like that, but one day . . .

"They could have had *us* laying the stones for next to nothing," Hat murmured to Lorand, obviously thinking along the same lines. "By the time they get around to realizing that, we'll be Highs and beyond menial jobs like that."

"And since we're the only two in the district who even came close to qualifying for Middle, they won't have local talent when they do make up their minds," Lorand agreed. "Some of the younger kids might strengthen as they get older, but there's no way of knowing it now. I wonder how much bigger Gan Garee is than Widdertown?"

"Probably twice or three times the size," Hat answered with a dismissive shrug. "Not that I really care. It's the positions available that I care about, and that's what I mean to check on first. As soon as I pass the test for High, of course."

Lorand nodded and let the subject drop, preferring not to think about Hat's chances of passing the tests for High.

Master Lugal, the district representative of the Guild of Magical Aspects, had let slip that he considered Hat a strong Middle talent, but didn't believe Hat would qualify for High. He'd certainly told Hat the same thing, but Hat tended to dismiss anything he didn't care to hear. Lorand ran a hand through his hair against the beginning discomfort of the day's heat, wondering if Hat might not have the right of it. Make up your mind to do something and then go after it, wasting no time at all on doubts and worries. Being like that would make life a lot more pleasant.

"Master Lugal ain't here yet," Phor Riven observed as he guided his team closer to the Guild building and then pulled them to a halt. "Th' man tends to keep big city hours, but I 'spose he'll be along in a little while. Hat, you take care and don't let 'em fox you none. Lorand, good luck to you, boy. Time for me t'be gettin' back to th' farm."

Phor solemnly shook hands with his son and Lorand, waited until the two of them had climbed down and gotten their cases from the wagon, then turned the team and headed back the way they'd come. Hat looked ready to wave if his father happened to look around one last time, but Phor never did. The wagon moved along the street until it disappeared, and then Hat sighed.

"I wish he'd done this because he really wanted to," he muttered, still staring in the direction the wagon had gone off in. "He told you what he believes, that it's a man's duty to see his sons off, so he did his duty. I still don't know if he'll really miss me, or just resent the fact that I'm gone."

"Well, at least I don't have to wonder about *that*," Lorand said with his own sigh. "I hadn't thought knowing it would be a benefit, but I guess it is. And I hope Master Lugal shows up soon. The coach to Hemson Crossing will be getting in in less than an hour."

Hat glanced up at the sun to confirm that, then shifted his case to his other arm. Hat's case looked heavier than Lorand's with more things packed into it, but that was only to be expected. Hat had been given regular wages for the work he did on his father's farm, while Lorand—

"What in the name of Chaos is *that?*" Hat demanded just as Lorand began to feel the tingle that meant magic was being worked. "If this is somebody's idea of a joke—"

By then Lorand was staring at the wide ball of flames

rolling at them, clearly the work of someone with Fire affinity. Joke or not, that fireball was coming *fast,* and there was no guarantee it would stop just short of them. Lorand shoved Hat one way and dived the other way himself, preferring to look foolish to standing there and being burned. He hit the ground and rolled, half expecting to hear the laughter of whoever had sent the fireball, but there *was* no laughter. Nothing but the fireball speeding through the place he and Hat had just been standing—and slowing to come around for another pass.

Shouts came from all around, but Lorand paid no attention to them. He felt blistered from the heat that had passed so close to him, and now the thing was coming back to try again. Most people with Fire affinity could light a lamp or a stove without much effort, but something like that ball—! Someone with *strength* had formed and sent it, and only strength would stop it—if he could just manage to do it right.

Lorand climbed to his feet just as Hat did the same and started to come close, but he waved Hat back and jumped out of the way again. The fireball roared by a second time, almost acting annoyed, and now it was moving even faster. If he didn't do something just as fast, it would soon be too late to do anything but burn. Blocking out fear as well as the distraction of shouting people, Lorand reached for his Earth magic.

Touching it was more than effortless now. For the last few years magic had stopped being something he could do and had started to be something that was part of him. Time slowed almost to a stop as he and the magic glowed together, one entity greater than the sum of its two parts. It was right and it was wonderful, but above all it was powerful—especially when under attack.

The large and hungry fireball roiled toward him, flames eager to consume everything there was. Lorand raised his arms and extended his fingers, fingers made *much* longer by the magic he had merged with, and thrust into the dirt of the street. Earth, everything of the earth, was his to employ, and the packed earth of the street leaped to comply with his desires. The dirt formed a whirlwind that spun around the fireball, surrounding it more and more until there was more earth than fire.

And then the earth began to close in on the fireball, merging with the flames while giving them nothing to burn. After a moment or two of that swirling, the fireball was denied air. Earth needed no air to survive but fire did, and that was the beginning of the end. The fire struggled and fought, striving to the end to reach living flesh. It died reluctantly but completely, and Lorand's "fingers" held the earth around it for another minute just to be certain. Not a single spark could be left, else the fireball would come alive again from that seed alone.

When it was finally over and Lorand withdrew, the first thing he did was take a deep breath. The air smelled of sifted earth and burning, and was filled with the shouts and exclamations of onlookers. But none of that disturbed Lorand as much as how hard it had been to sever himself from the magic. The stronger he got, the harder it grew, as though he were an adult constantly being forced to return to the life of a child. No one had ever mentioned that happening to *them,* but Lorand knew the time approached when he would have to speak about it to *someone. . . .*

"Lorand, Hattial, what's going on here?" a voice shouted, and Lorand looked up to see Master Lugal hurrying toward them. Right behind him came Jeris Womal, the town's resident Water talent, which finally let everyone relax completely.

"Somebody has a really bad sense of humor, Master Lugal," Hat complained to the Guild man, his voice still shaky. "We were standing here waiting for you, and suddenly that *thing* attacked us! If we hadn't been able to fight back it would have gotten us, so you'd better find out who's responsible real fast. If they try it again with those who *can't* fight back . . ."

Hat suddenly seemed to realize he was babbling and let the words trail off, but no one standing around laughed and pointed at him. Being attacked by magic like that was no laughing matter, but it *was* highly unusual. And Lorand saw no reason to correct Hat's use of the word "we." If Hat had tried to use his own magic Lorand would have felt it, so Hat had just let Lorand take care of them both. It made no real difference what other people thought; only he and Hat had to know the truth, and as long as they did there was no reason to speak of it.

"I should think a Fire talent with that much strength would already be on his or her way to the capitol," Lorand said just to change the subject, making sure the words could be taken only as an observation, not as a criticism. "Is it possible to hide that kind of strength?"

"I don't know exactly how much you're talking about, but offhand I'd say no," Master Lugal answered with a frown. He was a tall, spare man with thinning brown hair and very dark eyes that never gave his thoughts away. He always wore the tight breeches and colorful, wide-sleeved shirts popular in the capitol, and had told Lorand he would have to trade in his loose trousers and drab cotton shirts when he got there, else everyone would know him for a hayseed. He also wasn't quite as large as Lorand, and now looked up at him soberly.

"There hasn't been anyone with a strong Fire talent around here in twenty years," Master Lugal continued, still looking disturbed. "I'll need a little help to do a proper Search, but as soon as I get you two on that coach I intend to get started with it. Get your cases and we'll go."

That last was directed to Hat as well as to Lorand, and they both lost no time in complying. The coach would be there very soon, and only the suddenly building excitement over where they were actually starting to go kept Lorand from being disappointed over having to miss the coming Search. He had never seen those like Master Lugal—rare individuals who had a touch of all five of the talents, rather than just one—spread their senses out to locate a strong talent they'd somehow overlooked. Master Lugal couldn't *use* any of the five aspects, but he was able to locate those who could.

The coach to Hemson Crossing was coming up the street by the time they reached the depot, but Master Lugal had already bought their tickets.

"Now, don't forget," he told Lorand and Hat as he handed over those tickets. "Your fare is paid all the way to Gan Garee, but if you lose these tickets you'll have to walk—or dip into the silver in these pouches. If you do dip into the silver for anything but *modest* meals along the way, you won't enjoy your time in the capitol. The prices of *everything* there are sky high, even tiny attic rooms in falling-down hostels. Food is even worse, so don't forget what I told you to do."

Hat nodded dutifully as he put the pouch of silver in his shirt, but Lorand had the feeling his friend had dismissed all warnings of danger. Lorand put away his own pouch, but later he would distribute the silver into little pockets he'd painstakingly sewn into his clothing. It had been hard keeping the stitches from showing, briefly making him wish men wore dresses and petticoats like women. But he'd finally managed to do it right, swearing to himself that he would *not* get to the capitol penniless.

"Well, here it is," Master Lugal said as the coach pulled up, only a single passenger already inside. "Have a good trip, and best of luck with the tests."

He shook hands with each of them, watched them climb into the coach, then waved until he was out of sight. Actually having someone wave goodbye made Lorand feel considerably better, but not so much so that he could ignore the jouncing of the coach.

"By the time we get to Gan Garee our teeth will be loose," Hat grumbled, shifting around on the hard seat. "I never realized these coaches were worse than farm wagons."

"That's because you've never been in one," Lorand pointed out, then gestured to the third passenger. "But it has to be possible to get used to the bouncing, otherwise he wouldn't be asleep."

"He's probably just as tired as we'll be before the week is out," Hat answered, looking out the window on his side. "But I don't intend to be tired once we actually get to Gan Garee. I've heard you can find willing females on just about every street corner, and that's the *first* thing I'll be looking for."

Lorand smiled, but didn't comment on his own viewpoint. Girls were fine and he'd enjoyed the few private times he'd had with them, but right now he had no interest in women at all. The tests he would face were most important, and after that the position he would find. His father had turned his back on him, and one day he would show that man just how wrong he had been. He would come back to visit Master Lugal and say a proper goodbye to his mother, and then *he* would turn his back on his father.

But first he had to make something of himself, and he *would* . . . he *would*. . . .

Concerning Book One of the Blending

Well, that didn't go too badly. I think I showed you most of Lorand, at least as he was before he met the rest of us. It was hard to stay out of the story, but I did it because it isn't my turn yet. I expect my turn will turn out to be the best, so to speak, but that's only to be—expected. Hah! I do enjoy playing with words, but it's time to move on. Now you have to meet Jovvi Hafford.

TWO

JOVVI HAFFORD—SPIRIT MAGIC

"Do you promise, Jovvi?" Eldra Sappin begged while Jovvi checked her appearance in the mirror. "Will you really send for me once you've established yourself in the capitol?"

"Of course I will, Eldra," Jovvi answered smoothly, having her reflection send a reassuring smile. Her voice was usually like a warm caress and her smile was said to light up entire buildings, but those things were normally saved for the men. As the most celebrated courtesan in Rincammon and perhaps all the North, Jovvi had a certain image to maintain. And it never paid to make enemies where it was possible to make friends instead. "But don't forget it will take some time before I'm established," she added.

"Nonsense," Eldra came immediately to her defense, bristling with indignation. "Even those people in the capitol will have heard of you, and they may be rich but they aren't entirely stupid. They'll come calling as soon as you've opened your residence, and a week later you'll be everyone's darling, just as you are here."

"You may be overestimating my ability just the least little bit," Jovvi replied with the part of her laugh she couldn't manage to swallow. "Or at least my capacity, to have me known by everyone in just one week. And don't forget I have those wretched tests to take first, but hopefully I'll fail. And you can be certain I'll be more careful in choosing my patrons from now on."

"An excellent decision," another voice said before Eldra could comment. "A pity it wasn't made soon enough to be of real value. Eldra, dear, will you excuse us, please? I'd like to say my own goodbye to Jovvi."

"Of course, Allestine," Eldra said with a small curtsey, then wiggled her fingers at Jovvi before leaving. She would certainly be there to see Jovvi off, so final goodbyes were still ahead.

Jovvi turned from the mirror, and briefly examined Allestine while Eldra crossed the large room to close the door behind herself. Allestine was no longer young, but neither was she old. Her face was unlined beneath the tasteful touch of makeup she customarily wore, her figure was almost as good as it had ever been, and her dark brown hair was elegantly put up without a single lock or wisp out of place. And yet it was somehow perfectly clear that Allestine was no longer an active courtesan.

For a moment Jovvi thought it might be the demure day gown Allestine wore, a lovely fawn with tiny black embroideries, but that wasn't it. Jovvi herself wore a modest traveling suit of burnt orange with a snow-white blouse under the jacket and no full petticoats to waste limited coach space, but to her own eye there wasn't the least doubt of her station in life. Her golden-blond hair was also put up for traveling, but her blue-green eyes sent the same message they always did. It should be interesting to see what did happen in the capitol.

"Possibly *I* should have known rather than you, but that's no excuse for what happened," Allestine continued stiffly once the door had been closed and they were alone. "If you had warned me, I would have been able to take steps to avoid the situation entirely."

"How could I have warned you when I didn't know myself?" Jovvi countered, unimpressed with Allestine's sharp annoyance. "What do *I* know about talents and aspects and such? I still don't really understand what happened, or why I'm suddenly being sent to Gan Garee."

"There happens to be a law that says all Middle practitioners of magic—in any of the five aspects—have to go to Gan Garee to test for the position of High practitioner." Allestine's annoyance had grown rather than lessened, so she took a chair in an obvious effort to calm herself. "You happen to qualify as a Middle in the aspect of Spirit, something that Guild man discovered not long after he joined you in your suite. If I'd had any idea, I never would have given him that appointment with you."

"But how can I qualify as anything at all when I never *tried* to qualify?" Jovvi pressed as she took a chair of her own, needing the answer. The last few years had gone exactly according to her plans, but now it was clearly time for new plans. "And that man never did anything every other man doesn't do, so how did *he* know when no one else did?"

"He's a freak," Allestine said flatly with heavy disapproval. "I asked around afterwards, and found that out. Normal people are born with more or less talent in a single aspect, like mine with fire."

She turned very slightly to point at the fireplace, and flames obediently leaped high among the logs set in place against the cool of the evening. Then she made a small gesture of dismissal, and the flames disappeared again.

"Anyone born with Fire magic can do *that*, but the really talented can handle a hundred times more than I can," Allestine continued. "That goes for the other four talents as well, but freaks aren't like the rest of us. *They're* born with something of all five talents inside them, only they can't use any of the five. All they can do is tell when someone else is using one, and they're taught to recognize the level of strength. I was told that your extreme popularity among our patrons stems from the use of a very strong talent in the area of Spirit magic."

"And that's why my appointments always end so satisfyingly for my patrons?" Jovvi asked, brows high. "I would have considered body a good deal more important than spirit."

"You still don't understand," Allestine complained, her annoyance rising again. "I've heard it said that no Blending can be complete without the aspect of Spirit magic, since that's the talent that brings the other four together, makes them a unified whole, and smooths their efforts into successful completion. Without Spirit the other aspects fight each other for independence and dominance, and even when they deliberately work together there's still a whisper of disharmony present. Spirit magic quiets that whisper."

"I see," Jovvi commented, which was in part a lie. She now understood how important people considered her talent to be, but not what they expected to get out of her in particular. She knew nothing about Blendings, and that suited her perfectly. There were enough other things she did know about, like where *she* intended her life to go.

"So now we need to discuss how quickly you'll be back here," Allestine went on, the look in her eyes having sharpened. "The law may demand that you go and take the tests, but most don't come within a prayer of passing. Once your duty to the Empire is done, I'll expect you to return to me on the first available coach."

"You'd better explain that particular fact of life to Eldra," Jovvi said with an easy laugh, certain Allestine had overheard her conversation with the girl. "She expects me to stay in Gan Garee, set up on my own, and then send for her. She seems to have no idea how much gold it takes to even begin a project like that, so rather than explain I simply agreed with her. Allestine . . . you don't think I'll be gone so long that my patrons forget me? I mean, if I had to start all over, I'd simply cry . . ."

"No, dear, don't you worry about that," Allestine replied with a satisfied, assuring smile, leaving her chair to come and pat Jovvi's shoulder. "The testing shouldn't take long at all, so your patrons will probably meet your coach when you get back. You're not quite the most famous courtesan around here yet, but with my help that position will be yours in only another few years."

Jovvi stood so they might touch cheeks in farewell, and then Allestine left. Once she was gone Jovvi turned to the mirror again, but only to check her expression—which was still as innocent and sweet and guileless as she'd wanted it to be. Allestine had been her sponsor for three years, and fully intended to benefit from that position until Jovvi was too *old* to go off on her own. Not quite the most famous courtesan indeed! Her name was known for leagues beyond Rincammon, farther even than Allestine's name had been known. She'd be a fool to come back here from Gan Garee, and whatever else she might be, Jovvi was no fool.

She turned away from the mirror, having already mad
certain that the gold distributed in small pockets all over he
traveling outfit showed not at all. In the past three years she'
put together a good-sized nest egg, lavishly spending only
tiny portion of what loving and grateful patrons had give
her as gifts in addition to her fees. In the beginning Allestin
had tried to make her share those gifts, but she'd complaine
that she had to have *something* to spend, and then ha
supposedly thrown away every copper on frivolities. Tha
had satisfied Allestine, since the older woman made quit
enough arranging Jovvi's appointments.

"And what she really wanted was for me to be pennile
aside from the funds that are supposed to be put away fo
me," Jovvi murmured as she checked her trunk one las
time. "That way I'd *have* to stay with her, rather than findin
a place to set up on my own."

Leaving to do that would have been difficult, but now th
fates had accomplished what she'd only dreamed about. Sh
had a reason to leave that Allestine couldn't argue agains
and returning to Rincammon was out of the question. I
Gan Garee she would be unknown, but not for long. He
gold would rent her a house in the best district, and short
thereafter her patrons would supply her with enough to *buy*
house. And all the while Allestine would be picturing he
worrying about her position and patrons in Rincammon . .

Jovvi chuckled as she finished the last of her preparation
then called for the serving men to carry her trunk dow
stairs. She hated having to abandon the rest of her wardrob
and possessions, but her favorite things were going with he
and the rest could be replaced. *Would* be replaced, and wit
the newest styles as soon as they became popular. Tha
would be another benefit in living in the capitol.

Downstairs, everyone in the residence waited to sa
goodbye, even those girls who hated and envied Jovv
Allestine's handiwork, Jovvi thought as she exchanged care
ful hugs with those who really were sorry to see her go. Th
residence was the closest thing to a real home that Jovvi ha
ever known, and Allestine wanted her to remember that an
miss everyone. Well, she *would* miss some of the girls, bu
certainly not enough to come back to *that* place.

"Remember your promise!" Eldra whispered intense
when they hugged, and Jovvi gave her a reassuring pat befor

gently freeing herself. She certainly would remember her promise, even though there would be no way to keep it. Eldra was only fourteen and was used to run and fetch for the working courtesans, but she was already a beauty and Allestine had had offers for her from some of the wealthier patrons. As soon as Eldra turned fifteen she would begin the life of a courtesan whether she wished to or not, and Allestine would make a fortune. Believing that their sponsor would let her go just showed how innocent Eldra still was.

"All right, ladies, back to what you were doing," Allestine called with a clap of her hands. "Jovvi must leave now, or she'll miss the coach."

Everyone drew back at the order, freeing Jovvi to leave, which she did with as realistic an air of regret as she could manage. She made sure to keep glancing at Allestine, and once she had been assisted into the carriage carrying her trunk, she looked at the older woman who had come out onto the porch of the residence.

"Allestine, aren't you coming to the coach depot?" she asked in a frightened voice. "I was certain you would come with me . . ."

"Now, Jovvi, you're a big girl and I have things to attend to here," Allestine answered comfortably with a sleek smile when Jovvi's words trailed off. "I can't come with you now, but I'll certainly be there when you get back. All you have to do is write first, and you'll find me waiting. You'll like that, won't you?"

"Yes, of course, I certainly will," Jovvi murmured, pretending to hide the defeat and fear she had produced for Allestine's benefit. "I'll see you then . . . and I'm sure you won't forget me . . . will you?"

Allestine simply smiled, then stood waving a moment as the carriage began to move away from the residence. After the moment Allestine turned and went inside, but Jovvi sat turned and watching the residence until it was out of sight. Only then did she face forward, but still kept her expression under tight control. She would not be truly free until Rincammon was far behind her. Rincammon and Allestine's servants.

Two of those servants sat on the driver's seat, two men called Ark and Bar, who had worked for Allestine even longer than Jovvi had been at the residence. Now and then girls had been silly enough to say the wrong thing in front of one of them, and then had found out it wasn't possible to bribe them into silence. It had been suggested that the two were in love with Allestine and that was why it wasn't possible to reach them, but Jovvi couldn't believe it. That sort of love was a myth, not something that actually happened to people. In fact *all* love was a myth, and the wise courtesan simply used that myth to her advantage.

The residence, being in the middle of town, wasn't far from the depot, and Jovvi spent the ride pretending to be upset and miserable. The relaxed way in which Ark and Bar ignored her said her act was probably working, but there was no sense in taking chances.

When the carriage stopped at the depot, she simply sat there until her trunk was on the walk and Bar came to offer a hand. Then she hesitated for the briefest moment before accepting his help, as though reluctant to leave her last tie with the residence. Bar showed no expression at all, but Ark's faint smile told of his amusement and satisfaction. This one will be back, she could almost see him thinking, no need to worry about *her*.

But that didn't mean she was rid of them yet. Ark moved the carriage to a place around the corner from the depot and out of the way, then came back to join Bar in waiting with her. That Guild man was supposed to meet her there with her coach tickets to Gan Garee and fifty silver dins in coin, and then they would all see her safely onto the coach. Allestine didn't want her bothered by casual admirers before she left, so her two servants would stay to make sure of it.

It was a cool and comfortable morning, really pretty, but Jovvi was in no state of mind to appreciate it. In a matter of minutes impatience arose to demand where that Guild man could be, and a hint of fear followed over the possibility of the coach arriving before he did. If that happened she'd have to go back to the residence to wait until the next coach came in tomorrow, and that would be intolerable. It would give Allestine the chance to learn of her plans and ruin them, and the thought of that was more than intolerable. She simply couldn't—

At that point Jovvi noticed the shouts and screams suddenly coming from the people around them, which made her abandon her frantic thoughts to look up. At first there didn't seem to be a reason for the hysteria, but then Jovvi noticed the giant fireball rolling toward her. It was just beginning to pick up speed, and the people jumping and diving out of its way were the ones who were screaming. Bar's hand came briefly to her arm, as though he meant to pull her out of harm's way, then he changed his mind. The way that thing was picking up speed, she'd never be able to move fast enough.

Real, true fear wrapped itself around Jovvi, the sort she'd grown all too familiar with while growing up. The world had been her enemy and tormentor, and it hadn't been possible to avoid that world for long. So she'd learned to . . . *handle* it instead, in a way she still didn't fully understand. But she could do it without understanding it, even while frozen still with terror.

Bar and Ark had run to save themselves, but Jovvi paid no attention to their scrambling escape. All her attention was on the ball of fire, so very much more than the few sparks Allestine had produced. The thing stood as tall as Allestine did, which meant taller and wider than Jovvi. Small spurts of dust came from between the cobblestones of the street, and tiny streams of water rose from the nearest horse trough. Some of the onlookers were trying to fight the fireball with Earth and Water magic, then, but weren't able to affect it in any way that mattered.

So that left Jovvi to take care of herself, just the way she'd always had to. She gathered her inner strength in mental fingers then threw it out, making sure it spread as it went, aiming it at the fireball the way she usually aimed it at men. The fireball was almost close enough for her to feel its crackling heat, but when the leading edge of it met the strength she'd spread, it stopped dead in its advance. Its flames ravened against her invisible wall, trying to consume it, but it wasn't that kind of wall.

It was, however, a wall that did more than just stand there. Every lick of flame that touched it was . . . gentled and quieted, a state that fire couldn't bear. Even the smallest and most pleasant fire needs to rage and consume, otherwise it becomes something else. As soon as the edges of the fireball began to become something else, Jovvi's wall moved forward and spread around the rest of the fire like a blanket. Peace and quiet turned fire to ash just as it changed a patron's rougher intentions to concern, and the fireball was no more able to resist her than men were. She smoothed the furious ravening until it flickered in hesitation, then completely died out.

People were still screaming and shouting, but Jovvi knew it was all over, so she let herself begin to tremble with reaction. It had been so horribly frightening that she didn't know why she hadn't fainted, but she certainly knew she couldn't afford to faint *now*. It would probably mean being taken back to the residence, and that was out. An arm suddenly came around her shoulders and helped to keep her on her feet, then it began to urge her toward the bench in front of the depot. Going back to the residence was out, but sitting down might be a very good idea.

The arm helping her was attached to a man, Jovvi knew, but it wasn't until she'd settled on the bench that she discovered the man wasn't Bar or Ark. It was that Guild man she'd entertained, finally there and looking terribly concerned.

"What happened here?" he demanded, but gently in an obvious effort to keep from upsetting her even more. "When I turned the corner a minute ago, I thought the entire world had gone mad. And *you* look as pale as a ghost. What's going on?"

"A ball of fire appeared out of nowhere," Jovvi answered while fighting to pull herself together. "It came right for me but at the last instant something stopped it. Someone must have used stronger magic, but that doesn't explain why it was here to begin with."

"Someone's twisted idea of a joke?" the Guild man suggested, sounding as though he couldn't even make *himself* believe that one. "And you say someone stopped it with magic? What kind of magic, and who was it?"

"You're asking *me?*" Jovvi countered unsteadily, one gloved hand trying not to shake as it checked the position of her hat. "You're supposed to be the expert in this field, sir. Maybe you can tell *me*."

The Guild man, whose name Jovvi couldn't quite remember, didn't respond, but an odd look in his eye aroused her suspicions. That fire thing could have been a test aimed at *her*, something to confirm his decision to send her to the capitol. It made sense, but he'd never be able to admit it, no after all the trouble that fireball had caused. Some of the women on the street *had* fainted, and one or two of the men looked as though they'd come close to doing the same. Using magic so recklessly was against the law, and if anyone found out that the Guild man was behind it, he'd be in it up to his ears.

"Well, all that counts right now is that you're safe," he said after a brief hesitation, showing her a deliberate smile. "And I believe I hear the coach coming, so let me give you your tickets and pouch of silver. Watch them both very carefully, and your trip to the capitol will be a pleasant one. I've arranged to have the coach guards watch over you, so if anyone tries to bother you along the way, tell one of the guards and they'll take care of it."

"Thank you, sir," Jovvi said, putting the pouch of silver into her purse first. The coach *was* coming, and that made her heart beat even faster than the fireball had. In a matter of minutes she would be on her way, and *without* the company of one of Allestine's people to watch her. She'd been afraid that either Ark or Bar would be sent with her, but no one traveled without at least one change of clothing and the carriage had held nothing but her trunk. She would soon be *free* . . .

. . . and she was willing to do anything she had to to keep it like that.

Well, that wasn't quite as good as Lorand's introduction, but it should do for firsts. We all got to know each other a lot better later on, but at this point we hadn't even met. I sometimes wonder how things would have gone if it hadn't been for . . . No, that should come later. The hardest part of this task will be to decide on what to tell you when, but so far it's still relatively easy. The next of us you need to meet is Rion Mardimil, who still tends to put on airs.

THREE

CLARION MARDIMIL—AIR MAGIC

"But it *can't* be raining," Clarion said very reasonably to the fool servant, striving valiantly to hold his temper. "I can't possibly put the trip off any longer, and I was assured that today would be a nice day. Even here in the East, very few people consider rain to be part of a nice day."

"Nevertheless, Lord Clarion, it does happen to be raining," the nasty servant replied, his bland expression certainly hiding the pleasure he undoubtedly felt over contradicting his betters. "And the time grows short for when you must leave."

"I intend to speak to my mother about this," Clarion announced, then took his hat from the table. "We'll soon see, my man, we'll just see."

The servant bowed without saying anything else, predictably ruining Clarion's chance to laugh by refusing to ask what they'd see *about*. All the servants in the house were the same, vile creatures who refused to stay quietly in their proper places. Mother never hesitated to dismiss the worst ones, but that left so many of the peasants still there to bedevil him. . . .

Clarion brushed gently at his suit as he made his way to his mother's apartments, a suit he was very pleased with. Pale yellow silk trimmed with tiny amounts of black and orange, it was the height of current fashion in the capitol. The tailor had told him how nicely it went with his blond hair, how tall and broad-shouldered he looked in it, and that he would have to fight the ladies off.

Clarion hadn't said so, but for some foolish reason the ladies never had seemed interested—at least not here. At Court it was a different story, and if Mother hadn't been there a time or two . . . Clarion sighed and realized he hadn't been to Court in almost a year, but he still kept in touch with the important things like clothing styles. And he would have been delighted to see Gan Garee again—if not for the circumstances.

One of his mother's maids answered his knock, and he was shown directly to her bedchamber. She'd taken to her bed when word came through that she was absolutely forbidden to accompany Clarion, a decision that came directly from the Court. She'd laughed at the Guild man when he'd first told her that candidates for High were required to appear alone. She'd countered that the laws were for the masses to worry about, not people in *their* position, and she would travel with her son just as she had for his entire life. The Guild man hadn't argued, at least not with *her* . . .

"Oh, Clarion, the tragedy of it all!" she wailed as soon as she saw him, raising one hand for him to take. "It's unlikely that I will survive this, but you mustn't concern yourself with thoughts of *me*. Go and take their foolish little tests while life ebbs slowly from my body, and I will simply pray that you find it possible to return before the very last spark is extinguished. I'll try to hold on, really I will, just for *your* sake . . ."

She let her words trail off with a sigh, as though her meager strength had failed her. Clarion, as alarmed as ever he had been, held her hand more tightly.

"No, Mother, don't speak like that," he coaxed, brushing back a stray wisp of hair from her smooth, alabaster brow. "You'll be just fine, and I'll be back before you know it. Public transportation may be terribly rough and uncomfortable, but it does have the benefit of being much faster than a private coach. They change horses and drivers at regular intervals, I'm told, so if you sleep during the journey and stop only to eat during the changeovers, it's possible to get to Gan Garee in much less than the usual two or three weeks."

"Oh, my poor baby!" she exclaimed, her lovely face filled with pity. "Needing to use *public* coaches because *they* insist! But *you* must insist on being tested immediately, so you can start home again as soon as it's done. I'll never forgive myself for causing this horror, never!"

"Now, Mother, there was no way you could have known," Clarion soothed, patting the hand he held. "Lord Astrath was brought to your party by someone else, and he *is* a legitimate member of the lesser nobility. No one had any idea that he's also a Guild man without any proper sense of class distinction, but now *we* know. Once this is all over, we'll certainly have to speak to one or two members of the Blending. After all, they *are* the rulers of this Empire, so they should have *some* say in how it's run."

"My sweet baby, how delightfully strong you are," his mother said with a faint, amused smile. "And yes, darling, the Blending does need to be told how terrible it was for us that one of them supported that dreadful Lord Astrath. As soon as you're home I'll try valiantly to regain my strength, and if I succeed then *I'll* have a word with the Blending. I won't have you putting yourself out, not when that's what *I'm* here for. Call one of my ladies, dear, and tell her we'd like a bite of brunch to share, just you and I."

"If you insist, Mother," Clarion agreed smoothly, remembering the rain outside. "I *am* supposed to be leaving to catch that coach, but one more day more or less shouldn't—"

"Rot them!" his mother snapped, suddenly looking a good deal less delicate as she sat up. "This is the last day you were allowed, so you *must* go now, or—Rot them! They won't get away with this, you have my word, Clarion! I *will* find out who is behind this outrage, and when I do . . . ! Kiss me goodbye, darling, and then be on your way."

Clarion was disappointed, but he'd learned years ago not to disagree with his mother when she got into this kind of mood. Obediently he kissed her cheek, then glumly made his way out of her apartment. For a moment he wondered what she could possibly have been threatened with, to make her follow their schedule so scrupulously. It had to be something really extreme, and on second thought he might be better off *not* knowing. He knew his mother well enough to be certain there would be trouble once the testing was done, and no one in his right mind could want to be in the middle of *that*.

"Your trunk has already been taken down to the carriage, Lord Clarion," that same miserable servant told him as soon as he stepped out into the hall. "The staff wishes you a pleasant journey and much success."

Clarion paused to put his hat on, pearl gray with a band matching his suit, rolled brim, medium-high crown, and only one modest feather in yellow. While he adjusted the hat he ignored the servant, the man and the supposed good wishes of the staff together. The truth was they would all be glad to see the back of him, the louts, but not as glad as *he* was to be leaving. He'd hated that house and its servants ever since he was a boy, but for some reason Mother loved it. Maybe because the servants didn't spend half their time watching and laughing at *her* . . .

Clarion made a silent departure past what seemed like every servant in the house, but once he stepped outside his spirits immediately rose. It *had* been raining, but now the rain seemed done and the sun struggled to break through the clouds. Perhaps the Prime Aspect had taken pity on him after ignoring the balance of his prayers, and would at least give him a decent day to begin his travels. Possibly if he'd had even one sibling or friend to play with while growing up, he would not have made a game of his ability with Air magic. And had he not played that game so often, he probably would not have developed the strength that now forced him to travel to Gan Garee alone. Yes, the Prime Aspect did owe him a nice day at the very least. . . .

Once he had settled himself in the carriage, Fod shook the reins to get the team moving. Fod had driven Clarion often enough to know better than to attempt conversation, so that was one annoyance Clarion would not have to put up with on the way to the depot. Instead his thoughts dwelled on the fact that he had never traveled *anywhere* alone before except for an occasional drive in the country. He hadn't even gone alone to parties at the homes of those of his class here in Haven Wraithside. Mother had always been there to accompany him, even when she herself, because of the age group involved, had not been invited to the party.

But she'd always gone anyway, and when invitations had stopped coming for him, she'd taken him to the parties *she* was invited to. They were usually dull affairs, with no one even close to his age attending, but his going had pleased Mother so. And after the way she had given up *her* time to play with him as a child, refusing to force him to make do with other children as most parents did, she was entitled to be repaid with pleasure. That she had been too busy with her own affairs to give him a *lot* of time that way was a tragedy she had always regretted, and was certainly not something she should be blamed for.

Nevertheless, Clarion was now in the position of having to travel alone for the first time in his life. The prospect was daunting if not downright frightening, and at first Clarion had flatly refused to do it. Mother had spent the usual amount of time talking him around, but then a strange thing had happened. Rather than sulking over having to do something other than what he wanted to, Clarion had begun to think about being on his own—and the concept had held an odd appeal. As though it were something he'd wanted to do for quite some time, but hadn't *realized* he wanted it.

Clarion sighed as he looked around, noticing that they were almost to the coach depot. He hadn't noticed leaving the neighborhood of elegant homes which was his class's part of the city, but getting to the depot was taking his attention. If Mother had heard that she would have known at once that there was something wrong with him, and there certainly must be. Imagine, ignoring the proper for the highly irregular! What *could* he be thinking of?

Fod brought the horses to a stop in front of the depot, then saw to unloading Clarion's trunk while Clarion took his time getting his tall, fairly well-built body out of the carriage. That Lord Astrath was supposed to be meeting him here with the coach tickets and a trifling amount of silver, as though *he* couldn't afford to buy his own tickets even without their silver. Clarion had agreed to ignore the insult when he'd been assured that the law demanded the tickets and silver be provided, but ignoring an insult didn't mean forgetting about it.

Fod touched his cap respectfully before climbing back into the carriage, and a moment later he and the carriage were off back to Mother's house. Clarion had considered ordering the driver to wait at least until Astrath arrived, but then had thought better of it. Every servant in the house knew he had never gone anywhere alone, and having Fod wait with him would have been an admission of fear the whole staff would have gotten a good laugh over. And now that the thing was actually beginning, there was more than a slight taste of anxiety in his throat—

"Look out!" Clarion heard in a shout from behind him, along with screams and the sound of people running. Wondering what the peasants were up to *now*, Clarion turned— then had to move faster than he'd ever thought would be necessary. Someone had created a *fireball*, and if Clarion hadn't jumped out of its path, it would have rolled—and burned—right through and over him.

People were still running and screaming as the flaming thing stopped short and then began to come back again, but

Clarion was too angry to notice. Having to jump aside had mussed his suit, and even worse, his hat had tumbled into the dirt. Just on the day he most wanted to look his best, some *fool* came along and played tricks with a Fire talent. Whoever it was must be the sort to enjoy watching people scurry, but Clarion Mardimil scurried for no one! This time the wrong victim had been chosen, a fact he was perfectly ready to prove.

Just as the fireball began to come back toward him, Clarion reached out with both his hands and his mind. Air was the aspect of his talent, which made his reaching hands doubly foolish; if Clarion had cared enough about the opinions of others, he might have pointed out that he'd developed the habit as a child while playing alone, and had never felt the need to do otherwise. But Clarion didn't care, and no one asked in any event. He simply reached out with two hands and the talent of his mind—and the fireball was stopped in its tracks.

Manipulating thickened air to stop the thing pleased Clarion, but not for long. As soon as he allowed the air to thin again the fireball would be free once more, and even beyond that no lesson would be taught to whomever had formed it. The raging fire needed to be permanently stilled or the "game" would continue, an eventuality Clarion had no patience for.

So he immediately began to destroy the annoyance that had caused him to become rumpled. Using the thickened air as "gloves" for his mental hands, he formed a very tall cylinder around the roiling flames and then began to press inward. The narrowing cylinder forced the flames to narrow as well, making them very tall and thin rather than thick and round. They rose higher and higher as they were compressed more and more, but Clarion didn't need to see the top of the flames to keep them encased in thickened air. He knew where every inch of that blazing column was, through its contact with the air around it.

In no time the column was compressed so completely that it would have looked like the dot of an *i* from above or below. That was when Clarion began to use tiny ribbons of air to separate small sections of flame, then he sent a quick breeze across the areas one by one to blow out the tiny fires. In its original form the fireball couldn't have been extinguished with a breath even if it had been a giant doing the

blowing, but all stretched out like that . . . As the column
shrank it even became possible to see the sparks go out one
after the other, an amusing touch that quite lightened
Clarion's mood.

It actually took almost two minutes, but at the end of the
time there was nothing left of the fireball. Clarion relin-
quished his hold on the magic that was his oldest and dearest
friend, brushed himself to rights, then went to see what
condition his hat was in.

"Lord Clarion, what's been happening here?" a voice
demanded as he frowningly inspected his hat, somewhat
relieved to find it dirty but otherwise unharmed. "Some of
those people seem to be hurt. Are *you* all right?"

"Apart from being thoroughly annoyed, Astrath, of course
I'm all right," Clarion replied, finally looking at the other
man. "Although I must say it's no thanks to you, not when
you obviously took your time getting here. Perhaps, after all
this, it isn't beyond hope that today's coach has been
canceled."

"The coach is coming now," Astrath replied, glancing over
Clarion's shoulder with his own frown. "I have your tickets
and silver here, but you haven't yet told me what happened.
Everyone looks positively harrowed, but you—"

"But *I* am a noble of family and breeding," Clarion
interrupted with a faint smile. "Superiority lies not only in
the title, but in the doing, you know. I would love to stay and
chat, but I'm afraid the coach personnel might take a dim
view of such a pastime and simply leave me standing here.
Do feel free to question anyone else in the vicinity. I'm sure
they'll be able to tell you everything you want to know."

Clarion put his hand out then, and with the coach actually
pulling up beside the curb, Astrath had no choice but to
hand over both tickets and silly little purse of silver—
without asking any more questions. The look of frustration
in the man's eyes almost made that whole wretched situation
worthwhile, and Clarion was able to climb into the coach
with a smile after he directed the depot man in loading his
trunk into the boot.

The smile remained on Clarion's face until the coach
pulled away from the depot and there was no one about to
watch it disappear. The journey had begun, then, with no
miracle occurring to save him from it. Now he really was

completely on his own, and by the time he reached Gan Garee he ought to know if he hated the situation—or actually loved it.

Do you understand now about my comment concerning Clarion's habit of putting on "airs?" With his aspect being Air magic, how could he do anything else? I was punning, you see—Oh, all right, so I'm not doing this simply to amuse you. You want me to get on with the narrative. That's probably because you missed the pun and now you're annoyed, but that's all right, I'll let you go on simply pretending you're sophisticated. . . .

I'd intended to introduce Vallant Ro next, but for some reason everyone insists the turn should be mine. I'm delighted I'm the one writing this narrative all alone, otherwise people might feel free to come by and tell me how to do it . . . Oh, very well, if that will keep them from pestering me for a while. This is the story of me, Tamrissa Domon.

FOUR

TAMRISSA DOMON—FIRE MAGIC

My mother said, "Stop being stubborn, Tamrissa. You *will* marry again, since your father means to find you another suitable match as soon as you're home again. Which will probably be in less than a week."

"Meaning you don't expect me to pass the test for High," I responded without turning. "And what do you mean *another* suitable match? The first was a disaster, and I refuse to go through something like that again."

"The first was a matter of *business*, girl," she said slowly and distinctly, clearly speaking to someone she considered unfortunately simpleminded. "Gimmis wanted you badly enough that he was willing to leave his business interests to your father as long as there were no offspring from the match. It took gold to buy the information from the man's physician, but we did find out that there would *be* no children from the marriage, nor would it be long before we had our legacy. It all worked out just as it was supposed to, and now your father is probably the most well-diversified merchant in all of Gan Garee."

"Well, good for *him*!" I said with very false enthusiasm, finally turning to look at her where she sat. "And all it took to make it happen was throwing *me* to the wolves. But let's not forget I'll be rewarded for my sacrifice. Now that Father has what he wants, I've earned the privilege of letting him do it to me all over again. Well, guess what? You two may be ready for seconds, but I refuse to participate. This house belonged to my late husband, and since it isn't part of the business interests it now belongs to me. You and Father can find some other fool to sacrifice to his ambition."

"Why, Tamrissa, why do you refuse to learn?" my mother demanded wearily, briefly rubbing at her eyes. "This house doesn't *have* to be part of the business interests for your father to claim it, which he fully intends to do. This is an excellent neighborhood, and the house will bring in a tidy sum in gold when he sells it. That means you *can't* stay here, and we won't see a daughter of ours living on the street. You *will* come home to us, and I won't hear any further nonsense."

"Oh, won't you," I said in a growl, interrupting her preparations to stand. "To you it's all nonsense, and you don't care to hear any more of it? What a shame, since I'm really anxious to show off what I learned during the two years of this '*marriage*.'"

"Why do you always insist on making a scene?" she began in exasperation, light eyes clearly showing her annoyance. "You know that in the end you *have* to obey your father, the law says so. You tried to refuse the first time, and how far did *that* get you?"

"It got me to the point of thinking," I countered, a response that startled her. "I found myself wondering *why* the law was on Father's side even without his paying a bribe, so I looked into it. What the law really says is that I'm required to obey Father *as long as I live under his roof.* And since that doesn't happen to be the case any longer, we now understand why Father intends to claim this house. I'm sure it *would* bring him a tidy sum in gold, but even more to the point it would bring me back under his roof. Well, the two of you can forget about that, because it isn't going to happen."

"And how do you intend to *keep* it from happening?" she asked, back to the usual calm she showed the world. "Your father and I had children for a purpose, not to give in to their every wish and whim. You'll do exactly as you're told, just as your sisters have, or you'll find out what true suffering is. This wasn't the most profitable match your father could have found for you, but concern kept him from accepting any of the others. If you give him even one more bit of trouble, the next time that concern will be absent."

"Concern," I echoed, almost beyond speech—and starting to feel chilled. "You two don't know the meaning of the word. Which is why I've already arranged to put in my own claim to this house. If Father tries to do the same he'll have to plead his case in court, where I'll get to have *my* say. The law is clear there too, so tell him to save his bribes. The judges won't be able to find against me no matter *how* much he pays them."

"What an innocent you are," she said with the vilest amusement I'd ever seen, then she rose to her feet. "The law first supports the good friends of the court, one of whom is your father. This house will be taken away from you, and then you will be destitute. When your father offers to take you back into his care, the law will insist that you go. There are enough paupers on the indigent rolls that keeping someone off them is considered a public service. My advice to you is to withdraw your claim to this house as quickly as possible, and then apologize to your father and me. If you refuse, don't complain about what happens."

And with that she sailed out of the room, heading for the front door. In two years' time this was only her second visit, the first being when she and Father came as guests to my first anniversary party. Gimmis had still been fairly active then,

so they hadn't enjoyed the party or stayed very long. Now
that my husband was dead, their mood had improved
considerably.

"She's gone," Warla hurried in to say, obviously having
waited until the door closed behind our "guest." "What are
you going to do, Dama?"

I walked over to the chair my mother had been in,
smoothed my skirt, and then sat. The chair had belonged to
Gimmis, and was the only really comfortable one in the
whole sitting room. What a surprise that Mother had made
straight for it as soon as she entered the room.

"I refuse to simply roll over and play dead," I muttered,
rubbing at my arms to chase away the cold trying to cover
me. "I'd rather *be* dead than give in to them, so what have I
got to lose? I'm going ahead with the plans just as I told her I
would."

"But how can you?" Warla protested, wide-eyed and all
but wringing her hands. "You heard what the Dama your
mother said, you won't win. Why make things worse by
fighting if you know you can't win?"

"But I *don't* know that," I countered, forcibly pulling
myself together. "What my mother said and what the truth is
don't necessarily have to be the same thing. A successful
merchant always *acts* as if he's telling the truth, and most
customers will take his word for it without finding out for
sure. That's what my father says, and my mother has been
hearing it for much longer than I have."

Hearing it and following it, I added to myself. Father had
always chuckled and called Mother his best student, but I'd
never really understood the comment until a few minutes
ago.

"What if she *is* telling the truth?" Warla ventured, still
looking frightened and unsure. "You could end up being sent
back to them, and then you'd *have* to obey."

"Now, that's something that isn't true at all," I said,
reaching for the cup of tea my mother hadn't even glanced at
when Warla served it to her. "Two years ago they talked me
into believing I had no choice, but I *could* have refused to
obey. It would have meant a lot of trouble and pain, but I got
those anyway. I saved myself nothing by obeying, so I won't
make the mistake a second time. Even if it comes to that.

"You're still hoping you'll pass the tests for High pract

ioner," Warla said after a moment, a fairly safe guess on her art. "The Dama your mother never said anything about hat, even when you asked her."

"That's because she knows how these things work," I nswered sourly after sipping at the tea. "Now that someone as noticed that I qualify for Middle strength, I *have* to test or High. But they send people here from all over the Empire o do the same thing, and there are only so many positions as High awarded. You have to be absolutely tops, and even then ou might have to wait until a position is vacated. But if you re waiting, there are certain protections you enjoy until you nove into the position—as long as no one comes along to nock you out of line."

"It all sounds so . . . conditional and uncertain," Warla retted as she came over to freshen the tea in my cup. "If so ew positions as High are available, why do they keep ending people here from all over? Wouldn't it be better to ust leave them where they are?"

"And risk leaving some supposed Middle out there who's ctually stronger than their seated Highs?" I shook my head vith a very unamused smile. "They're not *that* stupid, not vhen there are people around who don't like the way this Empire is run. One of those unhappy people could conceiv-bly put together a Blending that would cause serious trouble efore it was stopped, so why take the chance?"

"That means they're doing it for themselves rather than or the people involved," Warla observed with a frown. That doesn't sound very nice, but—What happens to the eople who *don't* qualify for High? There must be an awful ot of them."

"That's something I *don't* know," I admitted, having lready worried at the question myself. "I tried to find out, ut people talk around the details or simply refuse to answer. he worst of the applicants are allowed to go home, I think, ut the rest? There's a good chance I may find out firsthand."

"And you *still* intend to try?" Warla exclaimed, back to eing really upset. "I don't understand you, Dama. Wouldn't t be so much easier just to apologize to your parents and do s they tell you? Maybe this time your father will find you a usband you really like."

"Of course he will," I agreed dryly. "Unless there's nother old sadist who wants me as much as my father wants

the man's business interests. A lot of them won't even car
that I'm no longer a virgin, just as long as they can d
anything they please to me. Warla, go and find out if dinne
will be served on time tonight."

Warla parted her lips, probably to remind me that dinne
was always served on time, then she got it. I wanted no mor
conversation from her, and hadn't simply ordered her t
leave because I don't believe in treating innocent people lik
that. She smiled tremulously, curtsied her agreement, the
left without another word.

Once she was gone I took a deep breath, needing it to fre
myself from the tendrils of helplessness Warla always spu
all around herself—and around those near her. If I hadn'
known better I would have thought it was a talent, but non
of the aspects covered such complete readiness to surrende
to anything at any and all times. Warla's born aspect wa
Water, which helped to make her a good companion an
lady's maid. The baths she drew were always the perfec
temperature, a pot of tea never grew too cold to drink, an
ice was always available when it was wanted.

But there were servants with other aspects able to do th
same things, and Warla had been engaged originally by m
husband rather than by me. He must have wanted her t
teach *me* the right attitudes, and her plainness had kept hir
out of her bed and saved her from what *I'd* gone through
After my husband died everyone in the house had expecte
me to send her away, but that was the last thing I'd do.
needed her horrible example constantly in front of my eyes
to show me what *I* could become if I ever let them have thei
way again.

Them. I'd learned from acquaintances that most peopl
don't think about their parents like that, lumped togethe
without personality and always on the opposite and enem
side of the line. No one quite understood why I had troubl
controlling my temper whenever it became necessary t
discuss *them*, but I found it equally impossible to under
stand other viewpoints. Your mother came to tend you
house and children when you were sick in bed? Why? Wha
did she expect to get out of something like that? She didn'
expect to get anything? She did it because she loves you
Sure, right, tell me another one.

I got out of the chair and began to pace, more disturbe

than I'd admitted to Warla. I don't need a mirror to tell me what desirable merchandise I am, with reddish-blond hair and violet eyes, an incredibly beautiful face and a lush figure. Every man I meet seems to want me from the first glance, especially the old, rich ones with no conscience or sense of right and wrong. At almost twenty I was getting on in years, but even aging didn't seem able to kill the attraction. My parents had no intentions of letting me out of their clutches until I became really useless to them, so it was either give in at once and completely, or get ready for the dirtiest fight of my life.

So I had to think about the fight, since giving in was completely out of the question. I did have a couple of weapons I'd never had the nerve to use, but two years in the hands of a brute either kills your nerve completely or toughens it to the point of iron. If Gimmis hadn't become incapacitated when he did, I wouldn't have just stood there letting him die in his own good time. I'd been no more than a step away from doing it myself and at once when he fell to that final illness, and the memory of my state of mind still haunted my dreams. If anyone ever pressed me that hard again. . . .

The house abruptly became stifling, and I just had to get out for some air. The street would be almost empty at that time of the afternoon, but the possibility of meeting even one person I knew was more of a chance than I cared to take. I couldn't have handled polite conversation if my life had depended on it, so I left the sitting room and hurried all the way to the back of the house and out to the gardens. Our gardens weren't as large as some, but they had a ten foot stone wall surrounding them.

It was possible to make myself slow down once I'd gone a short distance along the flagstoned path, but not because I'd managed to calm myself. On the inside my emotions still raged around, which meant it was a good thing Gimmis was dead. The agitation kept me from paying attention to the thorns on the bushes, and the catches and pulls they caused in my skirts would have had my husband reaching for his belt. A girl too fuzzy-headed to care properly for her clothing needed to be taught better, he'd always said.

And that brought on all the other memories, mostly of the times I'd run into the garden to hide. That had been right at the beginning, when I'd still thought it would be possible to avoid whatever my husband wanted to do to me. Once I learned the futility of that hope I stopped running, and simply crept out to be alone once he was through doing whatever he'd decided to. The time came when I also got past the creeping stage, and then I used the garden to brood in. It was also where I first decided to kill Gimmis. . . .

When my breath started to come in harder and harder gasps, I finally admitted it had been a mistake to come out here. Even having to engage in polite conversation with a neighbor wouldn't have been as bad as *that*, so I turned around to go back. I couldn't have taken more than two steps when I felt the sudden stirring of magic . . . *my* kind of magic . . . and then a really large fireball appeared. It hovered between me and the house, and then it stopped hovering and began to move toward me.

"What sort of stupidity *is* this?" I demanded out loud certain that whoever had created the fireball could hear me. I also stopped it before it could reach me, of course, but the mental command I gave for it to disappear wasn't obeyed Someone with a good deal of strength had created the thing and set it practically in my lap, and banishing it wasn't going to be possible.

And that managed to focus every bit of anger and fear and hatred and uncertainty inside me onto the latest intrude into my life. This whole thing could very well be something done at my parents' urging, to show me how futile my hope were in regard to passing the tests for High. You'll neve escape us, the crackling flames seemed to say, not until we'v burned every bit of use and humanity out of you. Even you talent won't free you, not ever, never, never. . . .

"I'll show *you*," I whispered, so lost to insanity that actually spoke to the flames. "I *will* get free, I *will*, I *will*!"

And then I reached to the fireball with my own talen causing a second fireball to come into being around the firs Fight fire with fire the old adage advised, and that wa exactly what I would do. But not in any ordinary sense, o no, nothing ordinary for *this* girl. Brute force combined wit exquisite finesse, yes, that's what would do it.

I seem to remember muttering darkly to myself while spread my own flames completely around the intrude flames. Encasing someone else's creation wasn't supposed t be possible for two people using the same aspect, but I was in no condition to remember that. Half the time it was my husband whom I surrounded with flames, and the rest of the time it was my parents. I was intent on showing them all, proving that they would no longer be allowed to do as they pleased with me.

And once the intruder flames were completely surrounded, I caused my own flames to burn hotter and hotter and hotter. Only a crazy woman would try to burn flames, but there was something else I did as well. With *my* flames using up all the air around the intruder, there was nothing left for *it* to burn in. The hotter my flames grew, the fainter its became, until there was nothing but a shrunken shadow left inside my inferno. I waited until even the shadow had disappeared, extinguished my flame and the small fires my efforts had started in the surrounding garden, then stumbled to a nearby stone bench. Once I'd collapsed onto it I began to shake, buried under the memory of what I'd done. The madness had disappeared with the intruder, and all that was left was unadorned terror.

"And that's what you can look forward to if they manage to get possession of you again," I whispered from out of the terror, knowing it to be the truth. "You'll go mad and use your talent to kill them, and then you'll be sentenced to the Demon Caverns for the rest of your life. Everyone left alive in the Caverns is mad, and no one ever escapes. You *have* to stay out of their hands, so you *have* to pass those tests."

A lot of have-to's for a woman already half crazy, but what choice did I have? None that I could live with, none that anyone else involved would live *through*. I had to stay free no matter what, *had* to . . . *had* to. . . .

That was harder than I'd thought it would be, and I'm glad it's behind me now. I'm not usually that intense, not out where others can see it, at least, but I'm supposed to tell the truth in this narrative. The others insist I was as biting as

*my flames when we first met, but I'm sure they're just
exaggerating. Or mistaken, which is perfectly possible. You
see, it all began with a plan and a misunderstanding,
when—*

*Oh, yes, I have forgotten somebody, haven't I? The last of
our five, the arrogant Vallant Ro. Well, if you insist . . .*

FIVE

VALLANT RO—WATER MAGIC

There weren't many people in Port Entril—or any other
Southern port—who didn't know the Ro family and their
fleet of transports, and most of the ones who didn't were
either drunk or children. Neither description fit the group on
the dock, so Vallant wasn't surprised when they made a
beeline for his ship as soon as the *Sea Queen* was docked.
Then they got close enough for individuals to be recognized,
and Vallant cursed under his breath. The man in the lead
was his oldest brother Torrin, which had to mean trouble.

Torrin was first up the gangway, but the group behind him
wasn't *far* behind. The deck was, as usual, a madhouse, with
seamen trying to batten down for port and getting the cargo
offloaded, and passengers clutching their belongings while
trying to debark. Torrin and his escort made an effort to
ignore it all, but they were swimming upriver against a
stronger current than they knew. Vallant leaned a shoulder
against the deckhouse, folded his arms, and watched their
approach with open amusement.

"I'm glad you're havin' such a good time, little brother,"
Torrin growled when he finally fought his way close enough
to Vallant. "Too bad the fun has to end—and so abruptly—
but you can't say you didn't ask for it. Get your things
together and start movin'. Captain Vish will take over from
here."

"The hell he will," Vallant answered, no longer amused at

he straightened. "The *Queen* is *my* vessel, and another man captains her over my dead body."

"Right now I wouldn't much mind arrangin' that," Torrin countered, his expression showing he wasn't joking. "And Daddy would probably name me sole heir if I did. He's been chewin' walls for the past week, which hasn't done his health any good. *He* wanted to come down here to meet you, but none of us would let him. Havin' the head of your family arrested for murder can be embarrassin'."

"What in hell are you talkin' about?" Vallant demanded, so out of patience that he forgot to watch his tone. The Master-of-the-vessel snap that made him a captain no one talked back to caused Torrin and the others to flinch, even that fool Vish. Vish the Fish, most seamen called him ... "Why in every blazing blue hell would Daddy be angry at *me*? I think you're tryin' to cod me, Torrin, and if you are—"

"Damn it, watch your mouth, Val!" Torrin hissed with a glance at the gaggle behind him, and Vallant finally noticed that there was a woman in their midst. She wasn't bad looking, especially with that faint blush now in her cheeks, but this wasn't the time for women.

"Answer my questions, big brother," Vallant ordered, this time using the tone of command deliberately. "Tell me what's goin' on, and why you're trailin' a pack of lubbers."

Vish bristled up at that and jutted out his bearded chin, but everyone managed to ignore him.

"Vallant, you're supposed to be on your way to Gan Garee!" Torrin answered with exasperation, but without any more bush-beating or hesitation. "It's the *law*, little brother, and you know how Daddy feels about the law. No child of his will ever break it and *stay* a child of his, not while there's an ounce of breath left in his body."

"You can't be serious," Vallant said with a frown, finally understanding. "I have no interest in testin' for High, and I told those fools that. I'm a seaman and captain of my own vessel, and that's all I *want* to be. Now take this pack and get off my deck."

"Val, you can't refuse to test!" Torrin said slowly and forcefully, clearly ignoring the way some of his followers started to turn away in obedience to Vallant's orders. "It doesn't *matter* whether or not you want to be High, the law

says every confirmed Middle has to test for it. There's a
coach leavin' on the Gan Garee circuit in less than four
hours. If you aren't on it voluntarily, you'll be arrested and
put on it with an escort. And Daddy will have to pay
expenses for the escort."

Vallant immediately looked around at the people behind
Torrin, and the way the two biggest men avoided his gaze
said they were the ones who would be arresting and escort-
ing. Or trying to do those things. That they weren't at all
eager to be about it showed how wise they were, but that had
nothing to do with the most important point. He hated the
idea of leaving the sea even temporarily, but he'd rather die
than bring trouble down on his family and disappoint his
father.

"Tell Daddy I apologize, and that I didn't understand," he
grudged at last in a growl without looking at Torrin. "I'll
pack my belongin's and be on that coach, but get Vish off my
deck. *You* supervise the offloadin', then put Palafar in
temporary command of the *Queen*. He's been my second
long enough to be in line for a captaincy of his own, and I
can trust him to take care of the *Queen* until I get back."

"Now you're bein' reasonable," Torrin enthused with a
smile, then lost his smile as he looked around. "But if you
don't mind, I'll put Palafar in charge of the offloadin' as well.
It's been years since I last stood on a deck, and I haven't
missed it. Not to mention that I never captained and
everyone knows it. You go ahead, and I'll see to what needs
seein' to."

Vallant nodded and turned away toward his cabin, noticing that the woman seemed to want to say something, but he
ignored her. Now he really wasn't in the mood for women, or
much of anything else. He would be land-bound for weeks,
and that was *his* version of a fate worse than death. Not to
mention the fact that he also had to collect a few things from
his rooms above the tavern in town. And pay his quarterly
rent. And say a temporary goodbye to Mirra. Mirra would
hate seeing him rush off again right after getting in, but she
would understand. She'd know he'd miss *her* as much as
he'd miss the sea, and that he wasn't leaving out of choice.

Torrin and his flock were gone by the time Vallant got back
to the deck with his seabag, and Palafar had everything
moving smoothly. Most of the crew came over to say
goodbye, and Vallant made sure they understood that it was

a *temporary* farewell. He would be back even if every blue demon in the universe tried to stand in his way. They seemed to know that already, so he left the *Queen* feeling slightly better.

More than the usual number of people stopped him on the way to the tavern where he lived when in port, and he had to be polite for the sake of future business. But that meant there was less than two hours left to coach time when he finally reached the Roaring Sailor Tavern. Realizing that darkened his mood again, so much so that when he went upstairs and walked into the first of his rooms to find Mirra lounging in a chair, he barely glanced at her. Stomping on through to his bedchamber without a word seemed more to the point, but that didn't keep her from following.

"Vallant Ro, how *could* you just walk past me without a word?" she asked, sounding mortally wounded. "I've been waitin' here for half the day, waitin' for a *gentleman*, but if this is the way you're goin' to act, you can find another girl to wait for you. *If* you think you can find one to match *me*, that is."

Vallant stopped pulling things out of a chest and took a deep breath, understanding that he'd made another mistake. Mirra Agran's father had almost as profitable a shipping business as his own family did, but where he had four brothers and two sisters, Mirra was an only child. That had spoiled her to a large degree, but she'd never been able to walk all over Vallant the way she did with other men and she seemed to like that. She would force him to be stern with her, and then she would let him take her to bed—where she gave him an experience much like being in a skiff in a rainstorm. He probably never would find another woman filled with as much passion, not to mention one with the sort of business connections his daddy had suggested he encourage. . . .

"Mirra, I really must apologize," he said as he turned, making no effort to smile at her. "Somethin' has happened, and I thought it best to spare a lady like you the weight of my mood. If you choose to leave at once, I'll certainly understand."

"*What's* happened?" she demanded, immediately dropping the great-lady-wounded attitude. "My daddy can probably help even if yours can't, so tell me right now."

"No one can help," he returned, just short of a growl. The idea that her daddy could do what his couldn't was usually amusing, but today . . . "I have to go to Gan Garee to test for High, the law insists on it. If I don't make today's coach under my own power, they'll arrest me and *put* me on it. But it shouldn't be long before I'm back, so don't you worry your pretty head. And don't let any of my brothers move in on you while I'm gone."

"No chance of *that*," she assured him with a sound of scorn. "They may all be as big and broad-shouldered as you, with the same platinum hair and light blue eyes, but none of them is like you on the *inside*. But I do recall tellin' you not to show off so much with your talent, and it seems I was right. If you hadn't brought yourself to their attention—"

"Nonsense," he denied, turning back to his packing chore. "I said almost the same thing when that Guild fellow first mentioned goin' to the capitol, and he set me straight. Guild people check *everyone* on a regular basis until the age of twenty-five, since no one has been known to develop significant strength past that age. They don't have to find you doin' somethin' complicated, even waterin' a garden with your talent can be enough. It has somethin' to do with the feel of the strength you put into the smallest effort . . . None of *us* can tell, but Guild people can. And they do."

"But this is awful!" Mirra wailed, suddenly projecting a sense of tragedy. "Your bein' away will delay your promotion from that awful boat to a proper office position, and that in turn may delay our weddin'. You told me yourself your daddy won't do anythin' for his sons that he doesn't do for his other employees, so—"

"Mirra, where on earth did you get the idea that I mean to give up my ship?" Vallant demanded, turning back to her again. "The one time we discussed the idea, I told you I had no interest in takin' a promotion to the office. You seemed to understand, but now—"

"Oh, Vallant, don't be silly," she interrupted, peremptorily gesturing away what he'd said with a shake of her auburn-haired head. "You have no idea what's really good for you, but when the time comes *I'll* make sure you do the right thing. And the first of those things is that you can't take the coach today. I couldn't possibly be ready to go with you so quickly, but the day after tomorrow should be fine. You just tell them that, and then we can enjoy the rest of today the way we planned."

Her smile had turned inviting with its usual promise and

she stepped forward to press herself against him, but Vallant was suddenly repelled. She'd been playing a game with him all this time, pretending to obey him while planning their life together to suit only herself. Any number of people considered him high-handed, but he'd never once tried to force a decision on her about something that concerned the two of them. That was the reason he'd told her he'd be remaining at sea right from the beginning, to keep from hiding things. Apparently she hadn't felt the same . . .

"Mirra, stop it," he said, gently but firmly pushing her back away from him. "Listen to what I'm sayin', and try to make yourself understand. I *have* to take the coach today, or I'll be arrested. It isn't a matter of choice, but of necessity. One thing, however, *is* a matter of choice, and that's the fact that I will *not* give up my captaincy for a place in an office. Since that doesn't agree with what *you* want out of life, I suggest that you see other men after all. You'll never get what you want from *me*."

"Oh, Vallant, you keep sayin' these silly, childish things," she told him with a sigh and a pout. "*You're* the man I've decided on, so why would I bother with anyone else? And once we're married you'll change your mind about that stupid boat, I promise you will. Right now I'm leavin', but only to go and speak to Daddy. *He'll* talk to those Guild people, and then they'll understand that they *can't* arrest you. Miss me while I'm gone, but have that special present waitin' for when I get back."

She blew him a kiss, her smile now radiant, and then she left. Vallant stood staring after her for a moment, feeling almost dazed. How could he have missed seeing what she was really like all this time? He must have let her beautiful face and lush body blind him to the truth, a blindness that could have trapped him for the rest of his life. He shuddered at the thought of that, then quickly went back to his packing. Like other men, he'd always been attracted to the most beautiful women, but he felt cured of that now. If he couldn't find a plain woman to suit him, he'd visit courtesans.

He finished the rest of his packing morosely, then went back downstairs. He had just enough time to have a meal before he'd have to leave for the depot, so he took a table and ordered. He'd put his packed seabag on the floor beside his chair, and that had brought him curious stares but no questions. If Jako, the owner of the Roaring Sailor, had been there it would have been different, but Jako was away and his current crop of serving girls didn't know him well enough to ask.

Which, in a way, was too bad. Questions might have distracted him from the hurt he could no longer deny, the unexpected pain of finding out that Mirra wasn't the joyously abandoned companion he'd always considered her. Being the center of a beautiful woman's universe was always pleasant for a man, but when she joined him there and teased him in that very special way . . . He hadn't realized how much he'd been looking forward to having that for the rest of his life, the togetherness, the sharing, the fun . . .

But she hadn't really felt any of those things, not in the same way he had. She'd marked him out as her private property, complete with deciding his entire future, just the way you would do with a pet you valued and were fond of. He wasn't a *person* to her, just another someone she could manipulate into giving her what she wanted, and that really hurt. She might well love him, but only as his "owner."

His food began to come, so Vallant forced away the brooding and applied himself to eating and planning. It would take about a week to get to Gan Garee, and the same coming home. How much time he would have to spend in the city itself was what he didn't know, but surely it couldn't be longer than a week. From what he'd heard it would be best if he were eliminated from the contests early, and then he'd be free to leave. And he *would* be eliminated early, he'd make sure of that.

"Excuse me, Dom Ro," a woman's voice said, causing Vallant to look up. "Since we have some business to take care of, I'm sure you won't mind if I join you."

"That's Captain Ro," Vallant corrected, watching the woman take a seat without waiting for permission. She was the one who had accompanied Torrin onto the *Queen*'s deck earlier, and she was prettier than he'd realized. Considering his most recent resolve, her presence was one he would have preferred to do without.

"Merchants like my daddy are addressed as 'Dom,'" Vallant continued, "not people like myself. That probably means whatever your business is, you'd be better off takin' it up with him. I'm gettin' ready to leave the city in just a little while."

"I know," she responded, a certain satisfaction hidden in

her eyes. "You've learned that you won't be allowed to disobey the law no matter how rich your family is, or how big and strong *you* are. I'm the one who was put in charge of getting you to Gan Garee, and finally it's almost done. I've brought your tickets and spending money in silver, and all that's left is to bundle you onto the coach."

She put the tickets and pouch of silver onto the table between them, then smiled at him with pretty, white teeth. The smile was probably supposed to look friendly, but all that enjoyment behind it turned it into something closer to a laugh. He was twice her size and could probably buy and sell her entire family without needing his daddy's help, but she'd still bested him and was now laughing about it. Vallant held his temper with fists of steel and tried to simply continue eating, but she wasn't through crowing—or pushing—yet.

"Actually, you weren't all that hard to handle," she commented, clearly trying not to drawl as she leaned back in her chair. "If I'd gone directly to *you* about the problem, I'm sure you would have smiled your very handsome smile and then tried to talk me around. So I went to your father instead, and explained how you would *not* be allowed to break the law simply because you were his darling boy child. I was surprised when he saved me the trouble of having to turn down a bribe, and simply agreed to take care of the matter."

Vallant looked up quickly at that, but he wasn't mistaken. The woman was deliberately insulting him and his family, hoping he'd—do what? Obviously she wasn't terribly fond of people with money, but she'd already gotten what she wanted. What else could she possibly be after?

And then he had the answer, which was really rather obvious. She *had* gotten what she wanted, but not quite in the best of ways. She would have been happiest if he had had to be put on the coach in chains and under arrest, so she'd decided to provoke him into doing something to make it happen. Like forcing him into blowing up and refusing to go after all. He didn't know the cause of her hatred and couldn't fully understand it, but that was hardly the first time he'd ever seen it.

"Yes, you were one of the easy ones," she went on when he stayed silent. "No trouble out of any of you, and now you're going to the depot like a little lamb. I'll really have to mention in my report what a good boy you are."

Under other circumstances, that would have done it for Vallant. He would have blown up with a roar, thrown the table across the room, and then would have sent *her* on her way with a smack to the bottom and his refusal ringing in her ears. But since that was exactly what she wanted, he smiled at her instead.

"I'm glad you noticed," he drawled, letting his eyes move over as much of her as he could see. "It's too bad we don't have the time for me to show you just how good a boy I am, but that can be seen to when I get back. Since I'm sure you'll still be hangin' around, just come up and remind me. I won't make you wait *too* long."

The arrogance of that speech turned her first pale and then flushed, as though she couldn't quite decide how to react. She parted her lips to say something, blushed even harder when she probably realized he'd turn anything she said into more of the same, then she gave it up. She stood and marched away without a single glance back, and Vallant was able to finish his meal in peace—while seriously considering the idea of giving up women entirely. Disillusionment had really set in, making him wish with all his heart that he was back at sea.

Vallant paid for his meal and left the tavern, having more than enough time to stroll to the depot that was only a few streets away. He intended to use the walk to take a last, remembering look at Port Entril, to make sure he had what to think about while he was away. He no longer had a woman to fill his thoughts, and memories of the *Sea Queen* would be almost as painful. Home port was a place he'd long since gotten used to leaving, though, not to mention thinking about without a sense of permanent loss. He could—

Screams suddenly came from some of the other people on the street, and Vallant turned fast to see what the trouble was. For an instant the sight of the raging fireball confused him, but then he realized what it *had* to be. That Guild female, looking for a more effective way to delay his reaching the coach. He would be so busy keeping himself—and others—unburned that he would lose track of time, giving her the perfect excuse to show up with those two bully boys and a set of chains.

But that wasn't the way it was going to happen. The woman had obviously forgotten what his talent was, which made her stupid as well as vindictive. Sending fire after someone with Water magic . . . Vallant snorted and put his seabag down, then began to reach for every bit of moisture around. The horse troughs, the clouds in the sky above, the very air of a port city only a few streets from the sea.

It was all his to use, in any way he cared to use it. The fireball had begun to roll at him, threatening to burn him down where he stood, but *it* was the one that had to veer off. He'd hung a fine curtain of mist in its path, but not so fine that the curtain hadn't begun to put out the leading edge of its flames. The fireball drew back and started to circle, trying to reach him, but it was already too late for that. By then he'd surrounded the thing with a ring of water, and the more water he called into the ring, the faster the fire began to shrink.

It took no more than minutes before the fire was completely drowned, and then Vallant was able to free the water to return to where it had been, retrieve his seabag, and continue on his way. He kept his eyes open for the woman's appearance with her men, but oddly enough the coach arrived before she did. Or maybe not so oddly. She must have seen her latest plan in ruins, and finally got smart enough to give up. About time, too, before he *really* lost his temper.

Vallant handed over his seabag and then climbed into the coach, grimly determined not to think about what he left behind. Soon it would be what he was headed back to, and *then* he could think about it. Now he just had to concentrate on making the interval in between the shortest it could possibly be.

All right, now *you've met all of us. Of course, things didn't start to happen until* we *met, or at least not much of anything. We all knew what we wanted and intended to have, but the prophecy had already begun to enter our lives to make certain things inevitable. And then there was what our ruling class wanted, and what our friends and relatives*

*and enemies wanted, and what our ultimate opponents
wanted. And let's certainly not forget about the Ancients
and what* they *wanted.*

*Goodness, it's a miracle we accomplished anything at all,
not to mention survived. There were all those times we were
sure we wouldn't, especially after we really got together.
That was a time, let me tell you . . . All right, all right, I'll
show* them. *It all began shortly after the others reached Gan
Garee, where I already was . . .*

SIX

"We made it, Lor, we're actually here!" Hat's voice was low
but intense, underscoring the way Lorand felt himself. "And
I can't believe how big this place is! It took an hour of driving
through the city for the coach to reach here."

"We'd better get our cases before the coach leaves with
them," Lorand told him, reluctantly pulling his stare away
from the immense walled area they'd been brought to. "I
wonder if that's where we're supposed to go."

"Sure is," the coachman unpacking their cases from the
rear of the coach said with a grin. "You go up to one of them
guards, tell 'im you're here for testin', and he'll let you know
where you go next. Good luck t'you, an' have fun."

Lorand thanked the man as he took both cases, Hat still
being too immersed in staring openmouthed to join him. But
once the coach pulled away, Lorand moved the few steps to
Hat and pushed his case at him.

"Take this thing, will you?" he said, nervousness making
him faintly irritable. "It feels like you packed half the county
along with your clothes."

"Well, I had to, now didn't I?" Hat replied with a laugh as
he took the case. "Since I won't be going back again, I had to
take what I'll need. I wonder if they'll give us time to find a
pretty lady or two first—or maybe they'll supply some after
we pass."

"First worry about passing," Lorand advised, beginning to

lead the way toward the gated wall. "If we don't, none of the rest will matter."

"Women will always matter," Hat countered, but not as lightheartedly as before. It was now really beginning, and Hat was starting to feel that as strongly as Lorand already did.

The immense wall clearly surrounded an area that wasn't open to the general public, the presence of sword and spear and armor-clad guardsmen reinforcing that observation. Lorand slowly approached one pair that were already staring at him and Hat, but when he reached them he didn't quite know what to say.

"We're—we're supposed to test," Hat stumbled in explanation, now sounding as uncertain as Lorand felt. "Can you tell us where we're supposed to go?"

"Let's see the coach tickets you used," one of the guardsmen rumbled without inflection, putting out a large, blunt-fingered hand. Lorand and Hat exchanged an uneasy glance, then dug for what was left of the coach tickets they'd been given. They'd had to relinquish an inch of ticket for each leg of their journey, which had left them with little more than stubs. But they produced those stubs and handed them over, and the guardsman inspected them briefly before handing them back.

"You go to the main building right behind this gate," the guardsman told them, drawling the words in a way that said he'd repeated them any number of times before. "Use the entrance second from the right, and turn in these tickets when you're told to. They'll let you know what to do next."

And then the two guardsmen were stepping out of their way, giving them access to the gate. Lorand felt the strangest urge to wipe his sweating palms on his tunic, but he couldn't stand the thought of doing it in front of the guardsmen. There was already a definite gleam of amusement in the dismissive glances he and Hat had been getting, as if the guardsmen knew these two bumpkins had no chance to pass the tests. Well, Lorand did have a chance, and he meant to make the most of it. Hat still stood unmoving beside him, so he took a better grip on his case and resolutely moved through the gate . . .

. . . only to stop again just a few steps beyond it. The wall had hidden the most—utilitarian area Lorand had ever seen. A very large building with arched entrances stood before them, made of uniform gray stone three or four shades lighter than the stoned approach. It took no effort to feel the controlled strength that had been used to construct the building and approach, but less had gone into the planting and care of the grass surrounding the stone of the approach. The grass struggled to survive without Encouragement, an odd situation where there were supposed to be so many strong talents.

"Look at all the people coming in," Hat murmured from his left, obviously having stopped when he did. "They're using all those other gates, but only a few are heading toward the entrance we were told to use."

It was strange that Lorand had actually missed noticing the people, but Hat's mentioning them brought sight and awareness of them. There were dozens of people moving in and out of the immense building, men and women alike. Those coming out moved briskly in a businesslike way, as did some of those going in. Most of the others, though . . . Most of the others seemed like himself and Hat, nervous, unsure, hesitant, maybe even frightened. And most of them were alone, which made Lorand grateful for Hat's presence.

"No sense in just standing here," Lorand said after taking a deep breath. "It's already past noon, and we'll have to find someplace to stay before it gets dark. Let's go tell them we're here and find out when the testing will start, and then we can go looking for a place to live until it's our turn."

"Which won't be *too* long after our silver runs out," Hat agreed sourly, joining him in walking toward the building. "I don't know why official doings have to take so long to happen, but they always do. Remember the five-year-old tests?"

It had been a long time ago, but Lorand did remember. Every child in every district went to registration at the age of five, when they were enrolled in school and given their first tests. Lorand could also remember his father muttering about fool wastes of time, the elder Coll hating the need to allow anyone else access to *his* children. And allowing them a say over those children. Camil Coll would have kept his children illiterate if the law hadn't refused to let him do it, but Lorand hadn't known that at the time.

All the five-year-old Lorand had known was how strange everything looked, since that was his first trip off the farm.

He hadn't been allowed to go along when his older brother had been registered, but he'd been a baby then, not even three. Now he was five and it was *his* turn, and his walk had become a strut every time his father wasn't watching.

The registration for school had taken only a few minutes, but then had come the wait for the testing. Lorand had started out eager to find out what would happen, then he'd grown impatient, and then finally he'd gotten bored. It was taking so *long* to get to him, and he didn't know any of the other boys and girls there, and his father was watching him so closely despite the conversations he had with some of the other fathers there . . . That was probably why Lorand had forgotten the strict orders his father had given him before leaving the farm.

"I'll never forget how long it took for them to get around to me at the five-year-old testing," Lorand answered ruefully. "It was so long that I forgot all about what my father had said about not showing off. I really wanted everyone to know what I could do, but if I'd remembered the orders I'd been given . . . Do you think that's *why* they made us wait so long? So we'd forget what we'd been told?"

"Since my father didn't tell me anything but to do my best, I doubt it," Hat answered distractedly, his gaze on the entrance they meant to use. "They were just acting true to form, and showing everyone how important they were by keeping us waiting. What do you think *these* tests will be like?"

"I . . . don't know." Lorand hesitated before answering the question they'd both been careful to avoid all during the trip. "And I'd rather not even think about it. Master Lugal said we have to be ready for anything and everything, and you can't do that if you decide something has to be a certain way—"

"Well, I *am* ready, and I'll bet I know what they're going to do," Hat interrupted as if he hadn't heard what Lorand had said. "I know what they'll do and I can handle it easy, so I don't have to worry about passing. I *will* pass, and after it's all over I'll be a High."

Hat spoke with such intensity that Lorand was sure he really spoke to himself, unaware of having actually voiced the thoughts. And he made no effort to share his conclusions with Lorand, which was faintly disturbing. It was true that

they would be competing against each other, but they were
supposed to be friends . . . Did their friendship come down
to so little that it was put aside so easily? Lorand didn't really
want to know what Hat had thought of about the testing, but
what hurt was that Hat hadn't even offered to share. . . .

Lorand was disturbed as they reached the archway they'd
been told to use, but once he stepped through it was awe that
suddenly filled him. The area inside was nothing less than
vast, the ceiling so far above their heads that it was difficult
to see. People walked as quietly as possible inside that
vastness, and those who spoke to one another whispered.
Every ten feet or so a torch burned in an ornamental sconce
on the walls, but the torches did little beyond making the
inner dimness a bit less intense. All the way down at the
other end of the building it was possible to see some daylight
through other arches, but that also did nothing to brighten
the place.

"Coach tickets, please," a brisk voice said, and Lorand
took his attention from the vastness to look at the man who
sat behind a small table just a few feet inside the entrance.
The man was dressed in the sort of wide-sleeved shirt Master
Lugal usually wore, and he hadn't spoken in a whisper. But
the silence around them seemed to soak up the sound of the
words so that no one more than five feet away would hear
them. Lorand moved closer to the table and produced his
ticket stub again, and he and Hat handed the stubs over
together.

"Well, well, you're both right on time," the man said,
looking at a long piece of paper that had what looked like
lists of names. He made checks beside two of those names
with a marker, then looked up at Lorand and Hat again
while reaching into a small box.

"I'm going to issue you identity tags," the man said slowly
and clearly, as if he spoke to those who weren't very bright.
"You'll wear these tags at all times, even out on the street.
They identify you as participants in the testing, and won't be
taken away again until and unless you fail your test. Do you
understand?"

"Of course we understand!" Hat snapped before Lorand
could answer a bit more civilly. "We may not come from this
city, but we're not complete idiots."

"The man was just explaining things, Hat, not trying to

insult us," Lorand said quickly and soothingly, putting his hand to Hat's shoulder. "A lot of the people coming here must be too frightened and confused to think, so spelling everything out is really a kindness. No sense in getting hot over something like that."

"He should have known we're not like that," Hat muttered as he shook free of Lorand's hand, but at least most of the belligerence was gone. Lorand saw that the man at the table was busy writing on the rectangles of heavy paper he'd taken from the box, but the tightness in the man's jaw said an apology would have been in order. Lorand briefly considered suggesting that to Hat, then immediately rejected the idea. Hat was too wound up to apologize to anyone, and trying to talk him into doing it anyway would just make things even worse.

"All right, here are your tags," the man finally said after another few minutes, pushing them toward Lorand and Hat. Once their names had been put on the tags, the man had attached a wide loop of fine chain to an eye in the middle top of the tags. Those loops would fit over their heads, and the tags would hang in the middle of their chests.

"Thank you," Lorand said with as much warmth as he could muster, taking the tag with his name on it. "Can you give us any idea of how long it will be before the first test? We know we're not the only ones here for the purpose, but even a guess would help us to—"

"I can do better than guess," the man interrupted, leaning back and looking only at Lorand. "I can tell you exactly when your first test will be, since you'll be going for it as soon as you leave here. We don't believe in wasting time here in the capitol, so you'd better get used to it. Take these papers, and Jamrin will show you where to go."

Lorand took his set of papers woodenly, shocked to hear that the testing would begin so soon. But it wasn't *his* expression that the man behind the table was watching. The man's faint smile was a reaction to the way Hat had paled, as well as to the visible unsteadiness of Hat's hands as he took his own sheaf of papers. The sudden appearance of another man, from a group of three in the dimness to the right rather than out of thin air, caught Lorand's attention, but Hat had to be nudged with an elbow before he could gather himself together well enough to follow the newcomer.

Their guide led the way across the vastness of the building without looking back, and Lorand had to deliberately keep himself from running to keep up. Lengthening his stride did the job well enough, not to mention keeping him from looking like a scatterbrained fool. He still felt shaken at the idea that the testing would start so *soon*, but he refused to lose himself to mindless fright.

Hat, though, seemed to be another story. Lorand's long-time friend *did* run a few steps in an effort to keep up, after having almost forgotten to take his case of clothing and possessions with him. And it looked like he *had* forgotten that Lorand was there. All his attention centered on the man they followed, his thin shoulders hunched as if in an effort to block out the rest of the world. Hat radiated terror, but this was the chance he'd been waiting for and he obviously had no intention of missing it.

Lorand would have tried speaking to Hat if they hadn't been moving so briskly, so he decided it might be a good thing they were. Hat clearly wasn't going to let *anything* interfere with his dream, not even someone who had been a lifetime friend. Lorand could understand his attitude to a certain degree, but beyond that his understanding broke down in confusion. He had no more intention of crawling home in failure than Hat did, but it didn't seem necessary to reject everything else in his life in order to get what he wanted.

At the brisk pace their guide Jamrin set, they crossed the wide stone floor rather quickly. Lorand wouldn't have been surprised if they'd been taken to one of the flights of steps that led higher in that gray stone building, but instead they were guided to one of the far archways leading outside again. Jamrin went down the two steps at the same brisk pace and headed across another stone walkway, which meant Lorand had no chance to stop and stare at the five buildings which stood in a circle beyond the building they'd just left. The five buildings were each rather large in their own right, but not as incredibly big as the one which guarded the approach to them.

Jamrin began to circle to the right, but they didn't have far to go. The first building on the right had a brass plaque with the symbol for Earth magic right beside its front door, and Jamrin stopped about ten feet in front of that door.

"That's where you go," he said, negligently throwing a thumb over his shoulder toward the building. "They'll tell you what to do next once you're inside. Now you can give me my tip."

"A tip for what?" Lorand began to demand. "You didn't do anything but race us here, so why—"

"Come on, Lor, don't be so bloody provincial," Hat interrupted with a strange grin, looking almost fevered. "We're here and we're about to test, and once we pass we'll have all the gold we want. What's a little silver more or less?"

He tossed a piece of silver to Jamrin before striding away toward the building's door, which meant he missed the flash of amusement in their former guide's eyes. Hat had fallen for some trick, then, but at least he'd saved Lorand from also being taken. Ignoring the expectant look Jamrin now wore as he held his hand out again, Lorand walked past the man and followed Hat to the building.

And now that Lorand had the time to notice, he could see that the building was made of oak resin rather than stone. The resin could only be extracted from trees by the concerted efforts of three talents, Earth, Water, and Spirit. It came out in a semi-liquid state, and hardened so slowly that it was possible to shape almost anything out of it before it reached its final solidified state. Lorand had never seen an entire building made out of resin, but he'd heard they were popular in areas which had regular earthquakes. Even solidified, the resin had a slight rubbery resilience which would let a building move *with* an earthquake rather than fall. But that left the question of why they had one—no, five—such buildings here in Gan Garee.

But Lorand had no time to consider a question like that, not when he'd reached the doorway leading into the creamy-white building. Hat was already inside, standing in front of another table with another man behind it, so Lorand joined him. The entrance area was fairly large and completely unfurnished except for the table and the chair the man sat in, but the lamps on the walls turned the area warm and friendly. The cream-colored resin was responsible for that, of course, being a good deal more cheerful than even light gray stone.

"All right, Hattial," the man behind the desk said, looking up from the sheaf of papers Hat had given him. "Everything is in order including Lugal's final evaluation, so we'll get right to the testing. Go through that doorway all the way to your left, and you'll be taken care of."

Lorand looked toward the doorway at the same time Hat did. The front entrance had had a large metal door on strong hinges standing open, but this inner doorway had nothing but a curtain covering it. The curtain was brightly colored in reds and yellows and oranges and pinks with white running through, which helped add to the friendly atmosphere of the room.

"Let's wish each other good luck now," Lorand began as he looked back toward Hat. "We may not get the chance later, so—"

He let the words break off as Hat just strode toward the curtained doorway, ignoring Lorand as if he weren't there. He'd heard what had been said to him, Lorand knew he had, but he'd obviously decided not to do even so little as exchange good wishes. Lorand tried to pity his friend, but annoyance and disgust were rising too sharply to allow much room for the kinder emotion.

"It often goes like that," Lorand heard once Hat had disappeared through the curtain. It was the man behind the table speaking, so Lorand turned back and handed over his set of papers as the man continued, "The ones with the smallest chance are often the ones who want it the most, and by the time they get here they can't see anyone or anything but those wants and wishes. He has every ounce of himself invested in what he's about to face, so don't think too unkindly of him."

"There's nothing wrong with wanting something with every fiber of your being," Lorand answered slowly with a faint frown. "I feel the same way myself, but I happen to look at it differently. I decided a long time ago that if you can't get what you want without stepping all over other people, you aren't a winner, you're a loser. A real winner doesn't *have* to sacrifice all sense of decency."

"There aren't many people in this world who would agree with that," the man returned with a faint smile. "They would point out that someone with your strength of talent can afford to be generous, since most will never be able to match you. But that's a philosophical discussion to be engaged in at another time. Your papers are all in order, so please go through the doorway on your extreme right."

Lorand nodded his thanks, but was suddenly aware of an uneasy feeling that wasn't for himself. Hat had been sent to the left, and the man behind the table seemed to know Master Lugal's opinion of Hat's chances. Were they going to put Hat through something that he couldn't possibly hope to handle? Maybe if he followed after he could do something to protect Hat . . .

"It's no longer possible for anyone to help your friend," the man said with faint annoyance as Lorand stared at the doorway to the left. "He'll be facing the same thing you will, the same thing all hopefuls face when they come here. Go and take your own test, and let the Fates see to the both of you."

Lorand took a deep breath and nodded, thanked the man, then walked to the doorway to the right. There *was* nothing left he could do for Hat, and he did have his own test ahead of him. But somehow the brightness of the curtain over the doorway had lost some of its warmth and welcome.

Stepping through the curtain brought Lorand into a hall, one that was well-lit by wall lamps. Three people sat in an alcove to the left, two men and a woman, and all three rose to their feet while one of the men nodded expressionlessly.

"Follow me," was all the man said before he headed up the hallway, the other man and woman coming along behind Lorand. They made a small parade to the end of the hall and around a gentle curve, until they reached a closed doorway made of the same resin as the rest of the building.

"Leave your case out here and go inside, then sit on the stool," the man who had been in the lead said, gesturing to the closed door. "You'll be given further directions in just a few minutes."

Lorand felt an odd tingle of . . . *something* in the air, but he put his case down and did as he'd been told. The resin door swung smoothly and quietly inward to show him a round, high room that was empty of all furniture, except for the stool which stood beside the wall directly opposite the door. Lorand headed for the stool and didn't notice that the door had swung shut again until he turned to sit on the stool. For some reason that bothered him and he half rose to go over and open it again, but instead he just sank back down onto the stool. The lamplight coming through the large squares of transparent resin which circled the room at several points showed there was nothing on the inside of the

door to open it with. It fit so perfectly in the space in which it
was hung, the door seams were almost invisible.

"That's right, you can't get out again unless we let you
out," Lorand heard, but from somewhere above. He looked
up to see that a large square panel high in the wall had been
opened, and the man he'd followed looked out of it. And
now that he'd noticed the one square, he could see the
others, smaller and still closed, which completely circled the
room well above his head.

"This is the first of your tests, but it can also turn out to be
the last," the man continued, sounding as if he spoke a
prepared speech. "It doesn't matter whether or not you want
to pass, you *have* to pass if you intend to continue living.
Failure in this test means death, so you'd better keep that in
mind during the next few minutes. Good luck or goodbye."

And with that the man shut the wide panel, leaving
Lorand shocked and disbelieving. They couldn't be serious
about that, about it being his life if he failed! That was
ridiculous and totally unreasonable, not to mention insane!
People don't *kill* you if you fail, they just—

All thoughts of protest died when the smaller square
windows opened all around, and soil began to pour through
them. Lorand was already on his feet, and reflex sent his
head down and his arms up to keep the cascading earth away
from his face. His last glimpse said they meant to drop tons
of earth on him, enough to bury him alive. But they also
hadn't told him what to *do*, what way they expected him to
save himself!

And that was when the chills hit, despite the dust and
closeness generated by the falling soil. How Lorand avoided
dying was for *him* to figure out, there on the spot, in the
middle of the cascading earth. It had already begun to pile
up on the floor, showing how little time it would take to fill
the room completely. He would be dead long before that
happened, of course, buried under the first tons of earth to
rise above his six-feet-plus worth of height.

Lorand had never been so frightened in his entire life, but
when he began to cough and choke on the dust rising into the
air he also began to get angry. He *wanted* to be there and
show what he could do, but no one had stopped to find that
out. They'd simply assumed he had to be forced into trying
his best, and had put his life at risk to accomplish that. They

were ignorant fools and would-be murderers, and he'd show them the error of their ways if it was the last thing he did!

And that was when he reached for the power, finding it leaping to join with him even more eagerly than it usually did. He used it first to cause the earth to fall around rather than on him, at the same time clearing the dust from the air he breathed. That gave him a place to stand and think in peace, at least for a handful of minutes. After that he'd start to run out of time, but he hadn't yet reached that point. He still had time to think of something . . .

He sent a searching gaze all around the room, looking for something, *anything* that would help to save him, and he almost missed it. With all that earth pouring out of the walls it was hard to see anything clearly, but he finally noticed that the large panel his guide had opened and spoken from wasn't joining the others in pouring dirt on him. Beyond the stream of earth he could just see that it remained closed and quiet, and even more importantly didn't have mounds of earth piled in front of it. The door he'd come in by did, and trying to clear it would have been futile even if he could have opened it. It was possible to do many things using Earth magic, but making earth go against its nature and *not* mound wasn't something that would work for long.

So that left the large panel as Lorand's only chance for escape. The biggest problem with *that*, however, was the panel's location, a good six feet above Lorand's head. The falling earth had already mounded knee-deep around Lorand and got deeper by the minute, but it wasn't deep enough—or firm enough—to stand on to reach that panel.

Lorand automatically pushed his clear space out a little farther as he looked around again, wasting no strength or effort on keeping his feet and legs free. When he thought of something to do he'd free himself, but right now he needed to figure out how to get a lot higher. If only there was something to climb on! The short stool was useless, of course, not to mention being half buried already. There had to be something—!

And then the obvious answer came to Lorand with a groan. The panel was the only way out of that room, and the only way to reach it was to climb something. The only thing available to climb was the falling earth, which he'd be able to fashion into a flight of stairs. It was just about certain he was *meant* to use the earth to fashion a stairway, but the solution wasn't as easy to do as it was to say. Magic had all the limitations of the element of its affinity, and earth was notoriously stubborn about not allowing the impossible.

Like stacking it up to make a stairway, for instance. Even a temporary stairway had to be properly and firmly based, otherwise the whole construction would come tumbling down at the worst possible minute. Even a ramp would need a usable angle, one that could be climbed in some way that wasn't straight up. That room wasn't big enough to allow the construction of a decent ramp so it would have to be stairs after all, but that brought up one very important question: was there enough earth to build a usable stairway *with*?

Lorand looked up at the earth pouring out of the panels and groaned again. It was already deep enough in the room that his knees were covered, but that didn't mean there was enough earth to construct a stairway almost twelve feet high. His base would have to be the entire width of the room, otherwise he'd run out of tread space before he reached the necessary height. Or run out of building material.

Lorand cursed under his breath, suddenly realizing what he would have to do but not knowing if he could. He'd have to begin to build his stairway with the earth already available, and then would have to hold it together until enough new earth fell through to continue and complete the job. It would be one of the hardest things he'd ever done, requiring as it did that he split his attention and ability. While knowing that if he faltered, it would all come crashing down to bury him . . . Right, no problem at all.

A small stream of falling earth hit Lorand in the face, showing him the direct way that he'd let his attention wander. He wiped away the dirt even as he reestablished full control, realizing it was a good thing the lapse in attention had happened. It had been a mild lesson in what would happen if he let his attention wander again, when he would pay for the distraction with more than a dirty face. He knew what had to be done, so he'd better get started doing it.

Another minute of thought before beginning brought Lorand a small revelation. If he made his stairway only wide enough to hold his foot, he'd need less earth to make it which would in turn take less time. He'd been picturing fairly wide treads, but those weren't necessary. He only needed enough width for stability, and a base as wide as possible would help with that. Now to get down to it . . .

"Me and my big mouth," Lorand muttered after many long minutes of sweat-filled effort. Getting "down" to it had proven to be the first of his problems, since the earth that had already fallen was neither properly placed nor solidly packed. Lorand had to move the soil away from where he meant to construct his base, hold it back while placing his building material properly, then begin the first treads. He also had to keep the newly falling earth from damaging his stairway, while at the same time keep it off his face so that he could see. Not to mention breathe, which was becoming harder rather than easier.

By the time Lorand had half a dozen steps built, the stairway was better than five feet high, all the available earth had been used, and he himself had turned to mud because of the sweat pouring out of him. The magic flowed into him just as strongly as it ever had, but his handling of it wasn't the same. The more tired he became the harder it was to control the magic, and suddenly a new worry added itself to the rest: would he *continue* to be able to stay merged with his magic?

A spurt of falling earth broke through the shield he had over himself, adding itself to the mud already smeared on his face. Lorand wiped at it with the back of his hand, making the mess worse rather than better, wishing he could be impatient with himself over the brief lapse. But what he felt now was more fear than impatience, since every childhood horror story he'd ever heard was suddenly coming back to him. All those warnings against trying to do more with the power than you were naturally able to . . . How naughty children who didn't listen turned themselves into mindless vegetables that people had to put down like the poor, maimed animals they were . . .

If Lorand had had the strength he would have shuddered, knowing as he did that all those stories hadn't been exaggerations on the part of adults trying to keep their children manageable. He could still remember that little girl at school, when he'd been nine or ten and she'd been about the same. Her talent had been Water magic, she'd been incredibly strong for her age, and the indulgence of her parents had made her more arrogant than anyone should have been allowed to be.

Lorand carefully filtered more of the dust out of the air around him, needing to take a deep breath without tiny pieces of grit filling his mouth and lungs. That little girl had ignored the words of caution from their teachers, and had constantly searched for new ways to show how good she was. When spring came that year with its thunderstorms, the little girl had been delighted. She decided to gentle a thunderstorm the way Middle practitioners sometimes did, not realizing it took more than one Middle and more than Water magic. Lorand could still see her quietly slipping out of the schoolroom with a triumphant smile on her face . . .

Her screams had brought everyone running outside, but by then it was already too late for the girl. Afterward their teachers had explained that she'd summoned enough power to handle the thunderstorm, but hadn't herself been able to handle that much power. It had filled her beyond bursting, raging through her when her control slipped. The teachers had quickly herded the other children back inside the school building, but not before Lorand had seen the girl.

She'd been sitting slumped on the ground, the most horrible blankness and slackness in her face, a still-breathing body with no one at home any longer. No one home now, and never, ever again. . . .

Lorand did shudder then, and then another spurt of earth into his face brought him a frightening awareness. The soil was now coming faster and harder out of the openings, almost as if it meant to batter down his stairway along with himself. Now it would be more difficult to shield everything, not to mention harder to slow the rain of earth in order to work with it.

Lorand felt the aching weariness in both his body and his mind, at the same time becoming too aware of the increasing strength of his magic. He would need that much strength and more to do what had to be done, but would he be able to handle it? A sickening picture of that little girl's face rose up before him, bringing with it a terrible chill. He'd have to *find* a way to handle the magic, but what if he failed and ended up the same way? How was he supposed to do what was necessary with *that* hanging over him? How . . . ?

SEVEN

Jovvi waited for the guard to come to the door after the coach had stopped, and then let the man help her to the ground. The neighborhood was odd, not the middle-of-town or residential area she'd been expecting the coach to stop in. A very large stone wall stood directly ahead with guardsmen in front of the openings, and it was even possible to see other coaches a short distance away to either side of her own. The coach to her right disgorged two men who were, by their bucolic clothing, obviously from the country, and neither one even glanced in her direction. They were too busy staring at the massive wall with their mouths open.

The single man leaving the coach to Jovvi's left was dressed in the height of fashion, and his annoyed movements and sullen frown directed toward the coach he'd just left told her he was probably newly arrived and therefore would be just as useless for her purposes. She needed someone who could tell her which neighborhood to rent her house in, something she intended to see to before getting around to that testing. That way she'd be all ready to begin her new life as soon as she failed that tiresome test.

"Just step this way, ma'am," the coach guard said to her gently and carefully, gesturing toward the closest entrance through the wall. "Hark and me'll carry your trunk that far, and then the gate guards'll get somebody to take over."

"That's *so* sweet of you," Jovvi told the man with a warm, encouraging smile, trying to remember what his name was. "I feel so safe and comfortable with you looking after me, but I must confess that this place frightens me. I was hoping to be taken somewhere . . . nicer, where I'll find it possible to rent a house. You don't happen to know a neighborhood like that, do you?"

The wistfulness Jovvi put into the question nearly melted the man where he stood, but he still found it possible to shake his head regretfully.

"We can't take you no place else than here, ma'am," he said, sounding as if he were admitting some terrible crime. "Your ticket says you're here to test for High practitioner, and this is where all applicants got to be taken. First you gotta register, and then you can ask about that house."

Jovvi felt thoroughly annoyed, but her small sigh of defeat and weak, tremulous smile told the man that she'd realized she had no choice. She *had* to register for that foolish test first, and only then would she be free to find her perfect house. Well, if she had to she had to, and she'd done harder things in her life. Besides, the people registering her might know more about the sort of neighborhood she wanted than a coach guard would.

Feeling considerably brightened by that thought, Jovvi followed the two men with her trunk to the opening in the wall, where the guardsmen who stood the post were already studying her. In point of fact they'd had their eyes on her since she'd left the coach, and their attitudes were perfectly plain. She'd seen the same on every man who had come to the residence and then had discovered her, which hopefully meant that the residences there in Gan Garee weren't stuffed full of courtesans of her caliber. When the gentlemen of this city found out she'd taken up residence here, she would hopefully have more gold than she could easily count.

"This lady's here for the testin'," the coach guard told the gate guards as soon as they were all close enough. "This here's her trunk, and you'll need to call somebody to carry it for her."

"Set it down just inside the gate, to the left," one of the gate guards directed, gesturing behind him without taking his gaze from Jovvi. "We'll keep an eye on it while she's inside, and when she comes back out we'll find somebody to help her with it."

The coach guard and driver did as they'd been told, then took an awkward minute saying goodbye and wishing her luck. Jovvi was as gracious to the two as she made a habit of being to all men, since a girl never knew which of them would turn out to be most significant in her life. When they finally went back to their coach Jovvi turned her attention to the gate guards, but before she could speak one of them held out his hand.

"I need to see your coach ticket, ma'am," he said, the words polite but the tone inflexible. "We heard what the coachmen said, but we have to see for ourselves."

The request surprised Jovvi, but not so far that it completely disrupted her plans. She reached into her bag for the stub which was all there was left of her ticket, and tremulously smiled as she handed it over.

"Everything here is so strange and frightening," she said to the guard, letting him see the helplessness in her eyes. "Are they going to . . . *hurt* me in there? If only I knew what to expect it might not be so bad."

"I wish I could help you," the guardsman said quite sincerely, apparently caught in the depth of her eyes. "If I knew what they did in there I'd tell you all about it, but all I know is what I tell every applicant: use the archway directly behind this post to enter the building, and then hand over this stub. They'll let you know what to do next. I'm really sorry."

"I understand," Jovvi said warmly and gently as she took the stub back. The man was really quite attractive, and although it was unlikely he'd ever be able to afford to become one of her regular patrons, there was no sense in hurting him. He would have helped her if he could have, after all. His inability simply meant she'd have to find someone else.

The second gate guard hadn't said a word, but he stepped aside just as quickly as the first when Jovvi moved toward the gate and through it. She could see the archway she was supposed to use to enter the very large building straight ahead, as well as other people heading for that building. Most of the others seemed rather hesitant about approaching, and although Jovvi could understand that, she didn't share the emotion. She wanted this registering business over and done with, and then she'd be able to get on with what was really important.

The archway took her from afternoon sunshine into lamplit dimness, but it wasn't so dark that she couldn't see a table to the right of the archway with a man seated behind it. The table was clearly being used as a desk, and when the man looked up, Jovvi produced her tremulous smile again.

"I was told someone in here is supposed to take what's left

of my ticket," she ventured, hesitantly holding out the stub. "Is this the right place?"

"It certainly is, my dear," the older man answered with a gentle smile, taking the stub. "Just a moment, and I'll locate your file."

There had been a number on the ticket stub, and the man searched through a box of papers, apparently looking for a match to the number. When he found it he put the stub aside, then reached into a box with cards of some sort. Another moment and he'd written Jovvi's name on the card, and then he looked up again.

"You'll need to wear this identification at all times, my dear," he instructed in a kindly way as he attached a chain to the middle of the card. "Just slip it over your head and take the paperwork, and then I'll have someone show you where you go next."

"But . . . my trunk is still outside near the entrance gate I used," Jovvi protested weakly and helplessly as she took the card and chain. "It's been such a *long* trip and I'm so very tired . . . It won't really hurt anything if I find a place to rest and leave my things first, will it? I'd be so very grateful . . ."

"For your sake, I wish it were possible," the man answered with a sigh, his sadness as real as any Jovvi had ever seen. "Unfortunately the procedural rules are very clear, but please don't let that disturb you. I'm sure they'll help you find a nice place to stay once you've finished speaking to them."

Jovvi voiced her own sigh, but the accompanying smile and nod of surrender were harder to accomplish. These people were really beginning to be tiresome, especially since she did need some rest. After days of traveling, it was difficult to remember what sitting still in one place for more than an hour felt like.

"Reshin here will accompany you the rest of the way," the man said, gesturing to the *woman* he'd called over from a small group of people to one side of his table. "Just go along with her, and you'll be on your way to proper lodgings before you know it."

Jovvi thanked him with automatic warmth as she slipped the chain carefully over her head, settled the card against her chest, then took the set of papers he'd held out. The card now blocked a proper view of her cleavage, but with another woman as her only companion, it didn't really matter. The woman crooked a finger and began to head toward an archway all the way over on the other side of the building, and Jovvi had no choice but to follow. The woman walked slowly enough to let her catch up, and once Jovvi did, the woman looked at her with a surprisingly friendly smile.

"I love that suit you're wearing," the woman Reshin said, sounding as if she really meant it. "Did you buy it here in Gan Garee?"

"No, actually I had it made for me in Rincammon, where I live," Jovvi answered, trying to put the same sort of friendliness into her voice. She never got along as well with women as she did with men, but that was usually because of their jealousy and resentment. Very few women were able to be successful courtesans with all the benefits which went with the position, and that naturally turned them resentful. Jovvi understood the feeling very well, and would have shared it if *she* hadn't been able to live the life.

"Well, that pale violet really suits you," Reshin continued in the same friendly way. "I wish it suited me as well since I love the color, but I've learned that it doesn't love me back. But that's just as well, I suppose. My husband-to-be likes to see me in red, and that color I do get along with."

The woman's black hair made that a given, and there was nothing really wrong with the red-trimmed gray dress she had on. It was a bit too severe for Jovvi's taste, but it seemed to go well with the dimness and distance of that building. Jovvi remained silent until they had almost reached the far archway, but then she simply had to ask about what lay ahead. Making decent plans without knowing what you were about to face just wasn't possible, and there was too much at stake not to take the chance.

"Reshin . . . what's supposed to happen next?" she asked diffidently, deliberately slowing the pace they'd both been walking at. "I'm . . . not really used to things like this, and I hate to admit it but I'm . . . frightened. Is there *anything* you can tell me?"

"I could tell you everything I know, but none of it would help you," Reshin answered, flashing her a compassionate smile before touching her arm to increase her pace again. "My job is to accompany applicants to the proper testing area, but I don't even get to go through the door. What goes

on in the building, I'm told, is none of my business, and if I'
tried to find out anyway they would have dismissed me
Since I'd rather not give up this position until I marry, yo
can understand why I've curbed my curiosity."

Jovvi nodded, understanding the woman's position per
fectly. There were few enough positions for women in th
business world as it was. Losing a good one for being to
nosy would have been horrible, but that left *her* swinging in
the wind. Well, there were bound to be people inside tha
building Reshin had mentioned, and at least one of them
would *have* to be a man. . . .

Stepping outside again was something of a relief, at leas
until Jovvi got a good look at the circle of buildings beyon
the wide walk separating them from the very large entranc
building. The buildings that were part of the circle wer
made of resin, a material Jovvi had seen only once before i
her life. It had been used by a very wealthy man to form hi
"playroom" just beyond his back garden, and Jovvi ha
almost ended up inside it. She'd been very young at the tim
and hadn't yet met Allestine, and hadn't known what tha
very wealthy man did to young girls in that room of his. If h
hadn't decided to take that other girl in first, and if Jovv
hadn't been lucky enough to hear the girl's screams when
servant had opened the door . . .

"Well, this is it," Reshin said, drawing Jovvi back from
nightmare memories. "Just go straight in, and try not t
worry. They really do need people like you, remember, s
they can't possibly do anything *too* terrible to them."

The point was a good one, and helped Jovvi pull hersel
together. Reshin patted her arm in comfort and support
then waited while Jovvi forced herself to walk inside. At leas
the door was open, and hopefully looked as if it would sta
that way.

Inside there were lamps to brighten up the cream-colore
resin of the walls, not to mention colorful hangings coverin
what seemed to be multiple doorways. Seeing hanging
rather than actual doors made Jovvi feel even better, enoug
so that she was able to approach the man at another tabl
with something like her usual confidence.

"Is this what you're supposed to have?" Jovvi asked th
man, shyly proffering the papers. When he took them with
smile Jovvi felt even more encouraged, and so decided not t

waste any more time. "I . . . was told you might be able to help me find a decent place to rest for a while," she ventured carefully. "I've been traveling for days, and I'm absolutely exhausted. It's—"

"All in good time, child," the man interrupted gently, his smile still very evident. "We'll make sure you have what you need, but first you have to speak to some of our people. Just go through that doorway all the way to the right, and they'll take care of you."

Jovvi was getting very tired of thanking people for being of no help at all, but she did it again anyway and then walked to the proper doorway. Beyond the hanging was a long hall, and in an alcove to the left sat three men. They got to their feet when they saw her, and the one in the lead smiled faintly.

"Come this way and I'll get you settled into a room," he said before Jovvi could try to get somewhere with him. "There are things we need to know, and after we get our answers we'll answer any questions *you* may have."

Jovvi sighed as she followed the man, but she wasn't so impatient that she didn't know the other two men also followed her. That made her faintly uneasy, but she forced herself to keep in mind what Reshin had said. People with talent like hers were *needed*, so it wasn't likely that the government would allow her to be savaged. They didn't know she meant to fail their very first test, after all, so she ought to be perfectly safe at least until that happened.

The man who walked ahead led her around a curve in the hall, then stopped in front of a door. It was made of the same resin as the rest of the building, but opened easily when the man pushed on it.

"This is the place," he said, stepping aside in the gentlemanly way to let her walk in first. She began to do just that, but stopped short only one step in. The room was as dark as a moonless night, maybe even darker. It wasn't even possible to see the floor under her feet where she stood.

"Oh, good grief, some fool turned down all the lamps," the man holding the door behind her said in annoyance. "If you'll just step forward one more pace, I'll be able to reach this lamp right by the door."

Jovvi didn't like the idea of moving forward into all that pitch darkness, but the promise of immediate lamplight helped her to do it. "Just stand still now," she heard the man

say, but instead of producing more light she suddenly ha‚
less. Rather than light a lamp he had closed the door, an‚
now even the feeble light from the hall was gone!

"Oh, no!" Jovvi tried to scream out, but the terrifie‚
protest turned into a whisper. She had been left in the dar‚
with who-knew-what, and couldn't even bring herself to tr‚
to retrace her steps to the door. Darkness like that ha‚
always terrified her, and it was so bad that she couldn't eve‚
begin to think of anything to do!

It seemed like forever that she stood trembling mindlessl‚
there in the dark, but then she heard a noise from some‚
where above her. It sounded like a scraping of some sort, bu‚
she was distracted from it by the sudden brightening o‚
lamps being turned up. She saw the lamps as soon as the‚
began to glow, and it didn't matter that they sat behin‚
windows of clear resin higher in the walls of that place. The‚
were providing the light she needed so badly, which soothe‚
her terror—until she was able to look around.

"That's right, you're perfectly safe as long as you stay o‚
the walkway," the man who'd led her there said over he‚
horrified gasp. That's who it was who had opened a smal‚
doorway in the wall above the lamps, a place she was no‚
afraid to look up toward. "The drop to either side of th‚
walkway is very deep and very deadly, but you'll be fine a‚
long as you don't fall off."

Jovvi wanted to scream that she was *about* to fall off tha‚
very narrow walkway, but she wouldn't have been able to ge‚
the words out even if they'd been true. Even as terrified a‚
she was, she would *not* let herself do anything stupid lik‚
fainting, which would certainly have plunged her off into th‚
unlit depths to either side of where she stood. Only the four‚
foot-wide walkway stretched across the abyss, providin‚
footing between the door she'd come in by and another doo‚
at the far end.

"In order to leave that room, you have to reach th‚
doorway you can see at the other end of the walkway," th‚
man above her continued. "The door behind you can't b‚
opened from your side, but the other one can be. All yo‚
have to do to reach it is exercise your talent. If you do i‚
properly you'll survive to reach the other side, but if yo‚
don't you'll die. The choice is yours, and I certainly hop‚
you'll make the right one. Good luck or goodbye."

Jovvi heard the sound of the small door closing again, but still couldn't make herself look up. And even beyond that, she was confused by what the man had said. Walking that four-foot-wide stretch would be nerve-wracking for her, but she wouldn't need her talent to do it. She'd simply get herself moving, and before she knew it she'd be on the other side. She took a slow breath, getting herself ready to start, and that was when *it* began.

Jovvi had served men of every aspect there was, and suddenly it felt as if the room were filled with every one of them—and all of them were either angry or upset. All those people were probably hidden somewhere below, but it did feel as though they were right there in the room. The heavy feelings battered at her where she stood, almost knocking her over, as palpable and real as if someone stood beside her pushing at her. Jovvi knew then she'd been wrong. She *would* have to use her ability, or she'd never be able to stand up under the assault.

And "standing up" had taken on a very special, very important meaning. Jovvi could feel the sweat begin to bead her forehead as the mass of projected feelings grew even stronger, threatening to knock her around like some invisible wind. When she almost staggered under the load her terror increased; staggering now could mean falling off the walk-way, into the depths and certain death.

Jovvi had been frightened many times in her life, and each of those times she had reached out blindly with her skill, learning the best ways to keep herself safe. Now she no longer reached out blindly, but with the experience of practice and a certain maturity. It was her place to soothe all those raging feelings, to calm them to a proper balance that would let her maintain her own balance. She had no more than about twenty-five or thirty feet to walk before she reached safety, but she needed to be steady on her feet to do it.

So she pushed her fear aside and reached out with that very special part of herself, knowing she first had to calm the storm before she might escape. There were women as well as men raging about, she could tell that easily, but reaching and calming them all wasn't quite the same. Bringing one or two or three to balance took no more effort than it ever had, but when she released them to touch the others they immediately went back to raging. It was like trying to gather up a bunch of frightened chickens without using an enclosure to hold them. As soon as she took her attention from the ones she'd caught to catch the others, the first bunch scattered again.

"But how am I supposed to catch them all at the same time?" she whispered, feeling like whimpering. "They're all running in a different direction . . ."

Which wasn't precisely what was happening, but the analogy was close enough. She had to touch and soothe and balance all those minds at the same time, something she'd never tried before.

And something she wasn't sure she could do. Her body had begun to tremble from being held so rigidly, but she didn't dare relax. And the storm felt as if it were growing stronger again, which would make it all that much harder to do. But if she didn't find a way to succeed she would die, and she didn't *want* to die. She wanted to live, but how was she supposed to accomplish that? How . . . ?

EIGHT

Clarion stepped out of the coach in a part of Gan Garee he'd never seen before, but that wasn't surprising. He'd never been the sort to frequent that kind of neighborhood, and especially not by public transportation. He turned for a final look at the coach, knowing he'd never forget the experience of traveling in it—and would do his best never to repeat it. He couldn't remember ever being so uncomfortable in his entire life.

But that statistic was in danger of being topped by

whatever his next experience would be. He turned to study the guard wall again as the coachmen struggled to remove his trunk from their vehicle, trying not to be incensed a second time over their refusal to take him anywhere near his and Mother's house there in the city. His ticket demanded that he be brought *here*, they'd insisted, and even an ordinary coach stop deeper in the city wouldn't do. He was supposed to "register" in this place, whatever that meant.

"Just follow us to th' guard post, boy," the coach driver said as he and his assistant carried the trunk past Clarion on his right. "They'll get you straightened out, or at least squared away."

The other man carrying the trunk guffawed at something he considered amusing, but Clarion couldn't see the joke. The commoners had been rude to him at every opportunity, usually in some indirect way that Clarion hadn't been able to protest, and he was heartily sick of it. They must have been related to his mother's house servants in some manner, but the time of indignity was finally over. At least that was one benefit in being here: he would never have to see those miserable commoners again. The thought of that let Clarion smile as he strolled after the two over to the guard post.

"This here one's yours," the driver said to one of the guardsmen before setting Clarion's trunk down just beyond the men and inside the gate. "You boys have yourselves a real nice day."

And then the men were heading back to their coach, depriving Clarion even of the pleasure of refusing to tip them! That entire situation had long since turned intolerable, but even the intolerable should have had limits.

"Let's see your ticket, friend," one of the guardsmen said, taking Clarion's attention. The hand he held out was large and meaty and blunt-fingered, clearly marking another member of the lower classes.

"Ticket?" Clarion echoed, thoroughly confused. "No one told me I needed a ticket to enter here. Are you trying to charge me for something I have no real need of, my good man? If so, then—"

"Your coach ticket," the guardsman interrupted with what looked suspiciously like a swallowed sigh. "I need to see the coach ticket you used to get here."

Clarion frowned in thought, trying to remember what he'd

done with the remnants of the coach ticket. It wasn't his habit to collect keepsakes even of pleasant occasions, so there was an excellent chance that he'd thrown the useless stub away. Searching his coat pockets was proving fruitless, but just as he was about to say so, his fingers finally brushed the thing. It was something of a surprise that he *hadn't* thrown it away, but at least it saved him from having to order the guardsmen to overlook the stub's absence.

"Okay," the guardsman grunted after inspecting the stub, now offering the useless thing back. "Take this inside to the archway just to the left of the one directly behind this post. When you give it to them, they'll tell you what to do next."

"Who do you mean to have carry my trunk?" Clarion asked as he reluctantly took back the ticket stub. "Since there doesn't appear to be anyone else around, you and your companion will probably have to—"

"The trunk will be fine right where it is," the man interrupted again, now appearing fractionally more impatient. "We're not about to let anyone walk off with it, and you can reclaim it once you come out again. Dragging it along with you would be a waste of time and effort."

Clarion would have enjoyed arguing that opinion, but it had become obvious that he *would* have to drag the trunk if he took it with him. These two oafs were clearly refusing to carry it for him, so it was either leave the trunk here, or look a fool dragging it behind him. So Clarion swallowed what he would have said under other circumstances, nodded curtly, then took himself through the gate the two men guarded.

Inside was one of those would-be grand administrative buildings one could find in various parts of the city, but this one lacked the doors of the last one Clarion had seen. The structure had nothing but simple archways, and the one he'd been told to use was the next one to the left of the archway straight ahead. Clarion had the urge to pick an archway at random and use that instead, but being frivolous would only delay his reaching Mother's house and some true comfort. He therefore strode to the proper entrance and walked inside.

Just to the right of the archway was a table with a man behind it, and when Clarion stopped in front of the table the man looked up.

"I'm told *you're* to be given this thing," Clarion said to

him, handing over the ticket stub. "Once you've done whatever it is you do with it, I'll require two strong men to carry my trunk, and the summoning of a public carriage to take me to my house."

"What you'll require is putting on this identity tag as soon as I finish filling it out," the man countered dryly without looking up from the rectangle of heavy paper he wrote on. "After that you'll follow the guide provided you to the proper building, and then the people inside will tell you what you'll require next. Do you understand that?"

Clarion's jaws were clamped together in anger when the man glanced up at him, but apparently that was enough of an answer to satisfy the lout. He continued writing for another moment, attached a thin chain to the paper when he was through, then handed the whole thing over. Clarion disliked putting on the foolish thing, especially since he had to remove his hat to do it, but better that than dignifying the man's remarks with words. When the thing hung around Clarion's neck the man silently handed over a small sheaf of papers, then gestured to one of two people who had sat a short distance away.

"This is Fellar, and he'll take you to where you have to go," the man behind the table said. "Give them that set of papers when you get there, and they'll tell you what to do next."

"You're repeating yourself," Clarion commented in as offhand a manner as he could manage while turning away from the man. "That's one of the first signs of old age, I'm told. Do have a nice day."

And with that he walked off after the man Fellar, who was already heading for the far side of the building. Nothing in the way of a countering comment was shouted after him, which made Clarion feel inexplicably good. He'd never before found it possible to use that smooth but distant and superior tone he admired so much, but this time it had come flowing out as if he'd used it all his life. The general situation was still intolerable, but apparently even the intolerable had its bright side.

Fellar moved at a brisk pace ahead of Clarion, but Clarion made no effort to hurry and catch up as he might have done earlier. He'd gotten to Gan Garee completely on his own without the least difficulty, and soon he would be free of these stupid people and their nonsensical requirements. With that in view he had no reason to put himself out hurrying after some nobody who was there for no other reason than to guide him. If the man found himself too far ahead of Clarion, he'd have to stop and wait.

Which was exactly what happened. Clarion reached the archway in the far side of the building which Fellar had disappeared through a pair of moments earlier, and stepped through himself to find the man waiting only a short distance ahead on the stone approach. Beyond him was a wide circle of rather large, odd buildings, and it took Clarion a moment to realize they were made of resin. Why that would be so he had no idea, but it wasn't possible to ask about them. That foolish guide had taken off again, and all Clarion could do was follow.

The man Fellar circled to the left, and eventually stopped in front of one of the buildings. Clarion strolled up to it a moment later, ignoring the fleeting expression of annoyance on the man's face.

"This is where you hafta go," Fellar said, jerking a thumb at the building before holding out his hand. He was obviously asking for a tip, something not quite unexpected. Clarion smiled faintly as he handed over the two coppers he'd already taken out of his pocket, then he entered the building without a backward glance.

The symbol for Air magic had been next to the door on the outside of the building, but the first inner room was perfectly ordinary. Soft lamps lit cream-white walls of resin, garish hangings covered various doorways, and another table held another man sitting behind it. This man was fractionally younger than the one in the other building, and he looked up at Clarion with a neutral smile.

"I was told these are to be given to you," Clarion said as he handed over the small sheaf of papers he'd been carrying. "Now I'd like to be told how soon I'll be free to go home for a bit of long-denied rest."

"All in good time, sir," the man soothed as he checked through the papers, his attitude more mollifying than dismissive. "There's just another question or two to be answered, and then you'll be finished. If you'll step through that doorway all the way to your right, they'll show you to a room where you can sit down for a while."

Arguing would have been a waste of time, so Clarion swallowed his annoyance and simply walked to the indicated doorway. He stepped through to find three people in an alcove to the left, two women and a man. All three rose to their feet at his appearance, and the man stepped forward.

"Follow me, please," he said, then began to lead the way up the hall they stood in. But at least this new guide moved slowly enough to be followed easily and looked back to be sure his charge was with him, so again Clarion made no protest. He followed the man while the two women followed him, and in a moment they reached a closed door.

"Just make yourself as comfortable as possible in here, and we'll be right with you," the man said, pushing open the door with very little effort. Clarion sniffed to show his displeasure, but still stepped inside to look around. A bare room of resin it was, lit by lamps hidden behind windows of clear resin high in the walls, with no furniture but a single low stool. Clarion turned to demand what sort of joke that was supposed to be, but the man was gone behind the door which had silently closed.

"This is far too much," Clarion muttered in instantly increased annoyance. His limit for accepting the unacceptable had now been reached, and he would stand for no more. He stepped back to the door, intending to throw it open and march out to confront the fools, but there was nothing on the inside of the door to grasp. And it was closed so tightly the joining of door and jamb seemed almost seamless, giving Clarion the fleeting impression it was also sealed.

"*What* is going on here?" he demanded aloud, turning back to the rest of the room to confirm his impression that there was no other door. His question had been rhetorical, but a moment later he got an answer anyway. A scraping noise from above made him look up to see that a small door had been opened in the wall well above his head, and the man who had led him to that room now looked out.

"Your first and possibly last test is now before you," the man told him solemnly. "You must find a way out of the dilemma you will soon be presented with, otherwise you will die. Only you can save yourself, and if you don't accomplish it, no one will do it for you. Good luck or goodbye."

Clarion was so appalled, the man had pulled back and pushed closed the small door before Clarion had gathered his wits together enough to speak. By then it was too late, of course, but that didn't seem to matter much. Any demand for further explanations would probably have been ignored, and even if they'd been given, Clarion would certainly have had trouble understanding. Never before had his *life* been threatened, and he couldn't believe it was happening now. The man must have been joking, if not simply lying . . .

But that was when Clarion became aware of something else that had never happened. The air in the room . . . although he no longer consciously noticed it, he was always aware of the air in any place he happened to be. The pressure and shape of it changed according to the elevation of the place where it was, but the volume of it had never varied. Now . . . now the volume in that room was changing and lowering, as if someone or something slowly drew out the air and refused to allow it to flow back in. If something wasn't done, he would eventually lack enough to breathe!

The shock of that reached Clarion more directly than any words could have. The man hadn't been joking or lying; Clarion's life *was* in danger! His skill was with Air magic, but if someone didn't do something quickly, he'd have nothing left to work magic *with*.

No, not someone, *me*, Clarion thought with fear clutching at his heart. He took off his hat, intending to put it carefully on the stool, but simply dropped it to the floor instead. He was faced with the need to save himself, and the preservation of a hat came a long way down the list of what had to be done first. But what could he do? What *was* there to do?

The answer to that came quickly, as though part of his mind had waited all his life to begin functioning. The first thing he had to do was keep from losing any more air, and stretching out the fingers of his ability soon found the place where the air was being drawn out. He thickened the air at that point to keep it from flowing through the set of tiny holes in the wall, and the stratagem worked perfectly. No more air was drawn out through those holes, but that was when he became aware of the second set.

A number of frantic minutes went by while Clarion located one set of holes after the other, and once he'd found them all, the fright began to touch him again. There were almost a dozen sets, and if he took his attention from any of them, he would begin to lose air again. Which meant he had

o keep them sealed, but he also had to have enough of his
ability free to search for a way out of that room. It had
become perfectly clear that only his talent would get him out
of that horrible situation, so he *had* to do two things at once.

Or maybe three. Clarion wiped at the sweat on his brow
with the back of his hand, suddenly aware of how hard he
was breathing. The air around him had grown just a little too
thin for his lungs to work without effort, so he'd have to
bring down what air there was up near the ceiling. It did him
no good there, but gathering it closer to his face produced
even more sweat. He now worked harder than he ever had in
his life, but it still wasn't enough.

For he still had no way out of that place, except for the
wild idea he'd gotten in passing. The small door his guide to
that room had looked out of; it had closed inwardly, so it
ought to be possible to push it open from his side. The only
problem with that idea was how high the small door was,
more than six feet higher than the top of his head. Standing
on the stool would be a waste of time, but what else could he
stand on?

And how long would it be before his strength gave
out, bringing an abrupt end to his life? Clarion tangled his
fingers in his hair, feeling the fear inside him grow stronger.
He *had* to find a way out of there, but how? How?
How . . . ?

NINE

I was given a very early appointment at the testing center,
just past daybreak, in fact, but that wasn't a problem. I didn't
get much sleep the night before anyway, and finally gave up

trying. Getting up and dressed and simply waiting whil
everyone else slept was much easier, and had the benefit o
letting me be sure I wouldn't end up late.

I had no real appetite for breakfast but I ate it anyway
stuffing down every last crumb without tasting any of it. I'
heard that the first test would be the hardest, and applicant
needed all their strength to pass it. I *had* to pass it, and wa
prepared to do anything I had to to make that happen.

And I'd also picked up a very interesting point. Housing i
Gan Garee is usually difficult to find for transients, but righ
now, with so many competitors around, it had becom
impossible. For that reason, any large residence that took i
applicants as roomers during this time of testing enjoyed
very special status, like being immune to court actions whic
would change its ownership. I'd registered my house for tha
purpose just the day before, and now should be able t
concentrate on the test without being distracted.

Should be able to. I sighed at that thought as the publi
carriage took me toward the testing center, the city ju
beginning to wake up all around us. At the moment all
could concentrate on was the knot of fear in my middl
which twisted and tightened with every breath I took. M
life and sanity depended on my passing that test, an
determination isn't quite the same as confidence.

I'd been given a small card along with the appointmer
time, and that card got me past the guards and through th
outer wall. I'd heard that people of lesser ability were alway
trying to sneak in to take one of the tests, most of them bein
convinced that their evaluations had been wrong and the
did have the potential to reach High if only they were give
the chance to try. I could understand that outlook all to
easily, but although I sympathized with those poor unfortu
nates I didn't think much of their intelligence. Even margin
al talents were sent for testing, just to be on the safe side, s
misevaluations weren't very likely.

There weren't many people around at that early hour o
the morning, and the coolness of the air made me glad I wor
a long-sleeved dress. I'd been directed to a particular arcl
way into the building, and when I stepped through it I saw
man to the right, sitting behind a table. Even as I watched h
patted back a yawn, and I knew exactly how he felt.

"Good morning, young lady," he said pleasantly enoug

when I stopped in front of his table. "Since you're here this early you must live in the city, so I'll ask for your appointment card rather than your ticket stub."

"Don't applicants from the provinces ever get here this early?" I asked as I handed over the card, trying to divert myself just a little. If I didn't calm down, I'd probably end up exploding.

"Applicants from the provinces have their journeys here planned very carefully," he answered, digging through a box of papers before pulling out a set of them. "They arrive sometime between just before noon and midafternoon, and they're brought directly here. No sense in turning 'em loose in the city to get into mischief before they have the chance to test."

He flashed me another neutral smile, then gave all his attention to writing on a larger card than the one I'd given him. He was being very polite and pleasantly distant, but I knew it wasn't simply good manners making him act like that.

The people who came here to test for High were all strong Middles, meaning they were nobody you wanted to get angry at you. It might be against the law for us to use our talents against ordinary people, but that doesn't mean it never happens. If a drowned body is pulled out of the bay, it's almost impossible for the investigators to determine if that person drowned *in* the bay, or because of someone with a Water talent.

And then there was the matter of the tests. No one knew in advance who would or would not pass, and insulting an applicant could turn out to mean having insulted a High. At that point the man who did the insulting would certainly be out of a job, and possibly even finding it difficult to get another. Those who claim gold and silver mean nothing have never been in the position of needing to support a family, otherwise they would have learned better.

"All right, here you are," the man behind the table said, recapturing my attention. "This is your identification as an applicant, and you must wear it at all times. You have a number of stops to make throughout this building, and then you'll be taken to the place you have to go. Don't lose these papers, since you'll need to show them at all the stops."

By then I'd slipped the chain attached to the card over my

head, so I accepted the set of papers as a woman came up to
the table. I'd seen the man gesture the woman over, so she
had to be the one who would show me where to go. She
touched my arm before heading toward a stairway, proving
my theory, so I quickly followed along.

The stairs were made of the same stone as the building,
and we climbed quite a few of them before reaching the
second floor. I would have asked my guide about where we
were going and how long the stop would take, but she moved
just far enough ahead of me to make conversation awkward.
She also had no trouble using both hands to raise her skirt
high enough to avoid stepping on it, but one of my hands was
full of papers. Also using it to hold up my skirt took concentration, which worked even more against getting involved in talk.

At the top of the stairs the woman turned left, walked a
short distance to a door also on the left, then opened it and
went through. When I followed I found myself in a small
room with a man behind a table, a row of plain wooden
chairs, and two closed doors behind the man and his table.
My guide waited until I was inside, then silently left, closing
the door behind herself.

"Please have a seat," the man behind the table said with
no more than a glance for me. "Someone will be with you as
quickly as possible."

After that he went back to being engrossed in whatever
work he was doing, so I had no choice but to do as he'd said.
I chose a chair and sat in it, but it had to be one of the most
uncomfortable chairs I'd ever experienced. It had none of
the padding it so badly needed, its seat slanted at an odd
angle, and its height was wrong for a chair. I didn't know
how long a wait I had in front of me, but even five minutes
would have been too long in that chair.

A lot more than five minutes went past, during which time
I tried two others of the line of chairs. Each of them turned
out to be uncomfortable in a different way, and that fact
upset me more than it should have. I had just about worked
myself up to asking how much longer it would be, when a
man came in the same door I'd used to enter. He also wore
an identity card on a chain around his neck, and the man
behind the table looked up at him.

"Please have a seat," he said in exactly the same tone he'd

used earlier. "Someone will be with you as quickly as possible. And you may now follow me, ma'am."

The relief was exquisite when I rose to my feet and followed the man to the righthand door behind his table. He opened it to allow me through, then closed it behind me without entering the room. It was smaller than the first, and had only another man behind another table without any other chairs in sight.

"Good morning, ma'am," this new man said with another of those pleasant but neutral smiles. "Your papers, please."

I handed over the set of papers, then stood there while the man read every word written on them. When he was through, he looked up with the same sort of smile.

"Everything appears to be in order," he said, handing the papers back. "You may now go through that door to room twenty-two, which is your next stop."

The thought that my next stop might well be the test itself kept me silent until I'd walked out the indicated door, and then I was occupied with finding room twenty-two. It turned out to be on the other side of the building, but when I opened its door I saw an exact copy of the outer room I'd so recently left.

"Please have a seat," the woman behind the table said to me. "Someone will be with you as soon as possible. And now you may follow me, sir."

The man with the applicant's identity card got immediately to his feet and followed the woman, then went through the door she opened. Once he was through she closed the door, went back to sit behind her table, and was immediately immersed in her work again.

"All right, tell me the truth," I said from where I stood, *knowing* the line of chairs would be just like the first group. "How long will I have to keep doing this, and *why* do I have to do it? You can't tell me it isn't pointless."

I knew the woman heard every word I'd said, but she let a moment go by before she looked up from her "work."

"Please have a seat," she said in exactly the way she'd said it before. "Someone will be with you as soon as possible."

Meaning she wasn't going to tell me a thing. My temper stirred at that, making me want to do something outrageous, but I simply didn't dare. I couldn't do anything at all that might jeopardize my chance to be tested, not even raise my voice to protest. I'd have to continue on with the pointles[s] and put up with it for as long as necessary.

"As long as necessary" turned into hours, most of it spe[nt] in one or another of those horrible chairs. At one point I ju[st] had to get up and walk around a bit, but the current ma[n] behind-a-table looked at me in a way that quickly sent n[e] back to a torture chair. I had to do things *their* way, his sta[re] said, and it still wasn't possible for me to argue.

When the time finally came for it to be over, it took [a] moment before I realized it. I'd had nothing to do all th[at] time but think, and it occurred to me that the governme[nt] wanted the tests to be as equitable as possible. That w[ay] fewer mistakes in evaluation would be made, since it was f[ar] easier to come in for testing from one of the city's neighbo[r]hoods than it was to come in from one of the province[s.] Some people spent a week in a coach before reaching Ga[ru] Garee, and their strength would necessarily be less than th[at] of someone who came from the other side of the city.

So they'd developed a method of wearing down ci[ty] residents to the point of *feeling* as if they'd spent a week in [a] coach. All that endless waiting in incredibly uncomfortab[le] chairs, of being sent from one side of the building to t[he] other for no reason other than being told to do it. Aft[er] countless hours I felt as wearily impatient as it was possib[le] to be, and that was why it took a moment before I notice[d] the first deviation from what had become the norm: when [I] was shown into an inner room, there were two men in [it] rather than one.

"Good morning, ma'am," the man behind the table sai[d] in the prescribed way. "Your papers, please."

I handed over the papers quickly, then spent the waiti[ng] time staring at the second man. He stood beside the tab[le] with his hands clasped behind him, staring at nothing an[d] remaining silent. But he was there, which hadn't happene[d] before, leading me to hope with all my heart that the time [of] torture might be over.

"Everything seems to be in order," the man behind t[he] table said far more quickly than any of his predecessors ha[d] done, holding out the papers toward me. "If you'll follo[w] this gentleman, he'll take you to your next stop."

His mentioning another "stop" made my heart lurch wit[h] disappointment, but that reaction turned out to be prema[ture]

ture. Instead of being led to yet another room in that building, my guide found a staircase and began to descend.

Going down a staircase in long skirts can often be worse than going up, but that time I think I discovered the secret of flying. The man I followed walked too fast for me to take my time without also taking the chance of losing him, so flying was the only way to keep up. I reached the bottom of the stairs without remembering anything of how I got there, and then I nearly ran to keep my guide in sight. If I lost him I'd probably kill myself, and I really didn't want to die.

I was led outside to the back of the building, and was shocked to discover it was only somewhere around noon. I'd been ready to swear I'd spent a long enough time on the second floor for it to be past sundown, but obviously I'd been mistaken. There were a lot more people around now than earlier, and some of them were moving as close to a run as I was. But I noticed that only in passing, since most of my attention was on the man I followed.

That man led me to one of the very large resin buildings standing in a circle beyond the testing center's main building, to a doorway with the Fire symbol hanging beside it. Rather than continue on in he stopped to one side with his hand out, so I automatically offered the papers I'd handed over so often today. Rather than take them he gave them back with a sigh, then began to retrace his steps while shaking his head and muttering. I didn't know what his problem was, but I also didn't care. I was already on the way into the resin building, trying to ignore the renewed thudding of my heart.

Inside the doorway was a rather large room, and once again there was a man behind a table. This one was slightly older than the others had been, and his smile looked a bit more real.

"Good morning, young lady," he said, holding out his hand. "And how are you today?"

"I'm not sure," I answered cautiously, giving him the papers. "I suppose it depends on how many more rooms I'll need to sit and wait in."

"Ah, yes, you're from here in the city," he said, glancing through the well-worn papers. At one point I'd tried to read them myself just to have something to do, but had quickly discovered it wasn't possible. They were filled with jargon of

some sort as well as meaningless abbreviations and refe
enceless numbers, and therefore were as informative as
child's scribblings.

"Well, I have some moderately good news then," he sai
looking up after putting the papers aside rather than retur
ing them to me. "There's only one more room you'll need t
sit in, and that for only a short while. There are some fin
questions we need answers to, and once we have the
everything will be finished. Just go through that doorway a
the way to your right, and you'll be shown where to go fro
there."

There was a rather loud-patterned hanging over the doo
way he'd directed me to, and I gave him something of a
answering smile and then quickly went toward it. I couldn
quite believe there was only one more session of waitir
ahead of me, but the hope of finding an end to that terrib
day was enough to keep me from hanging back. I steppe
through to see a long hall ahead and three men in an alco
to the left, and as soon as I appeared the three men rose
their feet.

"Please follow me," one of them said as he steppe
forward, and then he led the way a short distance up the ha
to the first door on the left, which he opened. "If you'll ju
wait inside, someone will be with you very shortly."

The other two men had followed along behind me, but
was alone when I stepped through the doorway. Or at least
thought I was alone. The room was too pitch black to se
anything in it.

"Oh, for goodness' sake, some fool has turned down all th
lamps," the first man said from behind me where I'
stopped, only half a pace into the room. "If you'll just ste
forward a bit more, ma'am, I'll be able to reach the lam
right beside the door."

The request was perfectly reasonable, but despite m
eagerness to see that experience over and done with,
suddenly found myself suspicious. Even in the perpetua
dimness of the main building, none of the rooms had bee
this dark.

"If you'll point to the lamp, I'll be glad to light it," I sai
wondering if the man could possibly have forgotten what m
talent was. "There's no need for you to—"

I'd been turning as I spoke, but that was as far as I got. Th man's hand came to my shoulder with a shove, and I was sent stumbling away from the door. Terror hit me then, the sort my husband had taught me so well, and I responded so quickly it would have been frightening at another place and time. I reached toward the man with one hand and all my ability, and a raging inferno roared toward him where he stood beyond the now-closing door. I could feel him trying to raise and hold a barrier with his own Fire talent, but his strength seemed only a small fraction of mine. I would reach him and keep that door from closing, and then I would—

And then I would run into a heavy sheet of rain produced by Water magic! The curtain of rain appeared right in front of the man my flames were about to reach, and the resulting steam made everyone flinch back. That included the other two men, who now stood behind the first, and it was obvious that they were the source of the Water magic. Not a very strong source even working together, and not one that could have stopped my flames for long, but they'd stopped them for just long enough. The resin door finished closing between us, and by the light of the fire raging uselessly against it, I was able to see that there was nothing I could use to open it again.

I slumped in defeat where I stood, the chill of fear spreading through my bones, and let all but a slender flame of fire die. Once resin hardens it refuses to burn, and even melting it takes hours and hours of effort by a team of Middles. I had no idea why I'd been locked into that room, but it couldn't have been for anything good. I'd learned that lesson from my husband as well, a thought which made me sick to my stomach.

The slender flame I'd kept alight didn't relieve more of the darkness than what was immediately around me, but I had the impression of a rather large area. It took a few moments before my trembling and agitation were under control, but once they were I intended to use enough light to see everything in that place. I was just about to start when the room began to brighten from a different source, so I let my last flame die and looked around.

Lamps were being turned up all around the room, but they stood in little niches high up in the resin walls behind windows of clear resin. And I'd been right about the room being big, I could now see, but more in its length than its width. Behind me was the door I'd come in by, to the left and right were the side walls about twenty feet apart, and ahead about fifteen feet was another door. I could see that door beyond the large U of metal standing between it and me, a construction that seemed to have no purpose. And the door seemed to have a bar of some sort on it, something to keep it closed rather than something to help open it.

"I sincerely hope you've regained control of yourself, ma'am," a voice said, and I looked up to see the man who'd pushed me into the room. He now looked out of a small door high in the wall, and he seemed almost as shaken as I felt.

"I demand that you let me out of here at once," I said, fighting to keep my voice from shaking. "I came here for a reason, and being manhandled wasn't it."

"You came here to have your talent tested, and so it shall be," the man retorted, now sounding more sure of himself. "Your task is to find a way to free yourself from there, and if you fail at the task you will die. If this test seems harsh, consider how harsh most failure is. In this instance, you will *not* live to regret the defeat. Good luck or goodbye."

He drew back and closed the small door again, and all I could do was stand and stare at the place where he'd been. *This* was the test, and if I didn't pass it I would die? If I didn't pass I would want to die, but what was there in this room to harm me? And in what possible way could my talent be tested?

That was when I heard the rumble and felt the vibration, and looked around to see that the walls to my left and right had begun to move inward! Each wall had ten feet to cross, and then they would meet in the middle of the room! Panic flared as I looked wildly from one moving wall to the other, but then I realized the two *couldn't* meet. That strange U-shaped thing of metal in the middle of the room would stop them.

Hope rose in me briefly, only to die out again as I made some mental calculations. The U of metal was narrow, so narrow I would barely have the room to stand when it stopped the walls. And I certainly would find it impossible to pass the U in order to reach that second door. Not that reaching it would help. The moving walls would end up covering most of it, hiding it behind the resin I could do nothing against.

Terror came again as those walls rumbled steadily toward me, a terror that screamed at me to *do* something! I wanted to do something, anything that was possible, but nothing was. I put my hands to my mouth to keep from screaming aloud, the words of defeat ringing in my mind: there's nothing to do! Nothing to do! Nothing to do . . . !

TEN

Vallant Ro felt stiff as he climbed down from the upper coach seat at what had to be his final destination. He was a man used to the freedom of the seas, so first he'd been stuffed into a box of a coach, and now he stood before a massive wall with guards at all of its openings. Someone had apparently decided to see just what it would take to break him, and that someone was actually making a damned good start.

But it still wasn't going to happen. Vallant's basic love of life pushed its way through his depression, making him smile faintly with self-ridicule. No one was trying to break him, they just didn't understand what true freedom meant. To them what they did was ordinary and everyday, not an imposition on a man's right to be unencumbered. Vallant could have felt sorry for them if he hadn't been working so hard not to feel sorry for himself.

"Just take what's left of yer ticket to them guardsmen, Val," the coach driver, Ennis, said as he handed over Vallant's sea bag. "They'll tell ya what t'do next."

"What I'd *like* to do next is go home," Vallant grumbled as he took his bag, then he held his hand out. "Thanks for makin' this trip better for me, Ennis. I've enjoyed knownin' you."

"Same here, Val," the driver responded with a crooked-toothed grin, taking Vallant's hand. "Ya made th' run a lot shorter with all them stories you got. Hope t'hear the rest of 'em some day."

"If we meet again, I'll see that you do," Vallant assured the man as they shook. "Most people back home have stories of their own to tell, so I always have to wait my turn. Take care, Ennis, and try to remember not to believe everythin' you hear."

Ennis laughed aloud at that, obviously remembering how he'd swallowed every tall tale Vallant had come up with at first, and then he went to climb back up on his coach. That left Vallant with nothing to do but head for those guardsmen, so he tightened his grip on his seabag and did just that.

"I'm told you need to see this stub," Vallant said to the guardsmen when he reached them, handing over the item. "What would have happened if I'd thrown it away?"

"You would have spent more'n a week waiting for somebody to get here to identify you," the guardsman answered neutrally as he handed back the stub. "You'd be long out of coin, livin' on the street, an' real hungry by then, but you'd still have to go through with the test. Use the second archway to the right of the one directly behind this gate, and give *them* the stub. They'll tell you what to do next."

Vallant grunted noncommittally and headed for the gate, glad he'd asked the question even if he hadn't liked the answer. Without the ticket stub he wouldn't have starved or had to live on the street, not when the bank his family used had its main office there in Gan Garee. It was the extra time he would have wasted that made him glad he hadn't tossed away the means of identifying him when Ennis had first told him about it. The tickets of applicants for High were special and different, and that's why those who were sent to Gan Garee weren't left to buy their own.

The sun above him told Vallant it was just about noon, and the people hurrying in and out of the large building he walked toward seemed to be ready for lunch. Vallant had already eaten his at Ennis's suggestion while they were still on the road. He'd bought the food at the roadhouse where they'd stopped for breakfast while the horses were being changed, and the sliced beef sandwich had been kept fresh because he'd thought to form and hold some ice around it.

He'd done the same for Ennis's sandwich and the driver had returned the favor by heating both sandwiches and melting some cheese on them when he and Vallant had been ready to eat. Lucky Ennis's coach guard had taken sick at the beginning of the run and hadn't been replaced. That had let Vallant ride on top of the coach rather than leaving him cooped up inside. . . .

The building was large on the inside as well, which came as a relief to Vallant. Small areas and crowded buildings tended to make him uncomfortable, especially when there was no easy access to the outside. His cabin aboard the *Sea Queen* wasn't enormous, but it had large bow windows which he usually left wide open. This building didn't have much in the way of windows, but its very high ceiling and open floor let Vallant ignore that fact as he walked up to the table a short distance from the archway he'd used to enter.

"I believe this is supposed to be given to you," Vallant said to the man behind the table, once again handing over his ticket stub. "And I would also appreciate knowin' how long I'll be here. After a week on a coach seat, I could use some place stationary to stretch out for a while."

"They won't be keeping you for any unreasonable amount of time, I'm sure," the man answered with a glance and a smile as he went through a box filled with papers. "I'll have your identity card filled out in just a minute, and then you'll be able to get on with it."

Vallant watched for not much more than the specified minute while the man wrote on a rectangle of heavy paper, attached a thin chain to the rectangle, then handed the combination to him with instructions to put it on. Vallant removed his cap before doing so, and by the time he'd replaced it there was a woman standing beside him.

"Vosin here will take you where you have to go," the seated man said, gesturing toward the woman. "You must wear your identification at all times, and you have to hand over these papers when you reach your destination. Good day to you."

The man was being polite about it, but Vallant knew a dismissal when he heard it. He looked for the woman who was supposed to guide him, and felt annoyed when he discovered her already on her way to the far side of the building. She kept going without a backward glance, and

Vallant had to stretch his stride a bit in order to catch up with her. That was something of a surprise, since none of the inn and roadhouse girls along the way had been that unfriendly.

But he wasn't here to involve himself with women, after all. He was here to fail a test and then head home, so he followed along behind the pretty little thing without complaint. If he wondered what she might look like under that very plain gown she wore, it was only to give himself something to occupy his mind. So far his first trip to the legendary Gan Garee was even more boring than being becalmed.

The woman led Vallant out of the large building and across the outer walkway, obviously heading toward a group of odd-looking buildings standing in a circle a short distance away. They passed two of the buildings before the woman stopped, and the relatively small doorway she gestured to wasn't particularly encouraging. But the door had the symbol for Water magic on the wall beside it, and it was standing open. That was enough to let Vallant walk inside, which he did without giving the woman more than one final glance. But she was already on her way back to the large building, so Vallant shrugged and forgot about her.

This smaller building immediately made Vallant uncomfortable, but not so much so that he was willing to show it. He walked up to another man seated at another table, and handed over the set of papers he'd been given.

"Good morning, sir," the seated man said with a friendly smile as he took the papers. "You've obviously traveled quite a way to be here, so we'll get right to the questions we have without delaying you very long. You can leave that bag here with me and go through the doorway on your far right, and they'll take you to a place where you can sit down."

Vallant tried not to hesitate very long before handing over his seabag, and a glance at the curtained doorway helped. Curtains were easy to go in and out of, and there were probably even windows in the room they would take him to. Ignoring the sweat beginning to bead his brow, Vallant went to the curtained doorway and through it. Beyond was a very narrow hallway, and if there hadn't been three people in an alcove to the left, Vallant might well have turned and run out. But he couldn't do that with people watching, especially since one of the three was a woman. He'd just have to grit his teeth and think about the windows the room he'd be taken to would have . . .

"Please follow me," one of the men said, and began to lead the way up that horribly narrow hall. Vallant followed, giving all his attention to the man rather than what they walked through. And it wasn't even a very long walk. In just a couple of minutes the man stopped and opened a door on the left, so Vallant immediately passed the man and plunged into the room. His breath wanted to come in gasps to match the whirling behind his eyes, but as soon as he found those windows he would be fine. He just had to shake his head hard enough to clear his vision . . .

And that turned out to be the biggest mistake yet. It took a moment for him to be able to see that room, but the first thing he noticed was the absence of windows. The room was fairly large and more than ordinarily high, with lamps burning in niches covered over with clear material. There was no sign of another door, and when Vallant turned back to the one he'd come in by, he found it closed. He lurched over to it, nearly frantic to get it open again, but there was nothing to hold to. He wanted to claw at the edge of it where it met the jamb, but there wasn't room in between even for his fingernails.

"You can't get out that way," a voice said, making him whirl around. The man who had led him to that trap looked out of a small door he'd opened fairly high in the wall opposite, too far out of reach for Vallant to get his hands on him.

"Let me out of here," Vallant demanded hoarsely, fighting to keep some vestige of control over himself. "Open this door and let me out *now*!"

"Finding a way out of that room is *your* job," the man answered, his tone and attitude neutral rather than gloating. "This is your first test, and if you aren't successful it will also be your last—the last of everything, including your life. Work hard to find an answer, sir, for your life most certainly does depend on it. Good luck or goodbye."

And then the man withdrew, an instant later pushing closed the small door he'd looked out through. Vallant shouted, demanding that he come back and explain himself, but the small door remained closed. The sweat of fear was so

heavy on Vallant's face that he had to wipe it off with his coat sleeve, at the same time struggling to understand what he'd been told. He had to find his own way out of there? But how could he, and what had the fool meant about his life being at stake?

That answer, unfortunately, was the first one given him when flames of fire suddenly erupted all around the circle of the room. Vallant reached automatically for whatever moisture was at hand, and found that the air was heavy with it. Somewhere close by was a rather large amount of water, a fact guaranteed by the heavily-laden air. He quickly gathered the moisture and used it to douse the nearest flames, then began to do the same with the rest of the ring of fire.

Began to. Vallant had only just gotten started with putting out the fires when the first of the flames began to burn again. Only this time they were somewhat closer to where he'd retreated to, the approximate center of the room. That had to mean the circle of fire would continue to tighten until it met inside him, and he would probably find it impossible to put out all of it. Even now sparks were beginning to fly at him, trying randomly to set him afire. He had to get out of that room in order to survive—not to mention stay sane— but how was he supposed to do that?

He stood with frantic intensity flaring all through his body, an ache already beginning in his muscles from the tension, a sickness deep inside his gut. In the name of everything right, how was he supposed to get himself out of there?

Now do you see what I meant when I said we all had a terrible time? There can't be anyone reading this who doesn't know we survived, but what it cost us to survive is another matter entirely. And not long after that was when we met, with not a single one of us at his or her best. The biggest surprise isn't that we survived the tests, but that we

*all survived the meetings. Now let's see, in what order did
we finish those tests . . . ?*

ELEVEN

stood staring at the walls that slowly but steadily came
oward me, almost too terrified to think. I really wasn't in
danger of being crushed, not with the U of metal in the way,
o why had that man said I would die? Fail the test, yes, but
lie?

That was when a terrible thought occurred to me, so I
moved over closer to that U and took a really good look at it.
ure enough, it wasn't made of steel the way I'd thought at
rst. It was made of some very light metal I wasn't familiar
vith, which brought my terror back full force. It might keep
hose grinding walls apart for a time, but if they continued to
ush on it they would crush the U between them. I could feel
hat the metal wasn't tempered with heat, which would have
nade it significantly stronger.

Which meant that I *was* in danger of being crushed, only
ot right away. I'd be able to stand there and watch the metal
eing destroyed, knowing my own destruction would come
mmediately thereafter. A shudder rippled through me, turn-
ng my knees weak, threatening to send me to the floor in the
nidst of swirling blackness. In just a few minutes I would die
orribly, proving my parents had been right to believe I'd
ever pass this test.

And that thought, strangely enough, immediately began to
ive me back some control over myself. I hated the idea of my
arents being right about *anything* that concerned me, know-
ng how scornful and demeaning their thoughts would be even
vhile they were being told I was dead. They would also be
urious that I'd escaped them, but that wasn't the way I'd
lanned to escape. I wanted to be there to see their faces when
hey learned I was free, *had* to be there to see it, so there was
nly one thing I could do. Pass that test and survive.

But that was more easily decided than done. I put
trembling hand to my hair as I *really* looked around, m
mind searching for ideas. I'd been thinking that nothing wa
possible, but that couldn't be true. There had to be some
thing, and the trick would be to find it. Maybe a closer loo
at the barred door would help . . .

I slid around the U of metal even though the moving wall
weren't close enough yet to be a real problem, and hurrie
over to the door. It was barred closed all right, but not with
metal as light as what the U was made of. In order to ope
the door the bar would have to be slid from the rings it ha
been run through, but there was no room on either side to d
that. The bar would have to be cut in two places at the ver
least, and the only thing available to cut it would be m
flames. It would take time and a lot of effort, but I suddenl
began to think it might be possible.

That, of course, was when I remembered about thos
moving walls. I didn't *have* a lot of time, especially since on
end of the door seemed to have some mechanism to open i
and the ends of the door were what would be covered first b
the walls. I had to stop those walls long enough to give m
time to work on the door, but how was I supposed to do that
The walls and floor and ceiling were made of resin, an
hardened resin can't be affected by the Fire magic of on
individual . . .

I came very close to giving up then, but the thought c
allowing my parents to win came back to help stiffen m
resolve again. It *was* possible to pass that test, so I just had t
figure out what that way could be. My talent could get m
through the door, but only if I stopped the walls long enoug
to give me the chance. But I *couldn't* stop the walls, not i
any way involving my talent, so what—

I'd been looking around frantically as I thought, and whe
the answer finally broke through my upset I felt really stupi
That U of light metal . . . There was no reason for it to be i
the room unless it was part of the problem—or part of th
solution. Since it did nothing to threaten it had to be there t
help, and that line of thought led me to understand in wha
way. If I opened the U out into a straight line, it would sto
the walls before they moved over the ends of the door.

But the walls would not be stopped easily and not for lon
I took a shaky breath as my mind raced, trying to estimat

ime and strength factors. I would have to heat the light metal to a high enough temperature to change its shape, and then I would have to temper it to higher strength—but without water. Whether or not it would work was questionable, especially since I'd also have to cut through the bar on the door. After the horribly tiring day I'd had, would I have enough strength to do it? Maybe being dead would be enough of a triumph over my parents . . .

My hands turned to fists at my sides, telling me in no uncertain terms that being dead would *not* be enough. I had to survive and pass that test, but the self-doubts I'd been taught all my life would not help to accomplish it. I had to get beyond the doubts and stay there, and plunging right in might let me do that.

So I turned my attention and talent first to the U of metal. Reaching out with fingers of fire I began to caress it, following its shape and learning the feel of it as it now was. Even as I explored I heated my flames higher and higher, and after a moment I was able to detect the beginning of the change. Everything changes when fire is applied to it, and awareness of those changes is all part of learning your talent.

It has always amazed me how sensitive a sense of touch I have through my flames. I can feel the very texture of what I'm in the midst of burning, follow every stage of its change, sometimes even anticipate what will happen next. Now I could feel the metal under my flame-fingers begin to soften, the first step necessary in changing its shape.

By the time I had both arms of the U flattened down to a more or less straight line, the walls were almost up to them and I was close to drowning in sweat. I'd not only been exerting a lot of strength, I hadn't been able to block all of the heat from my fire. Blocking it completely would have meant losing contact and control, so the only real choice I had was to sweat. But I'd slowly been lowering the temperature of my flames and feeling the metal begin to harden again, so it was time to withdraw from that part of it.

I took a moment to rest then, using the time to check on the position of the walls and judge their rate of speed. They were still almost two feet away from the ends of my metal brace, and the longer they took to reach it, the cooler—and therefore harder—it would be. What I didn't know was how long the brace would hold, how long it would take me to cut

through the bar on the door, and whether or not I wa
wasting my time. If I'd guessed wrong about what the prope
response to the test situation was . . .

But I couldn't afford to spend effort doubting myself, no
when there was so much left to do. I wiped the sweat fror
my eyes with the back of my right hand and turned to th
door, then gave the bar my attention. Four cuts would mak
removing it effortless, but I might not have the time to mak
that many. The only thing I could do was start with the tw
most important cuts, and see how things went when the
were done.

Concentrating my flames down to a very small poir
wasn't something I'd done before, and in the process
learned why it wasn't often done. It felt like compressing
living, squirming entity between my hands, balancing th
need to keep it small but hot and the need to keep it aliv
The flames actually almost fought me in that shape, but
had to concentrate them if the cutting wasn't to take foreve
Smaller and smaller but hotter and hotter would also kee
the bar from melting and sealing me in, so it had to be don

I was so deeply involved in cutting through the bar, tha
the arrival of the walls at the metal brace almost made m
jump out of my skin. The first cut was about three-quarter
done, but I left it to jump and whirl around at the *thud–
screech!* from behind me. The thud had come from the wall
hitting the ends of the brace, and the protesting screech cam
from whatever moved the walls. It disliked the idea of th
walls having been stopped, and apparently announced it
intention to change that state of affairs.

I used a very light and gentle flame to check on th
condition of the brace, and found myself less than encou
aged. It was holding for the moment, but the pressure of th
advancing walls strained the metal in a way it wasn't going t
be able to resist for long. If I didn't have the bar out of th
way before it collapsed completely, I'd never get out o
there—or pass the test.

That thought made me turn quickly back to what I'd bee
doing, but before beginning again I realized I couldn't simpl
ignore the brace. I had to stay aware of its condition, and d
whatever might be possible to hold off its final collapse. Tha
meant splitting my attention, something else I'd never don
before, but this was obviously a day for firsts. Fear returne
briefly as I fought to maintain flame in two places and at tw

intensities, but then insight came to make the new practice easier. Only a small part of my attention was necessary to simply watch the brace; the rest of it was free to control my active work.

I was almost halfway through my second cut when the first crisis came. The walls had been pushing at the brace relentlessly, and the time finally came when it began to buckle. I had no idea what they were using to move the walls, but it proved to be enough to begin forcing the metal arms back up, returning them to their original position.

For an instant I had no idea what to do, then a crazy idea came. If the lower side of the arms were heated to softness in a couple of places, the arms might buckle downward and counter the upward pressure they were currently under. Since I'd never worked with metal in quite this way before, I had no idea if the plan would succeed. All I could do was try, but at the same time I had to maintain the cutting. The test had now turned into a real race against time, and faltering would certainly mean losing.

By the time I had everything moving properly, I was beyond sweating. The flames on the underside of the brace had to be concentrated almost as narrowly as the flames cutting the bar, but the intensities remained different. If I became confused and altered the intensities it was probable everything would be ruined, so careful concentration became my foremost need. It felt as if I were in two places at the same time, living two different lives as I performed different tasks, but I couldn't think about that. Cutting through that bar was the only thing to consider, the only objective in a narrowed-down world.

And finally it happened! Heating the bottom of the brace *had* made the arms crumple downward, but I'd used that delaying tactic twice and wasn't sure if the metal of the arms was up to going through it a third time. It felt as if the metal was ready to fold into pleats, and that was when the second cut made it through the bottom of the bar. The part of the bar that had been threaded through the central brace on the door now sat there severed at both ends, and if I got it out of the way I could free the bar section at the side of the door and reach the opening mechanism.

I actually reached toward the small section of bar with my physical hands, but happily the residual heat was intense enough to stop me a short distance away. I couldn't touch the

thing as it was but I had to get it free, and then anoth
ridiculous idea came. Without wasting a moment I took o
my shoe, used a heavy fold of my skirt to push the larg
section of bar on the left as high up as it would go, then be:
at the small section in the brace with my shoe heel.

It felt as if I beat at the small section forever before it l
itself be knocked out of the way, but a frantic sense of hur
let me keep at it. The metal brace holding the walls apart w:
in the process of collapsing into a mass of useless tangle, an
I *had* to reach that door release before everything fell apar
Once the small bar section was out of the way I straightene
the lefthand section and pulled with all my strength—whic
at that point wasn't very much at all. But it proved to b
enough to move the bar section just out of the way, lettin
me reach to the small lever that was hopefully all that ke
the door closed. I fumbled the lever open, pushed har
against the door—

—and almost fell sprawling into the hall beyond the doo
The door itself had moved so easily once the lever w:
released . . . it was over and I'd gotten out . . . now I cou
let go . . .

All at once I found myself seated on the floor of the ha
my back against one of the walls, a dark and distant whirlin
just receding from my mind and eyes. When I'd final
released every last spark of flame, the relief had been :
exquisite . . . and now I could feel that I hurt just abo
everywhere, so I had no idea whether I'd seated myse
deliberately, or had simply fallen. Strands of my hair floate
well out of reach of the pins meant to hold it up, and I didn
even care. So what if I looked like a hag. I'd passed th
test . . . hadn't I?

"Just rest there, young lady, and drink some of this,"
voice came, and suddenly the man from the front room w:
beside me and holding a cup to my lips. I thought it w:
water and gulped at it greedily, but it turned out to be mor
than water. The taste of the drink was sweet, and once it sli
down my throat it seemed to spread all through me. Stil
tense muscles began to relax, and a small but steady influx o
strength began to return to my limbs.

"There, that's much better," the man said encouraging
once I'd drained the large cup. "Sit where you are fo
another moment or two and pull yourself together, and the
we'll get you back on your feet."

"I may never stand or walk again," I whispered, resting my head against the wall behind me. I felt almost too terrified to ask, but I just had to know. "Did . . . did I pass?"

"You most certainly did pass," the man said with a broad smile from where he crouched beside me. "I would have offered my congratulations at once, but you were more in need of refreshment. And it should please you even more to know that you're the only one to pass in this facility today."

For an instant hearing that did please me, but then I remembered what failure meant and felt ill instead. How many Middle talents had been tested here today? And how many hadn't lived . . . ?

"Why did you do that?" I asked in the strongest whisper I could, finding it impossible not to shudder. "I came here determined to pass your test, but you didn't care. You put my life on the line, then turned your back and walked away."

"Explaining is always so difficult," he said with a sigh, no longer smiling. "Please try to understand that not everyone looks at the matter as you did. Many come here with the intention of deliberately failing the test so that they might return to their former lives, and we simply cannot allow that. A High practitioner *must* be the best of the best, so we force all applicants to show their best with the most effective means at our disposal. A life-threat always brings out the most in people, no matter what they meant to show or hide."

"And if their best isn't good enough, they die," I summed up, no longer looking at him. "I can understand your need, but I hope you'll forgive me for not having much sympathy with it. When can I go home?"

"As soon as the coach we've sent for arrives," he answered with another sigh. "You should be somewhat returned to yourself by then, and you'll have a day or two to rest before your next session. Remember to wear your identification at all times, and please refrain from discussing your experience with anyone. Disclosure penalties are rather strict, and I would dislike seeing you incur any of them. And—oh yes, I'm also supposed to discuss your house."

"What about my house?" I asked, suddenly frightened again. Could it have been claimed by my father while I was in the midst of struggling to save my life? I wouldn't have been surprised . . .

"You've registered your house as a residence for applicants," he reminded me, smiling faintly again. "Now that

you've passed your own test, the registration is automatical
accepted. You've said you can accommodate eight lodgers
addition to yourself, so they'll begin sending people now ar
the testing centers will pay for their lodging. Any foo
clothing, or other needs will have to be paid for by th
individual applicant."

"What are they supposed to supply it from?" I aske
delighted and relieved that my house would be safe for
time. "Are they expected to find jobs?"

"Hardly," the man answered with a chuckle. "They'll t
too busy with their regularly scheduled sessions for that, ar
shouldn't need a job in any event. Assuming they continue
do well they'll be eligible for the competitions, the winni
of which will bring a bonus in gold. That, of course, goes fo
you as well as your guests. You'll be given the name
someone to contact in case of any difficulties with yo
guests, and that's all there is to it for the moment."

"At the moment, that's all I can cope with," I muttere
finally feeling enough recovered to look down at myself. M
dress was probably ruined beyond repair, part of my ha
was flyaway and the rest hung in greasy strands, and the sho
I'd used to hammer at the piece of bar still lay where I'
dropped it, just past the doorway into this hall. Whether
not it was usable, I still meant to wear it home. Looking lik
a hag was one thing; going half barefoot like some wil
woman was quite another.

"Let's see now if you're able to stand," the man sai
straightening to walk to where my shoe lay and bending
retrieve it. "This seems somewhat the worse for wear, but
should still serve to get you home. Dama?"

He'd come back to put his hand out to me, so I took it an
used his help to stand. I was still a bit unsteady, but his ar
about my shoulders helped to keep me erect until my balanc
returned, and then he bent to replace my shoe.

"A perfect fit," he commented with a smile after straigh
ening again. "But with a lady like you, that comes as n
surprise. Your coach should hopefully be here by now, so I'
take you to it. And I do hope we'll meet again after your tim
with the sessions."

He wrapped my right arm over his left, but suddenly th
look in his eyes said the gesture was for more than offerin
support. If I'd had the strength I would have shivered at th
intensity of his stare, but I'd seen the same so often tha

weariness won out over my usual reaction. Even after having been turned into a hag, I still held interest for the man beside me. The idea was very depressing, but right now I had too many other things to worry about. He'd said there would be "sessions" and competitions; what did that mean? Did I have enough strength left to stand *knowing* what it meant?

The answer to my last question was absolutely not, so I made no effort to question my companion as he guided me around the hall and finally to a door that led outside. Just beyond the door a coach stood waiting, and once the man had helped me inside, he paused to study me in a different way.

"One more thing before you leave," he said after a moment. "The way you reacted at the beginning of the test, being so quick to strike in attack . . . I'm sure you know that under other circumstances, the authorities might well have been informed of your behavior. Please do try to curb that particular impulse, as someone might mistake you for a talent out of control. That would surely interfere with any future meetings between us, so I'd hate to see it happen. Get some rest, but keep the point clearly in mind."

I could feel my cheeks go even more pallid as he closed the door and told the coach driver he could leave. The man had reminded me of what I'd done when I'd been pushed into the testing room, which was strike out with *all* my talent. Doing that to people was against the law, since most unpleasant situations can be avoided with the use of a good deal less than full strength. If I were charged with being out of control and then convicted, I could end up condemned to the Deep Caverns for the rest of my life.

I shuddered and trembled for a while at the thought of such a fate, but then I discovered that it *is* possible to be too tired to be afraid. I had no strength left to sustain the fear, so just let it go as I looked out of the coach window. I did have to be more careful in the future, which I should be able to do once I'd had a good night's sleep. And once I really understood that the first battle in the war with my parents was over, and I'd won it more completely than I'd dared to hope.

Smiling out into the late afternoon streets felt strange, but *I* felt strange. I'd wanted to pass that test more than anything in the world, and despite a small but intense core of doubt deep inside me, I'd actually done it. Even now that was hard to believe, but the thrill of the realization still felt marvelous.

I'd passed the test and survived, and my house would remain mine for at least a little while longer.

The coach took me right to my door up the winding driveway, and only after I'd gotten out did I discover that the driver had already been paid and tipped. Warla met me at the door with wide-eyed concern for my condition, but that changed to a stunned expression when I told her I'd passed. Apparently she hadn't had any more faith in my doing that than my core of doubt had, and it felt wonderful to tell her she'd been wrong. Then I sent her to my bedchamber to fetch a change of clothes, and spoke to the staff about expecting house guests until she returned. Once she had I told her the same, took the clothes, and headed directly for the bath house.

There are bath houses all over the city for the use of ordinary people, but those of my late husband's class took pride in never having to use them. Our private bath house stood just beyond the back of the main house in its own little bower, a pretty addition to one side just before the gardens. I'd grown up being used to a private bath house, so it had taken me awhile to understand Gimmis's pride in the one *he* had. Once I understood that my husband hadn't been raised by an affluent family, I began to understand more than one thing about him.

Paper lanterns had been lit along the short path to the bath house, and once I reached it I paused to hang the "occupied" sign on the door. Gimmis had always been very strict about that, always hating the idea of being disturbed in his bath. That was because of the physical abnormalities his illness had long since begun to cause in him, and his bath time had always been one of freedom for me. Short-lived freedom, perhaps, but treasured all the same.

All four of the lamps had been lit in the bath house as well, which was definitely a lucky thing for me. After what I'd been through I couldn't imagine lighting so much as a spark, and would have had to resort to mechanical means if the lamps hadn't already been lit. As I closed the door behind me and went to the towel cabinet, I tried to remember the last time I'd used a flint to strike a spark. I couldn't quite remember the time, but that wasn't surprising. At the moment I was having trouble remembering my own name.

Stripping off my filthy dress and ruined shoes was delightful, as was freeing my hair for washing. The bath house was just the right size, small enough to be cozy and intimate and warm, large enough that the polished wood of its walls gleamed only a little in the lamplight. It was dim and comfortable with padded chairs in bright floral patterns to sit on, thin cotton rugs to keep your feet from the tiled floor, padded mats to stretch out on, and molded areas inside the large bath itself that held your body gently while you soaked. That was what I really looked forward to: soaking some of the aches out of my body.

The water was delightfully warm as I stepped down into it, kept that way by the efforts of two of the house servants who had minor Fire talents. After submerging completely for a moment I moved to one of the molded areas and sank down into it, letting free a deep sigh as I did so. The water felt marvelous to my tired, aching body, and I thought about spending the entire night right there without moving. If I hadn't been so hungry I would have considered the idea more seriously, but I felt hollow all the way down to my toes. I had only a limited time to soak before dinner would be ready, but coming back again after dinner was always an option . . .

I must have drifted off to sleep for a while, my head supported and cushioned by the padded headrest positioned just above the molded area. The gentle current of the recirculating water—provided by another servant with Water magic—was more than lulling, and I remember thinking myself in some private underground cavern, being carried off by the warm waters of its hidden stream. I floated along, finding the experience delicious—and then I jerked awake at the sound of the door opening! At first I thought it was Gimmis and my heart began to race, but then I remembered that Gimmis was dead. The man who had simply walked in was a stranger, and fear suddenly changed to outrage.

"Who are you and what are you doing in here?" I demanded, trying to shield my naked body with my arms. "No, never mind about answering that. Just get out of here!"

"Not until I've had my share of that water," the fool replied in a deep voice, looking directly at me as he made his way to the towel cabinet. "I feel singed from head to foot, not to mention broken and stomped on and covered in old sweat. I *need* that bath, but don't let me hurry you. Stay as long as you like."

I almost sputtered in outrage at that, as well as at the way he glanced at me before starting to search for a towel. He was a very large man with long pale-blond hair, light eyes, a deep tan, and broad shoulders. Obviously he was very used to getting his way with women, but this wasn't going to be one of the times he did. I used the opportunity of his back being turned to scramble out of the bath and wrap myself in my towel, and then I turned back to him. What a shame I was too exhausted to do anything but talk . . .

"I don't care what you need, or even who you are," I told him firmly, more than simply annoyed. "This bath house belongs to *me,* and I want you out of it this minute. If you refuse to leave, I'll call the guardsmen and have you arrested for breaking in here."

"I didn't break in, I walked in," he countered calmly, having turned back to look at me as he began to unbutton his shirt. "And if you own this house, I was told you would be expectin' me. I'm Vallant Ro, here in this accursed town to test for somethin' I never wanted. If you dislike havin' me here, you can thank the fools in our government for my presence. If not for them, I'd already be on my way back home."

I stared at him openmouthed for a moment, suddenly so furious that it was a good thing I'd have trouble reaching fire now. I'd had to go through hell because of people like *him,* people who didn't want to test for High and therefore had to be forced into doing their best! I grew so furious that I barely noticed he now stood bare-chested, his body as well-tanned as his face. I did notice, however, when he reached to his trousers and began to open them without hesitation. I lost most of what I'd meant to say, and could only turn quickly to face the wall.

"I'm going to speak to someone about having you put elsewhere," I finally choked out, hating the heavy heat of embarrassment I felt in my cheeks. "You haven't the first idea about civilized behavior, and I refuse to have you in my house a moment longer than absolutely necessary. And if they can't find another place for you, I hope you'll need to sleep in the street!"

Rather than hearing words in reply, I heard the definite splash of water in the bath that said a large body had plunged into it. My cheeks flamed hot again, and not just because I'd never seen a naked male body despite having been married. Gimmis had always forced me to close my eyes, even in the dark of his bedchamber. It was the rudeness of this lout that disturbed me so, a rudeness made up of his intrusion and his stare and the way I hadn't been able to say what I wanted to him. I stepped barefoot into my shoes, gathered my clean clothes awkwardly with one hand while the other kept the towel closed about me, and simply got out of there.

But once outside, I paused to remove the "occupied" sign from the door. If this Vallant Ro didn't mind intruding on *me,* he shouldn't mind having someone else doing the same to him. And his presence guaranteed the other applicants couldn't be far behind, hopefully with one among them who was as rude and intrusive as Ro himself!

TWELVE

Vallant Ro looked around at the fire circling him, at the same time fighting to clear his thoughts. All his basic self wanted to do was escape the confines of that room, going straight through a wall if necessary. The fact that it obviously wasn't possible to go through the walls didn't seem to matter to that basic part of him, but it mattered to the rest. There did have to be a way out of there, and only rational thought would find it.

Vallant looked around for a third time, distantly finding it strange that the fire concerned him less than the confined space of the room. That had to be because holding off the fire was fractionally easier, even if it wasn't possible to put it out completely. He'd hung a curtain of light moisture all around himself not far from the inner ring of flames, and so far the flames hadn't gone past it.

But that didn't mean they wouldn't, so he had to get moving. A way out . . . a way out . . . As he continued to look around, he felt heavy frustration mounting. There didn't seem to *be* a way out, but he'd already decided that that was impossible. Something had to be there, but without a usable door and with no windows except for that small, windowlike door high in the wall—

Vallant briefly cursed his stupidity under his breath, at last understanding one of the reasons his recent guide had appeared at the window-door. *That* was Vallant's way out, but how was he supposed to reach it? He'd never managed to learn to fly like a bird, although people claimed he swam like a fish . . .

And of course that was it. Water, the element of his talent, what he was there to be tested in. In order to save himself he'd have to use his talent, an act he'd intended to refrain from. This time it was the government he cursed under his breath, hating the way they'd manipulated him into doing his best. It wasn't fair, and he meant to tell them so as soon as he was out of there.

But first he had to *get* out, which wouldn't be easy. That large amount of water he could sense somewhere nearby wasn't large enough to flood the room and float him up to the door, at the same time quenching those flames. It would have to be used differently, but how? How could that large but limited amount of water get him out of here?

Vallant noticed that he was sweating harder, and not just from his terror at being locked in such a small room. That ring of flames had somehow moved past his curtain of water, and now burned that much closer to him. It was circling tighter and tighter, intent on surrounding and smothering him as well as burning . . .

Once again Vallant had to fight blind panic, and this time pulling out of it was harder. The thought of being enclosed by the fire really was harder to deal with than being burned by it, but putting out one section of it and escaping the circle wasn't likely to help. It was logical to expect the fire to follow wherever he went, and would undoubtedly trap him against the wall if necessary. He had to get out of that room to escape the double trap, and he had to use his Water magic to do it. But how . . . ?

He began to wipe the sweat from his face again, wishing the room could be cooler, and just that easily he had his answer. Ice, he would have to form ice from the water, and that way he'd be able to reach the window door. But with most of the room's heat coming from that fire, how was he supposed to form and maintain ice? Curse those codding bureaucrats! *That* was why they threatened him with fire! To make forming ice that much harder!

Vallant briefly considered clamping down on his temper, then dismissed the idea with a snarl. He needed every advantage he could get, and anger—directed anger—often increased his strength. And took his attention from other things, like a crippling fear. He just had to stay angry long enough to get the job done, which would be hard enough even that way. Ice, in all that heat . . .

But it could be done in a small way, so it ought to be possible on a large scale with enough strength behind the effort. First he would have to establish some protection from those flames, and then he could start building his ice bridge. But what shape should it be in? And did he really want a *bridge* . . . ?

It would have been nice if Vallant could have spent a while considering those questions, but he simply didn't have the time. Everything including his own mind pushed at him to hurry, but he had to hurry cautiously. A serious mistake would mean needing to start all over again, and by then the flames would be right on top of him . . .

Reaching out to every bit of moisture in the air, Vallant caused a fairly heavy cascade to form over the arc of fire that was in the way of where he needed to put his ice platform. And platform was what it would have to be, since there might not be enough water—or time—for anything more involved. And if things worked properly, he'd even bypass the need to climb up to that platform.

But first he had to move around behind that cascade, closer to the wall where the window-door was. Everyone knew that fire melted ice without needing to think about it, but it took some people a moment to realize that pouring water did the same. He would have to protect his ice platform from both things, as well as maintain the cascade while he built the ice.

Just thinking about it was a waste of time and strength, not to mention taking the edge off his anger by increasing his fear. He'd never had to do so much with his talent before, but worrying about whether or not he could would just lessen his chances. For that reason he quickly reached to the large supply of water, established a bridge to the room he stood in, and began bringing the water through. As soon as it reached him he added frozen chips from way up in the sky, which froze the rest of what it touched.

And the ice began to form under his feet, or more precisely, under his shoes. He would have been happier about his balance—if more uncomfortable—if he were barefoot, but his body heat would make the problem a lot harder to handle. He'd keep one hand on the wall he built his platform in front of, and try to maintain his balance that way.

The plan seemed to work, although Vallant had to ignore how hard it was to do everything at once. Maintaining the cascade to keep the fire put out, channeling in the water from wherever it was being kept, and bringing down the frigid chunks of ice from high up to freeze what was forming under him. It was like a crazy game, where everything demanded your attention at once if you weren't going to lose and lose badly. Vallant played the game, but he came close to drowning in sweat.

It took a number of very difficult minutes, but his ice platform finally brought him high enough to reach the window-door. He reached out to it gingerly with his free hand, briefly afraid that it would refuse to open, but the wood pushed back out of his way with very little effort. The only problem *that* left was sight of the space behind it, an area only a little larger than his body. There was a much wider opening beyond the very cramped area, but in order to reach it he would have to go through that tiny, airless, *confining* space . . .

Vallant almost lost it then, so strongly did his terror surge up. He'd considered the room confining, but that tiny crawl space was a thousand times worse. He had to use it in order to get out, but could he? He'd spread his talent out in three different directions, almost emptying himself of ability, but crawling through that tiny area could well be beyond him. He swallowed from a bone-dry mouth, fighting to keep his eyes from closing—and suddenly felt his ice platform trembling under his feet. Fear was interfering with his talent, and a single mental touch told him the platform was about to come apart!

That time Vallant used fear to his benefit, letting it propel him toward the only path to safety there was. He plunged through the window-door before he could lose his footing, at the same time closing his eyes. *There's lots of room in here,* he told himself frantically, struggling to picture an area as large as the inside of that first building. *Lots of room, but you still don't have to be in here long. The other side of it is completely open, and all you have to do is reach it.*

Vallant kept repeating that to himself, even though crawling slowly didn't get him to the other side very quickly. But he *had* to crawl slowly, or he would have brushed up against the sides or top of that tiny area. His fear didn't really believe the lies he'd told it, but as long as he didn't actually touch anything around himself he could pretend to believe. If he lost even that pitiful amount of pretense, he'd probably lose control as well.

So he crawled carefully toward the opening ahead with his eyes shut tight, and because of that he almost crawled over the edge. His hand came down on nothing, throwing off his precarious sense of balance, but there was also a slight breath of moving air. That encouraged him to open his eyes, which heartened him even more. He would have to climb down a narrow ladder to reach the floor of the hall below, but off to the right only a few steps away, a door to the outside stood partially open.

Twisting around in the mouth of that narrow opening to get his feet to the ladder rungs was hard, but not nearly as hard as the rest of what he'd done. Once on the ladder he felt his mind begin to open out, filled with an agonized yearning for the outdoors that he hadn't experienced since childhood. He went down the ladder fast, stumbled to the door and out as quickly as he could move, then sank to his hands and knees in blessed relief. He was outside, finally and completely outside at last.

Vallant lowered himself to the meager grass on his left side, concentrating on nothing but breathing and trying to gather some small amount of strength. If for nothing else he'd need it eventually to stand up, and right now he felt completely emptied. He'd also closed his eyes again, but the sound of footsteps made him open them quickly. The man who had been in the outer room of this building now walked toward him, holding a cup of something.

"Don't be upset, it's all over for now," the man said quickly as Vallant began to struggle into a seated position in preparation for getting to his feet. "And I believe you need what's in this cup."

Vallant hated to take anything from these people, but unfortunately the man was right. Between sweating like a waterfall and using every bit of moisture he could touch with his talent, Vallant was as close to being a dried out husk as anyone with Water magic could be. So he hesitated only an instant before taking the cup and draining it, finding its contents to be more than simple water and a good deal more refreshing. After a moment he could actually feel some strength beginning to come back, so he returned the cup with a grudging nod.

"Thank you for that, at least," he allowed, less of an edge to his tone than he'd wanted it to have. "Now that your game is over, you can just point me to the nearest coach stop. I'm goin' home whether you like it or not."

"My likes don't enter into the matter," the man replied with something of a shrug from where he crouched beside Vallant. "If it were my choice you could go or stay as you please, but my employers tend to have a different view of the matter. And by the way, congratulations on passing the test. Not everyone does, you know, and in fact more don't than do."

"That must keep you people really busy movin' bodies out of here," Vallant commented, unimpressed by what he'd been told. "And I don't care what your—employers—want either. Give me my seabag and show me the way out."

"I'm afraid it isn't that simple, Captain Ro," the man said, looking only faintly apologetic. "Now that you've passed the first of your tests, you can't be allowed to simply return home. You must participate in and complete the sessions scheduled for you, or you'll be taken into custody by the guard—with the help of two High practitioners. You'll be given a trial, of course, but the mandatory penalty for attempting to flee before the tests are over is five years at hard labor in one of the empire's deep mines. Those with Earth magic can't bear to work in them, I'm told, so manual labor is necessary. We can't force you to participate in the tests, sir, but we can and will punish your refusal."

Vallant stared at the man, trying to read the truth under the words the way he did with the merchants he dealt with, but the effort was useless. Either the man was a most accomplished liar, or everything he'd said was the truth. Not that it really mattered. Even if their "punishment" had been something he could bear, he still couldn't have allowed himself to run that far afoul of the law. He had his family to think of and the possibility of ruining the excellent reputation they'd always enjoyed, which meant he was well and truly trapped.

"The bunch of you should be really proud of yourselves," he commented, letting the other man see his disgust. "You'd all better hope I *don't* pass all the tests you have . . . So where do I go now? The nearest jail cell?"

"Certainly not," the man replied, straightening from his crouch as Vallant forced himself to his feet. "You've been assigned lodging with someone of the city who volunteered their house as a residence. Others who pass their tests will be staying there with you, so please remember that discussing anything at all about your own test is strictly forbidden. We'll be paying the cost of your lodging, but you must bear the expense of your food and clothing and other wants and needs. But after the sessions you ought to be eligible for the competitions, the winning of which will earn you a bonus in gold. For that reason I would not let the current state of your funds distress you. We'll be in touch again in a few days, but at the moment I believe your coach has arrived."

Vallant could also hear the creak of wheels and springs accompanied by the clip-clop of hooves, which meant the coach was undoubtedly on the outer side of the building, but Vallant had had more than enough of that place.

"Meet me around front with my seabag," he directed as he made his own way toward the path that separated this building from the next in the circle. "I'd hate to tempt you people into tryin' me again, so I'll get to the front by the long way."

Vallant felt the man staring at him as he walked away, but he didn't particularly care. His fear of that building didn't show, he knew, and a bit of suspicion was hardly out of place. He would get to that coach the long way, and enjoy every painful step of the trip.

By the time Vallant circled the building, the man he'd spoken to waited beside the coach with his seabag. Vallant took it silently with a curt nod and entered the coach, which at this point looked more spacious than confining. Sitting down also felt incredibly good, especially when the coach began to move. He was finally on his way out of that place, even though it wasn't to go home.

And that part of it bothered him quite a bit. He couldn't

very well humiliate his daddy and the rest of the family by
getting himself arrested, and the thought of five years spent
underground—as well as away from the sea—couldn't even
be considered. That meant he had to stay there and take their
blasted tests, but there *had* to be a way to fail one yet still
survive. If he could just find it . . .

Vallant took a deep breath and let it out slowly, turning his
attention to the unfamiliar city he rode through. Finding a
way home couldn't be done right now, which in a way was a
lucky thing. What he needed most at the moment was a long
bath and a change of clothes, to rid himself of the clammy
feel of his underthings. He'd sweated hard enough to float a
skiff, and until he bathed he'd find it impossible to rest.

It wasn't a very long trip to the house that would be his
residence, but Vallant was able to see the neighborhoods
change before they got there. Official-looking buildings were
replaced by surprisingly large houses with drives, and when
the coach turned into one of those drives Vallant leaned a bit
through the window. The house they approached was at least
as large as his daddy's, a three-story affair with what was
probably servants' quarters under the gables. Gardeners
tended the front lawn carefully and lovingly, shaded by the
presence of large trees. It looked like it might not be *too*
much of a hardship to stay there for a while . . .

When the coach pulled up at the front of the house, a
young woman stepped out timidly to meet it. There was only
a single step between the drive and the approach to the
house, and the fact that Vallant noticed the one step said
quite a lot about the woman. She was a plain little thing in a
plain dress of gray, medium brown hair and eyes doing
nothing to add to her attractiveness. Actually it was her very
obvious timidity that put Vallant off most, but he still gave
her his best smile once he'd gotten out of the coach.

"I'm told I'll be stayin' here for a short while, ma'am," he
said gently so as not to frighten the poor little thing. "I'm
Captain Vallant Ro, and I'll be with you as soon as I see to
the coach driver."

But Vallant turned to see that the driver was already on his
way down the drive, which had to mean his charges had been
taken care of in advance. That was perfectly all right with
Vallant, since it let him turn back to the woman with a small
but gallant bow.

"Apparently I'm to be all yours without delay," he said

with another smile. "Are you the owner of this lovely house?"

"Oh, my, no," the girl said with a timid and embarrassed laugh, now looking even younger than she had. "This is the house of Dama Tamrissa Domon, and I'm Warla, her companion. We've been told to expect you, Captain Ro, and your room is ready. If you'll follow me?"

The girl said that as if she expected he wouldn't, so he smiled and bowed again and gestured her ahead of him. She kept glancing back as she moved, apparently afraid she might lose him, and once inside she did manage to lose his attention. The large entrance hall was decorated with paintings and obviously expensive tables with vases and statuettes standing next to ornate chairs, all of which managed to overcrowd the area. It was as if someone were trying to prove how much gold they had, and they'd decided to show the world rather than say the words.

"Your room is this way, Captain." Warla's gentle reminder that he'd slowed almost to a stop pulled Vallant away from the unkind assessment he'd been in the midst of. The girl waited at the foot of the very wide staircase, but she began to climb it as soon as it was obvious that he was ready to follow again.

"Dom Domon must be a very wealthy man to have furnished his house the way he did," Vallant commented as he moved up the stairs. "I assume I'll be meetin' him later at dinner?"

"Oh, but the dom is gone," Warla told him over her shoulder with more upset than the statement called for. "He's dead, I mean, and Tamrissa lives here alone now. Or at least she used to be alone."

It sounded to Vallant as if the girl had swallowed a giggle at the end of her comment, which made him sigh. So his hostess was a widow, probably an older lady who had no children, and that was why she'd offered her house as a residence. And Warla seemed to expect that her employer would take an interest in *him*, which wasn't the best of news. Back home a number of the older ladies had seemed to declare open season on him and his brothers, and when one of his brothers had decided to accommodate them, the young fool had barely escaped with all his parts intact.

"With me around, the dama will probably still think she's alone," Vallant commented carefully. "I'm under a vow for

as long as I stay away from home, and I'm sure you know
how things like *that* go. I've had cause to regret the vow, but
there's no getting out of it now."

Warla gave him an uncertain glance and a tremulous
smile, undoubtedly having no idea what he meant but was
too shy to say so. As a matter of fact Vallant had no idea what
he meant either, but the tale sounded good enough for
something made up on the spur of the moment. People
usually hesitated before trying to interfere with "vows," and
hopefully Vallant would have found his way out of the trap
by the time the dama talked herself into trying.

At the top of the staircase Warla led him to the left, and
then left again into the first room. Vallant was relieved to see
an entire wall of windows opposite the door, and that let him
stroll inside after Warla.

"This will be yours while you're with us," she said, already
edging back toward the door. "If there's anything you need
just ask me or one of the servants."

Vallant was about to ask where the bath house was, but the
girl left so quickly that she all but disappeared. He realized
then that they'd been alone together in a bedchamber, and
he chuckled in understanding while beginning to open his
seabag. It had been years since any female had disliked the
idea of being alone with him in a bedchamber, but that could
be because he hadn't involved himself with girls. Women
were more to his taste, but right now he needed a bath more
than he'd ever needed a woman.

Vallant took his coat off and dropped it to the floor,
knowing it needed cleaning as much as his cap and the rest
of his clothes. After his bath he'd have a servant see to all of
it, but first he had to see to himself. He carried his change of
clothes downstairs, found a servant and asked the way to the
bath house, then followed directions to the back garden.
Every room in that house seemed to have been furnished
with more money than taste, so Vallant had really high hopes
for the bath house.

He found the place easily and followed the path to it, but
stopped abruptly with a muttered curse when he saw the
"occupied" sign on the door. That was just the way his luck
had been running lately, badly and with terrible timing.
Well, he'd waited this long, so another five or ten minutes
shouldn't kill him.

Twenty minutes later, Vallant decided he'd waited long

enough. For all he knew the person inside could have died, possibly of old age. The wait had felt long enough for that to *him,* and on top of it all the sign might have been left accidentally on an empty house. But even if it hadn't, he'd waited as long as he intended to.

So Vallant opened the door and went inside, only to discover that the occupant of the bath house hadn't died, and certainly not of old age. The way the girl jumped said she'd probably fallen asleep in the water, and before her arms came up to cover her Vallant could see that she certainly had what to cover. A ripely rounded body despite the slender frame, long, shapely legs easily visible through the clear water, light hair darkened now from being wet, a face of unexpected and exceptional beauty. High yet gentle cheekbones, a straight and delicate nose, ripely full lips . . . Hadn't he already used that word "ripe" in connection with her? He wasn't sure any longer, not with those gorgeous violet eyes there to fall into . . .

"Who are you and what are you doing here?" the vision suddenly demanded, pulling Vallant back from the edge of stopping to stare. "No, never mind about answering that. Just get out of here!"

After what Vallant had gone through he was in no mood to take orders from anyone, not even an incredibly beautiful naked woman. Or especially not a beautiful woman. Every time he thought about Mirra and what her intentions had been, he quickly lost interest in all women. Happily the condition was temporary, but this time he was still able to use it for his own purposes.

"Not until I've had my share of that water," he answered her demand that he leave, spotting the towel cabinet and starting for it. "I feel singed from head to foot, not to mention broken and stomped on and covered in old sweat. I *need* that bath, but don't let me hurry you. Stay as long as you like."

Vallant had meant to sound casual and uncaring, but somehow the words came out more as an invitation than a challenge. Obviously he found the girl even more attractive than he'd first realized, but her reply helped to take care of that. She'd gotten out of the bath while his back had been turned, and now stood muffled in a towel.

"I don't care what you need, or even who you are," she came back, sounding as sharp-tongued as any harridan he'd ever met. "This bath house belongs to *me,* and I want you out of it this minute. If you refuse to leave, I'll call the guardsmen and have you arrested for breaking in here."

Well, of course the bath house belonged to her, how else could she justify ordering him out? Never mind that all the property belonged to an elderly widow, he probably wasn't supposed to know that. It bothered him that the girl would lie, but he'd obviously have to get used to being lied to by beautiful women.

So he said, "I didn't break in, I walked in," at the same time turning to look at her and beginning to remove his shirt. "And if you own this house, I was told you'd be expectin' me. I'm Vallant Ro, here in this accursed town to test for somethin' I never wanted. If you dislike havin' me here, you can thank the fools in our government for my presence. If not for them, I'd already be on my way back home."

Vallant felt a good deal of satisfaction at her appalled expression, certainly a result of having heard he was in the midst of testing for High. Most people refrained from starting up with strangers in any way, because it was impossible to know how strong their talent was simply by looking at them. This girl had started an argument with him anyway, but ought to be regretting it right now. Vallant was sure she would be, but her next words proved she didn't learn very quickly.

"I'm going to speak to someone about having you put elsewhere," she announced in a voice that trembled slightly. She'd also turned to the wall with supposed ladylike modesty when he began to take off the rest of his clothes, probably trying to impress him with the gesture. "You haven't the first idea about civilized behavior, and I refuse to have you in my house a moment longer than absolutely necessary. And if they can't find another place for you, I hope you'll have to sleep in the street!"

Vallant was too busy finally getting himself into blessed water to answer the girl's silly tirade, and by the time he came up again she was gone. He'd been ready to tell her that he knew she didn't own the house, but he'd have to save that for the next time they met. Which was just as well, since he was more ready for soaking than for arguing. So he moved through the water to the place the girl had been relaxing in, set his head into the headrest, then with a sigh let all his muscles release. He'd been tensed up for so long and for so many different reasons . . .

The warm water was delightful, and he closed his eyes even as he wondered again why he never minded the confines of a bath house. Every time he relaxed in one the same question arose, but he'd never found an answer. Other places could twist him into knots in an instant, but bath houses, even small private ones like this, never bothered him at all. The situation made no sense, and he really wanted to get to the bottom of it. Having the answer might help him with his problem elsewhere . . . especially since he'd never been able to talk to anyone else about it . . . admitting his weakness to others appeared to be beyond him . . .

But falling asleep proved to be anything but beyond him. With his eyes closed Vallant simply drifted off, floating away to a world where there *were* no problems. He stood again on the deck of the *Sea Queen*, the wind playing in his hair, gleaming water all around and as far as the eye could see. He was just about to turn to his crew and give the necessary orders, when someone dropped a belaying pin—

But it wasn't a belaying pin, and it wasn't one of his crew. Vallant opened his eyes to see that a stranger had entered the bath house, a man dressed in the most foppish clothing he'd ever seen. He also seemed to be carrying another outfit of the same sort, which made his purpose in coming in more than clear.

"Common courtesy suggests that you knock before comin' into a bath house that's occupied," Vallant said in annoyance over having been yanked back to the real world. "Or don't you know what that sign on the door means?"

"There *was* no sign on the door, but common is certainly the proper word," the fop returned in a baritone so pettish that Vallant expected the man to start fluttering a silk hankie. "Your courtesy is very common, my man, but I haven't the strength to argue with you. Nor do I intend to share that bath. I'm accustomed to bathing alone as a gentleman should, so you will take yourself out of there at once."

"Will I," Vallant murmured, studying the fool a bit more closely. His height was close to Vallant's own, but the delicate motions of his hands suggested there was nothing but flab under those ridiculous but very expensive clothes. Vallant had seen fops like this one before, the useless sons of those who considered themselves noble. He needed a real man's experience with life to get that petulant, little-boy look off his face, but chances were good that the fool would die of old age before that happened.

"What if I decide I don't *want* to get out of this bath?" Vallant drawled, letting his measuring stare tell the fop what he thought of him. "You'd then have to decide between throwin' me out and waitin' until I was ready to go. I really wonder which one you'd choose."

The fop colored at the very clear implication that he'd never try to throw Vallant out by himself, but he wasn't stupid enough to deny the claim. Instead he stiffened in insult, then straightened to his full height.

"A real gentleman makes his choices without being influenced by the lower classes," he retorted, the words as stiff as his stance. "If I had the strength I'd make an issue of your crudity, but at the moment I'm too badly in need of that bath water. Tomorrow, after I've had the opportunity to rest, we can discuss this matter again."

And with that he turned and walked toward the towel cabinet, leaving Vallant unexpectedly surprised. The fop had been embarrassed by what Vallant had said, but he hadn't really backed down. He'd obviously decided instead to share the bath, and since there was enough room for another six or seven people, the decision wasn't unreasonable. But to lower himself that far, the man must really be played out . . .

"I think I've been blind as well as insensitive," Vallant said with sudden insight, sitting up in the molded part of the bath bottom. "You're an applicant just the way I am, and you're too tired because you just passed your test. What did they do to force *you* to participate?"

"The Blending refused to listen to my mother's very reasonable and courteous request," the man answered, slamming the cabinet door after removing a towel. "Now they dare to threaten me with the unthinkable, but I refuse to be intimidated. I *will* find a way out of this insanity, and return to where I belong."

"It looks like we have somethin' in common after all," Vallant conceded as he rose to his feet. "I also intend goin' back to where I belong, so let's talk later. I'm Vallant Ro, Water magic."

"Lord Clarion Mardimil, Air magic," the man grudged, apparently finding the conversation distasteful but necessary. "And yes, let us indeed compare notes later. Getting free of this horror would be worth any price. A pity it can't be accomplished with gold."

"What makes you think it can't be?" Vallant asked, automatically ignoring the man's title as he stepped out of the bath and used what was left of his talent to remove the water from his body and hair. He sent it back to the bath with more effort than it had *ever* taken him, showing how tired he really was. He then picked up the towel to use on the bottoms of his feet, and that was an effort as well.

"I never thought about offerin' gold, which makes me feel like a fool," Vallant continued, looking at the man Clarion thoughtfully. "Since I can afford to pay any amount they care to name, and everybody knows bribin' is the largest industry here in Gan Garee, I wonder *why* I didn't think of it."

"Possibly you didn't think of it because you dislike wasting your time," Clarion answered sourly, beginning to remove his eye-hurting clothing. "I, on the other hand, must enjoy it immensely, as I spent much too much time engaged in the useless practice. If there's an answer, it definitely lies elsewhere."

"There has to be an answer," Vallant said, shaking his head stubbornly against the suggestion that there wasn't. "High practitioners are supposed to be willin' to do the job, so those who are unwillin' have to be let go at *some* point. That's the point we need, as long as it isn't one that involves dyin' . . ."

The comment was true enough that Clarion made no attempt to add to it. Or maybe the man was just too intent on getting into the bath water. Vallant had been dressing slowly while Clarion undressed, and with the last of his clothing tossed aside Clarion made for the water. Once again Vallant was surprised, because the man certainly wasn't built like your ordinary fop. His musculature was almost as good as Vallant's own, which had been developed by long years of hard work on the decks of various ships.

"We'll speak again later," Vallant said when he'd finished dressing, gathering up his dirty clothing but leaving the towel for the servants to see to. "Enjoy your bath."

Clarion made a sound of some sort that might have been agreement, so Vallant took it like that and simply left. If the man needed to relax as badly as he had, leaving him alone was the most considerate thing he could do. And Vallant meant to be very considerate to someone who apparently had access to the Blending. If they came up with the right thing to say, that access might well get the two of them out of that waking nightmare.

But in the meanwhile, Vallant trudged back to the main house wondering how long it would be before dinner was ready. He was hungry enough to eat a shark, teeth, fin and all. And maybe he'd even see that girl again. She was probably one of the servants, and would be embarrassed at the need to serve him. He'd let her squirm for a while, thinking he might have her fired, but then he'd . . . let's see, just what would he most enjoy doing to—or with— her . . . ?

THIRTEEN

Clarion stood in the middle of the resin room, sweating so hard that an observer would have thought him a common manual laborer. His talent still sealed off all those tiny holes that had tried to suck the air out of the room, and he also continued to pull down the air from the high ceiling so he might breathe more easily. Beyond that he was frantic, for he couldn't seem to think of a way to reach the only exit from that room. The small door in the wall so far above his head, the door he couldn't reach because there was nothing to stand on . . .

Nothing to stand on. Clarion's searching mind suddenly seized that phrase, just as if it were the answer he'd been looking for. But that was foolish. How could someone stand on nothing? There had to be something, and if there were, then that person would be standing on—

"Standing on the nothing that's only something to a

person with Air magic," Clarion muttered, actually disgusted with himself. He should have seen that at once, considering the experience he'd had with the phrase during childhood. Mother would come into his apartment and find him playing with his magic, and would ask him what he was doing. "Nothing, Mother," had been his usual answer, mostly to avoid one of those lectures on what a gentleman of quality did and did not do to fill his time. He should have remembered sooner . . .

But remembering still wasn't getting him out of there. The nothing he had to stand on was obviously supposed to be air, but simply thickening it enough to hold him wasn't the entire problem. He also had to keep the air from being drawn out of the room, as well as hold it near him so that he might breathe. Any one or two of those things might be managed, but all three? He could feel the strength draining from him by the moment, so even two tasks might soon be beyond him. What was he to do?

Fear tried to take hold of him again, but he brushed it aside almost impatiently. For the first time in his life he was expected to do something for himself, and as much as he detested the situation he also refused to lose to it. More than his life was at stake, since a man was nothing without his pride. He would take a moment to think things through, and only then would he act.

Clarion straightened to his full height, and began by examining the matter logically. He still had the strength to do two of the tasks necessary to free himself, so the obvious first question was which of the three actions were basically unnecessary? He couldn't very well dispense with breathing, and if he released the thickened air in front of the holes, he'd not only have nothing to breathe, but also nothing to work with.

But that left thickening enough air to climb on as the unnecessary act, which just wasn't so. He needed to get himself out of that room in order to survive, and simply standing there would certainly not accomplish it. Too bad there wasn't another means of escape, but obviously there couldn't be. The only other door was the one he'd come in by, and it was tightly sealed and locked—

Clarion paused for a moment with his brows raised, realizing that that wasn't entirely so. It was true the door *had* to be sealed if no further air was entering the room around its edges, but he'd seen both sides of the thing and hadn't noticed any sort of locking mechanism. With the building material being resin it wasn't likely there was any interior mechanism, so maybe the door *wasn't* locked . . .

That brought him to another line of thinking entirely, specifically what sort of effort it would take to break the seals. Opening the door without any inner handholds wasn't as impossible as he'd thought at first, not when he looked at the problem from the point of view of his talent. The matter of the seals did bother him, however, because they were sure to add a drag on the door that could mean the difference between opening it widely enough and simply moving it a little. Clarion considered the matter for another moment, then concluded that he had very little choice.

"And it will require quite a lot of strength, so I'd best begin at once," he muttered, taking his air supply with him as he walked to the stool. He might turn out not need the thing, but opening the door only to have it close again before he could reach it wasn't to be considered. Better to be prepared for all contingencies at the outset . . .

Happily the stool proved to be fairly light, so he would have little trouble pushing it into the doorway with his talent once the door was open. Clarion placed it directly against the wall a good number of feet to the left of the door, where it would hopefully be out of the direct line of his efforts. Those efforts would be at maximum strength, and anything with less than significant weight would certainly be caught up—

Along with the sealed door, Clarion hoped. He was very much tempted to doubt his plan, but couldn't afford the distraction. Time was running out, and soon the air he'd saved would become completely unbreathable. He was already beginning to detect a taint in it that threatened to make him dizzy, which meant he had to act *now*.

Pushing away all doubts and fears, Clarion gathered up every bit of air in the room and forced it together in front of the door. That left him able to breathe from the edge of the mass, while at the same time left nothing that could leak out of the now-unblocked holes. He forced the mass harder and harder against the door, compressing it so tightly that he soon withdrew his breathing supply. When that happened he quickly released the mass with a snap, also pulling with every ounce of his talent's strength.

And the sudden rushing away of the air around the door

did manage to pull the door open behind it! There had been a momentary drag and then a sucking snap as the seals were forced open, and then the door flew open violently against its stops. Clarion himself was fighting to keep from being swept back at that moment, which meant the door would have swung closed again before he could reach it. But with the opening of the door came a rush of new, fresh air, which he immediately grabbed and thickened and used to push the waiting stool into position by the door jamb.

The returning door tried to knock the stool out of its way, but Clarion had anticipated that and used his talent to keep the stool in place. If the door closed he'd have to start all over again, but this time with most of his strength already spent. Clarion swiped at the sweat on his face with the sleeve of his coat, forced himself into motion, and reached the door as quickly as possible. Opening it wide again would normally have taken very little effort, but right now Clarion could only just get it done. Then he staggered out into the hall and to the wall opposite the door, where he let himself fall slowly to a seated posture on the floor.

Clarion spent a few moments simply breathing, the only effort that wasn't currently beyond him. Then he heard approaching footsteps, and looked up to see the man from the outside room coming over with a cup in his hand.

"Don't worry, sir, it's all finished now," the man said soothingly as he stopped to crouch beside Clarion. "You've completed the test successfully, which means you're due congratulations. And I'm certain you're in need of this."

He held out the cup, and despite Clarion's reservations he couldn't refuse to take it. Every drop of moisture in his body must have fled in the form of sweat, and the need to replace even some of it had become a desperation. Clarion gulped the liquid, at first thinking it was water, but simple water had never been that refreshing. By the time he lowered the emptied cup, a trickle of strength was already beginning to return to him.

"This vileness will not go unnoticed," he said at last to the man watching him, finally able to voice his anger. "When my mother hears of what was done to me, the next ones to hear of it will be certain members of the Blending. After that you people will be properly punished, and you can be certain that I'll be present to watch. Get someone to fetch my trunk and summon a coach. I'm going to my house *now*."

"A coach has already been sent for, and your trunk will be on it," the man responded as he took back the emptied cup. "It won't be your own house you'll be going to, however, and you won't be discussing this test with anyone at all. There are further sessions you'll be required to attend now that you've passed the initial test, and not even the *entire* Blending can excuse you from them. Hasn't anyone explained this to you?"

"I was told nothing but that I was required to appear here," Clarion answered, still angry but now faintly disturbed as well. "What do you mean that even the Blending can't excuse me from further outrage? In case you've failed to notice, the Blending does anything it wishes to."

"Not when it comes to discovering the abilities of High practitioners," the man disagreed, a faint satisfaction to be seen in his eyes. "That process is inviolate, being the basis as it is for the ultimate choosing of the Blending itself. The only thing able to keep a man or woman from participating is their firm refusal, and then they're subject to the mandatory penalties. Mandatory, to be certain no one *can* avoid them."

"And what penalties are those?" Clarion asked, wondering how he could have missed the fact that the Blending had begun by passing these very same tests. It must have been because Mother had been so certain she'd be able to get him excused. It had obviously been wishful thinking on her part, with nothing of the clear logic she usually demanded from *him* . . .

"The penalty for refusing to participate is immediate arrest and trial, the culmination of which is that mandatory sentence I mentioned," the man obliged. "It consists of five years at hard physical labor in one of the empire's deep mines, working twelve hour shifts with rest days coming only once a month. The harshness of the penalty reflects the fact that the felon has attempted to steal the fruits of his talent from everyone in this empire. High practitioners work to the benefit of everyone, you understand, so refusing to exercise a High talent is—"

"Is stealing from everyone," Clarion interrupted impatiently, refusing to believe something like that could happen to *him*. No one of *his* class had to worry about such barbaric treatment . . . "But that would apply only to someone who passed the first test and refused to continue. How much will it cost me in gold for the records to show that I failed? Just name the figure, my man, and you'll have it within two days."

"You seem to have forgotten something, sir," the man said with the faintest of smiles curving his lips. "There are only two outcomes with these initial tests, and those who fail to pass end up dead. The cost of being recorded as a failure would be your life, and afterward the body would have to be identified by the guild master who sent the applicant here. Does that still sound like a viable alternative to you?"

Clarion made a sound of disgust to show his opinion of the ridiculous suggestion, dismissing the idea of finding a dead body to substitute for his own. Even if Lord Astrath, the guild man, could somehow be bribed into keeping silent about the substitution, Clarion would have to hide out for the rest of his life. He'd never again be able to show himself among the people of his class, and after the loneliness of his solitary childhood he'd find it impossible to withdraw from the company of others now that he had it. Even the presence of commoners was preferable to being alone, so for the moment he was trapped.

"We've arranged accommodations for you with someone who volunteered their house as a residence," the man said after a moment, taking Clarion's silence for the admission of defeat that it was. "Your place there will be paid for by us, but your meals and other requirements will need to be seen to by you. After the sessions will come the competitions, and if you qualify for those you will have the opportunity to earn bonuses in gold. You will be given a short time to rest, but the first of the sessions will be scheduled in just a few days. Please remember that you're not to discuss the details of this test with anyone, a caution that will have been given to the others at the house as well. Now let's see if your coach has arrived."

The man straightened and waited rather than beginning to retrace his steps, as though he thought Clarion incapable of standing without his help. For that reason Clarion struggled erect alone, and then followed the man back toward the front room of the building. Walking and standing straight *was* difficult, and Clarion blessed the exercises he did on a regular basis for helping him to accomplish it. That servant Mother had had for a while so long ago had done him a greater service than he'd known, showing Clarion the exercises that would fill part of the emptiness of his days. It had also kept him from developing the unsightly paunch of so many of his class-equals, and it now kept him from looking weak in front of his inferiors.

Clarion followed the man back out the front door of the building, to find that a coach was indeed waiting. His trunk was also stowed in the boot and secured firmly, so all Clarion had to do was climb into the coach. He did so without showing the aches the action caused him, and looked out the window once he was seated and the door had been closed behind him.

"I've just remembered that I left my hat in your . . . unusual waiting room," he told told the man who had been in the process of gesturing the driver to leave. "I have no intentions of waiting now until it's fetched, so you'll have to send it to me to wherever I'm being taken. Don't make the mistake of forgetting about it, for I certainly won't. Driver, you may now proceed."

His last sight of the man from the building was a casual nod accompanied by far too much amusement, and then the coach had begun to move away from that outrageous place. If Clarion hadn't been so tired, he might have ordered the driver to wait while he made a sharp comment or two about the building man's misplaced sense of humor. As it was he simply leaned back in the seat with a grunt, wishing local public coaches were better upholstered. It wasn't nearly as uncomfortable as the long distance coach had been, but discomfort came in too many degrees for that difference to be at all uplifting.

Clarion watched the streets as the coach moved along at a brisk pace, and wasn't at all surprised that they made no approach to the neighborhoods he was familiar with. He couldn't imagine people of his class being foolish enough to open their homes to a pack of unwashed strangers, which most of the other applicants must surely be. His time among them would be a great trial, but one he would do his utmost to shorten. There *had* to be a way out of that insanity, and he meant to find it.

After a short while the coach turned into the drive of a house, one of those that attempted to copy the regal splendor of the houses belonging to people of true quality. It was rather a smallish place, about the size of his and Mother's summer houses, but at least it wasn't the shanty he'd been half expecting. He wouldn't have put it past those people to house him somewhere impossible, just to add to his misery and humiliation.

"But one day I'll see the score evened," Clarion murmured as they approached the house, giving himself a solemn oath. "At the moment it's their turn to win, but one day the turn will be mine. And when *that* happens . . ."

Clarion didn't need to finish the thought for it to bring a smile to his face, not when he would certainly find enough time to decide on what the perfect revenge would be. The coach stopped, ending that train of thought for a while, and a young woman came out of the house, followed by two male servants. The servants went immediately toward the back of the coach, but the young woman stood waiting while Clarion left the vehicle. Once he stood before her, she smiled tremulously.

"Good day to you, sir," she said in a breathless, timid voice. "We've been told to expect you, and when I saw your trunk on the back of the coach, I brought two of the men out to carry it. I give you welcome in the name of my mistress, and will show you at once to your room."

"Room?" Clarion echoed before the woman could turn away. "Surely you mean apartment. No one could seriously expect me to survive in just one single room."

"I'm sorry, sir, but the only apartment is occupied by my mistress," the girl returned, her trembling voice now no stronger than a whisper. She also wrung her hands, and her very plain face looked close to tears. Clarion had never encountered a servant like her, nor any other woman for that matter. He was accustomed to grandly confident women, and this one made him feel like a gross and hairy bully.

"Perhaps it would be best if I discussed the matter with your mistress later," he said quickly, certain he would be completely out of his depth if the girl began to cry. "For now you may show me to this . . . room, an offer I greatly appreciate the kindness of."

Clarion added a small bow to his ridiculous little speech, and was then astonished to see that it worked! The girl blinked back her tears completely, and curtsied with the return of her timid smile.

"Yes, sir, thank you, sir," she said, acting as though he'd saved her from execution. "Please come this way."

The servants with his trunk had already entered the house, and the coach was already on its way back down the drive.

That surely meant the driver had been seen to in advance, which was just as well. Clarion had meant to send the man back to that building to collect his fare, as this destination had been none of his own choice. He believed in paying for his own desires, not those of others.

The house's entrance area had been decorated with a trowel, spreading expensive items everywhere one looked. The action was typical of those commoners who happened to acquire gold, and seemed to be painful only to those with decent taste. Clarion carefully looked away from the garish display to keep himself from growing ill, and followed the girl up the wide staircase and to the left. She proceeded up the hall to the first door on the right, threw it open, then stepped aside.

"I hope you find this comfortable, sir," she said with a brief curtsy and a blush. "If you need anything, just ask one of the servants."

With that said she left rather hurriedly, as though it might be improper in some way for her to remain longer. Clarion wondered at that as he stepped aside to allow the servants to carry in his trunk, then followed to tip each of them for their efforts. Their thanks were unexpectedly profuse, as though they hadn't anticipated being tipped, and that made Clarion glad he'd done it. These servants, at least, seemed to know their place, a delightful change from those who served in Mother's house.

But as he sat down in one of the small room's only two chairs, he still found it difficult to understand the attitude of that girl. She'd acted as though she didn't dare to enter a bedchamber with him, as though he were someone she might have cause to fear. His reaction to that assessment should have been heavy insult, to have his honor questioned by a mere slip of a serving girl . . .

But somehow he felt pleased rather than insulted. No female had ever seemed to fear him as a man before, most especially not the serving girls of his and Mother's household. Some of them had actually flaunted themselves before him when Mother hadn't been able to see them do it, their belief in their safety always perfectly correct. One of the first times it had happened, when he was still rather young, he'd caught the girl and pulled her into his arms. That, of course, had been when Mother had walked in, and the resulting scene was a memory which still caused him to flinch.

"For shame, Clarion, for shame!" she'd cried, nearly swooning where she stood. "That my own flesh and blood should act so! Oh, the humiliation of it, and after all I've sacrificed for you! Perhaps the fates will smile on me, and I'll fall dead this very moment!"

Clarion had rushed to her side and helped her to a couch, begging her all the while not to say that she would die. He would never be able to bear losing her, and would do anything if only she would return to her usual self. She'd rallied then and had made him swear that he would never look at or touch one of the serving girls again, and he'd been more than eager to give his word. Anything to keep from losing her . . . !

Well, he hadn't lost her, but he also hadn't been able to approach one of the serving girls ever again. Even if he'd wanted to break his word, Mother had always been right there to help him keep it. She'd also been right there the first and only time one of the girls of his own class had agreed to go driving with him, an excursion that had turned stiff and awkward. Mother had been the only one with anything to say, except for when the girl had asked to be taken home early. After that *all* the girls of his age group had avoided him, at the same time giving him the impression that they were laughing at him . . .

Mother had assured him that that was only his imagination, and then had gone on to explain why the girls avoided his company. She'd said the girls had quickly come to understand how high above them he stood, and didn't dare aspire to such exalted heights. Perhaps one day he would find a woman worthy of him, but until that day arrived he could rest untroubled, secure in the knowledge that he still had his mother.

"But at the moment I *don't* have Mother, and that girl feared being alone with me," Clarion murmured, experiencing the oddest feelings. "I am a man and by myself in Gan Garee, and suddenly the possibilities are endless. I think I'll bathe while I ponder my options."

He chuckled as he rose from the chair, and wasn't even more than mildly annoyed when he realized that without a personal manservant, he would have to unpack clean clothes for himself. He opened the trunk and took the first outfit to come to hand, each motion making him more and more aware of how badly he needed that bath. This would be another day he'd never forget, and certainly wasn't any less unpleasant than the rest of those days.

After retracing his steps downstairs, Clarion got directions to the bath house from one of the servants. Stepping outside he saw a modestly pleasant garden ahead, with a side path to the left that led to his destination. His stroll hurried itself a bit as he neared the bath house, the prospect of submerging himself in soothing water even more attractive than the thought of food. He was certainly hungry enough, he decided as he entered the bath house, but that could wait until—

His thoughts broke off sharply and he came to a halt when he realized the bath house was occupied. He was completely unused to that circumstance, of course, since Mother had only bathed in the morning after breakfast, and the servants had all used their own, smaller, bath house. The man in the water started, as though Clarion's entrance had awakened him from sleep, and then he frowned.

"Common courtesy suggests that you knock before comin' into a bath house that's occupied," the stranger growled, his accent marking him as one of those who weren't native to Gan Garee. "Or don't you know what that sign on the door means?"

"There *was* no sign on the door, but common is certainly the proper word," Clarion retorted, more than annoyed that the lout would speak to him so. "Your courtesy is very common, my man, but I haven't the strength to argue with you. Nor do I intend to share that bath. I'm accustomed to bathing alone as a gentleman should, so you will take yourself out of there at once."

"What if I decide I don't *want* to get out of this bath," the stranger returned almost immediately, looking Clarion over in a most insulting way. "You'd then have to decide between throwin' me out and waitin' until I was ready to go. I really wonder which one you'd choose."

Clarion was enraged that this creature would dare to question his manhood, but rage didn't carry him far enough back toward his usual store of strength. He'd simply expended too much of himself today, and there was no getting around it.

"A real gentleman makes his choices without being influenced by the lower classes," Clarion rejoined stiffly, determined to make his position perfectly clear. "If I had the strength I'd make an issue of your crudity, but at the moment I'm too badly in need of that bathwater. Tomorrow, after I've had the opportunity to rest, we can discuss this matter again."

Clarion saw startlement cover the stranger's features before he turned and walked toward the towel cabinet, a reaction which was grimly satisfying. Bullies had thought to take amusement from him before, but the strength of his talent had always let him teach them a sharp lesson. They all knew better than to try themselves against someone they weren't acquainted with, since it was always possible that a stran-

ger might prove to be stronger than them. Clarion had shown that even the familiar face could be dangerous to antagonize, and had earned himself peace from harassment without having to appeal to Mother.

"I think I've been blind as well as insensitive," the stranger's voice came suddenly, no longer sounding mocking. "You're an applicant just the way I am, and you're too tired because you just passed your test. What did they do to force *you* to participate?"

"The Blending refused to listen to my mother's very reasonable request," Clarion answered, anger at the memory making him slam shut the cabinet door. He wasn't sure why he'd responded to the fellow, unless it was because the man had actually apologized. And also sounded as unhappy about being there as Clarion felt . . . "Now they dare to threaten me with the unthinkable, but I refuse to be intimidated. I *will* find a way out of this insanity, and return to where I belong."

"It looks like we have somethin' in common after all," the stranger said with grim agreement, standing up in the water. "I also intend goin' back where I belong, so let's talk later. I'm Vallant Ro, Water magic."

"Lord Clarion Mardimil, Air magic," Clarion responded, disliking the need to converse with a commoner as though he were an equal, but finding it easier than he'd thought it would be. In point of fact he was receiving more courtesy from this Ro stranger than he got from his own class brothers, and honor demanded that he respond in kind. "And yes, let us indeed compare notes later. Getting free of this horror would be worth any price. A pity it can't be accomplished with gold."

"What makes you think it can't be?" Ro asked as he actually left the bath, ceding the possession of it without argument. The man was Clarion's own size and must be at least as weary if he'd also passed his test, which he must have done in order to be there. Ro had a look about him that shouted of a familiarity with physical labor as well as being accustomed to command, and yet he'd still given up the bathwater without needing to be forced to it. Clarion was even more impressed than surprised, and both feelings brought him to an attitude of indulgence which he'd never before experienced with an inferior.

"I never thought about offerin' gold, which makes me feel like a fool," Ro continued after banishing the water from his body and hair. "Since I can afford to pay any amount they care to name and everybody knows bribin' is the largest industry here in Gan Garee, I wonder *why* I didn't think of it."

So the man wasn't a copperless peasant after all. Clarion now felt a good deal more comfortable, especially since he'd discovered the perfectly logical reason behind his urge toward indulgence.

"Possibly you didn't think of it because you dislike wasting your time," Clarion answered, remembering his failure with a great deal of distaste. "I, on the other hand, must enjoy it immensely, as I spent much too much time engaged in the useless practice. If there's an answer, it definitely lies elsewhere."

"There has to be an answer," Ro responded, looking as determined as Clarion felt. "High practitioners are all supposed to be willin' to do the job, so those who are unwillin' have to be let go at *some* point. That's the point we need, as long as it isn't one that involves dyin' . . ."

Clarion almost paused in his undressing, suddenly remembering how close *he'd* come to dying. Somehow he hadn't really believed in the possibility at the time, hadn't considered his death something that could actually happen, but now . . . Looking back made him want to shudder with the realization of how close he'd come, and that in turn forced him to drop the last of his clothing and plunge into the water. At least it was as warm as it was supposed to be, and immediately began to warm the chill ice out of his blood.

"We'll speak again later," Ro said after a moment, and Clarion looked around to see that the other man was completely dressed. And rather than stand about gawking like some infantile voyeur, he added, "Enjoy your bath," and simply left. Clarion made a sound of agreement to the suggestion, finding he no longer had the strength for conversation. What he needed was to unwind in the warmth of the water, letting it soothe away all tension and fear.

Choosing a molded area in the bath diagonally opposite the one Ro had used, Clarion submerged for a delicious moment then leaned back into the head brace. He hadn't stopped to look for soap, but that could be done later. Right now he needed to soak the ache out of his bones . . .

Clarion fell asleep for a while, but not a long enough while. He was still tired when the sound of the door opening woke him, and he looked around to see another stranger entering. This one was dressed in what Clarion considered low-class farm fashion, and he apparently had no idea anyone else was in the bath house. He looked around at the cabinets ranged to the left of the door, and actually had to open each of them before he located the one with towels. Then he went back to the one with soap, and carefully withdrew a jar.

Clarion considered ordering the lout to wait outside until his own bath was finished, but memory of his conversation with Ro caused him to hold his tongue. Here was certainly another ally in the war to attain freedom, and Clarion was desperate enough to accept help from whatever source it might originate with.

"Good day to you, friend," Clarion said as he sat up in the water, startling the lout into whirling around despite his carefully pleasant tone. "I'm sure you're in need of this bathwater as badly as I was, so please don't hesitate about coming right in."

"I didn't intend to hesitate," the mudfoot answered, returning to removing the sacks he obviously considered clothing. "You startled me because I thought the bath house was empty, but it isn't as if I've never used a bath house before. Our town has a large one for the use of the public, and week's end night usually had the place filled to capacity."

"You've used a public bath house?" Clarion blurted, unable to help himself. "With *crowds* present? But surely your own home had a bath house?"

"In summer we used the creek's swimming hole, and in winter we used a tub in the kitchen," the mudfoot answered with a shrug as he made for the water. "What's the difference *where* you bathe, as long as you come out clean?"

Clarion couldn't answer that question, not in any words the mudfoot was likely to understand. It made a good deal of difference where one bathed, and anyone capable of questioning that truth would certainly be incapable of comprehending it. Instead of continuing with the subject, Clarion waited until the lout had settled himself in the place Ro had vacated, and then he spoke more to the point.

"I assume you're weary because of what was necessary to pass your test," he said after clearing his throat, then borrowed the rest of Ro's successful opening gambit. "What did they do to force *you* to participate? I'm Lord Clarion Mardimil, by the way. Air magic."

"Lorand Coll, Earth magic," the man responded, raising his head to frown at Clarion. "What do you mean, how was I *forced?* I didn't have to be forced to participate, I wanted very much to try."

"You *want* to be here?" Clarion demanded incredulously, finding it impossible to keep from rising to his feet. "Well, I don't know why I'm surprised. Of course someone like you would be eager to fight for that nonsense, it's worlds above anything you're likely to get under any other circumstance. A pity they don't believe in taking *all* their applicants from the lowest segment of our society."

"At least I'm not from the *useless* segment of our society," the lout had the nerve to rejoinder, his face darkened with anger as Clarion stalked past him on the way out of the water. "If *I* end up without a High position, I'll still be able to contribute more than I use up. If *you* end up without one, all you'll be able to do is go back to being a worthless sponge. If you suddenly lost all your mountains of gold, you'd starve to death in a week. Since I'd survive no matter what, I'd say you need to rethink your conclusion about which of us is really the lowest."

Clarion was out of the water by then, and he refused to dignify the lout's moronic claims by commenting. Instead he used air to force all the water from his body, finding that even so small an effort as that was nearly beyond him. He quickly used the towel on the bottoms of his feet and then dressed, still maintaining his silence. Of all the mindless, idiotic things to say, calling *him* low class and worthless! If he weren't so tired, he'd show that lout *exactly* how worthless he was!

Fury took Clarion out of the bath house once he was fully

dressed and had gathered up his soiled clothing. He also slammed the door behind him to punctuate his exit, and quickly strode back to the tiny accommodations he'd been forced to accept. He slammed that door as well, then hurled his soiled clothing away with every ounce of strength he had left. Calling *him* useless and worthless! Daring to question his ability to survive! Low class indeed!

Clarion stalked back and forth across the room countless times, fighting in vain to control his anger. It wasn't true that he was useless, the lout simply didn't understand. Those of his class had no need to justify their existence with crude manual labor, they were above such foolishness! And if the unthinkable happened and he and Mother did lose all their gold, he'd simply—why, he would just—

When the proper ending to his argument refused to come, Clarion discovered that he'd also stopped pacing. He didn't know *what* he would do if he no longer had Mother's gold behind him, but he'd do *something*. He was a gentleman of quality, and that lout had had no right to question his worth. Why, he'd passed that first test, hadn't he? That proved clearly enough what he was capable of, even though he'd had to use his talent to do it. The talent *was* his, after all, and no one had given it to him . . .

But the mudfoot had come far too close to thoughts of doubt that Clarion himself had had from time to time. When Mother had occasionally gone away without him, leaving him with a few of the male servants to see to his needs, he'd sometimes wondered what would become of him if she never returned. He had no idea where her funds came from, or how much was actually there. All he knew how to do was draw his allowance from the bank, that and how to spend it. . . . If Mother had failed to return he would have been completely on his own, without support and companionship, without funds, and without the ability to care for himself. Useless. . . .

Clarion threw himself into a chair and covered his eyes with his palms, struggling with all his might to force those horrid thoughts away. He didn't *want* to be where he was, bowing to the demands of others and risking his life at their whim, but perhaps this was the answer to his dilemma. If he did qualify as a High practitioner, he would have a career if he needed or wanted it, one that no one without greater talent could deny him.

Yes . . . that might be the best way to handle the matter.
Clarion lowered his arms to the chair's armrests, but didn't
open his eyes. He was too tired, and now felt a good deal
more at peace. He would continue to search for a way out of
the trap of *having* to compete, but in the interim would make
a point of showing what he could do. That way the choice of
direction in his life would be *his* rather than everyone
else's . . . Yes, that was the way. . . .

As he drifted off to sleep again, he was only distantly
surprised that his glimpses of the future included women
who were definitely not Mother. . . .

FOURTEEN

Lorand stared at his still-incomplete stairway of earth, trying
to figure out how to handle the increased flow of soil that
now poured down. Pulling in more power was out of the
question, not when he was so tired. But he'd have to do
something. The stronger flow of earth threatened to knock
down the steps he'd already built, not to mention trying to
bury him where he stood. He'd have to protect both himself
and the steps, but his strength was failing almost by the
minute.

He stewed mentally for another long moment, then could
have kicked himself when the obvious answer came. If he
stood *on* the stairway, he could protect both the stairs and
himself with the same effort. Cursing himself under his
breath, Lorand carefully mounted the first step then put his
left foot on the second step. The treads were too narrow to
hold both of his feet and he wobbled a moment getting his
balance, but then he had it.

Combining the two shields against the falling earth was

easier, and after clearing the air immediately around him of dust, Lorand took a minute to rest. He'd pictured building his stairway all the way up to that small wooden window-door, but by now he knew it wasn't going to happen. The strain of holding the stairs together—along with everything else—was getting to be too much, so as soon as he could actually reach the window-door he'd try to get through it.

The rapidly falling earth was now coming through in enough quantity to let Lorand hurry his building job a little. He formed another three steps of the same size as the first five, and then decided to try his luck. Every minute of delay meant a little less strength, and it would be stupid to wait until he was reduced to crawling. Not that he didn't feel like crawling right now . . .

Pushing that thought aside, Lorand began to climb his stairway to its top—where he then had to walk the top tread like an Airealist, one foot in front of the other while he maintained his balance. The shield against the falling earth kept him from being knocked off, and when he reached the wall he found that his face now looked directly at that window-door.

Lorand wiped his muddy right palm on his trousers before reaching to the square of wood, his left hand flat on the resin wall to help maintain his balance. If he found the square barred on the other side and unmoving he knew he'd probably cry, but happily he was spared that. The wood pushed in easily, and once opened stayed that way. Now all he had to do was climb through, and then he'd be able to rest for a while.

That last, simple "all" nearly undid him. Lorand had done at least as much climbing as any other child as a boy, but his boyhood was a number of long years behind him. And it had never been resin that he'd tried to climb, which offered nothing at all in the way of toeholds. The inside of the win-dow-door was just as smooth when it came to handholds, and that left only one thing to do: Lorand would have to use another, shorter step of earth to give him a boost up.

But that meant using even more of the power, and Lorand wasn't sure he had the nerve to try it. Every other adult he knew used their talent almost carelessly, either not knowing or deliberately ignoring what could happen if they drew in too much power. Lorand often did the same when it came to casual use, but something inside refused to allow that when he had to increase the amount of "usual" power. He knew he was good and could handle a lot more of the power than most people, but . . .

No, no buts. Another spurt of earth in his face, coming through the shield, quickly convinced him of that. He had to banish all doubts and use everything he had, otherwise he would end up dead anyway. Pushing himself to the limit wasn't much of a risk under the circumstances, and all the doubt did was waste time he couldn't afford to lose.

So he turned his attention to the earth which had fallen in the last few minutes, gathered it together between the hands of his talent, and formed it into a single step right up against the wall. He nearly covered his own foot doing that, but now he was seriously in a hurry. He could feel his strength draining out even faster than it had been doing, so there wasn't much time left.

This time he stood one foot on the mound against the wall before trying to climb through the window-door, and that made all the difference. A small jump got him far enough through that he was able to wriggle and squirm the rest of himself in, and then he looked around as he panted air that didn't need much cleaning. The area was narrow and not very long, but it was wide enough for his shoulders and there seemed to be a ladder below the opening on the other side.

Crawling the few feet to the far opening and twisting around to put himself feet-first toward the ladder was almost harder than everything else he'd done. But Lorand finally managed it, then slowly got himself down the ladder. Only when he finally stood in the narrow hallway below did he let go, sitting down hard on the resin floor and not even feeling it. Exhaustion had that one benefit of dulling the pain of other happenings, and Lorand meant to take full advantage of it.

Simply sitting still and breathing normally was marvelous, but after a moment Lorand's peace and quiet was intruded upon. The man from the front room of the resin building appeared carrying a cup of something, and when he got close enough he crouched beside Lorand.

"Congratulations, young man, on passing your test," the man said with a pleasant smile. "You performed excellently well, but now I think you need *this*."

He offered the cup then, and Lorand was tempted to refuse it just to show how disgusted he was. But he needed something to drink too badly to refuse, and once he cleared his mouth and throat he'd be able to put his feelings into words. The contents of the cup was more than just water, and Lorand felt some strength trickling back even before he'd drained the thing. That was great, since he knew exactly how he wanted to use that strength.

"How can you people do something like that?" he demanded as soon as he put the cup down. "I came here intending to do my best, but not to gamble my life! Why don't you give people a *decent* chance?"

"How much more decent a chance is there than winning your life along with passing the test?" the man countered blandly as he took back the cup. "It gives people the best motivation possible for doing their utmost, a level some might not reach without that strongest of drives. And you must also remember that some who come here plan to hide their ability, so they won't need to serve the public good. Don't the people of this empire deserve the best High practitioners it's possible to find?"

Lorand's sense of duty kept him from arguing that point, especially since he knew of someone like that. The boy had been two or three years older than Lorand and had been rated a strong Middle in Air magic, but he hadn't been happy about going to test for High. He'd told all his friends that he would be back as soon as they discovered he didn't quite measure up, and then he'd put his feet up again and let his widowed mother continue to support him the way she'd been doing until then. The boy never had come back, and everyone had assumed he'd found someone else to sponge off . . .

But that wasn't the most important point the man had made. The one that affected Lorand personally was the one about reaching a level he might not have reached if his life hadn't been at stake. He couldn't very well argue the truth of it, not when it had actually happened to him, but he still felt a formless yet definite sense of unhappiness.

"I understand all the reasons you've mentioned, but I still think you're . . . not doing it quite right," Lorand said hesitantly. "There ought to be a way to accomplish the same thing without risking people's lives."

"Well, if you can think of the way, by all means let us know," the man said as he straightened. "Right now your coach ought to be here soon, so let me explain a few things.

Now that you've passed this test, you'll be scheduled for other sessions in the applicant process. The first of the sessions won't be for a few days, so we've arranged for you to stay at a residence along with other applicants."

"How much will that cost?" Lorand asked as he struggled to his feet. "I don't have much left of the silver I was given, so I need to know how far it has to be stretched. And do you have a washbasin handy? Separating the earth out of the mud covering me is a little bit beyond me right now."

"Of course," the man answered, gesturing behind him. "We have a washbasin set up just around this curve. And as far as your accommodations are concerned, we'll be paying for that. What you have to pay for is your food and any other necessities, but don't despair about making ends meet. After the sessions you should be eligible for the competitions, the winning of which will provide bonuses in gold. That will help you to refill your purse."

Lorand nodded absently as he followed the man around the curve, delighted that he could soon have a source of income. He intended to pass all the tests they gave him anyway, so winning in competitions could be considered the same thing. And being paid in gold for the effort would be a great . . . bonus. Lorand grinned at the thought, then extended the grin when he saw the large basin filled with clean water and the towel folded beside it on the stand. He'd be careful not to spend the gold before he had it in his hand, but that water was about to be spent until he was completely mud free.

Washing in the water with mildly scented soap made Lorand feel a good deal better, but even as he dried his face and hands on the towel he knew he'd have to find a bath house as soon as possible. His body felt almost as covered as his hands and face had been, but trying to fit himself into the basin wouldn't have worked very well. He put the towel back down to find that his clothes case had been leaned up against the basin stand, so he picked it up and joined the man he'd been speaking to at the door the man had opened in the wall.

The doorway led them outside, where a coach stood waiting as if he were someone really important. Lorand climbed in and the man closed the door behind him, then looked up at him with a smile.

"I know you'll understand when I say that discussing the details of your test with anyone at all is strictly forbidden.

Enjoy your rest until the next session, and perhaps we'll meet again."

Lorand came up with something of a smile as he nodded, but he wasn't certain he *wanted* to meet him again. There was something . . . different about the man, an attitude that said he was engaged in an odd but interesting game rather than real life. Of course, it had been Lorand's life at stake rather than his own, which made the attitude more than a little cold-blooded.

The coach began to move when the man outside gestured , and Lorand settled back to enjoy the ride. He'd never been in any vehicle but a farm wagon where he was the only passenger, but the privacy wasn't hard to take. Especially when the coach simply rolled through one of the gates without being required to stop. They hadn't had it that easy on the way in—

They. Lorand suddenly straightened in his seat, finally remembering about Hat. Shame flooded him at the realization of how easily he'd forgotten about his friend, but then he felt the blood drain from his face. Those who didn't pass the test died, and Master Lugal had sent Hat anyway. Did he know? He'd been fairly certain Hat would fail, but did he know the cost of failure? If he did and had still sent Hat . . .

Lorand leaned back slowly, the urge to ask the driver to turn around and go back draining out of him. Right now he wasn't strong enough to face the reality of Hat's death; the possibility alone was almost more than he could handle. There was always a chance that Hat had survived and had even passed the test, and Lorand would end up seeing him at the residence he was being taken to. He'd wait, and ask discreet questions if necessary, and above all get some rest. After that he'd be able to decide what to do if Hat did turn out to be dead. Continue on as if nothing at all had happened, or turn around and walk away in disgust . . . ?

The rest of the ride wasn't as pleasant as Lorand had expected it to be, not with painful thoughts clanging around in his head. Gan Garee was a giant city completely filled with strangers, and Lorand had never known it was possible to feel so alone. He watched those strangers on the street as his coach passed them, dressed in their odd clothes and going about business he couldn't even imagine. Most ignored the vehicle as if it were invisible, but some, not as well-dressed or prosperous-looking as the rest, glared at it and him with a sense of personal insult. As if to say, "How dare you ride like that when we have to walk? Who do you think you are . . . ?"

Closing his eyes and leaning his head against the seat back for a moment let Lorand banish that foolishness. It was the tiredness inside him that caused those thoughts, that and the guilt he felt about Hat. Objectively he knew that Hat would have come alone if Lorand hadn't come with him, but emotionally Lorand was hearing one of his father's lectures on the damage it was possible to do by trying to reach too far above yourself. You hurt others even more than yourself, the elder Coll had been fond of insisting, knowing better than most how sensitive Lorand was over the well-being of others.

"Yeah, he always knew how to reach me," Lorand murmured, but memory of his father was lessening the feelings of guilt rather than increasing them. Hat had been just as determined as Lorand to escape the life they'd been born into, and the most telling point was the one he'd have to think about: would *he* rather have to go home a failure, or would he prefer to be dead? There were usually other options besides those two, but what if the others didn't count? And what would he have done if he'd known about the risk beforehand? Would he have tried anyway?

There was still too much weariness in him to make any firm decisions, so Lorand let the whole thing go while he looked at the scenery again. They'd reached a really nice neighborhood with big houses on both sides of the street, and Lorand expected the coach to continue on through it. When it turned into one driveway instead he was startled, but then the most obvious answer came to him. The coach was meant to take someone else to that residence, and this was where they'd pick them up.

So Lorand simply enjoyed looking around as the coach drove up to the front door. The lawn to either side of the drive was healthy and well cared for, but he couldn't detect any of the . . . hum of satisfaction, was the best thing to call it, of truly thriving greenery. The beautifully arranged flower beds were also only minimally happy, but that might be because of the soil composition. The earth mixture in this area wasn't—

"Excuse me," a woman's voice interrupted his mental rambling, and Lorand looked down at a rather plain girl who had apparently come out of the house they'd stopped near.

"You *are* one of the applicants for High practitioner, aren't you?"

"Well, yes," Lorand admitted, feeling confused. "Was there something you wanted to ask me?"

"Actually I was wondering why you aren't getting out of the coach," the girl confessed shyly, her cheeks faintly pink. "You *have* been assigned to this residence, haven't you?"

Lorand began to deny that with a laugh of ridicule, but then he remembered being told that the coach would take him to the place he was supposed to stay. He hadn't expected anything like *this*, but a lot of things were happening lately that he hadn't been expecting.

"I suppose I *have* been assigned here," Lorand replied, now feeling slightly foolish. "I didn't mean to sit here and daydream—"

He broke off the lame excuse before he made himself look even more like a backward hick, took his case, and left the coach. After closing the door he meant to ask the driver how much the ride would cost him, but the driver got the coach moving again before he could even open his mouth.

"It seems the coach drivers are paid in advance," the girl ventured, apparently knowing what Lorand was thinking about. "At least the other coach drivers all did the same thing this one did . . . If you'll follow me, I'll show you to your room."

"Is this house yours?" Lorand asked as he followed the girl. "I mean, does it belong to your parents or husband or someone like that?"

"Oh, no, I just work here," the girl answered with a timid laugh and another faint reddening of her cheeks. "I'm the companion of the lady of the house, and she's an applicant, too. I'm Warla."

"And I'm Lorand Coll," Lorand answered, suddenly distracted by the incredible number of expensive things arranged all over the entry hall. He couldn't judge the value of everything he saw, but just by the gold and jewels alone . . . half the farms in his county were worth less. Lorand had the definite urge to drag his feet while he stared openmouthed, but the humiliation of doing that would have been unbearable. He *had* to get rid of these small town reactions he kept coming up with, or he'd put his foot in his mouth for sure.

The girl Warla was already climbing the beautifully grand staircase, so Lorand hurried to follow even though the idea

of any sort of stairs still disturbed him. His hurry lasted
for all of three steps upward, and then he was forced to
remember how little strength he had left. He was also forced
to slow down, but Warla didn't try to lose him the way his
previous guide had. She waited at the top of the stairs until
he'd joined her, and then she led him to the left.

The door she opened was the second one up the hall on the
left, and the room it opened into threatened to take Lorand's
breath away. It had *real* furniture rather than handmade
make-dos without the least amount of craftsmanship, and
the size of it was three times what Lorand had lived in at
home. The curtains and quilts and linens were all embroidered, and the incredible bed stood on a real carpet. They'd
had a carpet in their visiting room back home, but it was
older than his brother Mildon and had probably been
threadbare even when it was new . . .

"I'll leave you to get settled in now," Warla said, and
Lorand turned quickly to see that she stood just outside the
door. But she wasn't laughing, even though she must have
seen him gaping like a fool. "If you should happen to need
anything, just ask one of the servants."

Servants. Lorand nodded mutely and watched her close
the door, then he went to a wide chest against one wall and
put his case down on it. He should have known there would
be servants in a house like that, and he didn't know how to
behave with servants. Obviously he would soon find out, but
the prospect wasn't as appalling as it should have been. If he
managed to live long enough to win to High, he'd eventually
have servants of his own.

Whether or not that meant Lorand had decided to continue on with the testing was something he didn't care to
consider at the moment. His first and most pressing need
was a bath and a change of clothes, but he hadn't seen any
bath houses in the neighborhood. He'd have to ask someone,
but the nearest bath house had better not be too far away. If
it was, he'd find a stream or something and use that instead.

Lorand unpacked a change of clothes, then went downstairs again and found someone to put his question to.
Happily the man misunderstood, and answered, "Yes, sir, I
certainly can tell you where the bath house is. Just follow this
hall to the back of the house, and step outside. A few feet to
your left is the pathway to the bath house, which stands
between this house and the gardens."

Lorand thanked the man and began to follow the directions, but how he managed to keep from muttering, "A private bath house. A *private* bath house!" was a complete mystery. He was really beginning to hate the way everything he saw impressed him, but he didn't know how to make the feelings stop. He *was* a hick from the boondocks, and as humiliating as that truth was, it also couldn't be denied.

The gardens made their presence known as soon as Lorand stepped outside, but his energy was draining out of him again and only the sight of the bath house interested him now. He headed for the building as fast as possible, happy that using it would cost him none of his small hoard of silver. He'd been told he had to pay for his own meals, and right now he felt as if he could eat himself copperless. If he hadn't needed a bath fractionally more, he would have asked about places to eat. The cheapest places possible . . .

He walked into the bath house wrapped in thoughts about just how little he could afford to eat without losing vital strength, but was yanked back to reality when he saw the series of cabinets to the left of the door. Soap and towels must be in there, but Lorand had no idea of what would be where. In the public bath house, he'd been given soap and a towel when he'd paid his use fee. Here, the only thing he could do was search.

Lorand was in the midst of doing just that, when a voice said, "Good day to you, friend." He whirled around to see that someone was already in the bath, a man he hadn't noticed when he'd first come in. The stranger continued, "I'm sure you're in need of this bath water as badly as I was, so please don't hesitate about coming right in."

The man was obviously trying to be friendly, so Lorand ignored the faint tone of condescension in his voice and tried to be the same.

"I didn't intend to hesitate," he answered, going back to the undressing he'd started after finding the towel and soap. "You startled me because I thought the bath house was empty, but it isn't as if I've never used a bath house before. Our town has a large one for the use of the public, and week's end night usually had the place filled to capacity."

Lorand wasn't in the habit of boasting, and certainly not about something as foolish as having used a bath house, but something in the other's manner had pushed him to it. The stranger's expression seemed to demand that Lorand justify his being there, but his choice of justification turned out to be another backwoods mistake.

"You've used a public bath house?" the stranger immediately demanded, sounding as if Lorand had confessed to murdering helpless women and small children. "With *crowds* present? But surely your own home had a bath house?"

The stranger made the lack of a private bath house also sound like a crime against nature, and Lorand suddenly found himself very annoyed. He'd been struggling not to look like a backward hick, but this easily-shocked stranger turned his mood perverse.

"In summer we used the creek's swimming hole, and in winter we used a tub in the kitchen," he returned with the most outrageously bucolic picture he could think of. But his need for a bath hadn't lessened, so he headed for the water as he added, "What's the difference *where* you bathe, as long as you come out clean?"

The stranger didn't seem to have an answer to that, so Lorand used the opportunity of his silence to duck completely underwater. It felt wonderful to be wet all over, but it felt even better to know that the stranger had believed him. Lorand's family had a tub installed in one corner of the barn, and that cramped area was where they all bathed. There was a small hearth near it to heat the water, which they'd used in the winter to also warm the area. It was crude but usable, which had always been his father's standard of good enough.

Pushing away thoughts of his father, Lorand headed for a corner of the bath where there was clearly a molded resting area. He'd never had the chance to try relaxing in one, not with all the older men in the bath house claiming the comfort first, but now he could. He had just gotten himself settled into it when the stranger decided to try starting a conversation again.

"I assume you're weary because of what was necessary to pass your test," he said, this time managing to make it sound as if Lorand had probably jumped up and down a little before being *given* the passing of the test, rather than having earned it like this very self-important stranger. "What did they do to force *you* to participate? I'm Lord Clarion Mardimil, by the way. Air Magic."

It had been obvious that this Mardimil was also an applicant, but the title he'd added suggested it, and the name.

would be familiar to anyone with the least pretensions of being civilized. The title meant little to Lorand, and he'd never heard of the man—happily!—but he *had* heard the rest of what he'd said and that got to him.

"Lorand Coll, Earth magic," Lorand responded with automatic courtesy, then dove straight to the really important part. "What do you mean, how was I *forced?* I didn't have to be forced to participate, I wanted very much to try."

"You *want* to be here?" Mardimil demanded, once again declaring Lorand guilty of some horrible crime as he rose to his feet. "Well, I don't know why I'm surprised. Of course someone like you would be eager to fight for that nonsense, it's worlds above anything you're likely to get under any other circumstance. A pity they don't believe in taking *all* their applicants from the lowest segment of our society."

That sneering ridicule was more than Lorand was willing to put up with. His home town might be small, but it still had its share of monied snobs who considered themselves too good to breathe the same air as common folk. Their children had been just like this Mardimil, but Lorand hadn't been allowed to tell them what he thought of them. His father had been afraid of reprisals and had refused to "mix in," but his father wasn't here right now.

"At least I'm not from the *useless* segment of our society," he growled at Mardimil, who was in the midst of leaving the bath. "If *I* end up without a High position, I'll still be able to contribute more than I use up. If *you* end up without one, all you'll be able to do is go back to being a worthless sponge. If you suddenly lost all your mountains of gold, you'd starve to death in a week. Since I'd survive no matter what, I'd say you need to rethink your conclusion about which of us is really the lowest."

Lorand expected the man to come back at him with *something,* but Mardimil maintained an infuriated silence while he dried and dressed, then left the same way. His anger had been perfectly clear, and Lorand wondered why he hadn't said anything in his own defense, even a flat refusal to concede Lorand's points. Mardimil could have laughed and called Lorand a jealous fool, and there would have been no easy way to defend against the charge. So why had he done nothing more than dress and leave? It made no sense, unless . . .

"Unless I told him something he'd been suspecting was

true," Lorand muttered, suddenly more disgusted with himself than with Mardimil. He'd been in a self-embarrassed mood, so he'd let the man's attitudes push him into speaking a very cruel truth. There was no denying that the vast majority of offspring from wealthy parents were useless, but most of them were perfectly happy to have it that way. What must it be like to be one of the minority, aware of feelings of worthlessness, but refused the chance to do anything about it?

"It would be like living with my father, only worse," Lorand decided with a sigh. For him, leaving home hadn't been much of a hardship, and wouldn't have been one even if he'd had to do it on his own. Aside from his mother and brothers, there hadn't been anything left behind that he would miss. He also had a trained ability to offer an employer, and hadn't been raised to consider honest work a shame and a scandal. And he hadn't gotten used to things that only a large amount of gold would buy.

Yes, there were times when wealth was more of a burden than a blessing, Lorand decided as he forced himself to leave the molded rest area in order to reach the jar of soap. He'd left it near his towel, and the jar was full enough to let him wash once now and then a second time before he left the bath. In between he intended to soak and nap, even though the warm water had already soothed away much of the ache in his body. Later he'd look up Mardimil and apologize, even if it meant accepting a belated and sneering rebuttal.

Lorand washed his body first, knowing his eyes would end up filled with soap when he did his hair. He'd been thinking his hair was too long, but most men in Gan Garee seemed to wear it even longer. If that was the current style he'd have to learn to live with it, or else stand out even more than his clothes would make him do. Master Lugal had been right about those clothes, and as soon as he won some gold he'd have to see about buying new ones. Tight breeches and wide-sleeved shirts, in all colors but drab green, dull blue, and lifeless gray. Those were the only colors his clothes came in now, but once he had that gold . . .

His hair seemed to be as full of earth as the testing room had been, so Lorand just kept scrubbing at it even when he heard the door open and close again. He thought it might be Mardimil coming back to get in his rebuttal now, but it

wasn't possible to open his eyes and look. When the silence
continued Lorand decided it was some other applicant
coming in to wash away the sweat of his efforts, and simply
continued scrubbing at his hair. Once he got his strength
back he'd be able to remove any still-present grains of earth
easily, but right now scrubbing was all that could make him
feel clean again.

Lorand rinsed and washed his hair three separate times
before deciding he'd done all he could. He'd been able to
hear the newcomer moving around without speaking, and it
was possible that this man would be friendlier than the last.
The least he could do was introduce himself, but that sort of
thing went better when you looked a man in the eyes. He
reached for the towel he'd positioned right at the edge of the
bath, but his groping hand couldn't even find the bath edge.
He must have moved too far the last time he rinsed, and now
he needed help to get back where he needed to be.

"I'm sorry to bother you, but I seem to have lost the edge
of the bath," he said, speaking in the general direction of the
gentle splashes he'd heard. The man had come into the
water, and wasn't far from where Lorand stood. "If you'll
guide me back to it, I'll introduce myself in the proper way
once I can see again."

Lorand heard a soft chuckle, and then there were two
hands on his shoulder and back, turning him in what was
hopefully the proper direction. He moved forward with arms
outstretched, searching for the edge even as he wondered
about the newcomer. The poor man seemed to have very
small hands, which must have gotten him teased as a child
and ridiculed as an adult. Lorand would have to be careful
not to say the wrong thing and upset the fellow; he'd already
had words with one of his brother applicants, and didn't
want to get the reputation of being a troublemaker. His
hands finally closed on the towel, so he used it to wipe his
eyes and soak up some of the water in his hair, then he
turned back to the newcomer.

"Lorand Coll, Earth magic, at your—" service, only his
mind finished, his tongue too frozen with shock to speak the
word—or any other. The man with the very small hands
wasn't a man at all. He was a woman—*She* was a woman,
and the most beautiful woman he'd ever seen despite the
obvious hardship she'd been through. Golden-blond hair

and blue-green eyes, an oval face with the most perfect features, a slender body with large breasts, a tiny waist, and beautifully shaped legs . . . Perfect was the only word to describe her, that and—

"Naked!" Lorand blurted, his tongue starting to work again at precisely the wrong time. "We're both naked, and you're a woman!"

"How lovely of you to notice," she returned in a warm, husky voice that reached down to caress him in a usually unmentionable place. "I'm a woman and you're a man, and we're both unclothed. Do people usually bathe *in* their clothes where you come from?"

As she spoke she moved toward the deep water, but still hadn't stopped looking up at him. She was such a little thing, not particularly short but slender and delicate, yes, that was it, delicate. And naked. Her having called it "unclothed" instead hadn't helped in the least.

"That was a silly question, and I'm glad you're ignoring it," she said with a tinkling laugh as she lowered herself a bit more into the water. "Ummm, this feels marvelous, Lorand Coll. I'm Jovvi Hafford, Spirit magic, and I have the feeling you've never bathed with a woman present before. I thought the custom of mixed bathing had spread everywhere."

"Not everywhere," Lorand answered hoarsely, frantically trying to decide what to do. What he *wanted* to do was stop staring at her like a virgin boy and casually turn his back to hide his own nakedness, but he couldn't think how to do that without appearing like an awkward child. And if there was anything he *didn't* want to look like in front of this incredible woman . . .

"Then I really must apologize," she said in that velvet voice, now sounding completely sincere. "If you're not used to mixed bathing, then you must be horribly embarrassed. I should have waited until you were through and gone, instead of barging in and intruding. I'll wrap up in a towel and wait outside, and you can—"

"No," Lorand interrupted, stopping her as she actually began to leave the bath. "I won't hear of you waiting for what I know you need so badly, not just to soothe my backward beliefs. It so happens I was just about through anyway, so please let me be the one to allow *you* your privacy. It's the least I can do for being so rude."

Lorand had no idea where all the flowery words and phrases were coming from, he just felt great that they were. He'd read a lot of things over the years that his father had considered trash, but some of the heroes in those books had spoken like that. Maybe that was where it had come from, and if so he blessed his teachers for having made him read them. That was because Jovvi Hafford now smiled at him in a way that made her even more beautiful, and seeing that was worth anything he could imagine.

"That must be the nicest thing anyone has ever said to me," she replied, speaking what had to be a lie, but a very pleasant one. "I'll accept your offer if you insist, but it would be perfectly all right if you stayed. I won't mind in the least."

"I'd mind staying even less than that, but I think it will be better if I go," Lorand forced himself to say, then turned casually to the steps. "I'll be out of your way in no time at all."

Jovvi didn't respond to that, so he was able to concentrate on wrapping the towel around his middle as if it were totally unimportant. In point of fact the towel now hid the extreme interest he'd found in the woman, something she'd happily missed seeing while he was in the water. He would have blushed like a firebloom if she'd noticed, but now he was safe.

Or relatively safe. He kept his back turned while he dried himself in record time, briefly wishing his magic could have helped the way Mardimil's magic had dried *him*. Jovvi certainly wasn't watching him, but that wasn't keeping him from imagining her gaze on him, rating what she saw. Rating what usually wasn't seen by anyone but other men. Damn it, stop thinking like that before you start to blush like a schoolgirl!

Lorand couldn't remember dressing ever taking so long, and the fact that he couldn't hurry in any obvious way just made it worse. But he wasn't going to add to that by saying anything, so as soon as he was ready he gathered up his dirty clothes and headed for the door. When he reached it he thought he was in the clear, but Jovvi's voice came just as he began to push through.

"It was nice to meet you, Lorand Coll," she said in a way that made his toes want to curl. "See you later at dinner."

"I certainly hope so," he managed to get out, then finally

escaped without looking back. But he'd wanted to look back, and after he reached his room he wondered if she would have minded. She hadn't seemed to mind when they were in the water, but it wouldn't have been the same with him fully dressed. No, he'd been right not to impose on her broad-mindedness, especially since he couldn't match it. Between the two of them, *he* was the overly-modest old maid.

But maybe that was something he'd get over. Lorand sat down in one of the room's very comfortable chairs, closing his eyes in order to look at Jovvi again. If he was smart he'd *work* at getting over his modesty, but meanwhile there was dinner to think about and look forward to . . . Good thing he hadn't made more of a fool of himself by asking for directions to a cheap place to eat. . . .

FIFTEEN

Jovvi stood in the middle of the four-foot-wide walkway and trembled, feeling all those emotions of anger and outrage batter at her. She had to calm those feelings and bring them to a peaceful balance, but reaching to them a few at a time hadn't worked. When she released one group of them in order to soothe another, the first group went back to raging. She had to cross twenty-five feet of walkway to reach the door that would let her out of that place, but if she tried it with all those feelings storming around her, she'd be knocked off the walkway to her death.

She was really terrified and desperate, but when her quaking mind began to think that she'd never been so frightened in her entire life, some tiny part inside her immediately denied that. Her father had been killed in a mining accident when she was nine, and her mother had been left with Jovvi and her two older brothers and the baby. Her mother, a very minor talent in Water magic, was already taking in washing to help make ends meet, and the death of her husband was a blow she'd never recovered from.

Some women fall apart when tragedy takes away the one source of strength and safety in their lives, but some grow hard and tough themselves as a replacement for what was gone. Jovvi's mother had been a pleasant and loving woman who scolded but smiled indulgently when her husband tried to spoil their children. That changed completely and without warning once her husband was dead, as though someone had taken her a great distance away without moving her body an inch. Parli, Jovvi's mother, turned as cold as an uncaring stranger, and never again looked at her children with love.

But that didn't mean she stopped looking at them, usually in a darkly musing way. The silver from their father's death price wasn't much, but Parli had been paid for each of the children. Jovvi had stood behind the door to their shack's second room, listening to the stranger her mother had become muttering aloud as she counted and recounted the silver. No matter how carefully the amount was stretched, it couldn't possibly last more than four or five months. After that they would all starve if she didn't do something, so she would *have* to do something.

For a very long time, Jovvi had no idea what that something would turn out to be. Living on almost nothing was very hard, and she and her brothers took to roaming around their part of town, searching the refuse of those who were wealthier. Almost everyone fell into that category, and occasionally they found things that were edible. When that happened she and her brothers shared the treasure, making no effort to bring any of it back to the stranger who pretended to look after them.

Jovvi wasn't sure just when she noticed that the baby was gone, but Parli certainly didn't mention it. Nor did she seem particularly upset, so Jovvi thought she understood. The baby had been the weakest of them, and simply hadn't been able to survive living on almost nothing. The little girl had died, and now Parli was pleased because there was one less mouth to feed.

But five months went by, then eight and more, and the

meager amount of silver still hadn't run out. They all wore
rags and usually went to bed hungry, but Parli still had silver
to count at night when she thought the children were asleep.

Then, about eleven months after her father's death,
Jovvi's oldest brother disappeared. She and her last remaining brother searched everywhere for him, but no one had
seen him nor did anyone see him again. It was supposed that
he ran away from what could no longer be called a home, but
he hadn't even said goodbye to her. They'd been so close . . .
had he been afraid she'd beg to go with him, and hadn't
wanted her any more than their mother did?

After that she and her other brother grew apart, so when
the day came that he also disappeared without a word of
goodbye, Jovvi wasn't surprised. It had become a matter
of everyone for himself, so Jovvi was surprised when she
returned to the shack and Parli smiled at her.

"The best for last," she murmured, stroking Jovvi's cheek
once before turning back to her cooking fire. "Come and eat,
Jovvi, so your beauty will come more quickly to full bloom."

Jovvi had had no idea what Parli was talking about, and
grew even more confused when decent food was available
more often than it had ever been before. She still wore rags,
but at least she now had what to eat every once in a while. It
wasn't until she was almost twelve years old that the man
and his bully boys came to get her, the man her mother had
sold her to. That was when she realized that the baby hadn't
died and the boys hadn't run away . . . and even though she
was a widow her mother was pregnant again. . . .

"Now, *that* was when I first understood the meaning of
fear," Jovvi whispered to herself, gathering together the
scraps of her courage. "But I survived it and the worse that
followed, so I refuse to not survive this. There's supposed to
be a way to win, and all I have to do is find it."

All. That had been easy to say, but doing it would prove a
good deal harder. The invisible wind of all those emotions
buffeted her mercilessly and with ever-increasing strength,
and simple determination would never get her across those
twenty-five feet to escape and safety. She'd have to calm and
balance the emotions, but the way she'd already tried hadn't
worked. Maybe if she ran . . .

Jovvi sighed, discarding the idea of running without any
further consideration. She'd been a very fast runner during

her childhood, and could have managed a good deal of speed even dressed the way she was. But the strength of the invisible wind would overcome even the fastest runner in the world, knocking her off balance and off the walkway. No, she needed to find a way to shield herself from the buffeting long enough to get across the walkway, but how could she do that?

In frustration she tried to soothe the raging around her again, and actually managed to calm a group, hold it, and then calm a second group. When she tried to hold those two and reach for a third, the whole thing fell apart and she was back to where she'd been. And she staggered a little under the renewed load, which brought the sour taste of fear back to her mouth. She had to get out of there, or all her plans would die along with her.

And that wasn't something she was prepared to let happen. She'd worked too long and hard to get where she was to let it all go to waste, not even if that gauntlet of unbalance stretched all the way back to Rincammon. There *had* to be a way to get past it—

Jovvi stood very still as the idea came to her, making her wonder if she could do it after all. The key to getting out of there had to be going *through* the storm, since it wasn't possible to go around it. Going through meant balancing the forces raging at her to keep from being knocked over, but that didn't mean they all had to be balanced at once. She supposedly could have drawn in enough power to do that, but her sense of preservation told her she'd never be able to handle it. No, she had to hold and balance only two groups at a time, and that way she might make it.

If she held one group on each side of her. If she released those two and took another two that would allow her to move forward. If she could stand fast until she had the second two groups balanced well enough to move between them. If, if, if . . .

But there wasn't any other choice and Jovvi knew it. Her face perspired freely now, echoing the strain the rest of her body felt, but there was no getting around it. She had to try her idea and make it work, or else her lifetime of struggle would have been for nothing. She took a deep breath, ignoring how uneven it was, and plunged into the first of it.

Balancing the first two groups of emotion on either side of her was fractionally harder than it had been the last time she'd tried, showing she was seriously beginning to tire. That meant she had no time to waste, so she moved to the far side of her small island of calm, dropped the two groups, and reached for two more. She nearly lost her balance before the second two groups were calmed, but she couldn't let herself notice that. She simply had to keep on with it, moving three or so feet ahead with every successful effort.

By the time Jovvi was almost to the door, she was drenched in sweat and lightheaded. She reached to the last two groups automatically, but calming the railing storm made her clench her teeth and fists with the effort. She'd almost lost the previous groups too soon, and if she hadn't been so exhausted she would have been terrified. But there was no strength to spare for terror, only for doing what *had* to be done.

The calm in the last two groups took forever to come to full balance, but once it did Jovvi was able to reach the door. It had a simple latch string coming from a hole drilled through it, but pulling the string didn't open the door. It lifted the latch so the door could be pushed open, and it took Jovvi a short while to figure that out. Once she did she stumbled through into what looked like a hall, finally able to let go of the power. If she'd had to hold it for even one more minute. . . .

Paying no attention to whether or not the hallway floor was clean, Jovvi used the wall opposite the door to help her sit down without falling down. The muscles in all four of her limbs had turned to quivering water, and she couldn't understand why she hadn't passed out. Fainting wasn't something she'd ever actually done, but passing out after a time of incredible harshness . . .

"There, there, my dear, it's all over now," a male voice soothed, and suddenly there was an arm around her shoulders helping to support her. "Here, drink this and it will make you feel better."

"This" was a cup of what looked like water, but when the man helped Jovvi to drink from it she found it was better than water. It began to return a small measure of strength to her almost immediately, so she drained it to the very last drop.

"Yes, you *will* feel more like yourself in just a few minutes," the man said as he took back the cup, giving Jovvi the chance to see that he was the man from behind the table in the outer room. "And now I can offer my congratulations for your accomplishment. Your first test is passed and behind you."

"First and last test," Jovvi corrected, making no effort to be in the least pleasant or pleasing. After that ordeal she certainly looked a complete horror, so there would have been no point in trying to play the game. "My life is mine to live, not yours to threaten, so you will never get another chance to do the same again. As soon as I've recovered my breath I'm leaving, so you may summon a carriage for me at once."

"A coach is already on its way," the man replied in something of a murmur, looking at her the way most men did when she stood fresh and lovely and smiling. "I'm afraid it won't be taking you where you think it will, though, because this is *not* the last of your involvement with us. A series of sessions have already been scheduled for you, and you *will* appear for them. The law is quite clear on the matter, and even a woman as breathtaking as you must obey it."

The man's hand had begun to stroke her arm where it had previously rested, bringing Jovvi as close to outrage as her exhaustion allowed. She quickly shifted out of reach of the fool who believed he could enjoy her without paying her price, and stared at him coldly.

"I've made it my business to have an adequate knowledge of the law, and I've never heard of the one you just referred to," she told him flatly. "If you think you can bully me into going along even further with this madness, you're very much mistaken. I'm not a fool and I never let myself be bullied."

"I quite believe that," the man responded, looking at her with faint amusement but making no effort to follow. "In this instance, however, your knowledge is somewhat lacking. The laws covering applicants for High practitioner positions are a specialized and specific group, and therefore aren't generally available to those people not directly concerned with the matter. If you wish, access to the main archives here in the city will be arranged for you."

"I do wish it," Jovvi replied stiffly, showing nothing of the agitation she felt. The awful man sounded so *sure* of himself, and had even offered her the chance to see for herself . . .

"But until the access is provided, there will be no othe 'sessions.' Furthermore, I'll be taking a house here in th city—"

"No, my dear," the beast interrupted, still unperturbe but also unmoving. "The law does not need to be held i abeyance until you confirm it. Refusal to participate in th program is not allowed, and should you attempt to do so yo are subject to arrest. Trial is swift and the sentencing man datory, which is five years at hard labor in the deep mines Only at the end of those five years would you again be free t pursue your life according to your own desires. Is this wha you wish?"

Despite what she'd so recently gone through, Jovvi discov ered it was still possible for fear to touch her. The man wa looking too smug for his speech to be a complete lie, whic probably meant the mandatory sentence was the truth. Fiv years at hard labor in the deep mines, where not eve starving miners worked voluntarily. Even if she survived, he career as a courtesan would be over, and survival would b far from certain. She would make it a point to check the la anyway, specifically for the loopholes this creature wasn likely to mention, but until then she had no choice but t cooperate.

"Your expression tells me you're prepared to be your usua gracious and agreeable self," the man said after a moment straightening from his crouch before offering her his hand "With that in view we'll get you on your way to the residenc where you've been assigned and where you may rest. Yo need only remember that discussing the details of your tes with anyone at all is strictly forbidden."

Jovvi reluctantly allowed him to help her to her feet, bu only because standing up alone was probably beyond her an she needed badly to be out of that place. But once erect sh was able to stand alone, and the man made no effort to retai her hand.

"Your accommodation at the residence will be paid for b us, but your food and other necessities must be paid for ou of your own pocket." The man had begun to walk around th curve of the hallway, and Jovvi lost no time in following "That may sound like a cruel burden, but after the sessions mentioned there will be competitions, the winning of whic will earn you bonuses in gold. Ah, your coach *has* arrived.

By then he'd reached and opened a door, which clearly le

out of the building. Jovvi stepped out behind him to find that a coach did indeed seem to be waiting for her, and one which had her trunk in its boot. These people seemed incredibly efficient, to get a coach there so quickly after her victory. And one that had also had the time to learn what luggage was hers and collect it. Such efficiency seemed to go beyond the normal bounds of the condition, but rather than mention it Jovvi decided to keep it in mind instead.

"There you are, my dear," the man said once he'd helped her into the coach. "The driver will take you where you're supposed to go, and you'll have the opportunity to rest before your first session. Perhaps we'll even meet again."

Jovvi made no effort to answer that suggestion in words, but the cool look she gave the man was designed to say it all. Whether or not they met again made no difference whatsoever; Jovvi would not, under any circumstances, remember him. His rueful smile said he understood her intentions perfectly, but that ever-present amusement also said that what would happen remained to be seen. Then he gestured to the driver, and the coach began to move.

It took only a few moments before they passed through an archway in the outer wall and were on the street, and then Jovvi was finally able to relax. There had been something disturbing about that entire area, and it was a positive relief to leave it. She hated the idea of not being able to get on with her plans, but there *was* a bright note in all that hampering fog: that bonus in gold the man had mentioned. It simply wasn't possible to have too much gold, and if it turned out she *had* to participate in those competitions, she fully intended to make the most of the time.

Once they left the area of the testing center, the drive became rather pleasant for Jovvi. The neighborhoods they passed through slowly improved to the point of being quite lovely, and possibly even the sort of area she'd been looking for. Large private houses were to either side of the street, but most of them couldn't be seen by the casual passerby. Only occasional glimpses were visible, but those glimpses suggested the necessary combination of large-scale privacy and good taste.

And then the coach turned into the drive of one of those houses, a pleasant surprise Jovvi hadn't been expecting. She'd been certain they would house her in a hovel somewhere, just to further exercise their authority. Those with

authority *always* exercised it, and sometimes those withou
authority tried to pretend otherwise. It was usually possibl
to tell the difference, especially if you studied the matter th
way she had.

The coach pulled up in front of a house that fit Jovvi'
mind picture perfectly, making her feel a good deal better
Her enforced stay here would not be a total waste of tim
after all, since living in a neighborhood let you look aroun
quite easily for property on the market. But first she badl
needed to refresh herself, not to mention spend a long, ful
night asleep in a real bed. If she'd been weary when she'
reached the testing center, now she was nearly done i
completely.

A woman and two male servants came out of the house
but one of the men stopped to help Jovvi from the coac
before joining the other at the boot. The woman waited a
the top of the steps with a sweet smile on her unfortunatel
plain face, and when Jovvi reached her she gave a smal
curtsy.

"Welcome to the house, ma'am," she said, sounding as i
she meant it. "I'm Warla, and as soon as the men have you
trunk I'll show you to your room."

"Thank you, Warla," Jovvi answered with automati
kindness, forcing herself to supply something of a matchin
smile. "I'm Jovvi Hafford, and I'm delighted to finally b
somewhere that has no wheels. The day has been rather mor
strenuous than I expected it to be, so please excuse me if I'r
less than completely cordial."

"Oh, you poor thing, you look as spent as my mistres
did," Warla sympathized, reaching a hand out but withdraw
ing it again before actually touching Jovvi. "She's an appli
cant too, and returned in the same condition. Oh, the me
have your trunk now, so we'll go directly to your room."

Jovvi had been about to mention taking care of the coac
driver, but the coach was already on its way out and Warl
had turned to lead the way into the house. That made on
less thing to worry about, so Jovvi simply followed the gi
inside. Warla was obviously one of those sweet, innocen
people the world sometimes produced, people whose sol
purpose in life seemed to be helping others. Right now Jovv
needed that help, and was grateful to find it so easily to hand

The hall inside the entrance made Jovvi blink, as it wa
decorated in the exact way she'd been taught *not* to decorate

Too much of anything—including expensive things—made a clutter, and gave people the impression that you were trying to prove something. And distracted visitors from really impressive things like that magnificent staircase. Jovvi examined it with pleasure as she followed Warla in climbing it, promising herself one just like it once that testing nonsense was behind her.

At the top of the stairs Warla led the way to the right, then stopped at the first door on the right. They'd passed a door on the left that probably opened into the master apartment, but the room behind the opened door was quite pleasant. It was about the same size as one of the ones in the suite she'd had in Allestine's residence, and should be perfectly suitable for the short length of time she would be in it.

She and Warla stood to one side while the men carried in her trunk, and once the servants were gone Warla turned to her with another of those shy smiles.

"If there's anything you need, just speak to one of the servants," she was told with true warmth. "Or, if you like, you can ask me. Is there anything you need right now?"

"At the moment I'd most enjoy knowing where the bath house is," Jovvi answered, again trying to respond to the smile. "If I have to wait much longer before getting out of these clothes and into clean ones, I'll probably cry."

"Well, of course you would!" Warla agreed earnestly, again reaching out then drawing back before touching Jovvi. "I'm sure I would do exactly the same. The bath house is not far out the back, along the path to the left and before the gardens. You really can't miss it."

Jovvi thanked the girl, hoping it wouldn't be difficult to send her on her way, and it wasn't. Warla performed another small curtsy and left without even being asked, and Jovvi was impressed. As she went to the trunk to find something clean to wear, she considered trying to hire Warla away to be her personal attendant once she was properly settled. A discreet attendant with a sweet, giving nature was a precious jewel, as Jovvi knew from having had to put up with too many who weren't.

But that thought was for later, and getting clean again was for as soon as she could reach the bath house. There weren't many people about as she made her way through the house, just quiet servants going about their business. Did that mean she and Warla's mistress were the only two applicants in the

house right now? That would be pleasant—or not, depend
ing on what sort of woman Warla's mistress was. And wa
there a master as well? She'd have to remember to ask.

The gardens were lovely and inviting, but not as invitin
as the path to the left leading to the bath house. Jovvi move
as quickly as she was able and stepped inside—only to fin
the bath already occupied. And by a man. The lack of sol
itude was disappointing, but far from discouraging. She'
bathed many times in the company of men, but wouldn'
have let his presence stop her even if she hadn't. Her need fo
that refreshing water was much too great, and besides—
what she could see of the man was far from uninteresting.

Jovvi lost no time in getting out of her clothes and into th
water, and her companion did nothing to acknowledge he
presence. He seemed far too involved with scrubbing hi
light hair, which probably meant he was another applican
Her own hair felt twice its normal weight from havin
soaked up her sweat, but the delightfully warm water woul
soon take care of that—once she'd soaked a bit.

"I'm sorry to bother you," her companion said suddenly
"but I seem to have lost the edge of the bath. If you'll guid
me back to it, I'll introduce myself in the proper way once
can see again."

He stood with his eyes closed tight against the soap he'
been using in his hair, which was clearly how he'd gotte
turned around and moved too far from the edge. Jovv
chuckled at the charming way he'd put his request for hel
and moved closer to do as he'd asked, but couldn't hel
being somewhat impressed. He was a beautifully large ma
with broad shoulders and rock-hard arms, a wide and wel
defined chest, narrow waist, and strong legs. He was impres
sively made in another way as well, finishing off a picture he
patrons had rarely matched. Wealthy men were rarely beau
tifully made as well, which might be why they'd had the tim
to become wealthy.

Jovvi carefully turned the stranger in the proper directior
then watched as he groped his way to the towel lying at th
edge of the bath. He used it first on his eyes and then t
interrupt the dripping from his stylishly long hair, an
finally turned back to her to say, "Lorand Coll, Earth magi
at your—"

And that was as far as he got before his mouth droppe

open and his lovely brown eyes widened. Obviously he hadn't been expecting someone like her, as his handsome face actually darkened with a blush. Jovvi found that delightful, but wouldn't have laughed aloud for any amount. The poor man was already horribly embarrassed, which his next words more than proved.

"Naked!" he blurted, clearly the foremost thing bothering him. "We're both naked, and you're a woman!"

"How lovely of you to notice," Jovvi couldn't help replying, tickled that he seemed to be worried about her virtue. She'd *never* met a man who'd worried about that before, at least not with her. "I'm a woman and you're a man, and we're both unclothed. Do people usually bathe *in* their clothes where you come from?"

She'd tried some gentle teasing to make him relax, and even moved away from him to help his distress. But he was such a lovely sight that she couldn't bring herself to look away from him, and so was able to see that her teasing hadn't helped. Possibly a little flirting then, which most men usually appreciated and responded to.

"That was a silly question and I'm glad you're ignoring it," she said with her most attractive laugh as she bent her knees to let that deliciously warm water reach more of her. "Ummm, this feels marvelous, Lorand Coll. I'm Jovvi Hafford, Spirit magic, and I have the feeling you've never bathed with a woman present before. I thought the custom of mixed bathing had spread everywhere."

"Not everywhere," he disagreed, his pleasant voice somewhat strained, and once again Jovvi was impressed. Another man in his place might have tried to claim that he wasn't disturbed by the situation at all, but this man seemed more inclined to speak the truth. That was a rarity beyond price in her experience, since people—and especially men—never spoke the actual truth to her. Her first urge was to continue flirting the way she usually did, but this man deserved better.

"Then I really must apologize," she said instead, trying to give back the honesty she'd gotten. "If you're not used to mixed bathing, then you must be horribly embarrassed. I should have waited until you were through and gone, instead of barging in and intruding. I'll wrap up in a towel and wait outside, and you can—"

"No," the man interrupted, both her words and her exit,

his tone firm and no longer uneven. "I won't hear of yo
waiting for what I know you need so badly, not just to sooth
my backward beliefs. It so happens I was just about throug
anyway, so please let me be the one to allow *you* you
privacy. It's the least I can do for being so rude."

Jovvi was certain the man must be trying to impress he
with false gallantry the way men usually did, but one look a
Lorand Coll told her it wasn't so. The man was still bein
absolutely sincere, and there was no doubt that he reall
would leave.

"That must be the nicest thing anyone has ever said t
me," she told him with her own honesty and the sort of smil
her patrons had never gotten to see. "I'll accept your offer i
you insist, but it would be perfectly all right if you stayed.
won't mind in the least."

Jovvi realized her basic distrust of people had made he
test Lorand's sincerity, but amazingly she didn't end u
disappointed.

"I'd mind staying even less than that, but I think it will b
better if I go," he said, flashing her a very handsome smil
before turning to the steps. "I'll be out of your way in n
time at all."

See, he really did mean it, she gleefully told her suspicion
watching Lorand leave the bath. There were those wh
claimed that men like him could be found all over, but unt
today Jovvi had considered the claim a fairy tale. Men ha
always been quick to do things for her, but always for wha
they expected—or hoped—to get in return. This man coul
have bartered the opportunity for privacy, asking for her us
now or some time later, but he hadn't said a word about it

But he also isn't gone yet, her suspicion pointed out i
rebuttal, and you can't say you didn't notice how interestin
he found you. Let's see what he says before he does leave.

Jovvi was content to wait and see, especially since she ha
the back of Lorand to look at while he dried himself. And
lovely back it was, so broad and nicely muscled and leadin
down to hard, firm buttocks and those strong, well-shape
legs. He was a desirable man, all right, but Jovvi didn'
realize completely just how desirable he was until he was a
dressed, had gathered up his dirty clothes, and was headin
for the door. *Without* saying anything else, she smug
pointed out to her suspicion. But that didn't mean she had t
stay equally as silent.

"It was nice to meet you, Lorand Coll," she said as he was almost out the door. "See you later at dinner."

"I certainly hope so," he responded without turning, and then he was gone just as he'd said he would be. His clothing was awful, not just out of style but never *in* style, but that meant nothing. Jovvi was usually surrounded by sophistication, and knew better than most how quickly it became tiring.

But once dressed, Lorand had somehow looked familiar. Those two men who had arrived together at the same time she had; could he have been one of them? It didn't really matter, unless one looked at the coincidence as some sort of sign. She and Lorand might be meant for each other, especially since she'd need someone like him once she had her residence established. His presence would discourage patrons from trying to stay beyond their allotted time, and then she could find her own pleasure spending the night with him. She'd never actually had extreme pleasure from a man, but something told her Lorand was one who could supply it. . . .

Jovvi suddenly laughed at herself, interrupting the daydreaming to get down to the business of washing. She was still stuck with having to go through those "sessions," and so, obviously, was Lorand. Until she found a loophole in the law to free the two of them, making plans was a foolish waste of time. Time that could be used more profitably napping while waiting for dinner to be ready.

It would have felt good to soak in the bath for the next hour or two, but Jovvi knew that the longer she waited, the harder it would be to get herself moving out of there. So she washed her body and hair, being careful not to lose the edge of the bath, then dried and dressed. On the way back to the main house she passed another woman obviously heading for the bath house, a tall woman with reddish-brown hair who was pretty in a hard, obvious way. The other passed Jovvi without a word or a glance, so Jovvi shrugged to herself and simply returned to her room.

Stretching out on the bed felt wonderful even if she *was* fully clothed. Getting in and out of her things was completely beyond her, and there was still dinner to look forward to. But not before she'd napped a little . . . and then added a few touches of makeup . . . brushed her hair . . . hid her gold. . . .

So you see some of us had an easier time of it than others. Meeting each other, I mean. None of that first part was easy, nor were the times that followed. I often found myself wondering if it was really worth what we were putting into it, but most of that came later. It was when—Oh, all right, I'll tell it in the order it happened. There were other things happening as well, much of which we either heard about later, or put together with guesswork. You see, it was—All right, all right, I'll stop telling them about it and show them! But if you feel so strongly about my innocent comments, I'll just have to make fewer of them in future.

SIXTEEN

The room was large but austere, containing nothing but a long table with chairs around it, and half a dozen lamps on the walls lit the surroundings but failed to warm them. The lamps were lit because of the lack of windows, but the six men who entered seemed not to care. The last of them closed the door firmly, then went to take his place at the head of the table. He was quite ordinary looking, from his appearance no more than a prosperous businessman. He wore silk trousers in gray which flared at the ankles, a pale blue shirt with just a hint of ruffles, and a darker blue coat which reached no longer than his waist. An ordinary businessman who carried some papers, his unremarkable features showed nothing of an expression.

The other five men present were not the same. They were clearly individuals, but the resemblance each had to the others was quite noticeable. All of them were of middle years or approximately so, each had a pleasant, oval face which inspired trust and friendliness, and none of them was remarkable in any negative way. All had medium brown hair and unprepossessing brown eyes, average builds on bodies of average height, and hands unmarked by any sign of manual labor. They dressed in varying colors, but all wore the same sort of loose-sleeved shirt and cloth trousers. Nothing remarkable, except for the remarkable resemblance.

"You may begin your reports," the man at the head of the table announced, removing a pen and jar of ink from the inner pockets of his coat. "Am I mistaken, or have we finally reached the end of the flow? Air?"

"Yes, sir, we *have* reached the end of it," one of the five responded with a faint smile. "The last of the applicants arrived and were processed, and now we're almost ready to move forward. Would you like the figures?"

"If you please," the man at the head of the table agreed, his pen already inked and now poised over the papers set before him.

"This month, the final month, the Air magic applicants totaled twenty," the other man obliged. "Three of them proved to be no more than ordinary Middles, incapable of drawing in more of the power than that level calls for. We rescued them before they died, thanked them gently for coming, then sent them home. One of them cried, but they all went."

All five of the men who resembled each other chuckled, adding to the impression of similarity, and then the man representing Air magic continued.

"Of the remaining seventeen, fifteen died. Nine of them were flawed potential Highs without the proper capacity, so they weren't able to handle the amount of power necessary to solve their dilemma. The summoned power burned them out, and we disposed of the bodies as usual. The other six might have been the same, but there's no way of knowing. They lost their nerve at some point, which made them lose control of their ability, and then they died. Only two passed the test and survived, one not long after the first of the month, the second today."

"Well done," the man at the head of the table commented, most of his attention on the figures he wrote. "And those two were given the proper drink, were they not? Along with the proper instructions?"

"Should it become necessary, they will certainly respond to the orders given by someone in authority," the second man agreed comfortably. "Neither of them noticed a time lapse, so they had no idea almost an hour had passed from the moment they took their first swallow of the drugged water, to when they finally drained the cup. They'll be no more of a problem than any of the others."

"Excellent," the man at the head of the table said, taking the two sets of papers handed to him. Then his glance went to another of the five. "Earth?"

"The applicants in Earth magic did about the same," the third man supplied easily. "Five were Middles and therefore rescued, ten died and were disposed of, three survived and passed. All three responded properly to the drink, and none of them noticed a thing."

The man at the head of the table wrote again, accepted the three sets of papers passed over, then said, "Fire?"

"Fire magic had twenty-two applicants this month, and five turned out to be Middles," the fourth man answered with a faint smile. "Thirteen died trying to do more than they had the ability to, and four survived and therefore passed. The ordinary people of this land don't know how grateful they should be to us. We cull those who are born unfit before they're able to pass on their handicaps, thereby keeping their numbers manageably low. If not for us, every town and village and city would be knee-deep in flawed Highs."

"Making the general population that much more difficult to control," the fifth man agreed with a short laugh as the fourth handed over his sets of papers. "Water magic applicants were just as cooperative, with thirteen of the nineteen dying. Two were Middles and were rescued, four were unflawed and therefore passed. At least to this point. What they'll find it possible to do next remains to be seen."

"Especially when they find themselves competing with other applicants who have been here and practicing for months, if not all year." This from the last of the men, who wore his own faint smile. "At least a third of them won't survive, and another third will try to withdraw. My figures for Spirit magic, by the way, are seventeen applicants, two Middles, another thirteen dead, and two who were successful. Successful, that is, for the moment."

All five of the men chuckled at that, but the one at the head of the table was too busy finishing the figures and gathering up sets of papers to do the same. By appearances he neither approved nor disapproved of the banter, and when he'd put everything in order he looked up again.

"So much for the substantive part of your reports," he said, glancing around. "Now I will ask you for the final time: has any of you seen *anything* that might match one of the Prophecies? It won't necessarily be anything overt, remember, as some of the verses refer to happenings that are quite subtle. The more obvious signs will come 'out of the sight of the Five's enemies,' which at this point would be us. Is there anything to report?"

"My report is that there's nothing at all to report," the man representing Water magic replied calmly but confidently. "I've been watching carefully, and none of the applicants seemed especially heroic. Some, in fact, appear to have personal flaws which will see them quickly eliminated. No one has asked this before, so allow me to put the question which is surely in all our minds: Is this matter of the Prophecies something that should concern us to this great a degree? I know of no one who actually believes that the infamous Four will return, or that it will take a special Blending to defeat them. These are children's stories, and it's almost inconceivable that anyone in authority can take them seriously."

"These . . . children's stories, as you put it, have come true more often than you know," the man at the head of the table answered bleakly, apparently unsurprised by his underlings' skepticism. "It has been the firm policy of our superiors and their predecessors to claim otherwise, to weaken the belief of the populace in the Prophecies. But we ourselves know better, and you had better know the same. When various Blendings compete for the Throne in a short while, the special Blending mentioned in the Prophecies is supposed to be among them—and even more, is supposed to win."

"Then they must be among the talents who will form Blendings from those applicants who are nobly born," the man representing Air magic offered in a calm and reasonable tone. "They're excused from going through this same nonsense required of commoners, so what would be more logical? And since it will be one of *their* Blendings which will win as always, that fits as well."

"Are you all *deliberately* missing the point?" the man at the head of the table demanded irritably, for the first time showing more than equanimity when the other four murmured their agreement with Air. "Of *course* noble Blendings have won the Throne for the last seventy-five years or more. No other outcome has been allowed. This time, however, is not meant to be the same, for it's *the time spoken of in the Prophecies!* Is none of you able to take that in? The Prophecies are not to be dismissed, they're to be worried about!"

The other men sat back with raised brows over the outburst, not quite daring to exchange glances among themselves. Their superior was obviously not joking, which made the entire situation extremely bizarre.

"But . . . that makes for greater confusion rather than less," the representative of Fire said at last, speaking slowly. "If the Prophecies do come true after all, then somehow the infamous Four will return to take over. They turned everyone into virtual slaves before they were defeated by the first Fivefold Blending, and if they return and regain their position, they'll do the same again. With that in mind, why are we searching for the Five meant to stop them? To give them our support? But that doesn't—"

"Enough!" the man's superior interrupted, slamming his hand down hard on the table. "This is precisely why the matter has been kept from the populace, to avoid their jumping to such emotional and illogical conclusions! And you of all people should know better than to interpret *all* the Prophecies so literally. They've been correct in predicting some sort of crisis during the twenty-five year reign of each Blending, but what about the rest of it? The Prophecies claim that any Blending not seated in 'full fairness' will fail to survive and find victory on the 'blackest of days,' but has that happened? Hasn't every crisis been successfully met during the last century?"

This time the five did exchange glances, for their superior was correct. The contest to seat a new Blending had been carefully controlled every twenty-five years for the last century, and none of the seated Five had had any difficulty with their "crisis." That was what made the populace believe the contests *were* fair, the lowborn fools. What they didn't know let their betters live the lives they were born to and meant for.

"Forgive my momentary naivete," Fire said after a moment, his expression rueful. "Emotionalism is a heady wine, and I clearly drank too deeply. May I ask, sir, what the true state of affairs is? Explanations will aid our ability to assist in the matter."

"Yes, I suppose they will," his superior grudged sourly, now sitting back. "Although each of you is the Seated High in your respective aspects, you've been given little or nothing of the details. That was because you worked with the applicants who came here to unseat you, and the Advisors to the Five had no wish to distract you from so important a task. Knowing in advance the weaknesses and bad habits of your opponents will let you defeat them during the challenges, an outcome we all wish to see."

The five men smiled with pleased amusement, enjoying the jest as much as they always did, but their attention had not strayed from their superior. They were about to learn things they needed to know, and those who meant to survive in their world always listened carefully at such times.

"Our disturbance over the Prophecies is really quite simple," their superior began, putting the tips of his fingers together before his face. "Somehow or other the threat of the Four *will* come to pass, but just how that will happen doesn't concern us at the moment. What does concern us is the very unreasonable—but easily reached—conclusion that our chosen Blending will fail against the threat. Past experience has shown us that the opposite is true, as there's no reason to believe that *this* 'crisis' will be any different from previous ones.

"And yet a 'special' Blending will appear to do the job for them. Not only will such an appearance be unnecessary, it will threaten the very successful arrangement we and our predecessors have enjoyed for the past century. They won't be found among the nobility, not when they're described as 'springing from all corners of the land,' so they *must* be among the commoners. And they're certain to appear at the worst possible time from our point of view, so we're trying to identify them before then. Do you still feel you've seen nothing to indicate which ones they are?"

All five of his listeners shook their heads slowly, considering the matter with similar frowns. Then Earth stirred in his seat.

"Possibly we would do well to study those applicants who are most likely to actually fit into a Blending," he suggested thoughtfully. "Most Highs can be forced to work in a group of five, but that doesn't make them a Blending. My cousins here and I all tried to qualify for the last appointed Blending, but none of us was able to be truly effective in the framework. Our strength is best exhibited when we practice alone, which has to be the case for many of the applicants. The rest will be a much smaller number, and therefore more easily investigated."

"That point has already occurred to the Advisors," their superior replied with a nod. "Once the common Blendings are thrown together for the contest, there will be many eyes examining them. We'd hoped to save ourselves the trouble, but apparently that's not to be. Ah well, we'll find them eventually, and then they'll be gotten out of our way. Thank you for your reports, gentlemen, and do enjoy yourselves watching the final sessions and practices of this last batch of applicants. The time ought to be most amusing."

The five smiled their agreement and rose to their feet when their superior did, then watched him leave the room. Once again he seemed the ordinary, successful businessman, rather than one of the Advisors' best and most dangerous agents. He came from one of the most powerful noble families in the empire, and hadn't let his handicap of low-talent status keep him from a most successful career.

"I really dislike that man," Fire murmured, the look in his eyes no longer mild and unperturbed. "One day I'll find him in just the right place, and then I'll leave him as nothing more than a pile of ashes."

"You won't touch him, and neither will the rest of us," Water disagreed with a sound of ridicule. "We all detest him and the others like him, but each and every one of those cripples is safe from us. If we ever did anything to one of them, we'd be barred from studying the dross who came to unseat us. Then we would lose to the peasant, humiliation heaped on top of injury. Of course, then some other nobly born High would displace the peasant, but that would be of very little comfort to *us.*"

"So we accept being treated like commoners by a cripple, and simply ignore the insult," Earth added while Fire continued to fume. "The day may well come when one of them falls out of favor, and then he becomes fair game. Until then we see to our own most pressing business, and hope that the proper Blending is appointed this time."

"One of my sons managed to qualify, as did my brother's youngest daughter," Air commented, sounding rather smug. "If either of them is Seated on the Fivefold Throne, our difficulties will be over. They both have an incredibly strong sense of family, and will support us even against the Advisors."

"I'd very much like to see that," Water said with a chuckle, obviously enjoying the idea. "Seated High should be a position revered as well as envied and well compensated, and our own blood would make it so."

All of them agreed to that with laughter, all except Spirit. The man had been very quiet, and Water studied him for a moment.

"What disturbs you, cousin?" he asked at last. "You seem to be—preoccupied."

"I am," Spirit admitted with a sigh, then he looked about at the others. "We've been told that this special Blending will be gotten out of the way because they're unnecessary, but a rather disturbing question comes to mind. What if our oh-so-clever superiors are wrong, and the chosen Blending *isn't* victorious over the Four? I still can't see them coming back from the dead, but what if they do appear and win? What happens to *us,* when the Four was careful to destroy every High they were able to find?"

"Don't let the hysteria of those fools disturb you, cousin," Water replied soothingly, putting a hand to the other's shoulder. "They've talked themselves into believing that the Prophecies have actually come true, when anyone with the least amount of intelligence knows that that isn't so. They're worried because a common Blending is supposed to defeat their noble choice, so they're peeking under beds to calm their nervousness. Nothing will come of any of it, you mark my words."

The others agreed with Water, and Spirit finally unbent enough to join them in a ridiculing laugh. Then they left to find some excellent wine and even better female companionship, and no longer worried about something that would never happen. The infamous Four, returning to enslave everyone in reach! Really . . . !

SEVENTEEN

I didn't know I'd fallen asleep until I felt a hand shaking my shoulder. I opened my eyes to see Warla bending over the chair I'd just meant to rest in for a few minutes, her expression concerned.

"You look so tired that I hate to bother you, Tamrissa, but dinner is almost ready," she said at once. "And not only that, but you have a visitor. A lady from the testing people, here to make sure everyone's arrived who should have arrived."

"Did you tell her that that part of it should be discussed with you rather than me?" I asked, fighting to wake up the rest of the way. "I'm lucky I know that *I* got back here."

"Oh, I never would have told her anything like *that*," Warla protested, now looking upset. "It isn't my place, and what if *you* were supposed to do it? Saying something different could have gotten us both in trouble."

I sighed on the inside while conceding her point with a nod, but not because the possibility worried me. As long as all their applicants were accounted for, those people shouldn't care *who* did the head-counting. Warla *always* worried about getting in trouble over something, and right now I had no strength to argue with her. It was easier to simply let the point go, and take myself down to meet my visitor.

I'd gotten dressed once I'd returned to my apartment from the bath house, so all I had to do was smooth my skirts down against possible wrinkles before heading for the door. Warla followed behind me, but at the bottom of the stairs she slipped past to lead me toward the library. Inside was a pleasant-looking woman in her mid-thirties, who got to her feet with a smile when Warla stepped aside to let me walk in.

"Dama Domon, I apologize for intruding so close to dinner time," she said, stepping forward to offer a gloved hand. "I'm Eltrina Razas, and I'll be your liaison to the testing authority. I'm here so late because some of your lodgers were sent rather late, and we wanted to be certain they got here."

I took her hand somewhat gingerly, never having shaken hands before. It had always been something that only men did, but this Eltrina Razas acted as if it were perfectly natural. She wore an emerald green suit and cream blouse, with a matching cream-and-green hat on her carefully styled brown hair. There was a line of tiny embroidery all along the hem of her skirt where it brushed her shoes as well as along the cuffs of her jacket, an indication that her outfit was rather expensive. But her manner was open and friendly, so I tried to return her smile.

"It's a pleasure to meet you, Dama Razas," I said, ending the handshake as soon as was decently possible. "If you'd like to find out about the people who were sent, you'll have to ask Warla here. She met them as they arrived, and assigned them to rooms."

"Because you yourself are one of the applicants, which means you had to be too worn out to see to it personally," she added with a pleasant nod. "Yes, I quite understand, and in fact expected something of the sort. I'll just take a moment to speak to Warla, and then you and I will have a brief chat. And it's Lady Eltrina, not Dama Razas."

She said that last as if it meant less than nothing, then bustled Warla to one side in order to speak to her. I stood where I'd been left and watched them, not quite knowing how to behave. The woman was a member of the nobility, and dealing with the nobility was something else I'd never done. On a day with so many firsts, it would have been nice if I hadn't felt half asleep.

I went and sat in a chair to wait, and watched while Warla nervously counted things off on her fingers. When she reached eight she stopped and looked frightened, but Lady Eltrina soothed her with a quick smile and a few words. Then Warla curtsied and left, closing the door behind her, and Lady Eltrina came over to me.

"No, dear, don't get up again," she said quickly with another of those smiles as she took the chair opposite mine.

"We'll certainly be friends long before this is over, so you'll call me Eltrina and I'll call you Tamrissa. I'm delighted to say your Warla is wonderfully efficient. She knew the names of every applicant and in what order they arrived, and even listed you first."

"Yes, Warla is an excellent companion," I agreed, leaning back in the chair because I really needed to. "I've never relied on her quite this much before, but I don't expect to be disappointed. I wonder if I might—ask something."

"Of course, child, that's one of the reasons I'm here," she replied warmly, beginning to take off her gloves. "What do you need to know?"

"I'd like to have one of the applicants—transferred to another residence," I forced myself to say. The woman now sat in the chair my husband had always used, and I was too tired to push away all the unsettling feelings brought back by old memories. "The man was extremely rude to me, and actually admitted that he didn't want to be here for the tests. He's hateful, and I'd like to have him out of my house."

"Oh, dear," Eltrina said, and now she looked disturbed rather than encouraging. "I'm devastated to hear you have one of *that* sort, but I'm afraid there's nowhere else *to* put him. All the other residences are full, and we aren't arranging for any others since all the applicants for this year are accounted for. He hasn't gone beyond rudeness, I hope. I mean, he hasn't tried to *really* insult you?"

She'd begun to look anxious and seriously concerned, asking without words if he'd tried to . . . do what men always seemed to. I couldn't keep from blushing at the thought, especially after the way he'd stared at me, but happily the situation wasn't *that* bad.

"No, he made no effort to go beyond simple rudeness," I admitted, more than a little disappointed. "If that changes I'll have to insist he be sent elsewhere, but I suppose I can live with the situation for now. Is there anything else I need to know about?"

"One or two things," she answered, that warm smile flashing again. "And you're so reasonable, I can't tell you what a pleasure it is to deal with you. Some of the others who volunteered their houses . . . Well, I'm sure you know how stubborn some people can get. In one case we actually had to withdraw *all* the applicants, and cancel the agreement making the house a residence. That's one of the reasons we're so short of space, but I know we won't have to do the same thing here."

She was obviously trying to reassure me, but the thought of losing the protection of residence classification for my house made me want to shiver. Right now that could be the only thing keeping my father from taking it away, so I *couldn't* lose the protection. If the arrogant Vallant Ro grew even more rude, I'd simply have to avoid him rather than complain.

"Now let's discuss one of those things you need to know," Eltrina continued, her good mood completely restored. "It's come to our attention that you've used the lodging fees we paid to buy food for the applicants. There's nothing wrong with doing that to start yourself off, but those fees are meant for other things. I'll be setting a figure they'll have to pay weekly in order to eat at your table, and the silver will go directly into your food budget. If one or more of them are unable to pay, I'm afraid you'll have to refuse them a place at the table."

"Do I really have to be that . . . hardhearted?" I asked, at the last moment deciding against saying "uncharitable." The woman was on my side right now, and I didn't care to do anything that might change that. "They'll be living here, after all, and watching people starve while you eat is very—"

"Difficult, I know," she agreed when I paused to find a substitute for the word heartless. "A sweet, kind girl like you would find it very difficult, and that's why you won't be given the choice. Your staff will have strict orders before I leave here, and since their wages will be paid out of the lodging fees along with the rest of the house's maintenance, I expect they'll obey completely. In other words, for the remainder of the time that this house is a residence, you'll no longer really be in charge of it."

Hearing that was something of a shock, but not an overwhelming one. I'd never been allowed to have anything to do with running the house while Gimmis was alive, and I'd only recently begun to get the hang of how it was done. Not having to bother now was actually more of a relief, but then an uncomfortable thought occurred to me.

"Am I mistaken, or does that mean *I* can be barred from the table as easily as anyone else?" I asked, *now* feeling disturbed. "It sounded as if the lodging fees would be disbursed by someone else, and if so I don't know where I'd get the necessary silver. I don't have any money of my own, you see, so—"

"No, no, that won't be a problem," she soothed, quickly leaning forward in her chair. "You're correct in believing that you'll be subject to the same rules as the others, but you haven't yet been given the silver for living expenses that all applicants are given. I have yours and Pagin Holter's, who also comes from Gan Garee. He's one of your seven guests, and if you haven't met him yet you soon will. And don't forget about the bonuses in gold that will be offered during your future competitions. If you earn the bonus, you'll be able to keep it and spend it—but only on yourself. Sharing with other applicants is strictly against the rules."

Yes, it would be, I realized with a sigh. The bonuses in gold were there to tempt people like Vallant Ro into doing their best, or simply to keep themselves eating if temptation didn't enter into it. It was an idea easier to get along with than the pass-or-die of the first test, so I couldn't quite bring myself to criticize it.

"I'm glad to see you're wearing your identification," she went on, gesturing to the chain and card I'd put back around my neck. "No one not wearing the same will be served or fed, and I'll make that clear to the other applicants as well. And the last thing we need to discuss right now is clothing, yours and everyone else's."

"There's something wrong with my clothing?" I asked, glancing down at the peach silk blouse and green silk skirt embroidered with peach that I wore. "This outfit isn't as good as your suit, I know, but—"

"No, child, you have it backwards," she said with a very pleased laugh. "Your skirt and blouse are lovely examples of just-less-than top quality effort, but that's the entire point. Your outfit is still quite expensive, and not all of our applicants can afford to wear the same. That's why we have a dress code for the sessions, and I'll explain in more detail in a few minutes, when the others are also able to hear it. Right now I'll give you your silver, and then we'll go to the dining room to meet your fellow applicants. Warla was given instructions to call them all down."

And Warla certainly must have obeyed, I realized as I took the small pouch she removed from the silk handbag which matched her suit. Even Warla wasn't completely mine any longer, but I swallowed the urge to protest as I rose to put the pouch of silver in a safe place. There was no turning back now, not from the testing and certainly not from my plan to escape my parents. Nothing could be worse than what they had in mind for me, so going forward was nothing but a step in the right direction. It would *not* turn out to be just as bad . . . it *couldn't* . . . !

Vallant Ro walked into the dining room slowly, still beyond moving quickly despite the nap he'd had. Nothing short of a full night's sleep would help, he knew, but first he had to get something to eat. His insides were rumbling like a thunderstorm in the distance, and sight of the table set for eight was enough to make his mouth water. If the food wasn't brought quickly, he just might attack whoever did bring it eventually.

The thought of attacking anyone or anything right now made him chuckle to himself as he looked around. The room's walls were papered in a boring floral pattern, but at least the dark rose drapes matched one of the colors in the paper and the seats of the chairs. The hardwood floor was polished to a spotless gleam, and the sideboard was a perfect match to the table and chairs. The chandelier was a bit much though, especially with most of its candles lit. That much crystal could easily blind the unwary, but once again it was a matter of cost taking precedence over taste.

"Good evening, Dom Ro," the girl Warla said, turning away from the two people already at the table. "Your place is here, between Dom Drowd and Dama Lant."

The empty chair she gestured to stood in the third and farthest place on the lefthand side of the table, just beyond a woman with dark red hair and next to a quiet-looking man who sat at the foot of the table. At least Vallant assumed that that was the foot. The head of it would be reserved for the woman who owned the house, and that brought to mind the girl who had lied in the bath house. Next to her, this redheaded woman who had been seated beside him looked brittle and slight in her prettiness. But if she didn't lie, she would turn out to be the more attractive of the two. Warla bustled off to do something else, so Vallant went to his chair and sat.

"It feels marvelous to get off one's feet, does it not?" the man to Vallant's left commented with a sigh. "I arrived here so late, I barely had time to use the bath house before being summoned to the meal. I'm Eskin Drowd, Earth magic."

"Vallant Ro, Water magic," Vallant replied with a nod. "I've been here long enough to have gotten in a short nap, but it wasn't much help. As soon as I've eaten as much as I can hold, I'm headin' for bed."

"I intend to do likewise," Drowd agreed in his pedantic way, and then he looked beyond Vallant. "And you, my dear? Would you care to introduce yourself to us?"

"You must be joking," the woman said with a small laugh, more ridicule than amusement. "You heard the girl tell you part of my name, so you have to know who I am. Everyone has always known my name and what I can do."

"My dear young woman, you really must be adult about this," Drowd said to her gently but with inflexible firmness. "This empire happens to be extremely large, and not even the *Seated* Highs are known to everyone in it. To expect a mere applicant to be known beyond the boundaries of her own area is folly, and there is folly enough for each of us in this life without our deliberately adding to it. Others hearing your remark might well have laughed, but Ro and I are gentlemen. For that reason I repeat: would you care to introduce yourself?"

"Ah, I understand now," the girl said, finally settling into a smug expression. Her complexion had darkened with embarrassment while Drowd spoke, but that had abruptly changed. "You people must come from such tiny hamlets that you're all but closed off to the world, and you're trying to cover *your* lacks by pretending everyone knows as little as you do. You should have said that to begin with, and I would have understood. I'm Beldara Lant, Fire magic."

"And where do *you* come from, Beldara Lant?" Vallant couldn't keep from asking. If there was anything more annoying than someone who always found a reason why *they* were right . . . "I'm from Port Entril myself, and I captain a trade ship up and down the coast. From what I've seen, Port Entril is kind of big to be called a hamlet."

"As is Regisard, my own place of birth," Drowd said, smiling when Vallant raised his brows. "Yes, it's also sometimes called University, as no less than five institutions of higher learning may be found there. As you may have surmised, my family has a tradition of teaching in those institutions. Should I find my current undertaking of sufficient interest to hold my attention, I may well be the first to break that tradition."

"*May* well be?" Beldara immediately snapped, back to being red-faced with embarrassment. "Now, that's less of a surprise than it might be. Anyone who doesn't know that being a Seated High is the only worthwhile thing to be in this life . . . ! No wonder you haven't heard of me. You aren't bright enough to have found out about the really important things."

"Let me speculate a moment," Drowd said with a faint smile as he sat back in his chair, studying the angry woman. "Either one or both of your parents have told you that all your life, about how no endeavor but being a High is worthy of your attention. They're undoubtedly the same ones who constantly praised your use of the power, and assured you that you're known both far and wide. Am I mistaken?"

"Now you're suggesting there's something wrong with my parents telling me the truth?" Beldara snapped again, obviously trying to hide confusion. "They also said people here in Gan Garee would lie to me, so they were right there, too. Now you can save your breath, Eskin Drowd, because I'm not listening to lies any longer."

And with that she turned away to look at the other people who had been entering the dining room, throwing up an invisible wall that would allow nothing of "lies" to penetrate. Drowd sighed and made no further effort to reach the girl with simple common sense, but Vallant found himself disturbed. His own parents had always been supportive, but the only things they'd made their children believe in was the value of their own individual worth and the unacceptability of dishonorable behavior. That people could twist their children to satisfy their own desires was upsetting, and Vallant was more than happy not to pursue the subject.

Especially since almost everyone else had now come in and taken places around the table at Warla's direction. A man sat silently to Beldara's right, dressed for all the world like a farmer and looking extremely uncomfortable and out of place. Directly across from Vallant was the fop Clarion Mardimil, dressed in another of those ridiculous outfits, this time in blinding green. But the man nodded to him in a stiff but civil manner, so Vallant nodded back.

And then he forgot about Mardimil to look at the woman

seated to the man's left. She had golden-blond hair and light eyes, and was as beautiful as the girl Vallant had seen in the bath house, just in a different way. This one seemed to be laughing silently at the world, her flawless skin glowing with the amusement. Even Mardimil was finding it hard not to stare at her, but the girl didn't seem to mind or notice. She simply smiled and nodded to the farmer on Vallant's side of the table, who darkened slightly but managed to smile back.

The last of their number was another man, seated to the beautiful woman's left, next to the empty chair at the head of the table. He was slight and dark and looked almost as uncomfortable as the farmer, which wasn't hard to understand. His collarless shirt must have been matched by knee breeches and hose, the usual dress of grooms and stablemen. Vallant had never come into direct contact with one of them, not when he preferred a deck under his feet to a saddle under his rump, but he'd certainly seen enough of them.

But none of that was causing any of the food to be brought out. Vallant stirred in his chair, more than willing to go looking for sustenance on his own if they weren't served soon, but then two other women walked in. One looked to be in her mid-thirties with the bearing of someone who considered herself really important, and that despite the smile she showed so obviously. The other was the girl he'd seen in the bath house, and Vallant was startled to realize that he hadn't remembered just how beautiful she really was. Delicate and fragile, soft and helpless . . .

And not looking happy at all. That observation filled Vallant with guilt, since *he* was probably the source of her unhappiness. The older woman was undoubtedly the owner of the house, and the girl now expected to be exposed as a liar. She stood lost in thought while the older woman called the stableman over to her, probably expecting Vallant to say something that would embarrass her even more, just as he'd planned to. *Had* planned to, but no longer did. It would be enough if he and the girl were the only ones to know what had passed between them.

"Good evening, ladies and gentlemen," the older woman said suddenly, pulling Vallant out of his stare. The stableman had already returned to his seat at the table, and Vallant hadn't even noticed.

"I'll begin by introducing myself to you," the woman

continued, looking around at all of them with a smile. "I'm Lady Eltrina Razas, and I'll be your liaison to the testing authority. The first thing you must know is that you'll be expected to pay three silver dins a week if you intend to eat at this table—starting tonight. When I'm through speaking you'll go and fetch the silver, and then give it to me."

There wasn't quite a murmur at that, but Vallant thought it was only because none of them really knew each other. Sending people to live in a place after threatening their freedom, and then making them pay to eat! If Vallant had had any doubts about whether or not he wanted to continue associating with those people, that would have settled them.

"Another thing some of you will have to fetch is your identification as an applicant," the Lady Eltrina went on, now looking at them with a shade less friendliness. "You were told to wear it at all times, but half of you have come down here without it. From now on anyone appearing without identification will not be fed, even if he or she has already paid the necessary silver."

Now everyone looked around, to see that Mardimil, the beautiful woman next to him, the stableman, and Vallant himself no longer wore those chains and cards. Vallant had simply forgotten about his, but it looked like none of them would forget again. Score another direct hit on the possibility of a reasonable relationship with the people behind all this.

"As a final matter, you must all be ready just after luncheon tomorrow for the carriages which will come for you," Lady Eltrina said. "You will be taken to a tailoring shop which is familiar with our requirements, and there you will have fitted two outfits each for attending sessions in. The gentlemen will be given gray trousers and white shirts, and the ladies gray skirts and white blouses. You will also be expected to pay for the clothing, but a mere token rather than full price. If you use the shop afterwards to buy other, more usual clothing, *then* you'll pay full price. Now be so kind as to fetch the silver—and your identification, if necessary—so that I may leave you to your meal and the rest you undoubtedly crave."

It wasn't a happy group which rose from the table, but it also wasn't a slow-moving group. Everyone was obviously just as hungry as Vallant, and the only way to make the food start coming was to pay. Tomorrow Vallant would visit his family's bank and draw some gold, to replace what he would spend tonight and tomorrow at the tailor. He still had some silver left from what he'd been given at the start of the trip, but not all that much.

And as he watched the girl from the bath house leave the room along with everyone else, he finally had to admit that he owed her an apology. Warla had told him that the owner of the house was named Tamrissa Domon, and the older woman had called herself Eltrina Razas. That left his bathing companion as Tamrissa, especially since she'd also worn her identification. He'd finally noticed that as well, after spending most of his time staring at her face. And that beautiful reddish-blond hair. . . .

Vallant sighed as he headed for the stairs along with everyone else. Tamrissa Domon attracted him in a way no other woman ever had, but he hadn't come to Gan Garee to find a woman. In point of fact he'd decided against ever becoming entangled with a woman again, and he'd be a fool to forget that. So he'd simply find an opportunity to apologize to her, and then he'd be polite but distant. That ought to please *her,* at any rate; she hadn't seemed to like him very much, which was actually a damned good thing.

But which would have been a better thing if it hadn't annoyed him so much. . . .

EIGHTEEN

Lorand was among the first to get back to the table after paying over his silver, but no one actually took their time. The hollowness inside him had to be present in everyone, even that pompous fool Mardimil. The "lord" had stopped to speak to the Razas woman on his way out of the dining room, but the conversation couldn't have lasted very long. Mardimil had returned only moments behind Lorand, and he didn't look the type to run.

But he seemed to be a lucky type, having been seated next to Jovvi Hafford. Lorand wished he had the nerve to ask the man opposite to change seats with him, but they'd been assigned those seats and the man seemed to be as taken with Jovvi as Lorand felt. But at least she'd smiled and nodded to him, which was more than she'd done with any of the other men there.

"Ladies and gentlemen, thank you," Eltrina Razas said at last, hefting the pouch she'd put the silver in. "Our business is concluded for the moment, so I wish you hearty appetites and a pleasant night. When I return, I'll have your session schedules. Warla will name each of you for the others, and then you'll be left to your own devices."

No one said anything to that, just the way they'd said nothing to any of her other comments. She wasn't only a noble, she was someone who could make a hard time for them with the testing people. And she'd hesitate not a heartbeat to do it, that had been clear from the first despite her smiles. Lorand meant to stay well out of her way, a decision he probably had a lot of company in making.

"Ladies and gentlemen, the names are as follows," the girl Warla said, sounding frightened to death rather than sure and confident the way Eltrina had. "At the head of the table is Tamrissa Domon, owner of this house. Beside her on her left is Lorand Coll, then Beldara Lant, then Vallant Ro, then Eskin Drowd, then Clarion Mardimil, then Jovvi Hafford, then Pagin Holter. Please enjoy your meal."

Her curtsy was hurried and very self-conscious, and the Razas woman was amused when she followed Warla out of the room at a much more leisurely pace. Lorand heard a very faint "Finally!" along with a sigh from the girl who had been named Tamrissa Domon, so he smiled at her.

"I agree with that sentiment completely," he told her in a soft voice. "In case you missed it I'm Lorand Coll, and I can remember a time when I wasn't a mere shadow of my former self."

"I don't think I qualify for the term, 'mere shadow,'"

Tamrissa answered with a smile that made her even more beautiful than she was naturally. In fact she was just as beautiful as Jovvi in a more innocent and open way, which made Lorand wonder where he'd gotten the nerve to speak to her.

"I still weigh too much to call myself a shadow, but completely empty is another matter entirely," the girl continued. "I was ready to eat as soon as I got back from the test, but at least the staff is beginning to serve now."

"I wonder what those sessions will be like," Lorand remarked, mostly to keep himself from noticing the bread and cheese and soup that hadn't quite reached the table yet. He would *not* make a pig of himself by immediately bolting down what was put in front of him . . . "I intend to pass whatever they throw at me just the way I did today, but I can't help wondering what that whatever will turn out to be."

"It can't be worse than what they did to us today, so I have very high hopes," Tamrissa answered, obviously keeping herself from staring at the incredibly good-smelling soup that had been ladled into the bowl which had been put in front of her. "I also intend to pass, no matter how hard they try to make me fail."

"I *will* pass," the red-haired girl to Lorand's left put in, joining the conversation as if she had every right to do so. "To say you 'intend' is to say you have doubts, and I have none. Since you heard my name you now know who I am, which certainly confirms what I said. I *will* be the Seated High, and nothing and no one can stop me."

"That's all yer after?" the man opposite Lorand, Pagin Holter by the name on his identification card, put in hesitantly. "Wouldn't mind havin' thet m'self, but only fer consalayshun. It's bein' part o'one a them challenger Blendin's I mean t'try fer, this bein' a twenty-fifth year 'n all. Din't you folk r'member thet?"

Lorand thought the man had asked his question because of the way everyone was staring at him, even the people at the other end of the table. Holter was a small man and obviously far from the sort to push himself forward, but the fact that his voice had been hesitant hadn't stopped it from being deep and carrying. Everyone seemed to have frozen in the midst of whatever they'd been doing, shock or surprise showing on each of their faces.

"Yes, that's right, I'd forgotten it was a twenty-fifth year,"

Tamrissa said, apparently less affected by the announcement than Lorand and the rest. "Those of us who live in Gan Garee tend to be more aware of things like that, since the contests are always held here. I've heard they're really something to see, but as far as being a part of it goes . . . The winning Blending *rules* for twenty-five *years!*"

Her tone of voice said she couldn't quite picture herself ruling at all, let alone for twenty-five years, and Lorand knew just how she felt. It was one thing to aspire to a High position, another thing entirely to try for the Fivefold Throne. There had been plays and books written about people who'd dreamed about that, and most of them were either comedies or tragedies.

"Of course, that explains everything," the red-haired girl to Lorand's left breathed, apparently having missed what Tamrissa had said. The girl looked as if she'd been struck with revelation, and a delightful one at that. "Now I understand why I qualified for testing *this* year rather than any other. I'm meant to be part of the winning Blending, to fulfill my full destiny and *rule.*"

"I'm afraid your destiny comes up a bit short for *that*," a voice drawled, and Lorand glanced around to see that it was the fool Mardimil who spoke. "All members of the current Blending are from the nobility, which you would know if you moved in the proper circles. As the members of most of the Blendings before them were also the same, you should have chosen your place of birth a bit more carefully. Destiny favors those with *all* the proper qualities."

"Obviously you're all too jealous to admit the truth," the girl said smugly, somehow managing to be even more annoying than Mardimil. "But now that I know what my purpose in life really is, I don't care how jealous you are. When I'm crowned as one of the new Blending, I may even forgive you."

And then the girl turned with a smile to her food, dismissing all the rest of the world as beneath her notice. Lorand exchanged a glance with Tamrissa, who wrinkled her nose in distaste and shook her head, then he began to pay attention to his own food. Even if he hadn't been so hungry, there was nothing left to say to the red-haired girl who thought so much of herself. The idea she'd latched onto was tempting, but only a fool would think about it seriously. . . .

* * *

Clarion was so hungry he all but inhaled what was put before him, barely even noticing that the house cook was more than adequate. He'd been prepared to eat anything at all, even lower-class food, just so long as it filled him. And diverted him from that fool of a girl across the table. To think that a female dressed in *cotton* would consider herself a possible candidate for the new Blending! She was as blind and empty-headed as the rest of her class—and seemed to match at least one member of his own class.

The memory of his conversation with Lady Eltrina still nettled, enough so that under other circumstances it would probably have ruined his appetite. As a courtesy he'd stopped to introduce himself, and then would have mentioned how inappropriate his current surroundings were. He'd expected a member of his own class to understand, possibly even without having to be told; what he hadn't expected was to be cut short before the first word might leave his mouth.

"You've been told to go and do something, sir," she'd said coldly when he'd stopped in front of her. "In your case you've been told to do two somethings, which should mean you have even less time to accomplish it. Beyond that, we have nothing to say to one another."

Rather than argue, Clarion had bowed stiffly and continued on his way to fetch that idiotic identification card and the piddling amount of silver the woman had demanded. There wasn't much of the silver left after that journey, so tomorrow he'd have to pay a visit to Mother's bankers here in Gan Garee. A good portion of his last allowance still remained credited to him, enough so that silver would be the least of his worries.

He reached for another cut of bread, and found himself glancing involuntarily again at the girl sitting to his left. Jovvi Hafford, they'd said her name was, and the one at the head of the table was Tamrissa Domon. Both of them were dressed in silk and showed surprisingly good taste as well as something of well-filled purses, but that wasn't what seemed to attract Clarion to them. He honestly had never seen two women more beautiful, and for the first time in his life there were stirrings within him which weren't being banished by Mother's presence. The stirrings were decidedly uncomfortable, but for some reason it pleased him that they remained.

Perhaps he would even find it possible to do something about them . . .

But not at the moment. Right now it was his hunger that he assuaged, a prospect made even more pleasant by the appearance of platters of meat and bowls of vegetables in various sauces. The one lack was a decent wine to go with the rest, but in all honesty Clarion wasn't certain he could manage wine right now. A single sip of it would likely stretch him out for the night, leaving all that marvelous food to go to waste. The tea they'd been provided with would have to serve, at least until he returned to himself.

And until he had a tighter rein on his thoughts. Even as he let another bite of the tender roast melt in his mouth, his mind insisted on pursuing the thought that this *was* a twenty-fifth year. The present Blending would soon be replaced, and *he* happened to be right on the spot among those who would vie for the honor. Of course, his current companions were beyond consideration, but there were certain to be noble Blendings assembled for the contest. If he should decide that the effort wasn't unsuitable for a gentleman like himself, perhaps . . .

"The mind of man is an amazing instrument," a voice commented softly, and Clarion looked up to see that it was the man to his right, Eskin Drowd, who spoke musingly. "Before this excellent fare was placed before us, I could think of nothing but its imminent arrival. Now that I've consumed enough to assuage part of my hunger, my thoughts have found another topic to cling doggedly to."

"The matter of the upcomin' contest to seat the new Blendin'," Vallant Ro, across from Clarion, said with a nod around his latest mouthful. "I have no real interest in it myself, but even I can't stop thinkin' about it. I have no true yearnin' to rule anythin' but the deck of my ship, but the idea of bein' this close to and in the midst of the process that will seat the next holders of the Fivefold Throne . . . I must admit the concept is somewhat . . . thought provokin'."

"It's a bit more than that," Jovvi Hafford put in with a sigh before Clarion was able to repeat what he'd said earlier about commoners being unfit for the honor. "I've also been thinking about it, and all it's done is bring me a great deal of confusion. I came here knowing exactly what I would do with my life once I'd put this test behind me, but now the test *is* behind me and my plans are in danger of crumbling to ruins. Part of me knows I haven't a chance of winning to the Fivefold Throne, but thinking about the power and safety such a position would bring. . . ."

She left the thought unfinished, but Clarion found himself nodding along with the other two men. Power and safety, two things the Seated Blending enjoyed above everyone else in the empire—and beyond. The adjoining realms of Gracely to the east and Astinda to the west had begun with their own Seated Blendings, but somehow the process had broken down through the centuries and now it was said that every High capable of drawing power had his own small area over which he ruled. The borders of their own realm Gandistra had been steadily growing over the years at the expense of Gracely and Astinda, which proved the point. The Fivefold Throne represented power and safety impossible to match anywhere on the continent.

"It's been projected that in another thirty years or so, Gandistra will encompass this entire continent," Drowd said, nearly reading Clarion's thoughts. "Our expansion has been more rapid than most people realize, and I've even heard mention of the fact that across the seas are lands inhabited by unregenerate savages. If our expansion should become more rapid still, there may well be a place other than quiet retirement for this new, incoming Blending to go when their service to the empire is done. Savages need to be ruled by those with experience in ruling, and where would one find greater experience than among a retiring Blending?"

For the second time there was no overt comment on what had been said. Everyone seemed as taken by the concept as Clarion himself, even the fool of a girl sitting beside Ro. She'd held herself aloof from the conversation, undoubtedly to avoid more of their "jealousy," but her eyes gleamed in a way that said she pictured herself eventually bringing a large number of savages to their knees before her. The idea was absurd, at least with *her* in the picture . . .

"I'm not sure I approve of the idea of expanding to the next continent," Jovvi Hafford said suddenly, a faint frown marring her beautiful brow. "I knew a seaman once who visited the Tondron continent at least three times a year, the freighter he served on plying the trade route which has been used for centuries. The people in Tondron aren't savages, they simply have a way of life that doesn't include being ruled by a Blending. Not a single Blending, at any rate. I had the impression that most people became part of one, but I never got the details involved."

"That's because the man had to be lying to you," the red-haired girl said immediately with a sound of ridicule. "Only savages would consider getting along without a ruling Blending, and if you don't believe that ask anyone in Gracely or Astinda. They don't have Blendings either, and soon they won't even have separate realms. You really must learn not to be so gullible."

"Listening without preconceived ideas isn't being gullible, my dear," Jovvi corrected gently with an amused smile before Clarion could jump to her defense. "I can see how well you like the idea of lording it over everyone for the rest of your life, but just because you were allowed to do that until now doesn't mean you're guaranteed to continue doing it. For your own sake, *you'd* better stop being so gullible."

A definite sound of scorn came from the redhead, and then she was back to being aloof and no longer a part of the conversation. The behavior was obviously typical of her, but happily it supplied a reason for Clarion to speak to the vision on his left—but not in a way she might find daunting.

"Nicely done," he complimented Jovvi, smiling as warmly as possible while pretending to be just another ordinary person at the table. "It's quite obvious the girl will never learn the truth of her position, but fear of being put in her place might manage to keep her quiet. I'm Clarion Mardimil, Air magic."

"So your identification says," Jovvi replied with a marvelous smile, sharing the jest with him rather than making him the butt of it. "And what do *you* think of the plans to extend our influence, Clarion Mardimil? Are you for allowing people the freedom to do as they please, or for smothering them with your own definition of what's right?"

"Definitely freedom," Clarion replied immediately, startling himself. He had been raised to accept the idea of a completely directed life without question, but something odd seemed to be happening to him. Just exactly what that was Clarion hadn't yet figured out, but it earned him an even more delightful smile from Jovvi.

"I would have expected no less from such a handsome gentleman," she murmured, the words tingling along his spine like a caress. The power of her lovely blue-green eyes

began to bring an uncomfortable hardening to his groin, bu
then she looked away to the servants who had reappeared
with another offering.

"Is that sherbet?" she asked, then made a sound o
satisfaction when her observation proved itself to be true
"How delightful. Now my palate will be cleared for the nex
course."

That was the purpose of sherbet, of course, and Clarion
was delighted to see that she knew it. That certainly took her
firmly out of the category of peasant, something Clarion
didn't *want* to believe of her. Nevertheless he meant to avoid
stressing his true place in life, to also avoid the loneliness o
standing aloof. The Lant female had done that to herself
obviously not having grown up in the sort of isolation which
Clarion had. But he had no intentions of repeating that, no
again, not here . . . Clarion turned to his own sherbet, but in
a moment the conversation was taken up again in a differen
quarter.

"I'm inclined to agree with Mardimil and the lovely Dama
Hafford," Ro said from across the table, looking at Drowd
"If people in other lands have found a way to live that please:
them and does *us* no harm, what right do we have to interfere
with their lives? It would be the most colossal arrogance to
assume that we know better about what's right for them."

"My dear Ro, arrogance doesn't enter into the matter,"
Drowd returned with a deprecating laugh. "As the more
civilized of the two groups, we *do* know better about what':
right for them. If you wish, you may think of them a:
children and ourselves as adults. You do agree that adults are
best suited to know what's proper for children?"

"Not under all circumstances," Ro came back immedi
ately, dismissing the claim with a sharp gesture. "Som(
parents twist the lives of their children to satisfy their own
wants and desires, a point we agreed on not many minute:
ago. The child who grows up to live accordin' to othei
people's ideas of what's right usually ends up completely ou
of touch with the world as it really is. A truly wise adul
teaches a child to rely on his or her own talents and abilities
and supports the child's ambitions. To substitute your own
ambition means you're really an overgrown child yourself
not an adult."

"What you say is quite true," Drowd agreed with a
gracious nod as he applied himself to his own sherbet. "The

overgrown child, impressing his or her own narrow viewpoint on a true child, usually produces an offspring out of touch with reality. That, however, doesn't hold true for the actual adult, who tends to teach proper attitudes rather than false ones. Were you taught not to steal as a child?"

"Of course," Ro answered with a snort. "I was also taught what happens if you try it anyway. When you're a child, you tend to think of yourself as the only one with magical ability. You learn better when you try to sneak away with a cooling cherry tart, and Cook uses her own talent to show you your mistake. So what's your point?"

"The point, my dear Ro, is that small children may *consider* a particular action pleasant and therefore proper, but that doesn't necessarily *make* it proper. The adult knows better from having lived longer in a proper way, and therefore is entitled, no, honor bound, to teach the child. You do believe in adults fulfilling their duty?"

Drowd now wore a rather self-satisfied smile, but Clarion was too distracted to be annoyed by it. The conversation between Drowd and Ro had been strangely disturbing, but before Clarion was able to discover in what way, Ro responded to the question put to him.

"I most certainly do believe in adults fulfillin' their duty," Ro replied, not in the least daunted. "But before you can call such fulfillment a grand and wonderful thing, you first have to learn their definition of what's right. But the easiest way to discover whether *you're* right is to take the situation and turn it around. You think well of forcin' other people to live accordin' to *your* concept of right, but how much would you enjoy bein' forced to live accordin' to theirs? As long as their way doesn't harm you, the best—adult—solution would be for everyone to live accordin' to their own beliefs."

"That's begging the question," Drowd countered, no longer as pleased or self-satisfied. "If something is right, it's right for everyone. If it's wrong, it's wrong for everyone. *That's* something you can't argue with."

"It's something *I* can argue with," Jovvi said before Ro was able to respond, startling Clarion. The beautiful woman was still serene, but no longer amused. "As Dom Ro said earlier in a different way, what's right for you doesn't necessarily have to be right for me. For instance, I know someone who doesn't want to let me out of her sight. She pretends that her actions are for *my* benefit and protection, but in reality she's serving herself. And since even stealing can be considered right under the proper circumstances—as, for instance, to save your life—I seriously doubt if there are many universal rights and wrongs to begin with. You'd do well, Dom Drowd, to reexamine the basis of your beliefs."

Drowd came back with something to continue the argument, but Clarion no longer listened. He'd been shaken by Jovvi Hafford's words even more than by Ro and Drowd's, but the confusion buzzing around his head refused to let him understand why. What they'd said didn't apply to *him* in any way, so why were his hands cold and nearly trembling, and his mouth dry? The situation was quite ridiculous, but banishing it was apparently beyond him.

Clarion sat back in an effort to regain control of himself, and had almost managed it by the time the next course was brought. Chilled fish with a tangy sauce it was, just the thing to attract his weakening but still-active appetite. The others also let themselves be somewhat distracted by the newly arrived dish, but not to the point of abandoning their discussion. Their pointless, ridiculous discussion which had nothing to do with *him,* and which he therefore ignored. Leave it to the lower classes to upset a gentleman without even knowing they did it.

After the chilled fish came tidbits of chicken and various sauces to dip them in, and that finally settled Clarion's hunger. A light dessert of banana slices mixed into buttercream topped it all off, and by then no one at the table was still part of a discussion. Everyone seemed to feel the waves of exhaustion rolling over them as strongly as Clarion did, so he wasn't the only one to finish his tea, rise and bid a general good night, and then head for his room. Clarion had meant to discuss the size of his quarters, but at the moment it was simply too much trouble. Tonight he felt he would find it possible to sleep propped in the corner of a broom closet, but tomorrow would surely be another matter.

Yes, tomorrow he would speak to the lovely Tamrissa Domon, possibly with as much success as he'd had with Jovvi Hafford. Clarion climbed the stairs to his room with a smile of anticipation on his face, but that uncomfortable hardening had returned to his body. He usually had to exercise hard to rid himself of the condition, but possibly tonight his exhaustion would see to the matter. Tomorrow, however . . . Yes, tomorrow would definitely be another day.

NINETEEN

Jovvi awoke to moderate sunshine coming through the curtains, and spent a moment enjoying the feel of the bed and the lack of a servant determined to wake her. That happened only rarely at Allestine's residence, as Allestine believed in allowing her ladies only enough sleep to keep the blush of good health in their cheeks. Perhaps twice a year a holiday was declared and everyone was permitted to do as they pleased, but usually that happened only during some terrible storm that no one was able to get through. With Allestine even a shopping trip was business, as it let the girls show themselves off around town to men who might not know what marvelous courtesans her residence housed.

Jovvi's enjoyment evaporated at the thought of Allestine and the confinement she was determined to escape. So far her plans hadn't gone well at all, especially since she'd begun to wonder at those plans. Her ultimate aim was to be so wealthy and powerful that no one would ever be able to control her life again, and last night she'd been shaken to realize that she stood within reach of the ultimate place of wealth and power. Being a member of the new Blending . . .

"But that's more fantasy than reality," she protested to herself, trying to bring her imagination down from the heights. "Do you really think *you* could qualify as a member of the new Blending? Don't you remember what the boy said about it being nobles who were chosen? You may have nobles as patrons, but you can't be silly enough to think you're one yourself."

Jovvi sighed as her practical nature refused to let her lie to herself. Her family had been about as noble as an old shoe, something she refused to let herself forget. Her talent with

Spirit magic was just an asset to be used like any other, not something to use in an effort to pretend she was better than everyone else. Those who talked themselves into believing they were superior in every way usually proved just the opposite with everything they did.

Like that silly girl Beldara Lant, last night at the table. Jovvi made a face at the memory, wondering how anyone above the age of five could be so self-centered. Or any woman, at any rate. Men with money and power usually demanded that life accommodate them, but most women were too practical to do the same. Money and power most often ended in the hands of men, and only the occasional woman was able to take them for her own.

Which was what Jovvi had planned to do, before delusions of fantasy had begun to turn her head. In all practicality it would never be possible to become a member of the new Blending, but the temptation to try for it was so unbelievably strong. She'd better remind herself again about what the boy had said, repeating it over and over as necessary.

"And stop calling him 'the boy,' even in your thoughts," she chided herself as she sat up and ran her hands through her hair. "He's obviously older than you, and his name is Clarion."

Yes, Clarion Mardimil, she recalled with another sigh. He was actually more than ordinarily handsome, but there was a . . . lack, perhaps, or some kind of innocence that made him feel more like a boy than a man to her talent. His balance was so precarious it was difficult to understand how he'd passed his test. Most adults with so little self-possession rarely found it possible to cope with ordinary life, not to mention extraordinary situations like his test must have been. But he *had* passed, and was now in the process of developing a crush on her . . .

Jovvi smiled as she got out of bed, wondering if Clarion even knew what was happening to him. He'd dropped out of the table conversation early and had been one of the first to go to bed, but every time he'd looked at her she'd felt him reacting the way men always did. The odd thing about it had been the distance of his own awareness, as though he'd somehow been kept from learning a normal masculinity. Jovvi didn't understand that, but there were enough other men in the house to keep Clarion from pestering her. She'd use one or two of the others as shields, and—

Her thoughts broke off as she heard a very small but unexpected sound, at the same time feeling a wetness on her bare left foot. She looked down expecting to find herself imagining things, then blinked at what should have been imagination but wasn't. About halfway between her knee and her ankle a tiny cluster of thunderclouds floated in mid-air, dark and threatening with lightning flashing through them and thunder rumbling around. And rain coming down from them, which was what had wet her foot and part of her nightdress.

"But all we drank last night was tea," she protested in a murmur, staring down at the miniature thunderstorm. It was actually rather adorable, if you liked that sort of thing. What she didn't enjoy, though, was having her foot inundated, so she stepped back to get it out of the rain. That helped for a very brief moment, and then the clouds followed to rain on her again.

That was the point she realized someone must be playing a joke, but who they might be and how they were doing it was beyond her. The only ones at the table with Water magic were Vallant Ro and that shy little stableman, Pagin Holter, and neither of them seemed the type to play jokes. She'd expected a frank and direct suggestion from Ro because of the way he'd looked at her, but using a practical joke to get her attention? It wasn't at all likely, and the same held true for Holter. His yearning interest had been quite clear, but all traces of intent to follow up on the feelings were entirely absent.

Jovvi's foot was beginning to get cold, so there was only one thing to do: get rid of the clouds no matter how adorable they were, and then act as if nothing had happened. That should make the prankster reveal himself, to find out what had happened if for no other reason. And it *was* faintly amusing, that she was willing to grant.

Dispersing the cloud wasn't difficult. Thunderstorms were a careful balance of water and dust and air all in turbulence, and without the turbulence it wasn't possible to have a storm. Jovvi soothed away that roiling violence with very little difficulty, and once it was gone the clouds quickly dissipated and disappeared. Her foot was now safe from the threat of drowning, but it and the carpeting could use some drying. Not to mention that small part of her nightdress.

Mopping up didn't take long either, and then Jovvi went

to work on the problem of where to hide her gold. If she were going to be fitted for new clothes today, she couldn't very well carry it with her. But she also had no intention of leaving it lying around for the house servants to find. It had to be well hidden but easy for her to get to, and then she'd be able to dress and go looking for breakfast. Dinner last night had been quite substantial, but she'd slept for many hours and was now ready to sit down to another meal.

And possibly to speak to that nice Lorand Coll again. He was certainly handsome enough with a lovely body, but the unusual steadiness inside him was even more attractive to her than his looks. Not that she was in the midst of searching for a steady male friend. That fit not at all into any of her plans, not even the fantasy ones. . . .

Lorand walked slowly down the stairs on his way to the dining room, glancing around to see if he could spot the practical joker. He'd awakened somewhat earlier feeling well rested and back to his usual self, and had gotten up with the intention of dressing and going to breakfast. Halfway across the floor he'd suddenly discovered that someone had put together a tiny thunderstorm in his room, and the thing was raining all over the back of his nightshirt. He'd found it possible to see the miniature clouds and their lightning only by twisting around at the waist, but he hadn't had any trouble hearing the small thunderclaps.

But he'd done quite a bit of hopping around trying to see the thing before it occurred to him to stand still and simply twist at the waist. He hated to feel foolish even if no one seemed to be around to watch, so he'd quickly removed the dust motes that kept the tiny thunderhead together. Without that cohesion the storm had ended, spreading out and then disappearing. It had managed to get him good and wet first, though, and he'd actually had to wring out his nightshirt.

So now Lorand looked casually around, trying to spot the one who had tried to make him look like a fool. He intended to indulge in some practical-joke-getting-even by pretending nothing at all had happened even if the culprit confessed, no matter which one of them it happened to be. Ro and Holter were the two with Water magic, and it had to be one of them. He'd find out over breakfast, and then it would be his turn to laugh.

Lorand walked into the dining room to find only two of

the others there before him, the man Eskin Drowd, who already sat in his place at the foot of the table and ate, and Clarion Mardimil. The latter stood at a long table set up on the side of the room, a number of odd, covered dishes with long legs arranged on the table. Small containers of what looked to be some sort of oil bubbled gently under the tall dishes, no doubt thanks to some servants with Fire magic. But none of the servants were currently in the room and Mardimil was helping himself from a dish he had uncovered. That had to mean it was proper for Lorand to do the same, which came as something of a relief. He expected to get used to being served by someone other than his mother eventually, but he hadn't yet reached that point.

Walking around Mardimil to the left showed Lorand a stack of empty platters and a neat row of forks, so he took one of each and began to look in each of the covered dishes to see what they held. The first two held things Lorand wasn't able to identify in their cooked state, so he continued on until he reached the chicken livers in the third. They seemed to have been fried somehow and smelled wonderful, so he spooned some out onto his plate and went on with his search for eggs, potatoes, and bacon. *That* was what breakfast meant to *him,* but it didn't seem to mean the same to these people.

Mardimil paid no attention to him as they both moved along their own sections of the table, but Lorand couldn't help remembering what he'd decided. He owed Mardimil an apology for what he'd said in the bath house, and putting it off wasn't likely to make the effort any easier. If he kept his voice low, the conversation would be private even from Drowd, who sat at the far end of the eating table. Eating table, dish table. Lorand shook his head over people who made them two different places, then used his finally having made a hoped-for discovery to start the conversation.

"I was beginning to think I'd have to find some chickens and *coax* my breakfast out of them," Lorand commented to Mardimil, gesturing at the eggs he'd just uncovered. "Liver is a nice addition, but without eggs it just doesn't seem like breakfast."

"My eating habits apparently agree," Mardimil said after something of a hesitation, his words a bit stiff but still representing a response. "Mother's servants always place the eggs first on the buffet, even when she takes her own meal in bed."

Lorand nodded, glanced at a Drowd who paid no attention to them, then lowered his voice. "I'd . . . like to apologize for what I said yesterday," he forced out in a murmur. "It was entirely uncalled for, and you can be sure I won't do it again."

"But it wasn't uncalled for," Mardimil responded at once, at the same time looking surprised that he'd said such a thing. "It . . . made me think . . . about subjects I'd tried to avoid, even though my survival could well depend on them. You spoke the truth to a stranger, and this stranger is very . . . grateful."

"I would call it being gracious instead," Lorand replied slowly, studying the man who had briefly looked at him with such naked openness and loneliness. "Very few people in this world will thank someone for telling them what they consider a painful truth, and *I* consider myself lucky for having met one of them. But I don't think you can call us strangers, not any more."

"Why, I do believe you're right," Mardimil said, looking surprised again. "Those who are involved in a group undertaking can be considered comrades, and this undertaking *is* a group one, despite our various areas of expertise. How odd this is, to go from a distant awareness of the state to being a comrade oneself."

"I'm more familiar with the idea of friends in adversity," Lorand remarked as he happily located fried potatoes. "I'll admit I know nothing about being a comrade, but we all have experience with being friends so I'll think of it that way."

"I've . . . never had a friend either," Mardimil said without looking at him, the words sounding like an embarrassed confession. "Mother has always said that having many acquaintances is far superior to having a small number of friends, but occasionally I've wondered what friendship is like. I've heard that too often friends impose on one, and if one refuses the imposition he loses the friend."

"Whoever told you that lied," Lorand answered, feeling shocked and hurting for this very innocent victim of life. "A true friend is someone so close to you that you don't *mind* helping them, because you know they'd do the same for you. A friend is someone you care about, and—"

Much stronger shock cut Lorand off in mid-sentence, all but leaving him openmouthed. He'd forgotten about Hat, he'd actually forgotten all about his best friend!

"Is something wrong?" Mardimil asked, still speaking hesitantly. "I don't mean to pry into something that's none of my affair, so if you'd rather not discuss it . . ."

"No, I'm just in the midst of cursing my own stupidity," Lorand answered heavily, feeling very depressed. "I came here with a friend, someone who's been a friend for most of my life, and we tested at the same time. I . . . was afraid to ask about him after the test was over, hoping I'd find he'd been sent to the same residence I was, but he's not here. That became obvious last night, but I didn't even think about him. Makes me a really great friend, doesn't it?"

"Is it wrong not to want to admit that someone you care about could well be dead?" Mardimil asked, now sounding more sure of himself. "If I had someone like that, aside from Mother, of course, I'd certainly want to keep from admitting it. The pain of such a loss would be intense."

"Yes, it is," Lorand admitted, giving Mardimil a glance of gratitude. "I appreciate your trying to make me feel better about this, but Hat is dead and I'd better learn to accept it. And figure out a way to let his parents know. We can talk again later."

Mardimil nodded before Lorand turned away, actually looking faintly sympathetic. That was quite a change from the man Lorand had met yesterday, but right now he was in no shape to appreciate the difference. He had a friend to mourn, and a meal to eat despite no longer having an appetite. He'd been raised to never waste good food, so he had to stuff down what he'd already put on his plate.

But how was he ever going to find a way to tell Hat's parents that he was dead? *Without* going into details about the way it must have happened. Lorand reclaimed his place at the table from the night before, but it took a few moments before he was able to reach for the fork. Hat would have loved that residence and its upper class ways, but Hat would never see it. He was gone, and the blur of tears helped to take away the sight of what Lorand simply shoveled into his mouth.

Clarion watched the man Coll head quickly for the table without investigating the rest of what the buffet held, and Clarion sighed for him. He could only try to imagine what it would feel like to lose someone close to you, since he'd never had anyone close but Mother. And he'd done quite a bit of thinking about *her*, both last night and this morning.

The final warming plate on the buffet held a lovely cheese sauce, so Clarion spooned some over his eggs and then headed for his own place at the table. Teacups had been arranged in front of each place, and steaming pitchers of tea stood at intervals along the table. Drowd already sat at the table to Clarion's right, but the man had his nose stuffed into a book and didn't seem aware of anyone else's presence. Clarion was tempted to feel slighted, but he had too much to think about to regret the loss of another conversation right now.

After pouring himself a cup of tea, Clarion began on his meal and his thinking at precisely the same time. The conversation he'd heard the night before had disturbed him, centering as it had on parents who raised their children to satisfy their own needs rather than those of the child. Someone had once taunted Clarion with the charge that he was only around as a backdrop for his mother, and the insult had hurt twice as much because Clarion hadn't ever been able to find a different purpose for himself. They'd started to add that his mother had planned it that way, but then Mother had come by and chased the nasty children away.

Not that they had been *small* children. They and Clarion had all been sixteen or so, and Mother's explanation of their behavior had fit the situation. They were Clarion's social peers, she had said, and they naturally resented having been deprived of Clarion's presence among them. They were old enough to know how precious his company really was, but not yet old enough to realize that they couldn't possibly be considered fine enough to merit it.

Clarion had believed the explanation just as he always believed Mother, but some small kernel of doubt had remained. The boy who had spoken for the group hadn't sounded deprived and jealous, he'd sounded ridiculing and amused. The rest of the children had seemed the same, and Clarion had never quite forgotten the incident. But he *had* continued to believe that his welfare was Mother's first and only concern, just as she'd always told him it was.

And then he'd heard that some parents only pretended to act in their child's best interests, and he hadn't been able to chase the contention from his head. Clarion paused briefly in his eating, remembering how the thoughts had come flooding back once he was in his room. He could have held them off a bit longer if he hadn't been so tired, but instead he'd had to admit to himself that much of what Mother had done *hadn't* been for his best. He knew almost nothing of the world and the people who inhabited it, and that was a horrible lack rather than a benefit.

But then another thought had occurred to him, one that had permitted him to fall asleep quickly and sleep soundly. It was inconceivable that Mother would deliberately act against his best interests, so she must have done it by accident. He was her first and only child, and lack of experience at something can turn the best of intentions quickly to the reverse. She'd *mistakenly* done things that had put him at a disadvantage, and now it was up to him to correct that.

Clarion sighed as he paused to sip at his tea, remembering how distressed he'd felt over that decision earlier this morning. At first he couldn't think of a thing that would help him accomplish his aim, and that included a place to start. After all, how can you repair your lacks when you don't even know exactly what those lacks are?

And then that practical joke had been played on him, which at the time had seemed to make things worse. He'd gotten out of bed to pace while he considered his problem, and after a moment or two he'd noticed the oddest thing: a tiny thunderstorm raining all over his right arm. Where the miniature clouds had come from he had no idea, but the sleeve of his nightshirt was becoming drenched along with his arm.

Trying to move away from the thing had been useless, as it had followed relentlessly with its small lightning flashes and matching rumbles of thunder. After another moment Clarion had lost patience and had used his talent to separate the components of the little storm. With air surrounding those components and refusing to let them come together again, the storm had had no choice but to dissipate completely. Clarion had been outraged that someone would play such a foolish trick on a man of *his* place in life—but then another thought had come to him.

"Could this possibly be the way members of the lower classes make overtures of friendship to one another?" he'd muttered aloud. "If the person chosen as victim protests in anger or upset, they're rejected as being too stuffy to associate with. But if they laugh, or possibly turn the tables by pretending nothing has happened, they're considered acceptable."

It was only a theory, but Clarion needed very badly to be considered acceptable to join *some* group. Only by observing and listening would he discover those areas where he lacked knowledge or experience, and then he could see to repairing the lack. It would have done him a good deal more good if he were among members of his own social class, but the proper people weren't here just now and these lower class representatives were. He would simply have to cope as best he might, and then, at the first opportunity, move his efforts to the vicinity of those who really counted.

And so Clarion had dressed and gone down to breakfast, only to be delightfully surprised when that fellow Coll made the opening advances for him. The apology had been totally unexpected, and it had thrown Clarion far enough off balance that he'd responded unthinkingly in what had turned out to be the best way possible. Clarion's admission of ignorance over certain matters had brought a sympathetic and helpful reaction from Coll, and possibly would do so again once the man was over his distress at what had become of his friend.

Clarion pushed his empty plate away and sat back with his teacup, satisfied in more ways than one. He would have to encourage as many conversations with these people as possible, during which he would strive to learn what had been kept from him by accident. And in the interim he would consider what he'd decided about his current position, which could well change his mind even more in relation to those tests.

Becoming a member of the new Blending . . . of *course* it was a position for a gentleman, how could he have thought it might not be? And it was also one that no one could possibly consider useless or foolish. . . .

Vallant came down the stairs feeling faintly annoyed, but that feeling disappeared entirely when he caught sight of his hostess standing in the hall below, speaking to two of the servants. Today she wore a dress of pale yellow embroidered with small ivory flowers, and the night's sleep seemed to have worked really well for her. Incredible as it was, she looked even more beautiful than she had yesterday, something Vallant would have sworn was impossible. He slowed his pace on the stairs, deciding that that would be the perfect time to offer that apology he'd decided to make. As soon as the servants were through speaking to her, he would take their place.

But in the meanwhile he had a few minutes, so he used them to wonder what could have gotten into that man Pagin Holter. The little groom hadn't seemed to be the sort to play practical jokes, so maybe the tiny thunderstorm that had tried to drown Vallant in his room had been more of a challenge. It could have been a matter of, "Look at what *I* can do," but if so even that matter was taken care of. Removing all the moisture from the miniature clouds had ended the storm and any challenge together, the whole thing done firmly but quietly.

Which ought to end the matter completely. Vallant had decided against mentioning the incident if Holter didn't, and the groom probably wouldn't. When your challenge is accepted and met with very little fuss, it doesn't become something to boast about. Vallant would have enjoyed knowing why Holter had challenged him in the first place, especially if it had been the matter of becoming one of the new Blending. He himself had very little interest in the possibility, but maybe Holter hadn't realized that. If so, he really ought to tell him—

Vallant's thoughts broke off when he saw the servants getting ready to walk away from Tamrissa Domon, his signal to start moving closer. His timing was good in that he'd just finished descending the stairs, so he ambled over and stepped into the place the servants had just left.

"Excuse me, Dama Domon, but I'd like to speak to you for a moment," he said when she raised those incredible violet eyes to look up at him. "I owe you an apology, and I'm always rather strict about payin' my debts."

"Are you really," she said rather flatly, a tinge of pink coloring her cheeks. "I should think it would be easier to do things that don't require apology. Then you would have fewer debts."

"If I ever become perfect, I'll certainly follow that advice," Vallant answered, not at all encouraged by her manner but determined not to let the matter go. "At the moment I'm still an ordinary human, however, so the apology is in order. Yesterday, in the bath house, I doubted your word about bein' the mistress of this house. As I've since been proven mistaken, I offer my deepest and most sincere apologies."

"Is that it?" she asked, interrupting Vallant's most charming bow. "You're apologizing for doubting my word?"

"What else is there to apologize for?" he asked in turn, feeling somewhat confused. "I covered the matter of bargin' in on you at the time, a circumstance which you should have understood since you shared it. What else did you have in mind?"

"If you need *me* to tell you that, then I'd be wasting my breath," she returned, looking up at him defiantly. "By all means have your fun, Dom Ro, but don't make the mistake of getting in my way when the tests begin again. Unlike you, I mean to go through to the very end of them, and I refuse to let some overgrown child upset me. I *will* win through, do you understand me?"

"Overgrown child?" Vallant demanded, well on the way to being thoroughly outraged. "Yes, Dama Domon, I believe I understand you all too well. You're clearly used to gettin' your way in life, through your beauty if not through the sharpness of your tongue. I've known other women who believed their beauty excused any action they took, but they were just as mistaken as you are. And if you think there's somethin' wrong with occasionally havin' fun, you must be a good deal older than you look."

"You're quite right, Dom Ro," she said, her face now pale rather than flushed, her voice trembling faintly. "I'm completely used to getting my own way because of my beauty, and the practice is much too pleasant to give up. Unlike you, I dislike giving up, preferring instead to stand victorious and proud. And now, if you'll excuse me—"

"Just a moment," Vallant said, moving to his left to keep her from stepping around him. "That's twice you've said somethin' about not bein' like me, and I don't care for the tone of your insinuations. Just what do you find so terrible about me?"

"I can't stand someone with talent being too afraid to exercise it," she answered, now clearly fighting to keep her voice steady. And her eyes, the indescribable look in those breathtaking eyes . . . "It may *sound* good to say you have other things to do with your life, but I think the truth is you're just too afraid to try something you may fail at. Warla is like that, and a lot of other women, but I'll *never* be. That,

Dom Ro, is what I dislike about you, and now I will appreciate your getting out of my way."

Vallant felt a very strong urge to continue the argument, but the girl's trembling had become more visible and he could almost feel the tension in her. It had to be his imagination that he could see a hint of flames beginning to burn in her gaze, but he still bowed curtly and stepped aside. After what she'd said to him he didn't *want* to talk to her, maybe not even to continue the argument. A quitter and coward, that's what she'd called him, and how do you speak politely—or even argue evenly—with someone who thinks *that* about you?

As soon as her path was clear she moved toward the dining room, her back straight and her head up but her pace a little too fast to be called a stride. She all but ran to get away from him, possibly to keep from contracting the dread disease that *he* suffered from. She'd sworn she'd never be that pitifully low and despicable, but she did seem to think the condition might be catching. . . .

Vallant turned away from the door she'd disappeared through, fighting to control the emotions exploding inside him. How *dare* she call him such terrible things without knowing anything about him? Even if she *had* known him she wouldn't have had the right to judge, not when he was the one who had to live in his skin. He *wasn't* a quitter, and it *wasn't* cowardice . . .

It was just fear. Vallant took a deep breath, then admitted to himself what he would never admit aloud. He *was* afraid to try for anything but being what he was, the captain of a ship. Almost everything else required being indoors too much of the time, possibly even being *inside* some place that wasn't easily gotten out of. That idea was enough to frighten the manhood out of him, to turn him as weak and helpless as that child she'd named him. He couldn't help it, couldn't control it—and couldn't make it stop.

"So why bother thinkin' about what I might do under other circumstances?" he murmured, the bitter end of the argument he would never put into words. "Go ahead and call me a quitter, it won't change anythin'. I can't change what I am even if the most beautiful woman I've ever met disapproves. I'm used to bein' a disappointment to beautiful women, especially the ones accustomed to gettin' their own way."

Vallant made a sound of sour amusement, wondering why he always seemed to attract that sort. Or be attracted by them. Her violent refusal to join his counter-illustrious ranks was something different, but the rest of Dama Tamrissa Domon was probably just like Mirra, the girl he'd thought he would be happy to marry. Happy, certainly, he would surely be happy. But not with Mirra and not there, in stifling Gan Garee. He would get back to the Sea Queen, and *then* he would be happy.

He waited a few moments until he was completely back in control of himself, and then he went to the dining room to join the others for breakfast.

TWENTY

By the time I got my plate filled with the breakfast I really needed, I almost had full control of myself again. But that didn't mean I'd figured out what that Vallant Ro was up to. First he puts together a tiny thunderstorm to rain all over my nightdress, and I have to get rid of it by using my flames to evaporate the moisture in it. That makes me determined to tell him off properly, but before I can, he comes over to apologize.

But not for playing that childish joke. He apologizes instead for doubting me the day before, when I hadn't even known he was doing it. Giving him the chance to apologize for the joke as well turns out to be a waste of effort, since he then pretends he knows nothing about it. And after everything he's done, he then has the nerve to ask why I don't like him!

Only the fact that there were other people around kept me from shaking my head as I sat down at the table. One word had led to another with Dom Ro, and when he'd gotten angry I'd felt that very familiar clutch of fear in my middle. But this time I hadn't let it paralyze me the way it usually had with Gimmis, and I'd been ready to protect myself with everything I had. The man must have seen that because he'd stepped out of my way, and I'd been able to escape here to the dining room.

Able to *continue on* to the dining room, I amended as I began to eat. Gimmis was dead, so I no longer had to think in terms of escape. I was now a free woman and would stay one, no matter how many people tried to change that. Vallant Ro hadn't liked being called a quitter, but I'd suddenly seen he was precisely that. A grown man of his size, handsome and charming and filled with an unconscious but very forceful authority; what could *he* know about fear, and how hard some people had to fight not to fall victim to it? Winning my way through the tests could well mean escaping the fear for good, so that was a goal I refused to abandon.

I spent a few moments simply eating, but then an anomaly in my private arguments pushed forward to take my attention. I'd accused Vallant Ro of being afraid to exercise his talent to the fullest, and then I'd silently demanded to know what he could possibly understand about fear. If the man pretended disinterest in the tests to keep from finding out how far his ability could take him, he had to be afraid of *something*. It was impossible to imagine what that something could be, since Dom Ro appeared to have enough self assurance to supply a small town.

And enough size and presence to protect himself from anything. I glanced at the man where he sat, almost at the other end of the table, and a pang of guilt came when I remembered everything I'd said to him. He ate as silently as everyone else, giving full attention to his meal, but he no longer looked angry. Disturbed, yes, but no longer angry, and it came to me that it might be my turn to apologize. Even in spite of silly practical jokes.

Breakfast continued along in the same silent way, as though all of us were too wrapped up in private thoughts for casual conversation to divert us. Many of them must have been thinking about my own main topic, which was the reminder we'd been given about this being a twenty-fifth year.

Funny how I'd known that without having considered it,

as though it were so far out of reach that it wasn't worth thinking about. Now it was no longer that far out of reach, even though my becoming a member of the new Blending wasn't very likely. No matter how much gold my father had we still weren't members of the nobility, and all of the most recent Blendings had been composed of nothing else. What I now wondered, though, was the possibility of a way around that. . . .

Breakfast broke up in almost the same order it began, except for Vallant Ro being one of the first to leave. I decided to try to find him in order to offer that apology, but he wasn't in his room or anywhere else I could find. Then I was captured by members of my staff who needed instructions on various dealings with our guests—in spite of my no longer being in charge of anything—and that took up most of the rest of the morning.

By the time I escaped from updating household records and approving menus and setting up service rotations—it was *such* a relief not to be in charge for the length of the tests—it was time for lunch. This time there was some small amount of conversation, but none of it touched the topic of the new Blending. It seemed we were all saving that for another time, and even before we rose from table we were told the coaches had arrived to take us for those fittings for our new clothes.

Two coaches were pulled up in front of the house, backdropped by the storm clouds which had been gathering for the last hour or two. We three women took one of the coaches together, which meant one of the men had to ride with us. It was something of a relief when that turned out to be Eskin Drowd, the young academician and Earth magic applicant. I'd been afraid it might be Vallant Ro, who hadn't given me the chance to apologize—but who had taken to staring at me in a very odd way.

"My goodness, what a terrible burden this is to bear," Dom Drowd said with a grin as he settled himself beside Beldara Lant. Jovvi Hafford sat to my right, the place she'd chosen after Beldara had taken the seat opposite mine. "Three exquisitely lovely ladies, and myself the only man amongst them. Ah well, life demands that we take the bad with the good."

"I sympathize with your suffering, Dom Drowd, and

admire your strength in bearing up under it," Jovvi said to him with a small laugh. "I'd be curious to know the device which caused you to be taken by such misfortune."

"The device was quite simple, dear lady," Dom Drowd replied with his own laugh. "I realized almost immediately that each coach would only seat four comfortably, and therefore made certain to be the last of the group. I'd hoped, you see, that you ladies would travel together, and fortune smiled on my carefully thought out preparations."

"How odd," Beldara said, giving him a very cool look. "I could have sworn you'd forgotten to bring your silver down to lunch with you, and had to be reminded to return to your room to fetch it. Or wasn't that you who was nearly out the door ahead of everyone else?"

"I would never think to cast doubt on a lady's word," Dom Drowd returned, his tone still easy but all amusement suddenly gone from his eyes. "If that's what you wish to believe, please continue to do so. My previous remarks stand as they were made."

"As if that alone makes them true," Beldara returned with a smile of ridicule. "Nothing you say rings true, especially what you've had the nerve to comment about *me*. A man with true intelligence would know enough to sit quietly and not make a fool of himself."

"It takes wisdom to recognize foolhardiness, Dama Lant, which means you don't qualify," Dom Drowd countered in a drawl, smiling at the girl without true humor. "I suspect your jealousy now begins to get the better of you, since you're no longer among those who worship you as unique. Haven't you yet realized that your only true competitor among us is the lovely Dama Domon? You and she share the same aspect, after all, so why do you spread your vitriol among the rest of us? Do you fear, perhaps, that we will prevail while you do not?"

"I fear nothing where *you're* concerned," Beldara returned with scorn, but then her rather intense gaze came to me. "But I must say I *hadn't* realized that Tamrissa and I shared the same aspect. I hope you won't be too upset when I outdo you, dear. I'm sure you're really very good, but I'm better. You'd be wise to accept that truth now, to spare yourself disappointment later."

"Truth and opinion are *not* interchangeable words," I

pointed out, forcing myself to say that despite the drumming of my heart. "When it comes to proving which of us is best, we'll save the opinion and let the test results show the truth."

"You can't really expect to make a decent showing against *me*," Beldara said with a small laugh of incredulity, obviously believing every word she said. "I'm the best there is, girl, and no one has ever been able to prove differently. If you think those flashy dresses of yours will make the difference, guess again. We'll all be dressed alike for the sessions, so no one will know you currently have more gold than I do. And that's *all* you have going for you, take my word on it."

I didn't want to take her word for anything, but her self-assurance was so like what my parents usually showed that I actually felt myself beginning to have doubts. I *had* to do well in the rest of the tests, my future life and sanity depended on it, but what if she turned out to be right . . . ?

"It wasn't wealth that brought her through the first of the tests," a voice commented as I stared down at my hands, watching my fingers twist about each other. Surprisingly it was Jovvi who spoke, a definite hint of amusement behind the words. "I think you're deliberately forgetting that, Dama Lant, in an effort to ease the fear Dom Drowd mentioned. No one ever told you you'd be meeting your equals during the tests, so they certainly never mentioned meeting superiors. Now you're worried that everyone may have been lying to you all these years, and you'll end up failing and making a fool of yourself."

"I'm worried about no such thing!" Beldara spat, her face twisted up into something harsh and ugly, her hands curled into claws in her lap. "No one lied to me, and no equals or superiors were mentioned because I don't *have* any! All of you hate my superiority and envy it, so you're trying to talk me out of it. Well, once the tests start again you'll be forced to admit you were wrong, so I won't have anything more to say to any of you until then."

And with that she leaned back in her seat and gave her attention to the places and people our coach passed, clearly prepared to carry out her promise. Personally I felt grateful for the proposed silence, but not as grateful as I felt for the help Jovvi had given. I looked at her, trying to find a way to express my thanks, but she smiled and shook her head and patted my hand. Apparently she felt thanks weren't neces-

ary, which convinced me they certainly were. Later I'd have
o find *something* . . .

But right now we were on our way to the tailoring shop,
and the route the coach driver took became something of a
surprise. We'd driven through the neighborhood I lived in
and then passed a section of the business district, but after
hat we took a sharp left turn. That put us on a street I'd
never traveled before, and after two blocks it was actually
possible to see refuse scattered here and there on the walks.
The farther we went the more refuse there was, along with a
growing conglomerate of smells that began to turn my
stomach.

"This must once have been a fairly nice neighborhood,"
Dom Drowd commented, gesturing toward the predomi-
nantly stone buildings. "The street was decently cobble-
stoned, but no one has bothered to fix those holes our wheels
keep falling into in quite some time. And those small shops
and stalls of wood between the buildings may be relatively
new, despite the fact that they look old and ready to fall
down."

"Most shops and stalls like those are made with scrap
wood," Jovvi said, also looking out at what we passed.
"That's why they seem so old, even if they were only just put
up. Those who put them up can't afford paint or any other
decorations, of course. . . . What they earn selling their
wares goes to keeping them and their families alive."

"With existence always so precarious for them, I've often
wondered why they bother," Dom Drowd said, sounding as
if he discussed a pack of wild and unimportant animals.
"They can't hope to better themselves, not when they have
no education, no talents, and nothing of any real value to
offer. The government would do us and them a service if
they took people of that sort and put them out of their
misery."

"Well, you may be right," Jovvi responded, her voice still
sweet and even but now far from amused. "I've heard that
very opinion expressed many times, but there's always some
trouble in defining exactly who can be considered expendable. Why, I've even heard the suggestion that most academics fall into that category."

"What?" Dom Drowd exclaimed, obviously outraged.
"That's preposterous! Academics are the ones who educate
the populace to a knowledge and appreciation of the impor-

tant things, so how could anyone dare to suggest that we're expendable?"

"Now, *that* was the interesting part," Jovvi said, looking as if she were trying very hard to remember the point and get it right. "One gentleman pointed out that he learned what he knew about business practices from his father and uncles, so what good had academicians done *him?* He paid someone to choose and buy the artwork hung in his house, had paid them to decorate it, and even paid to have someone organize his parties and balls. He himself was able to read and write and do his figures—which he'd learned from his parents— so all things academic were completely useless to him."

"The louts of this world always tend to believe that," Dom Drowd said with a deprecating gesture. "You call the man a gentleman out of the goodness of your nature, dear lady, but clearly he was no such thing."

"Perhaps not, but the three nobles he spoke with agreed with him," Jovvi said with a very sweet smile. "The three lords saw no reason for places of learning and people to work in them, since they'd all had private educations. They were also of the opinion that educating anyone who wasn't nobly born was a waste of time, since the lower orders weren't capable of really appreciating what was taught. They added that all academicians knew that, but spent their time holding classes so they might have an excuse for feeling superior to their low-class brothers."

"Of all the absurd—!" Dom Drowd swallowed the rest of what he'd meant to say, but that didn't mean he wasn't thinking it. People learned not to speak against the nobility out loud in the company of strangers, since too many had thereafter been called to account for their indiscretion. No one ever admitted to passing on tales to the nobility for the silver the action brought, but admitting it was hardly necessary.

"And, of course, there are always those misguided souls who consider the nobility themselves unnecessary," Jovvi continued blithely on, apparently seeing nothing of the mottled color now staining Dom Drowd's face. "I'd venture to guess that everyone feels that way about someone, and deciding who is right would be a terribly confusing affair. Don't you agree?"

Dom Drowd made some sort of sound deep in his throat, then returned to looking out the window the way Beldara continued to do. Jovvi glanced at me from beneath her lashes, a vast amusement visible in her eyes, and it was all I could do not to cover my mouth and laugh uproariously. It had obviously never occurred to the highly intellectual Dom Drowd that a sweet woman like Jovvi might be making up everything she said. And crediting it to those whose opinion Dom Drowd couldn't simply brush aside. . . .

There wasn't anything in the way of conversation after that, but the trip didn't last long enough for the time to become uncomfortable. In the midst of the soot-covered stone buildings and rickety wooden stalls and shops was a sturdy two-story house with a walled-in back courtyard. The front of the house obviously faced on another street, but the gate into the back courtyard had been opened to allow our coaches to enter.

By the time we pulled up to the back entrance, people had come out of the house. A moment's worth of study showed that although one of the men gave all the orders to the servants who were there to help us from the coaches, the woman standing to his left and just behind him had authority of her own. She studied we women as Dom Drowd and one of the servants helped us from the coach, her expression far from dissatisfied.

There was a short time of confusion when we were led inside, the men being directed to the left and the women to the right. Beyond the door leading from the back entrance hall was a spacious workroom with seven seamstresses sewing away at a rather brisk pace, and a small cluster of comfortable chairs just to the left of the door. A tea service stood on a table near the cluster, and the woman I'd seen outside came in to gesture to the chairs.

"Welcome to our house, ladies, and please make yourselves comfortable," she said in a voice like starched sand. She was in her middle years with dark hair and eyes, a buxom rather than overweight body, and a bearing that strove to be regal. The end result was more stern than regal, though, like the headmistress of an academy teaching deportment.

"The girl will serve you all some tea, and then we'll begin," the woman said, now gesturing to a servant. "I am Regensi, the one who designed the clothing you will soon be fitted for, and I am delighted to see that two of you are the ideal I had in mind. The style was meant for silk, of course, but cotton

has been decreed and so cotton it will be. With you two
ladies, it won't matter in the least."

"With them," Beldara said flatly, certainly noticing the
way Regensi spoke only to Jovvi and me. "Are you saying
that your marvelous creations won't look just as good on
me? Since I happen to be the best in this group or any other,
that doesn't say much for your supposed talent."

"Don't be ridiculous, girl," Regensi answered with a
withering expression and a dismissive evaluation in a quick
up and down examination of Beldara. "Your average prettiness looks cheap beside the glowing beauty of these two, and
that would hold true even if you were smothered in silk.
They, on the other hand, will be just as outstanding in
cotton, so kindly seat yourself and refrain from discussing
matters you know nothing about."

"I was referring to my ability," Beldara began to grind out
with gritted teeth and a flush to her cheeks, but by then it was
clear that she'd wasted her breath. Regensi had turned away
to snap orders at two of her workers, which obviously turned
her deaf to any and all rebuttal.

"Don't let this silliness disturb you," Jovvi began in turn
to Beldara, clearly trying to soothe the girl's embarrassment
and anger. Regensi's speech had been horribly tactless and
insulting, but Beldara apparently had no interest in being
soothed. She glared hatred at Jovvi and me before turning
abruptly and heading for the chair farthest away from us,
and Jovvi gave up her attempt with a sigh. If we and Beldara
hadn't precisely been friends before, now we had probably
become enemies.

"We really must remember to thank Regensi," I murmured, definitely vexed. "Without her help it might have
taken us another two or three days to make Beldara hate us
this much."

"The feeling was already there inside her, only partially
buried," Jovvi murmured back with a small shrug. "As long
as she was able to consider herself completely superior she
didn't care about our respective appearances, but now I'd say
she's begun to develop . . . less assurance. I can't say doubt
because she doesn't doubt her beliefs, but this comparison of
physical attraction has accessed her rage. From now on she'll
probably be even less pleasant to us than she has been."

"Wonderful," I said with my own sigh. "As if she was all
that pleasant to begin with. And what a surprise that this

happened over something as hateful as physical beauty. If I could trade my appearance for hers, she'd probably never believe that I would do it in a minute."

Jovvi frowned at me and began to say something, but Regensi came back then to remind us about sitting down and having tea. While the tea was served and sipped at for a time, she lectured about how important she was in the world of fashion even if most people had never heard of her. Then she interrupted herself to direct Beldara into a fitting room with one of the fitters, but resumed the lecture once that was seen to.

Beldara wasn't kept in the room very long, not by usual fitting standards, but the same didn't hold true for Jovvi and me. Regensi saw to each of us personally, which lengthened the process almost to the point of exhaustion. The basic skirts and blouses had already been cut to a large, wide fit, and only had to be tailored down to our individual sizes. But that meant checking the draping of the skirt to make sure it fell properly, and opening basted seams to assure that darts would not be too deep and extreme. All of it had to meet Regensi's concept of perfection, which meant fitting and fixing, fitting and changing, fitting and refixing.

Jovvi was taken in last, and by the time she came out again even I was tired of sitting and waiting. Beldara had divided her time between pacing all over the sitting area and returning to her chair to stare expressionlessly at the skirts and blouses being worked on by the seamstresses. During one of those times I caught the look in her eyes, which made me want to shiver. If she wasn't considering the possibility of "accidentally" setting every piece of cloth in the room on fire, I've never seen the urge toward vindictive revenge. Or felt the same myself. . . .

Regensi insisted on making Jovvi sit down for some tea before finally letting us leave, and as much as Jovvi needed those few minutes off her feet she was just as relieved to get out of there as the rest of us. We stepped outside with me, at least, feeling as if we'd been released from prison, unsurprised to find that it was almost evening. Our new clothes had been promised for delivery the next day, and even if they turned out to be ill-fitting rags I had no intention of complaining. *Anything* to keep from having to go back for another fitting . . .

"That was rather expensive for what we'll supposedly be

getting," Jovvi remarked softly as one of the servants went looking for our coach driver. "I've been left with two solitary silver dins."

"So was I," I agreed, surprised by the coincidence. "I wonder if I should be glad I brought only a small portion of the silver I was given yesterday. Do they make a habit of leaving people with only two coins no matter now much they bring in? How would they manage something like that without seeing inside our purses?"

"I've heard that those with Earth magic sometimes have a special affinity for metals," Jovvi said, her brows lowered as she considered the point. "Apparently that sort can tell how much you have of copper, silver, and gold by sensing them, so there's never any guesswork involved. Businesses enjoy having someone like that as a clerk, which keeps them from lavishing attention on customers who look likely but actually have nothing to spend. Did they leave you with the same two dins, Beldara?"

I joined her in looking toward our third, but we might as well have spoken to the wood of the building behind us. Beldara gave no indication that anyone in the world retained life but herself, and she had no interest in talking to herself. Jovvi's latest attempt to smooth things over between us and Beldara had failed as badly as the first one, but this time Jovvi was more exasperated than sympathetic.

"People who refuse to accept the world as it is sometimes manage to make it over according to their own specifications," Jovvi commented, looking at Beldara's turned back with no approval at all. "More often they find themselves plowed under when the world gets around to remaking *them,* and usually because those fighting it have no idea of what accommodation means. Some people and situations have to be accommodated if you mean to change the rest, and pretending that that isn't so is the worst kind of self-delusion."

I expected Beldara to respond to that at least, but she continued to stand there hearing nothing and saying even less. I felt tempted to admire her singlemindedness, then decided to wait until I saw how far it got her. My own determination now seemed pale in comparison to hers, but it also seemed a lot more reasonable.

"I wonder what happened to the second coach," Jovvi said, bringing my attention to ours and the driver now beginning to drive it over to us. "I know it takes less time to fit men, but there were five of them and only three of us. If they're already back at the residence, I just may throw a temper fit."

"Let's ask our driver," I suggested, more than ready to join her in throwing the fit. As the coach pulled up in front of us I added, "Driver, what happened to our companions? And how long ago did they leave?"

"'Twaren't long, ma'am," the man answered, quickly pulling off his cap. "They come out here an' talked a bit, then asked if'n they culd go somewheres besides back t'th'house. We wus hired fer th' day, so it makes no nevermind t'*us* where y'go. When they heared thet, they set the littlest feller up with Zom, an' then went off."

"That sounds like they made Pagin Holter their guide, and went to have a look at the city," Jovvi said. "If I weren't so played out from being used as a lifeless dressform, I'd be interested in seeing the same. You do know the city well enough, don't you, Tamrissa?"

"I suspect I don't know it nearly as well as Dom Holter," I replied wryly. "My excursions away from home were always carefully supervised and chaperoned, so I know nothing of the sections the men will find most interesting. I do, however, have one small item of interest back at the house, and you ladies are more than welcome to share it with me."

"Now you've piqued my curiosity, so let's go back," Jovvi said with a laugh and one of her brilliant smiles. "Even if it doesn't turn out to be as good as what the men will find, I intend to tell them it was better."

I had to laugh at that, but Beldara was still in her own private world. The servant had already helped her into the coach, and although I'd included her in on the invitation it was fairly clear she had no intention of accepting. Which was just as well, since I had no real interest in sharing my secret pleasure with anyone but Jovvi. I felt certain she would enjoy it as much as I did, and I didn't care to waste it on someone who was sure to find fault no matter how good it really was.

And it would be nice to have another woman I could really talk to. As I settled myself on the seat beside Jovvi, I wondered if it would turn out to be possible for us to be friends. I'd never had a real friend, my parents had seen to that, and even my sisters and I had been discouraged from growing too close. We'd been like a group of strangers who happened to live in the same house, but now . . . maybe freedom wasn't the only priceless thing I'd finally have a chance at.

TWENTY-ONE

Lorand stood outside the tailor shop with the other men, trying not to show how fascinated he'd been with the experience just past. He'd actually had clothes *fitted* to him, by a professional who did nothing but produce clothes. All his life his mother had made his clothes, and if they hadn't fit quite right, well, at least they were too big rather than too small. During his growing years the clothes had usually become too small too fast, so his mother had gotten into the habit of making things too big to be outgrown before they were worn out. And the material that was supposed to be so cheap . . . he hadn't the nerve to admit the clothes would be the best things he'd ever owned.

"Is *thet* whut you gotta go through if'n yore a rich man?" Pagin Holter asked everyone in general after letting out a very sharp, deep breath. "If'n so, I gotta think agin 'bout tryin' t'be one. Don't like bein' mauled around like thet, I surely don't."

"Then you ought to make a very successful rich man," Clarion Mardimil told him with the heavy annoyance that wasn't aimed at their group. "Those people were quite impossible, treating us like so many cattle from a nearby field. My personal tailor would have screamed in horror had he been here to watch them."

"Even *my* tailor would have been outraged, and he's normally a very calm man," Eskin Drowd agreed, his tone dry and almost as annoyed as Clarion's. "Not to mention what they charged for the rags they'll be delivering tomorrow. All I have left is a single pair of silver dins."

"That's all I have left as well," Vallant Ro put in with a frown. "Did they leave any of us with more?"

Lorand shook his head along with everyone else, momentarily surprised, but then he understood.

"They must have had a clerk with Earth magic and metal affinity go over us," he said, drawing everyone's attention. "I knew someone like that back home, and even learned the trick myself. I know how much silver, gold, or copper goes into a penny or din, so by feeling how much of each metal a man has on him, I can tell exactly what coins he's carrying. Do they usually use that talent to rob people here in Gan Garee?"

"I have a feelin' this was done especially for *our* benefit," Vallant Ro said with a growl, glancing back at the tailor shop with an angry glare. "If I thought they were doin' it on their own I'd go back in, but somethin' tells me it has to do with those people runnin' the tests. They don't want us havin' money, but that's too bad about 'em. As soon as I get to the bank, I'll have all I need."

"And I," Clarion agreed with matching satisfaction. "If today and tomorrow weren't rest days I'd go straight there right now, but since they are I'll simply have to wait until the day after. In the interim I'll need to think of myself as penniless, for what can one do with just two silver dins?"

"Plenty, if'n y'know where t'spend 'em," Pagin Holter said, interrupting the muttered agreement of Ro and Drowd. "I got th' same two silver and nuthin' more I gotta spend it on—'cept a real good time. 'Pears t'me like I earned one."

"As did the rest of us," Drowd said firmly in support, finally dragging his attention from Lorand. The way he'd stared for a moment had been odd, as if he were trying to swallow down some kind of jealousy. "We all passed those wretched tests, and I for one would enjoy celebrating rather than returning to the residence for another early night. Are we all in agreement about that?"

"I think I might be best off not joining you," Lorand forced himself to say amid the general happy agreement. "Two silver dins are a lot better than none, and for me going to the bank would be useless. Why don't I just walk back to the residence, and—"

"Nonsense, man, I won't hear of it," Mardimil interrupted, actually looking outraged. "Your efforts were no less than those of the rest of us, which means you're entitled to the same good time. When I visit the bank I mean to withdraw gold, therefore allow me the privilege of pledging to replace your dins. That should allow you to spend your own now with an easy heart."

The others all added their own words of encouragement, which quickly ruined Lorand's resolve. He did want to celebrate with them, and Mardimil had seemed sincere about replacing the dins. It was even possible he might not need anyone else's silver, since there would soon be bonus money in gold to earn . . .

"Thanks," he said to them all with a smile. "I guess I'll be going along after all."

A half-teasing cheer went up, and then they were calling over the driver of their coach along with his vehicle. It turned out that the coach was theirs for the rest of the day, so another problem was neatly solved. Holter said he'd ride with the driver to direct him, but then turned back to those about to enter the coach.

"I know we wus told t'wear these here idents all th' time, but it might not go over so good where we's goin'," he told them in a low voice. "Mebbe it might be a good idear t'sorta slip 'em inside our shirts, like . . . after we leave this here place."

Since Holter had become their guide and mentor, they all nodded agreement before continuing on into the coach. When they were settled the coach began to move, and once they left the tailor's courtyard everyone began to look out eagerly for the first glimpse of where they were going.

"I must admit that this will be a new experience for me," Drowd said, absently slipping his tag on its chain inside his shirt. "My friends and I often met to drink tea and discuss any number of fascinating ideas and facts, but never to . . . carouse. In my circle it simply wasn't done, but I've always been curious."

"Then let me give you a word of advice," Ro said amiably, the only one of them simply enjoying the idea of what was ahead rather than brimming over with eagerness. "Carousin' is a lot more fun if you keep one eye on your purse, one on what you're drinkin', and never agree to gamble with the friendly stranger sittin' next to you. Especially if you think you can beat him at his own game. You can't, and the lovely lady whisperin' in your ear tellin' you you can is most likely his partner. And be especially careful with all the lovely ladies. Get the price firmly set before you go with her, and don't drink *anythin'* she might offer includin' tea."

Lorand felt a slight warmth in his cheeks at the mention of lovely ladies, since he'd only been thinking in terms of drinking with the others. Drinking had usually been a pleasant pastime on the few occasions he'd indulged, because his talent was able to neutralize strong drink no matter what it was made of. The degree he neutralized it to depended on whether or not he needed to be completely sober, or could allow himself to be pleasantly relaxed. But getting involved with professional women . . . that wasn't an approved undertaking with the people he'd grown up among. . . .

"That's another practice I've never indulged in," Drowd said, nodding thoughtfully to what Ro had said. "Paying lovely ladies for their favor, I mean. The established courtesans were too expensive for a young man who had yet to make his mark, and Regisard is a city which discourages droves of street-strollers. Only the occasional amiable female acquaintance was available, the sort who indulged for her own pleasure and curiosity rather than for gain. That means I have no idea what a fair price would be."

"Here in Gan Garee, I don't either," Ro said with a shrug. "There's usually a big difference between what the traffic will bear and what the lady will settle for, so you'd do well to ask Holter. When you're on another man's stampin' grounds, always follow his lead."

"I hadn't expected to follow Holter's advice about anything, and yet here I am," Drowd said with a small laugh. "I feel like a small boy on holiday in a sweets shop, determined to enjoy myself until I'm too stuffed to move. It's amazing what a strong sense of freedom one acquires when one first escapes strong parental restrictions."

"That's why my Momma and Daddy made sure my brothers and I weren't restricted at home," Ro said, now gazing sightlessly out the window. "They raised us to know right from wrong and how to make our own decisions, then turned us loose. When we first left home there was nothin' out in the world that we were crazy to try because we couldn't try it sooner, so we got into a lot less trouble."

"Your parents sound like wise and wonderful people," Lorand ventured when Drowd simply lifted one brow and remained silent. "You must miss them quite a lot."

"Yes, it so happens I do," Ro answered, his gaze still directed out the window. "I'm used to leavin' home on voyages, but somethin' tells me this won't be any ordinary voyage. We'll have to get past a lot of jagged rocks and sharp reefs before we reach clear sailin' to home."

That time no one commented, since even Lorand was thinking about home. It occurred to him to wonder how dedicated he would have been to making good during the tests if he'd had a home like Ro's to return to. Possibly not having a pleasant fall-back position gave him an edge over most of those he would compete against, but it was an edge he would have preferred not to have. What must it be like, to know that there were people at home waiting to greet your return with love and laughter . . . ?

"I believe I shall also admit that I have no experience with this thing called carousing," Mardimil said abruptly into the thickened silence. "Those of my class never indulge in such things, of course, so I find myself curious to know what will be involved."

"Surely you're joking," Drowd said, examining Mardimil where he sat beside Lorand in a way that suggested the young noble was an amusingly odd insect. "Those of the nobility indulge in carousing more often and more thoroughly than any of the so-called lower classes ever do. How is it you don't know that?"

"It could be he and his group of friends don't believe in that kind of behavior," Lorand suggested when Mardimil simply colored and didn't answer. He couldn't help remembering Mardimil saying he'd never *had* any friends, which could well mean he lacked experience in other areas as well. But just how far did those lacks go . . . ?

"I've never met a noble yet who didn't believe in indulging himself," Drowd said with a snort for Lorand's suggestion. "They tend to believe that the world and all the people in it are theirs for the taking and using, and most often they can prove the contention. Not that I'm really complaining, of course. When I become one of them, I mean to do the same myself."

"So you've decided the game is worth your full effort?" Ro

asked, finally turning from the window to examine Drowd. "I thought you considered the life of an academician the best a man could strive for."

"I believe I said I would have to find something of more interest to change my mind," Drowd corrected with a cool smile for the man sitting beside him. "I've discovered that the very strong possibility of becoming a member of the new Blending provides that interest, at least for me. I take it the situation holds no attraction for the rest of you?"

He looked around at all of them then, and not even Ro spoke up to agree. Lorand realized they *were* all thinking the same, no matter how farfetched the prospect really was.

"What about Mardimil's earlier objection?" Lorand found himself asking, just to hear Drowd's view of the matter. "Every Blending I've heard about for the last century or so has come from the ranks of the nobility. What makes you believe that things will be different this time?"

"What can there be beyond a belief in your own ability?" Drowd countered with an easy wave of his hand. "If the competing Blendings from the nobility are less able this year, those from the lower classes will have their chance. And how do you think the people who call themselves noble got that way in the first place? At some point in time, their ancestors were just as common as everyone else—until they found it possible to prove otherwise. It was *their* efforts which gave their descendants the free ride they now enjoy, so why can't I do the same for *my* descendants?"

"Now you're the one who must be joking," Mardimil said, looking downright scandalized. "Members of the nobility have *nothing* to do with commoners, not to mention starting out as one of them! Where could you possibly have gotten such a ridiculous idea?"

"The idea—and the indisputable facts—come from studying history," Drowd replied with his own ridicule. "It's possible to research every one of the noble families, and discover in what year they were ennobled. If that doesn't mean they were commoners before that, I'd like to know what it does mean."

Mardimil looked at Ro and then at Lorand, apparently waiting for one of them to say Drowd was either joking or lying. When Lorand shrugged to show that he'd been taught the same thing, Mardimil's expression turned stunned.

"You can't mean you've never heard that particular truth before?" Drowd said to him with a short laugh. "My dear boy, you *have* led a sheltered life, haven't you?"

"Some people do," Ro commented, looking out the window again. "And I think we've arrived."

Lorand glanced around to see that they'd all put their identification into their shirts, and then he joined the others in looking at the destination they'd reached. The street was narrow and its cobblestones uneven, but there was a good deal less refuse than other neighborhoods had contained. They'd come to a stop in front of a dirty brick building on the left with a swinging sign showing a horse in front of it, a pair of unlit lanterns hanging to either side of the sign. A short way down the street was what looked like a stables, presumably where the coach would wait for them.

Holter had gotten down from the box and come around to open the door, but Lorand had to nudge Mardimil when it was the lord's turn to leave the coach. Mardimil seemed really upset, and Lorand couldn't understand that. No noble wanted to admit that his ancestors had been commoners at one time, but they certainly all knew it. All but Mardimil, apparently, who looked like the sky had fallen on his head.

When Lorand finally made it out of the coach, the others were already following Holter through the unpainted wooden door of the brick building. Inside it was a lot dimmer than the late-afternoon sunshine, and it took Lorand's eyes a moment to adjust. Then he was able to look around to see a place that seemed little different from the posting house the men in his home district gathered in on rest days.

The area they'd come into was one large room, with hearths to both the left and the right separated by scattered tables and chairs. The hearth to the right was unlit and the benches near it unoccupied, but the one to the left had the usual workers preparing for the upcoming meal. A good-sized pig was spitted above the fire, and the way two of the workers kept glancing at it while they prepared salads and such said they were the ones turning the spit. Air magic was useful for that sort of thing, letting the workers turn the spit without actually touching it. And usually there was one with Fire magic, who oversaw the cooking fire to be sure the animal on the spit roasted evenly.

The pleasant, homey feel of the place told Lorand there

was probably more than one worker with Spirit magic present, and the comfortable temperature of the room said both Water and Fire magic were being used to adjust the air. Near the back of the room, where the long bar stretched, a boy was using Earth magic to freshen and smooth the wood shavings covering the floor. Lorand could feel his efforts to separate clean shavings from fouled ones, a harder job than one might expect. The clean shavings "felt" different than the dirty ones, but you needed to pull in a good deal of the power to make the difference instantly obvious. The boy didn't seem able to reach more of the power than any other ordinary user of Earth magic, which made the job both difficult and time consuming for him.

"Hey, Holter, you cur, where you been?" a deep voice boomed out from behind the bar. "We ain't seen you in almost a week, an' some been sayin' yer too good now t'mix with yer old friends."

"Too overworked an' too tired's more like it," Holter answered with a laugh, now leading the way to the bar. "I done it, Ginge, I passed the first o'them tests, an' now I'm on my way to th' big 'un. Wouldn't stop now if'n I could, but I did bring sum friends by t'help me celebrate. Don't know when I'll be gettin' back here, so I came t'say a proper g'bye jest in case."

"Never goodbye, Pag, boy," the big florid-faced man behind the bar corrected seriously. "Jest say til th' next time we meet. An' now I'd like t'meet these here gents."

Holter introduced everyone to the tavern owner Ginge, but Lorand noticed that neither man went into details about who Holter's friends were. Ginge looked to be a shrewd businessman behind the open friendliness of his facade, so it wasn't likely that he'd missed guessing they were all there to test for High positions. But saying that out loud might have made all of Ginge's tavern guests uncomfortable, especially the already-respectable number of ordinary customers scattered throughout the room. Best for everyone to say nothing, and just let them all enjoy themselves.

Ginge came out from behind the bar to personally lead them to a large table to the right, far enough away from the cooking and preparing that they wouldn't be disturbed by it. He also gestured to a boy standing behind the bar, who then came out to take up a complex-looking stringed instrument.

The music the boy produced with the instrument was marvelous, but Lorand was willing to bet he used more than his two hands to do it. With all those strings, easily more than a dozen, the incredible chords *had* to have more than four or five fingers producing them.

Holter interrupted their appreciation of the music by demanding the silver dins each of them had been left with. Once he had them he went to the bar where his friend had already returned, and engaged in a brief, low-voiced conversation. At the end of it he handed over all the silver including his own, then returned to the table with a very satisfied smile.

"This's gonna be a night we don't soon ferget," he confided with a small laugh. "Ginge'll keep us in brew long as we're still standin', an' he'll even feed us some. Th' girls is upstairs awready an' fresh as posies in a field, an' Ginge swore t'make sure they do us right. Let's have us sum brew b'fore we start visitin' 'em."

Ro and Drowd agreed with that as quickly as Lorand did, but Mardimil had to come out of distraction before adding his own agreement. Lorand had the distinct feeling that the young noble had more than one thing upsetting him, which meant he'd have to find the opportunity to speak to Mardimil alone. Lorand could believe that Mardimil had never had any friends, and he'd all but promised to be the first. It was enough that he'd let one friend down, if only by forgetting about him when he was certainly dead. Lorand now needed to *be* a friend as badly as Mardimil needed to have one.

But the first cups of brew served turned out to be really good, almost as good, in fact, as the music. Lorand sat back and decided to wait a short while before looking for a chance to talk to Mardimil privately. That was mostly because he now knew the time with the ladies was really going to happen, and the thought of visiting the girls upstairs had warmed him a bit. It still felt faintly wrong, but being in Gan Garee also made it oddly acceptable. Nothing a man should do at home, but here in the wicked big city . . . which was supposed to end up *being* home. . . .

Lorand took another swallow of brew, which helped him to ignore the confusion his thoughts were turning into. Tomorrow he'd sort out which was what, but tonight he'd have a wonderful time, if only to honor the memory of Hat.

TWENTY-TWO

Clarion sat and listened to the music filling the sleazy tavern, distantly surprised that it wasn't all that bad. Neither was the drink they called brew, a distillation far superior to the one of the same name once given to him by three of Mother's carriage drivers and grooms. The three had laughed when the very young Clarion had thrown up from the vile taste of the liquid, but Mother's sudden appearance—and immediate dismissal of the three—had ended their laughter.

It was now becoming possible to hear laughter among the patrons of that tavern, and Clarion nearly marveled at the experience of *not* being the cause of the amusement. He was instead a part of one group contributing to the laughter, which was an even more unique experience. For the last several minutes he had been using that to distance himself from the shock of what he'd been told—and the increasingly greater disturbance he felt over what lay ahead.

And that, of course, was the heart of the matter, not *knowing* what lay ahead. His companions had all spoken of "visiting the ladies," but Clarion was certain they had more than just visiting in mind. He'd nearly asked what that was, but some vague instinct warned him that admitting ignorance in that area would be far different from the supposed ignorance Drowd had admitted to. That Drowd fellow was a liar, Clarion knew it in his heart, but separating out the lies from the occasional truth the man spoke was difficult.

". . . sure you two don't mind?" Clarion heard the words from quite near, and came out of his thoughts to see that it was Ro who spoke, mainly to Coll but also to himself. "I'd be more than willin' to wait a while if you or Mardimil would rather go now."

"No, I'm perfectly willing to hold the table while you three visit the ladies first," Coll answered him, then looked toward Clarion. "You don't mind keeping me company, do you, Mardimil? We can have our turn with the ladies later."

"Of course we can," Clarion said, hopefully not too quickly. "I'd be pleased to stay and keep you company, Coll."

"Then it's settled," Coll said with a smile and a shrug. "You three have a good time, but make sure you don't wear them all out. We do want *something* left for us."

Holter, Drowd, and Ro laughed as they stood, each man solemnly promising not to "wear the ladies out." They then made their way toward a staircase to the left of the bar and the right of the cooking area, and quickly climbed out of sight. Clarion returned his attention to his brew, but stirred in faint annoyance in his chair rather than simply drinking. What *were* they going to be doing up those stairs?

"Mardimil, I think we need to talk," Coll said slowly with a good deal of hesitation. "I waited until we could have privacy, because the topic is a delicate one."

"You should have told me sooner that you wanted to speak with me privately," Clarion said with a smile, remembering with gratitude how Coll had defended him in the carriage against that odious Drowd. "Where conversations are concerned, privacy is easily had."

And then Clarion thickened some of the air around them in that special way he'd developed. Sounds became as muted as a thick door would make them, and even heavier odors were excluded. The remaining air inside their invisible bubble also began to circulate, constantly refreshed by what drifted through the delicate barrier he'd established.

"The first time I did this, I made a small error," Clarion confided to an amusingly surprised Coll. "I also turned the air of my barrier opaque, so that no one could see inside. Unfortunately that meant I was unable to see out as well, so I had no idea that everyone in the house was frantically trying to 'rescue' me from the unexplained horror that had swallowed me up. When I finally dispersed the barrier and reappeared, Mother was in the midst of hysterics. I had to promise never to do that again before anyone was able to calm her."

"Some mothers do tend to overreact," Coll said with a chuckle of appreciation. "My own mother had a fit once when she came out of the house and discovered how high I'd climbed into one of the shade trees. I'd seen my older brother do the same thing, you understand, so I couldn't comprehend why it was so terrible for *me*. The fact that he was seven while I was four wasn't a point I considered important."

"I wasn't permitted to climb anything at all," Clarion said with a sigh after sipping more of that brew. "In fact I wasn't permitted to do anything but behave like a gentleman, even at the age of four. Mother was usually too busy with society matters to play with me very often, but she was somehow always there if I wanted to try something forbidden. It didn't take long before I gave up on trying."

Clarion took another swallow of the brew to wash away the taste of depression. Mother had only been trying to protect him, of course, but because of that most of his life had been sheer monotony.

"I . . . take it then that you had . . . very little chance to do things most boys do," Coll said, looking faintly embarrassed but also determined. "Things like . . . getting together with girls very often . . . or even at all?"

The question was as delicately put as anything Clarion had ever heard, but it told him Coll had penetrated to the secret he had meant to keep private. Clarion felt tempted to be angry, but the opportunity to learn what was going on was too good to be missed.

"You're quite correct," Clarion admitted, finding it impossible to keep the stiffness out of his voice. "A gentleman such as myself is required to have very little to do with women beyond occasionally speaking to them politely. Even that was an extremely rare occurrence, as most of the ladies seemed reluctant to speak with me when Mother was there. A rudeness, Mother said, which proved them completely unsuitable for me."

"And a rudeness they always showed, I'll bet, because your mother was always there," Coll said, for some reason looking very sympathetic. "Didn't you ever . . . feel a need to be near women *without* your mother? To be alone with them somewhere private, and investigating the . . . urges you began to feel when your body changed and you became a man? Didn't you ever have to . . . do something in private when the women weren't available and the . . . urges became too strong to bear?"

"But no young man should be abandoned to privacy with his mother around," Clarion protested, automatically repeating what Mother had said from the time he was very, very young. "When my body changed I did feel certain odd but unimportant urges, and Mother stayed with me almost constantly while I learned to ignore them. A real gentleman does ignore them, you know, but most often has to struggle alone. I was fortunate in that I had Mother's help and support."

"Fortunate," Coll echoed, for some reason now looking faintly ill. "Smothered to suffocation, and I have to figure out how to get around that. But maybe there's a way . . ."

Clarion understood nothing of the muttering Coll was doing, but he'd just emptied his cup of brew. That was a much more important and immediate problem, but one that was quickly solved when Clarion spotted the pitcher which had been left on the table. He wasn't used to serving himself with anything, but critical situations called for unusual solutions. Pouring more brew into his rather nice pewter cup was actually very easy, and when he sat back after the satisfying accomplishment, Coll was apparently ready to abandon his muttering.

"Mardimil, I'm about to tell you something you obviously don't know," he said quite clearly, proving the point. "It will come as a shock, so I'd like you to brace yourself."

"Certainly, braced," Clarion acknowledged after another swallow of that marvelous brew. "Please do go on."

"Mardimil, there are some things about men that women never find out," Coll said, happily speaking slowly enough that Clarion was able to follow him. "Your mother, the dear soul, *thought* she knew what men do and are and so tried to teach those things to you, but she was mistaken. It was no fault of hers, of course, because men do keep these things secret from women."

Clarion nodded his understanding, congratulating himself on having discovered that point earlier. Mother did have his best interests at heart, but had mistakenly put him at a disadvantage instead.

"Yes, the poor dear did try her best for me," Clarion agreed with a fond smile. "It isn't her fault she doesn't know about—what?"

"That men are *supposed* to feel certain urges for women," Coll supplied, leaning forward a bit. "There are certain things a man does when he's alone with a desirable woman, and I'll describe those things for you in detail so you'll know what to do when we go upstairs. But what *you* must do right now is convince both your mind and your body that doing them is perfectly natural. If you don't, you'll find disappointment rather than pleasure."

Clarion nodded again, then obediently worked on his mind and body while Coll began to tell him what men and women did together in private. Distantly Clarion had the thought that at another time he would have found what Coll said to be extremely embarrassing, but right now it was merely fascinating. He'd never dreamed it was possible to do *that,* or particularly desirable even if it *was* possible. Before Coll was through, a hardening and tightening had begun in Clarion's body, and for the first time since he'd started to experience that feeling, he made no effort to ignore and dismiss it.

". . . so try to remember what I told you," Coll said, apparently winding up his lecture. "It's perfectly acceptable to touch the girl anywhere you please, but you mustn't hurt her in any way. Once you've completed your first experience you may feel the urge to cause her pain, but that will be anger stemming from having been unfairly denied so long. One of the town boys was raised by a mother like yours, and when he finally had his first woman the guilt and rage were too much for him. He beat up that poor girl something awful, and in school they had to take all the boys aside to explain why he'd done it. Just remember that it *isn't* wrong, only natural, and there's nothing to feel guilty about."

"Nothing for guilty," Clarion agreed with a smile, partly for Coll and partly for the brew. That sleazy tavern must have found the best vintage brew ever made.

"I'm going to keep enough alcohol in your blood to make sure you continue to look at it like that," Coll said, returning his smile. "I'll lower the amount a little when you join the lady to make sure you can perform, but a man's first time ought to be nothing but pleasure. If guilt gets involved, you can deal with it later."

"Later," Clarion agreed heartily, looking fondly down at his cup. Coll was such a fine fellow for a member of the lower class, but now that was completely understandable. At one time *everyone* was a member of the lower class, and Mother was sure to shriek and faint when he told her. Nobility were now obviously superior, but at one time. . . .

Clarion lost himself to his thoughts, but was pulled back

briefly by Coll to remove the barrier of air he'd constructed. He did that with slightly less ease than usual, then sat back to enjoy the music and the brew. He was part of a group, and although the group was low-class and therefore not good enough for him, he still enjoyed being a part of it. He'd never admit that to Mother, of course, not with *her* precarious health, but he didn't mind in the least admitting it to himself. . . .

Clarion had difficulty keeping his thoughts on one subject for very long, but when a girl appeared and began to dance to the boy's music . . . Watching her movements took no effort at all, except that his discomfort grew when she wiggled her body in his direction. She was a very attractive young lady indeed, and Clarion wouldn't have minded joining her in that dance. Once the idea came he began to get to his feet to do it, but Coll's hand on his arm kept him seated and then he changed his mind. He would look foolish dancing with the girl, and gentlemen weren't supposed to look foolish.

After a while Clarion noticed that people had approached their table, but not just any people. Drowd and Holter and Ro were back, and all of them looked thoroughly satisfied.

"That was rather different, but pleasantly so," Drowd announced as they all resumed their chairs. "Now you two may take your turns—unless one of you has decided not to indulge after all?"

There was something sleekly ugly behind the man's tone and question, but Clarion couldn't quite make out what. Ah well, it didn't really matter, not when it was now his and Coll's turn.

"You haven't changed your mind about indulging, have you, Coll?" Clarion asked with concern as he pushed himself to his feet. "I mean, I would never dream of interfering with the decision if you've made it, but—"

"No, Mardimil, I haven't decided against going upstairs," Coll interrupted, also rising to his feet. "Drowd seems to have a—strange—sense of humor, but I think from now on he'll work to curb it. Won't you, Drowd?"

"All I did was make the most innocent of remarks," Drowd replied, looking just as innocent, but then he glanced around and shrugged irritably. "Oh, very well, as you all seem to think it was inappropriate. I suppose it *is* unfair to jibe at a man in his cups, and Mardimil is clearly unused to spirits."

"That, sir, is another untruth," Clarion said as he drew himself up, determined not to let Drowd get away with lying again. "I have been accustomed to drinking wine with dinner for many years, so imbibing is far from unfamiliar to me."

"It's the brew," Coll said hastily as he began to urge Clarion away from the table with him. "Many people have no idea how potent it can be. He'll be just fine, especially after we make our visit upstairs."

"Yes, our visit upstairs," Clarion said happily, no longer interested in remaining at the table and showing Drowd up as the liar he was. "Let us indeed begin our visit upstairs."

There was a small amount of chuckling from the men they left at the table, but Clarion quickly dismissed all that from his mind. His need right now was to stay on his feet and reach the stairway, after which he would concentrate on climbing it. But the floor of that low-class place was so ridiculously uneven, much more so than he remembered it being when they'd first walked in . . .

"Here, let me help you a little," Coll said from his left, and then the man's hand was on Clarion's arm. Oddly enough Clarion immediately began to feel better, and even the floor became flatter.

"Thank you, but I'm perfectly all right," Clarion said to Coll with a smile, warming to him more and more as time passed. "I may never have been on my own before, but I'm discovering a definite talent for it. Don't you think I have a talent for being on my own?"

"Absolutely," Coll agreed with a return smile. "I can't remember ever meeting anyone with a greater talent for being on his own. Watch your step now, we don't want any broken bones I'd have to help mend."

Clarion looked down to see that they'd reached the stairs, so he did pay careful attention to climbing them. He'd expected them to be rough and splintery, but instead they were worn smooth and even looked shiny. Wood did behave like that, he recalled, although he was far more used to marble stairs. But if he did fall and break something, he wanted Coll to tend him. He'd never liked that Middle practitioner of Earth magic Mother had always summoned to tend them both. The man was a fool who always pretended to be better than he was, as though everyone didn't know the real truth . . .

"Okay, here we are," Coll said, and Clarion raised his eyes

from the top tread to look around. This second floor had a fairly wide hall with doors every few feet along the walls, some of which were closed. Lamps lit the area well enough to show imitation Denigan carpeting on the floor, a poor imitation in ghastly colors that were thankfully almost worn away. The walls and doors—and ceiling—could have used whitewashing at the very least, but Clarion lost the chance to comment on any of that when he noticed something far more important.

Someone—possibly Coll—had rung a small, tinkling bell, and now the open doors were beginning to show filled doorways. Girls were coming forward to stand where they could be seen, more unaccompanied women than Clarion had *ever* seen. Small, medium, and big women, young and not so young, dressed in . . . in . . . Clarion's body hardened so abruptly it made him grunt.

"Go ahead and choose the one you like best," Coll's voice urged, reminding Clarion that he was there. "Then you can join her in her bedchamber rather than standing around uncomfortably out here."

"Of course, choose one," Clarion echoed, finding that his fight for a bit more clarity of mind was actually succeeding. Clarion needed clarity and was getting it, and that made him laugh. The whole thing was silly, but he could scarcely wait to begin. First, however, he had to choose a girl.

Clarion was in such a state that he should have settled for the closest girl, but something deep inside refused to let him do that. He'd had to settle for far too many things in his life—like living without friends or a real knowledge of the world—that now he would exercise his first real choice. He walked from doorway to doorway and girl to girl, finally stopping in front of one lovely little pixie with long black hair and dancing green eyes.

"Dear lady, would you do me the honor of—entertaining me?" he asked her with a bow, the courtly words somehow coming effortlessly. "If you agree, I promise to be forever grateful."

"Oooh, I'd love to," the girl answered in a voice as sweet as her smile, offering him her hand. "Just you come with me."

Clarion took her hand and let her draw him into a bedchamber filled with lace and satin and perfume and softness, all in reds and pinks and white. She reached behind him to push the door firmly shut, and then she produced a delightful laugh.

"All the girls will hate me now, but I don't care," she said in that silken voice, looking up at him adoringly. "I'm just glad I'm the one you chose, and I intend to give you the most marvelous time you've ever had."

"Why would they hate you?" Clarion asked, raising her small hand to his lips. Her flesh felt so warm and wonderful in his hand, but not nearly as good as it felt to his lips. He had no idea that girls could be this magnificent, and was now eagerly looking forward to discovering even more marvels.

"They'll hate me because of what you said," the girl informed him, pressing herself ever more closely to his body. "You were so beautifully gallant, like a real gentleman, not like the rough bulls *they'll* get. I know it's what they're here for, but even girls like them need a little niceness every now and then."

Clarion looked down at her, and it was almost as if he could feel the pain this girl had experienced in life. So small and harmless she was, and yet there were those who would hurt her with blows as casually as he had been hurt by words. Distantly he remembered someone telling him to be gentle with her, but the caution had been unnecessary. He'd never find it possible to harm her . . . or anyone even remotely like her . . .

"Come to the bed," she whispered when he put a hand to her lovely face to experience the feel of her silky skin. "I want to give you pleasure, but these clothes are in the way."

She drew him along to the large bed the chamber boasted, one hung about with gossamer curtains of pink beneath tied-back drapes of red velvet. She parted the curtains to let him sit on the white linen, urging him to lean back against the red and pink cushions scattered across the white. Clarion did as she asked, then had the delightful experience of being undressed by someone who was neither his mother, his nurse, nor his valet.

When she found his identification on its chain around his neck, Clarion expected to have to explain what it was. But all she did was remove it and toss it after his clothing, not even pausing to glance at it. Her lips kissed each part of his body as she exposed it, and by the time she was through, his manhood threatened to burst the flesh it was made of.

"I can see you enjoyed that," she told him laughingly as

she joined him on the bed, her fingertips on his desire sending unbelievable flashes and tingles through his body. "Would you like to kiss me first, or would you prefer to be eased?"

Clarion had no real idea what she meant to do to ease him, but that made no difference. He took her in his arms and touched his lips to hers, once, twice, then took them strongly for a good deal longer. Her velvet lips answered his kiss with one of her own, passion bringing a moan to her throat. It felt so *good* to be doing that, so wonderful and right, even when he left her lips and pushed aside the sheer pink robe she wore to kiss one of her breasts. Her moan grew even louder, matching one of his own. Women were marvelous, and he couldn't imagine ever having enough of them.

When he'd finished tasting both of the girl's breasts, she squirmed out from under him, pushed him flat to the bed, then began to return the way he'd treated her. Only she did it to his desire, which quickly brought Clarion *beyond* the moaning stage. The pleasure was so intense that he felt he might well pass out, but the idea of missing even a moment of the sensation of her hand, lips, and tongue . . . No, Clarion knew he couldn't possibly allow himself to pass out, but stopping the explosion was completely beyond him.

He lay panting and throbbing for an unknown number of moments, and just as he felt he was returning to himself she also returned to him. It took her very little time to bring him back to the state he'd first been in, and then she was in his arms again, sharing another kiss.

Clarion wanted to investigate every inch of her, so he eventually pushed her flat and began to remove *her* clothes. She wore the strangest outfit he had ever seen, a corset which did nothing to hold in her breasts, a very small breech-sex in white cotton over her womanhood, cotton stockings in red held up by—*things*—coming down from the corset, and a sheer pink robe over the rest. Clarion touched and looked and kissed and toyed as he slowly unwrapped her, marveling at the differences between her body and his, and finally her whimpering and squirming changed to words.

"Please, love, please do it now," she begged, running her hands over his chest. "You're obviously made of steel, but you've turned *me* into pudding. Please do it now before I die of wanting you!"

She'd spread herself out as she'd spoken, her legs to either side of his body in an arrangement that brought his blood to the boiling point. Instinct howled in an effort to tell him what to do next, but suddenly Clarion had an idea how to avoid the clumsy gropings of inexperience.

"Guide me, sweet girl. Take me in your hand and guide me." He whispered the words as he kissed and nipped at her ear, making her slender body shiver where it lay beneath him. "Show me what pleases you most, and I will return the pleasure you gave me earlier."

"Here, I need you here," she responded in a moan, reaching between them to grasp his renewed need. Then she guided it to the entrance of ultimate bliss, which was the heat and slick moisture of her own desire. Clarion thrust within the incredible tunnel, experiencing feelings he had never even dreamt of, not only grasped tight but also pulled even closer when her legs locked about his waist.

"Stroke deep, my fleeting love," she murmured, already beginning to move her hips in the most marvelous way as her fingers buried themselves in his hair. "Our time together will be over much too soon, but for the precious few moments we remain here, make me yours completely."

Clarion had begun to match her movements with his own, and was so lost to the flood of new and incredibly wonderful sensations that he found it impossible to reply to her. Instead he simply kissed her, loving her deeply for this precious gift she gave with no hint of reluctance. He now knew why the others had been so eager to visit with these ladies, and knew as well that next time he would take his turn with those going first.

Their motion went from slow to rapid to frenzied, and after a time it culminated in that indescribable explosion that left pulsing tremors tingling through him. The girl seemed to experience the same, and after they'd rested side by side for a short while Clarion turned to her again. He felt there was more to learn about this wonderful new undertaking, and that conviction led him to a determination to discover the rest. They began again, and this time Clarion asked to be shown the little things that pleased her. He would learn and learn, and then . . . when he felt a bit more clearheaded . . . he would exhibit his knowledge to one whose face had taken to invading his dreams. But not *this* dream. Only this girl beside him belonged in it, and he would remember it forever. . . .

TWENTY-THREE

Vallant looked up when Coll rejoined them at the table, pulled back out of his thoughts by the arrival. He'd been reviewing conclusions and decisions—and feelings—since he'd gotten back himself, and was still too deeply enmeshed to notice what Drowd did immediately.

"The lordling isn't with you?" the academician said to Coll, the usual smirk in his voice. "What's wrong, wasn't he able to perform? If the ladies laughed him off the premises, we'll have to make an effort to search for him."

"If you intend to search, I can show you which chamber to begin in," Coll returned immediately, paying more attention to the cup of brew he reached for than he did to Drowd. "I happened to be right next door, and as I was leaving, they were starting what sounded like seconds. If you ask him nicely when he finally does get back, he may agree to give you pointers."

"Don't be absurd," Drowd responded with a snort, clearly ignoring Holter's muffled amusement. "The day will never come that that *boy* can teach anyone about anything. Can't you all see he's completely out of his depth in most things? He doesn't even know the realities of his own class."

"He knew enough to pass his initial test," Vallant pointed out, too annoyed with the man to keep silent. "And someone really should have told you the followin' truth sooner, Drowd: anybody who needs somebody to laugh at as badly as you do marks himself as a man who's afraid he's inferior. You talk about other people's lacks and faults just to make sure no one notices yours, but it's a really annoyin' habit that I'm mighty tired of. If you don't have somethin' good to say, just sit there without sayin' anythin'."

246

Drowd's face had gone red by then, but the growl Vallant hadn't been able to keep out of his voice apparently convinced the man not to argue—along with the way Coll and Holter stared soberly and silently. If either of them had disagreed with Vallant's assessment, their expressions at the very least would have shown it. They were clearly just as tired of Drowd's digging, and realizing that kept the young academician quiet.

So Vallant was able to go back to his thoughts in peace. It had taken him some effort to get around being called a coward and a quitter by Tamrissa Domon, but once he had he'd been able to really notice the rest of what she'd said—and the way she'd said it. When she'd announced *she* would not be too afraid to do things the way other people were . . . Vallant was surprised he hadn't been knocked over by what she said she was determined not to feel.

That girl is terrified of somethin' Vallant told himself for the dozenth time, *and that could be why she came down so hard on* me. *She sees givin' up as a threat to* her, *but why would that be? And why did she sound so strange when she agreed that her beauty always let her get her own way? There was bitterness in her eyes, and some kind of mockin' that had nothin' of amusement in it. . . .*

Those observances had bothered Vallant, so much so that they had even interfered with his pleasure. It wasn't until he found himself calling the girl under him Tamrissa that he noticed he'd chosen a light-eyed blonde, and he'd barely managed to finish what he'd started. That seemed to be because the girl *wasn't* Tamrissa Domon, a cooling realization he'd never before had trouble with. The thought of Mirra had never kept him from enjoying himself in other ports, and he'd known Mirra a good deal longer and better.

So why had the thought of a girl he barely knew and had never had—and one who clearly despised him—affected him so deeply? It was ridiculous and meaningless and puzzling and disturbing, and he couldn't seem to stop thinking about it—or find any reasons for it. He wasn't an inexperienced child, after all, falling in love with the first pretty face he saw without knowing anything about what lay behind that face. Hadn't he learned *anything* from his association with Mirra, like being wise enough to stay uninvolved? What in the world was *wrong* with him?

Asking himself useless questions became a rut too deep for

Vallant to climb out of, at least not easily. He was pulled out again when Mardimil finally returned, after a surprisingly long passage of time.

"You look like you enjoyed yourself, Mardimil," Coll commented as the young noble resumed his seat at the table. "If you died right now, it would take the burial people a week to get that smile off your face."

"At the moment I feel as though the smile is a good deal more permanent than that," Mardimil replied with a small laugh as he reached for his cup of brew. "That girl was the most delightful creature I've ever encountered, and I couldn't seem to tear myself away. Perhaps I'll return a bit later, once I've restored my energies."

Mardimil emptied the cup of brew down his throat, missing the amused glances Vallant exchanged with Coll and Holter. Which was a lucky thing, since he wouldn't have understood that their amusement was aimed at Drowd, who pretended to be too absorbed in the music and dancing to comment. To say Mardimil had been successful with the lady would have been to state the obvious, something Drowd clearly wasn't prepared to concede. It would have meant losing the butt of his nasty jokes, an end he'd apparently refused to accept.

With all of them back at the table, the landlord Ginge sent a girl over to ask if they were ready to eat. The answer was a unanimous yes, so they were supplied with a thick vegetable soup, hot pork sandwiches on fresh, seeded bread, small salads, and generous wedges of apricot pie topped with clotted cream. Not quite two silver dins worth from each of them even with the brew and girls included, but Mardimil asked for and was freely given another sandwich and a pot of tea. The rest of them were told to ask if they decided on seconds as well, which meant Ginge was an openhanded host. He would definitely make a profit on them, but not at the expense of their good time.

The meal put them all in a nicely mellow mood, and when a group of musicians came out to relieve the boy and his instrument they sang and clapped along with everyone else. The trio played the most popular tunes that were known all over the empire, but Vallant noticed that Mardimil didn't seem to know the words to any of them. He clapped and laughed and even hummed the refrains, but clearly didn't know any of the words. Maybe that was because of the mild drunk he was in the grip of, something that had been true even when he'd come downstairs.

The evening wore on pleasantly, despite the fact that the tavern had long since become full. Most of the patrons seemed to be regulars, and most of them came over at one time or another to greet Holter. The little groom seemed pleased to see them, but even though he laughed and joked with them he made no effort to introduce them to Vallant and the others. After a while Vallant realized that was to keep from having to invite all those strangers to join them, which was very thoughtful on Holter's part. He'd brought them to the tavern so they might enjoy themselves in peace, not to go on display for gawking outsiders.

Vallant heard himself think that, and couldn't hold back on a quiet snort of self-ridicule. Anyone coming over would be a gawking outsider, but he himself was part of the special inner group. Never mind that he knew where every door out of the tavern was located, but still had to fight feelings of confinement almost constantly. He was still *one of them,* and was obviously considered better than some. He found it ludicrous that even Mardimil, tipsy and innocent as he was, was still doing better than the dashing Vallant Ro. Maybe *he* ought to ask Mardimil for lessons . . .

That thought pushed Vallant back down into depression, a state which perversely kept him from getting anywhere near as drunk as he would have liked. Why depression kept him sober was a question he'd never been able to answer, but that didn't stop it from being true. He didn't even notice when the trio of musicians paused to take a rest, and no one came forward to replace them.

But he did notice when the half-dozen customers at one of the tables began to loudly demand that the music start up again. The six seemed to be relative strangers to the tavern, sitting apart from everyone else and doing nothing in the way of exchanging greetings the way most of the other patrons had. They were all dressed in rough trousers and shirts and coats, looking not only well-worn but dirty. That description fit both them and their clothes, and their manners were a perfect match.

"Just keep yer shirts on," the landlord Ginge called from behind the bar when their noise refused to stop. "They'll be back after they get a bite t'eat and swaller some brew, so jest—"

"We ain't payin' fer *them* t'have a good time," one of the six interrupted Ginge in a loud, belligerent voice. "We's here fer our own good time, so you c'n jest get 'm back out an' playin' like they's supposta be doin'."

"They'll be back when they's done," Ginge tried again, obviously working to hold his temper. "You all got full cups t'hold yer interest while yer waitin', so—"

"No!" the same man shouted, wobbling to his feet. "This stinkin' brew needs all th' help it c'n get, so you haul them three on out here! 'R mebbe you'd like *us* t'do sum entertainin'."

With that he took his cup and hurled it across the room, wetting everyone it passed and landing on a table to spill the two cups sitting on it. People all over began to come to their feet with a roar, and that seemed to be what the six were waiting for. The five still seated jumped up whooping and laughing, and a moment later a melee was in progress. Small bits of sand and wood shavings flew everywhere, small clusters of flames tried to set everything on fire, small gouts of water turned everything they touched soggy, and small winds blew the various messes directly in men's faces. Ginge and his people dropped everything and tried to break it up, but after a moment it was clear they didn't have a hope of accomplishing it.

"I'm gonna help Ginge," Holter said over the shouts and bellows, looking around at the rest of them. "If'n any a you feels like doin' th' same, it would shorely be 'preciated."

That was because more and more of the patrons were being drawn into the free-for-all, Vallant knew. He'd seen the same any number of times before, the exercising of ordinary talents in a way that was designed to let the combatants neutralize an opponent to a certain extent before the fight turned physical. The six who had started it all looked to be really practiced in the technique, which meant the landlord and his people needed all the help they could get.

"I'm with you," Vallant said as Holter began to turn away. "But before we start anythin', let's see how much more help we've got."

Coll nodded immediately when Vallant looked at him, and Mardimil apparently took Coll's willingness as a signal to add his own. They all then turned to look at Drowd, but the academician had somehow left the table without their noticing. Where he'd gone was something they didn't have the time to wonder about, not when the fight was already beginning to go physical.

"Let's work this together," Vallant said quickly, addressing the other three. "Mardimil—do you think you can use air to circle and separate out the six who started this? Good, because that's the most important part. Next comes surrounding them with wood shavings which Coll will do—to let the other patrons know something is happening—and last but not least will come Holter's and my contribution. Let's get started."

Mardimil raised his brows, obviously wondering what Vallant meant to do, but then he shrugged and turned to look at the six main rioters. He'd apparently decided that he'd find out Vallant's intentions soon enough, and got down to doing his part. Vallant watched with a good deal of satisfaction as the six troublemakers were suddenly and forcefully separated from everyone else, most probably thinking some invisible giant was to blame. That was pretty much the way it looked, with the defenders being shoved back away from the six, and the six themselves pushed together. Vallant had never before seen a High practitioner of Air magic work, but knew he was certainly seeing one now.

Once the separation was complete, Coll took his turn with Earth magic. Not only did he use almost every wood shaving on the tavern's floor to surround the men, he also seemed to have used them to separate each of the six from the others. Again, the amount of strength and control necessary to do that was impressive, but since it was now Vallant's turn he left being impressed for some other time.

Instead he opened to his own magic, and brought down the coldest, most chill water he could reach that was still liquid. Holter chuckled as he followed suit, obviously having waited to see what Vallant had in mind. Together they gave the six men the coldest baths they could ever have had, ignoring the men's howls while they made sure none of the icy deluge ran off onto the tavern's floor. If the six had started that trouble because they were drunk, the treatment they were now getting ought to sober them up to the point of peacefulness again.

Once each of the six had been thoroughly doused, Vallant returned the water to the upper skies. When Holter followed his example, Vallant was then able to signal Coll to release the wood shavings. As soon as the shavings had settled back in place Mardimil withdrew the fence of air, and they were able to look at the six again.

The men stood shivering and white-faced, obviously scared sober and calm, which was what they'd been trying to accomplish. When all six broke and ran for the door, fighting each other to scramble through, Vallant joined Coll, Mardimil, and Holter in laughing uproariously.

The laughter felt good, but suddenly it came to Vallant that they were the only ones in the large room laughing. Everyone else, patrons, servants, workers—and Ginge—stood and stared as though looking at ghosts. The laughter trailed off as one by one Vallant's companions noticed the same thing he had. The six men who had run out had been terrified, and the ones who remained weren't far from being the same.

"Whut's wrong with th' buncha you?" Holter suddenly demanded into the thickened silence, looking around from face to face. "You sayin' you wanted them bungers t'tear this place apart? Since we got it stopped, you oughta be thankin' us!"

"We do thank you," Ginge said after a long hesitation, during which no one seemed to move except for the requirements of breathing. "Leastways *I* thank you, this bein' my place 'n all. It's jest . . . I ain't *never* seen nothin' like that, or felt it neither. The power you used t'bring that there water down . . . both a you . . . it felt like a pair a kicks from a giant! How d'you pull in that much, an' why ain't you all burned up 'cause you did?"

"An' whut you gonna do wiv it next?" a voice whispered from somewhere, a man's voice trembling like a frightened girl's. That seemed to be the question bothering everyone there, even though they all surely knew the law. Using the power to harm someone usually got you sent to the Deep Caverns—but only if you weren't really strong. It was unheard of for a High to be condemned, and the whispers claimed that that was so no matter what they did. Vallant had heard—and believed—the whispers himself, so their next move was obvious.

"I think it's time we thanked you for your hospitality and said good night," Vallant announced as he rose to his feet, trying to keep his tone light and friendly. "This is surely the best tavern in Gan Garee, and I believe I also speak for my friends when I give you thanks for makin' us welcome here. We'll remember our visit fondly."

By then the others had also gotten to their feet, so Vallant led the way to the door. Men stepped back out of their path without saying a word, and every face showed the same trembling uncertainty. Were they serious about going without harming anyone, or would they suddenly turn around and lash out with furious anger behind the monstrous power they controlled? No one seemed to know, possibly not even when they were all outside and had pulled the door to behind them.

"I never expected *anyone* to look at me like that," Coll said after a moment, sounding somewhat shaken himself. "They were afraid of us, but all we did was help them. Why would that make them afraid?"

"Probably because they've never known anyone even as strong as a Middle," Vallant offered when the others remained silent. "I never knew a Middle, not personally, and I remember agreein' with people that you just can't trust the ones with real power. Since I wasn't into showin' off, no one really understood how strong *I* was. That made me one of *them* rather than one of the faceless group with *power,* and I never saw myself any other way. Now . . ."

Now he and the others had suddenly had the ground cut out from under their feet, changing their stance in a way that would never let them go back to what they'd been. Realizing that made Vallant feel horribly lonely, and led to another disturbing question: he'd been hoping that something would happen to let him go home, but *could* he go back? If his own family ever looked at him the way those people in the tavern had . . .

"We better get th' coach an' go back to th' house," Holter said in a defeated voice, giving Vallant the impression that the small man had already been barred from ever going home again. "Wouldn't want Ginge t'look out an' find us standin' here, not after how nice he wus t'us . . ."

No one seemed willing or able to argue that, so they began to trudge along the street toward the stable where the coach was supposed to be. For an outing that had started out so well, the only way it could have ended worse would have been to have guardsmen witness their performance.

Vallant had finally remembered something the others had

clearly also forgotten, certainly because of all the brew they'd had. Individuals might be sent to the Deep Caverns for using their ability to harm others, but those of different aspects who tried to act together were summarily executed. Vallant and the others hadn't exactly acted together and all five aspects hadn't been represented, but the fine point of difference wasn't one Vallant would have enjoyed arguing before a court. Not when they weren't yet Highs, just a handful of hopefuls. . . .

"That reminds me," Vallant said suddenly as they approached the stable entrance. "Drowd is still missin'. If he hasn't already come out ahead of us, we'll have to send the driver back to the tavern to look for him."

The others muttered something in agreement without looking overly concerned, and Vallant couldn't blame them. A man like Drowd was usually popular, but only because those flocking around him were afraid of what he might say about them if they *weren't* his friend. With no one in their group willing to hear barbs against any of the others, Drowd's popularity had taken a severe beating. If he ended up gone for good, it was unlikely that anyone but the testing authority would be upset.

The large stable doors stood open with a small amount of lamplight pouring a short way out into the dark. Just inside to the left, in a space about three stalls wide and deep, was a sitting area fixed up by and for the stablemen. Old, mismatched wooden chairs stood around a splintery wooden table with almost all of its finish gone. A large stable lantern illuminated the area, showing an old man and two boys along with their driver, all four sipping brew from battered cups and smoking pipes. When their driver saw them he rose to his feet, murmured something which the old man nodded to with a cackle, then proceeded to empty his pipe.

"Thought ya might be along soon, so I had th' horses hitched t'th' coach," he drawled as he made sure the dottle hadn't a single spark left to it. "That other 'un, he tried t'tell me you wusn't comin' out t'night atall, so I oughta take him back alone. Got mad when I said I'd wait some t'be sure, an' now here you all is. Sure glad I waited."

All that was said without looking at Vallant or any of the others, and then the man ambled back into the stable proper to get the coach. He used a small glow in the palm of his hand to light his way, one that wasn't likely to frighten any of the horses.

"And you were worried about Drowd," Coll said to Vallant, his air of disgust clearly aimed at the academician. "The man was ready to abandon us here, without even knowing whether or not someone would call the guard down on us. We ought to ask them to put him in a different residence."

"They won't agree," Mardimil said, still showing a bit of that dreamy air that suggested he hadn't yet thrown off the effects of the brew. "Since they don't yet know which of us will win High positions, they won't take the chance of really offending any of us. And I meant to ask: why did we have to leave so early?"

"I'll explain it all tomorrow," Coll told him, which made Mardimil smile and nod agreeably. Vallant thought it was a shame that they couldn't keep Mardimil permanently drunk. He wasn't nearly as pleasant when he was sober. . . .

Their driver brought the coach forward to where they could board without worrying what they might be stepping into before stepping into the coach. A shadowy figure already sat inside in one corner, but that presented no problem at all. Holter wordlessly climbed to the box beside the driver where he'd sat on the way there, leaving just enough room inside for the others.

"Well, I'm very relieved to see you all again," Drowd said in an uneven voice once everyone was settled and the coach had begun to move. "Would you believe that that fool of a driver wanted to take me back alone, leaving the rest of you here? I refused to allow it, of course, and stayed in the coach to be certain he didn't leave with it anyway. We should all report the man tomorrow, to be certain he isn't used again."

Vallant simply looked out his window without replying, leaving it to the others to tell the man what they thought of him. When the others also remained silent, Vallant smiled faintly into the darkness. Drowd would have no idea whether or not they believed him, and that would turn out to be worse for him than simply being told off. Maybe tomorrow one of them would get around to telling him what they thought of him, but right now the pain was still too fresh and intense. As if by the stroke of some magic wand, they had all suddenly become outcasts! Even if he found a way to go home, wouldn't people take to pointing at him and whispering among themselves? They hadn't yet realized how different he was before he left, but now, after they'd had a chance to think about it. . . .

Vallant sat staring out the window at the dark streets of a dozing city, the tears in his eyes blurring the scene's details but matching the light rain which had started. He hadn't cried since the time he was very young, and probably wouldn't be crying now if he hadn't had so much brew. But he had had the brew, and the pangs of loneliness and homesickness were very strong and painful. Never to go home again . . . how were you supposed to think about that *without* crying?

Vallant felt very small and very helpless and alone, almost the way he'd felt once before in his life. Back then he *had* been small and helpless, and he'd been certain things would have been different if he'd been a grown man. Well, he was a grown man now, and things certainly were different . . . so different he almost couldn't stand it. . . .

TWENTY-FOUR

Jovvi felt more rested by the time they got back to the residence, which meant her annoyance was harder to control. Beldara Lant flounced off to her room without a single word to anyone, determined to stick to her beliefs or die trying. And without the men the house sounded almost empty, which reminded Jovvi that they were out having a good time. She would have enjoyed doing the same, but not without a guide who knew which areas to avoid. At least Tamrissa had been honest enough to admit she knew nothing about the city where partying was concerned . . .

And thinking about Tamrissa, Jovvi saw her heading for the small library after gesturing that Jovvi should follow. The girl had mentioned something about a secret she wanted to share, and Jovvi really was curious. The secret wasn't likely to be anything really forbidden like bramleaf juice or holban resin, not when those two drugs left their mark clearly on users. Tamrissa wasn't a drug user, despite the extreme pain Jovvi could sometimes feel inside her.

So Jovvi followed her hostess into the library, where Tamrissa rang for tea. The service was brought rather quickly, and Tamrissa took a moment to ask the serving girl to tell the cook that the men probably would be absent for dinner. Then she closed the door behind the girl, and turned to Jovvi with a smile.

"Let's fix ourselves cups of tea, just in case Cook decides to come by raging and crying," she said. "If it's still quiet once the tea is ready to drink, it will be safe to bring out my hidden treasure."

Jovvi laughed, liking the way Tamrissa was trying to provide an adventure for her, then joined her in pouring and sweetening cups of tea. It didn't take long, of course, but apparently it took just long enough.

"If Cook were coming, he would be here by now," Tamrissa said, turning to give Jovvi a look like an eager child. "The coast is therefore clear, so make yourself comfortable while I fetch the treasure."

Jovvi took her cup to the table between a pair of leather-covered chairs, put her purse and hat on the table as well, then followed instructions about making herself comfortable in one of the chairs. Tamrissa had gone to one of the bookshelves and removed two of the books, then reached in behind them. What she withdrew was a small leather-covered box in red, the sort which usually held writing paper of good quality. The two books were returned to their places on the shelf, but the box was carried over to where Jovvi sat.

"You must promise never to tell anyone about this," Tamrissa said, not yet opening the box. "I bought it the day after my husband died, using some of the gold he kept in there. If any of the others find out they'll expect to share it, and I no longer have the gold to replace it. It's horribly expensive, but I think you'll agree it's worth the price."

"Good grief, girl, what *is* it?" Jovvi couldn't help demanding. "Diamonds would fit in that box, but I can't imagine people expecting to share them. Beyond that I can't think of a single—"

Jovvi's words ended abruptly when Tamrissa opened the box, showing something that Jovvi had heard about but had never tried. It was something the nobility most often kept to themselves, paying outrageous sums which even many merchants couldn't afford to match. It really was a treasure, and it was—

"Chocolate," Tamrissa said with a smile for the stunned expression Jovvi certainly wore. "Someone brought a tiny amount to Gimmis once, trying to bribe him somehow in relation to some business deal. My husband was rather narrow and uneducated, so he had no idea what it was. After he threw the man out, he tossed the gift into the trash without giving it a second look. I rescued it when he went for his nap, and ate every bit of it myself. He eventually found out what it was and cursed himself for throwing away a small fortune, never guessing it hadn't been wasted after all. Try a piece."

Jovvi hesitated only an instant, politeness quickly falling under the wheels of driving curiosity. A patron of hers had once promised to bring chocolate as a gift, but he'd never returned after making the promise. She'd heard later that he'd killed himself after losing his fortune to gambling and fast living . . .

But the uneven chunk of brown stickiness was now between her fingers, and Jovvi could wait no longer. She brought it to her lips and licked it gently, then took a very small bite. Pleasure exploded against her taste buds as the tiny bite melted along her tongue, spreading indescribable ecstasy all through her. She hummed a little with the delight of it, and the sound came out like a moan. It was marvelous, well beyond anything she could have imagined, and she meant to savor every small crumb and smear of it.

"Don't be ashamed to lick your fingers when the rest is gone," Tamrissa said with a laugh, having taken the other chair after helping herself to her own small chunk. "I always do, and I don't care how unladylike it's supposed to be. Letting any of this go to waste would be worse than a crime against humanity."

"Yes, let humanity take care of itself," Jovvi agreed, speaking only after all trace of the first taste was gone from her mouth. "And to the Deep Caverns with supposed ladylike behavior. This is almost as good as being with a man."

"How can you compare the two?" Tamrissa asked with a strange sound, giving most of her attention to the brown chunk she nibbled at. "Being with a man is vile and unending pain. Chocolate is the most marvelous thing ever created. The two can't possibly be discussed in the same breath."

"It's . . . becoming increasingly obvious that you weren't happy in your marriage," Jovvi said, approaching the subject carefully. "Did your husband change after you married him?"

"If at all, only for the worse," Tamrissa answered, now deliberately looking at the chocolate rather than at Jovvi. "My parents didn't care what Gimmis was like, they just cared that he was willing to name my father as his heir if they married me to him. But that won't ever happen again, because I won't let it. I'd rather be dead than be married off a second time."

"That's what you meant when you said you'd be willing to give up your beauty to Beldara," Jovvi suddenly remembered, studying the girl. Tamrissa had that fragile sort of beauty that aroused most men, either for good or ill depending on their individual natures. Jovvi was quite glad her own beauty was completely different; if she'd looked like Tamrissa, she might not have survived.

"It looks like we have something in common then," Jovvi said after a brief hesitation, now studying her own piece of chocolate. "My mother sold me when I was very young, but not into anything as nice as this house. The men who bought me expected to pass me on to one of their regular customers, someone who bought young girls rather often. I learned he bought so many because he tended to use them up, so I escaped before they were able to deliver me. Afterward I spent a very long time hoping they went back to my mother to reclaim my sale price."

"That would have served her right," Tamrissa said with a faint smile, raising those vulnerable violet eyes to Jovvi's face. "I've always wanted to see something of the same done to *my* parents, but they're much too careful to be caught like that. How did you live when you escaped? If you were that young, who did you find to protect you?"

"There was a family I lived with for a while," Jovvi

answered, unsurprised that she told this girl what few others had ever learned. A bond seemed to be growing between them, almost a sisterhood . . . "The father of the family caught me trying to steal some food, and forced me to sit down and eat it along with more than I'd had the nerve to try for. They weren't rich people by any means, but they said that if anyone saw me leaving their place looking half starved, they'd never live it down. I stayed with them for almost two years, and when I finally began to earn more than coppers as a courtesan, I sent them silver on a regular basis."

"You were a courtesan?" Tamrissa asked, raising her brows before wrinkling her nose. "How did you stand it? Oh, of course, you were probably forced into it. Isn't it wonderful that now you won't ever have to go back to it?"

"My dear girl, I *wasn't* forced into it," Jovvi said gently with a sigh, knowing she had an almost impossible job on her hands. "You have to understand that not all men are like the one you married, and being with them is pleasure rather than pain. My first man was really a boy, the oldest son in that family I stayed with. He was beautiful and I fell in love with him immediately, but he refused to touch me until I grew old enough to join him rather than be used by him. He taught me what pleasure there was to be had, and then he left home to make his own way in the world."

"He left you just like that?" she asked, wide-eyed again. "I knew men were no good, and you're just too nice to understand it."

"He first asked me to go with him," Jovvi said with a fond smile of memory, remembering the night they'd said good-bye. "But I knew he didn't really love me, he was just trying to be gallant about it all. By then I was no longer *in* love with him, so I refused to go along. He didn't need two mouths to feed while trying to make something of himself, and I had plans of my own. The agent of a courtesan residence had seen me and given me the card of his principal, so I decided to see if I could make a go of it."

"Obviously you did," Tamrissa said, looking Jovvi over from head to foot. "Your clothes are as beautiful as your face and figure, so you must have earned a *lot* of gold. But if you weren't forced to be a courtesan and you enjoyed it, then . . . maybe you aren't as glad to be here as I thought . . ."

Jovvi could feel the girl's inner drawing away, and

strangely enough it had nothing to do with her being a courtesan. It had to do with wanting to be there to take the tests, something Tamrissa was more than passionate about. Taking and passing the tests was nearly an obsession with her, and Jovvi couldn't bear the idea of ruining the closeness they'd begun to feel.

"Actually, I'm delighted to be here," Jovvi said quickly, to keep Tamrissa from withdrawing to the point of refusing to listen. "Being sent to Gan Garee got me away from my sponsor Allestine, who had made up her mind to keep me in her residence until I grew old and gray. I'd planned to open my own residence here when I failed the first test, but if I'd failed I wouldn't have opened anything. Now . . . Tamrissa, what do you really think our chances are to become part of the new Blending? I mean, it's just a silly dream, isn't it? *We* aren't members of the nobility, but if we ever won a place . . . no one could try to own us again."

"That's exactly what I've been thinking," the pretty child said with a sigh, her emotions relaxing back to where they'd previously been. Pretty child . . . Jovvi was just about the same age as Tamrissa, but felt decades and centuries older. Her own life hadn't been easy, but she'd learned it was possible to escape things at a very young age, and then she'd had the love and support of her foster family. Tamrissa's twisted emotions said she'd had none of the same, which made Jovvi wonder how she'd managed to stay sane.

"I keep telling myself that thinking about becoming part of the new Blending is foolish, but some bit of me doesn't want to listen," Tamrissa said, idly licking melted chocolate from her fingers. "I can't imagine that any of us here have the least chance, but Jovvi—wouldn't it be wonderful?"

Jovvi was in the midst of tasting her own chocolate again, so she didn't answer immediately. Once it was all down, though, she said, "Being completely free would be wonderful. Being a member of the new Blending would be—what? What do we know about the life they live, or what they're required to do? From time to time I asked some of my noble patrons, but even they didn't really know. They repeated the latest gossip about this or that threat having been overcome, but there were never any details. Do *you* know anything more about it? Have you ever even *seen* any of them?"

"Once or twice," Tamrissa said, frowning now. "Two of

them came to the inn my parents and I were staying at when I was a lot younger. We were on our way back to Gan Garee, and so were they. Those who had accommodations on the top floor of the inn were put out of them, to make room for the Blending members and their entourage. Mother and father and I were forced to sleep in the same room rather than in the three we'd had, because places had to be found for those who'd been put out. And after all that, we only got the briefest glimpse of the two in the morning when they left. That was actually the closest I've ever gotten."

"So we don't really know what's involved with being members of a Blending," Jovvi said, just about thinking out loud. "High practitioners, on the other hand, are very visible, and live like and among the highest nobles when they aren't needed for the most important jobs. But come to think of it, I've never seen a High at work, or met anyone who has. Middles are everywhere and doing what has to be done, but you just hear stories about Highs."

"The same way you hear them about the Blending," Tamrissa agreed, the beginnings of suspicion clear behind her nod. "I don't like the sound of that, since High is supposed to be what we're trying for. If Highs don't *do* anything, why do they go to so much trouble gathering us in?"

"Not to simply put us out of the way," Jovvi decided after thinking about it for a moment. "If that was all they wanted, they could have had us killed as soon as we were located. Accidents happen all the time, and if some of them had happened to us before we knew we were candidates for High, no one would have thought a thing about it."

"And they do need challengers for their Seated Highs," Tamrissa pointed out. "The law says they have to win against a variety of challengers, otherwise they're automatically ejected from their positions and never allowed to hold them again. That's part of the law that can't be changed, but it's not likely to be all they're after. If it were, saving a few potential Highs to do the challenging would be the only thing necessary."

"So Highs are needed for *something,* but not necessarily the something we had in mind," Jovvi said slowly, then looked directly at Tamrissa. "If it would do any good, I'd suggest we rethink our plans to participate. I don't like dealing with people who have private objectives in mind, but participating has stopped being our choice. We have to go on with it, but we'll also have to do some serious thinking. Maybe we'll find a way to protect ourselves."

"And still get what we're after," Tamrissa said, the words grim. "Without the protection of this competition, my parents will come after me again. They'll arrange another marriage like the first, I'll refuse, and shortly thereafter, when they realize they can't change my mind, I'll be dead. That's better than going along with them, but dying isn't my first choice of desired outcomes. I'd rather fight to get a place of my own . . . even if I'm not always sure I can do it. . . ."

Jovvi's brows raised at that strange combination of feelings, so unusual was it to find the two together. When Tamrissa spoke of refusing her parents, her emotions were steel-hard and twice as determined. But when she mentioned gaining something for herself using her abilities, the doubt and lack of confidence turned her determination to water. At first Jovvi couldn't understand how the two fit together, and then the answer became obvious.

"Of course you can do what you want to," Jovvi said, doing her best to project utter conviction without actually using her talent. "I'd guess that your biggest problem is having no one on your side, no one to occasionally lean on. Standing alone is very tiring, and when the weariness comes it brings memories of the lies you've been told. Your enemies want you weak and helpless, so they've always insisted that you were nothing else. Most of the time you know better, but when you tire you become afraid that they're right."

"At one point they *were* right," the girl forced herself to say as she leaned back and closed her eyes. "I let them force me into the first marriage, and if I'd really been strong I wouldn't have. If something happens once it can always happen again, even if you decide not to let it."

"I repeat, it only happened because you had no one on your side," Jovvi said slowly and clearly, fighting off the waves of defeat coming from the girl without trying to change them artificially. "You now have *me* on your side, which gives you more than a single choice. If we decide we don't like what those people are up to and there's a way to get out in one piece, we'll take it and set up a residence together. With the two of us in it, we'll soon have so much gold we'll have to give it away to keep the banks from breaking under the load."

"That's a lot of gold," Tamrissa said with a laugh that broke her painful mood, but then she reddened. "I really like your idea, but *me* in a residence . . . pretending to be a courtesan . . . I wouldn't have the first idea of what to do. Not to mention never being able to stop blushing. I can't imagine many men wanting a woman who looks as though she's fallen into a vat of red dye."

"You'd be surprised what men want and like," Jovvi said with her own laugh. "Most of my former patrons would be delighted with your blush, since it makes you even lovelier than you are. And you can be sure no one like your late husband would be allowed through our doors. I never have trouble telling that sort, and no longer even bother making the effort to keep them from hurting me. I simply refuse them, and spend my time with men who have no sickness in their minds. And speaking of *that* sort, stay away from Eskin Drowd. I knew he was one from the moment we first met."

"I'm not surprised," Tamrissa said, no longer quite as flustered. "He really enjoys hurting people with his words, just the way Gimmis did. But I still can't imagine finding it pleasant to be with a man, so I'm going to try to find a way to make this High practitioner thing work. Maybe no one ever sees them doing things because what they do is secret. What I can't figure out is what that sort of thing would be."

"If their work is secret, there are only two possibilities," Jovvi answered, delighted to feel the balance which had returned to Tamrissa. "Either they're working against the enemies of our empire, or they're working against our own people. Nothing else I can think of would require secrecy."

"In what way could they be working against *us?*" Tamrissa asked, looking thoughtful rather than disbelieving. "People would notice interference that strong, and there would be rumors and gossip and guesswork flying everywhere. Have *you* ever heard anything like that?"

"No," Jovvi admitted with a sigh, forcing down her annoyance over not being able to figure the thing out. "And right now we're the ones flying everywhere, but without solid facts there's nothing else we can do. Let's find another subject to talk about for a while, specifically one *you* can talk about while I finish my chocolate. It's just about all melted between my fingers, and I want to eat it before I lose any."

"Go ahead," Tamrissa invited with a laugh, watching as

Jovvi did just that. "And if you'd like another piece, just help yourself."

Jovvi was tempted to accept the offer, but couldn't quite bring herself to do it. Tamrissa had been more than generous sharing the treasure in the first place, and to take more of it just wouldn't be fair. Maybe another time, after dreaming and remembering for a while. . . .

Tamrissa didn't have a second piece either, but instead replaced the leather box in its hidden niche. After that they shared the tea, rewarmed to the proper temperature by Tamrissa's talent. And they stayed away from important or unpleasant topics, to give themselves a chance to think clearly. Their futures depended on what they would learn or figure out, which made it something they'd be idiots to rush.

Jovvi returned to her room to freshen up just before dinner, taking the opportunity to check on the safety of her gold. It was still just where she'd hidden it, but the place under the loose floorboard in the corner of the room no longer looked as safe as it had. That business at the dress-maker's had disturbed her, leaving each of them exactly two silver dins. If they'd used Earth magic there to deplete the applicants' resources, they could just as well come to the house to do the same thing. She would have to find a better place to hide her gold, one that couldn't be found even by someone with Earth magic. And there might be just the place . . .

By the time Jovvi went down to dinner, she felt a good deal better. The golden statuette on a wooden pedestal out in the hall had been pure gold rather than simply gilded, and the beautifully carved pedestal had been constructed of lacy lengths and sections joined together to make its pattern. That meant there were empty places inside the pedestal, most especially in the almost-solid portion the statuette stood directly on. Putting her savings in that portion and wedging it in with rags brought the gold of her coins close to the gold of the statuette. If that didn't disguise and protect her cache nothing would, short of depositing it in a bank once they reopened. That was something she'd have to think about, but not right away. She might end up being glad her gold was close to hand . . .

Dinner consisted of small game birds baked in a variety of sauces, vegetables with complementary sauces, bread, cheese, and wine. Jovvi took the chair next to Tamrissa's rather than her own, but Beldara Lant sat in her usual place and still pretended to be alone in the world. Her anger and spitefulness hadn't eased in the least, nor did it seem like it would. Apparently Beldara was someone who never changed her mind once she'd made it up, and telling her about the suspicions Jovvi and Tamrissa had would have been a waste of breath. Ah well, the girl was too singleminded to have been much help anyway.

After the mostly silent dinner, Jovvi proposed that they all use the bath house together. Beldara got up and left the room even before Jovvi finished speaking, which made *her* response perfectly clear. For some reason Tamrissa also tried to beg off, but Jovvi wasn't in the mood to be alone so she insisted. Tamrissa finally gave in and agreed, and the two of them went for lounging wraps and slippers, then walked together to the bath house.

"I still think we should have brought clean clothes rather than wraps," Tamrissa said as they reached the bath house door. "We don't know when the men will be back, and they could find us parading around almost naked. Which reminds me . . ."

What the girl had been reminded about was the "occupied" sign, which she found pushed to the wall to the left of the door. She readjusted it to hang directly on the door in plain sight, then led the way inside.

"I hope it works better this time than it did the last," she said over her shoulder as Jovvi shut the door behind them. "That annoying Vallant Ro walked in on me while I was trying to soak the aftereffects of the test out of my poor, abused body, and refused to wait until I was out of the water and decently clothed again. I could feel him staring at my body until I got it covered, and I've never been so embarrassed in my entire life."

"That was obviously because you're not used to being appreciated when being looked at," Jovvi said comfortably, beginning to get out of her clothes. "That makes all the difference, and eventually takes all the embarrassment out of it. How did *he* look without clothes?"

"You don't think I tried to find out?" Tamrissa protested, coloring again the way she had earlier. "I was taught that seeing a man in the altogether is wrong for a girl, unless the an is her husband and wants it that way. Gimmis didn't, hich was just about the only good thing in our marriage."

"Are you saying that men are the only ones who should be lowed to choose?" Jovvi asked, working to keep the onversation light. "I happen to feel I have just as much ght, which I exercised when I walked in on Lorand Coll. e's not only a darling man, he's also beautifully made. And ould you believe he felt as embarrassed as you say you id?"

"Yes, I'd believe it," Tamrissa replied, more serious than mused. "He's really nice, and what's more he wants to be ere. But what you said . . . about women having as much ght to choose as men . . . I never looked at it that way efore. Do you really think it's a matter of choice rather than matter of right and wrong?"

"Right and wrong always depend on where you're stand-ıg," Jovvi said, eager now to be in the water. "Stealing is rong if you're the one being stolen from, but it's right if our only alternative is to starve to death. Choice is an easier oncept to handle, especially if no one else is affected by your ıoice. That doesn't often happen, but I still believe we're all ntitled to live according to what *we* want rather than what thers do. If it's proper for men to look, then it's proper for omen."

"I think calling it proper makes it easier yet," Tamrissa ıid, her brows raised. "I've always thought it was horribly nfair for some things to be proper for men but improper for omen. Like being able to refuse the marriage your parents rrange. It's proper for a man to decide he doesn't like the rrangement, but not for a woman."

"That's what they *want* us to believe, but it isn't so," Jovvi ıid, beginning to enter that marvelous bath. "If you remem-er that most people have ulterior motives when they tell ou you have to do something, you'll find it easier to refuse. nd if I happen to fall asleep in here, wake me up when ou're ready to leave. I'd hate to come out tomorrow morn-ıg looking as shriveled as a prune."

Tamrissa laughed and promised not to leave without aking her, if Jovvi would do her the same favor. The two of ıem took pleasure in the warm water and swimming about little before choosing corners to soak in, but Jovvi's leasure was slightly dimmed. The poor child's body was :arred in one or two places, giving Jovvi some idea of what that marriage had been like. No wonder she was shy about being seen without clothes.

They both enjoyed a nice long soak, but neither of them actually fell asleep. The relaxing warmth made them ready for bed, though, and going back to their rooms was uneventful. The men still hadn't gotten back, which Jovvi found faintly disappointing. She'd decided it shouldn't hurt to get to know Lorand Coll a *little* better, as long as she didn't do anything silly like fall in love with him. And that she certainly wouldn't do, not when she had so many other things to decide about.

Would they ever get to the point where they would no longer have to pass the tests to stay alive? That was Jovvi's most pressing question as she snuggled down comfortably in bed. After that came all the other questions she and Tamrissa had discussed, a list too long to be considered when she was half asleep. Tomorrow she'd think about it again, and maybe even discuss it with one or two of the men. It would be a good excuse to get Lorand Coll alone, but not Vallant Ro. Tamrissa actually liked him, although she wasn't up to admitting it even to herself.

Tomorrow, tomorrow she'd think about all of it. . . .

TWENTY-FIVE

Clarion awoke slowly, which let his memories of the night before return just as slowly. He had a small headache somewhere behind his eyes, but lying still seemed to placate it enough to keep it from being a problem. The ache made no effort to interfere with his thinking, which was definitely a blessing; the confusion he felt was interference enough.

Thinking about it now let Clarion appreciate just how much he'd had to drink the night before, which simply added to his confusion. He'd been told that drinking to excess would make him ill, cause him to embarrass himself dreadfully, and then would lay him out as if he were a very small child. Having no wish to encounter any of those eventualities, he'd made a habit of following the advice he'd been given: to drink only the best wines, and no more than half a cup even then. But last night he'd all but swum in brew, and none of the expected had happened.

He raised his arms and gently ran both hands through his hair, his thoughts centering instead on the *un*expected. He'd decided that if he watched the others and did as they did he'd begin to learn what he needed to know, but he'd never anticipated anything like last night. He felt as if he'd floated through it, half a participant and half an observer, actually performing those acts while at the same time watching it all from a short distance off. That must be because of the way he'd acted, unlike anything someone who knew him would have recognized.

"And I'm still not sure where it came from," he muttered, gingerly touching the memories with his mind as if they were soap bubbles, delicate and apt to burst to nothingness if handled too roughly. "Maybe one of those foolish books. . . ."

The same servant who had taught him how to exercise his body had given him books to read, but not the sort he got from his tutor or Mother. Those were fantastic adventure novels with strong men rescuing beautiful, delicate ladies from peril, and then doing obscure, enigmatic things that they both enjoyed. Clarion had never understood what those things were, so he hadn't been overly upset when his mother had found him reading one and had insisted that he promise never to touch another of that sort again. But now . . .

Now he knew what those enigmatic things were, and felt a brief but very intense burst of outrage that he'd been kept from them so long. He'd lain with that lovely, dark-haired girl the way those heroes had lain with the ladies they'd rescued, and the writer's words hadn't been nearly adequate enough to describe the pleasure to be had. Men did that with ladies all the time, Coll had said, but before last night he hadn't even known it was possible. And after having had the

experience he felt different, somehow, more relaxed and i
some obscure manner not the same man. What he'd turne
into wasn't clear at all, but there was no doubt about hi
being different.

But he also remembered something else Coll had said
which still made no sense at all. Clarion sat up slowly an
massaged his left shoulder, wondering what Coll coul
possibly have had in mind when he'd warned Clarion not t
hurt the dark-haired girl. After the pleasure she'd given hin
he would have had to have been a twisted beast to harm her
even if provoked. But there'd been no provocation, only he
gentle voice wishing him well just before he left her. And i
any event it was Mother's lacks, not the girl's, which ha
kept him from learning the truth sooner . . .

For a moment Clarion felt a jolt of shock that he'
considered Mother as someone with lacks, and then a toucl
of guilt came. Yes, he'd thought of Mother as lacking, an
couldn't deny that truth no matter how upset learning of i
would have made her. He was less of a man, less of a person
than even his lower-class companions, and the fault was n
one's but hers. She should have found a gentleman of thei
own class to tutor him, not that stiff, elderly female creatur
who had lived her life in semi-seclusion amid her textbooks

Clarion got out of bed and went to wash his face, needin
the touch of cool water when his thoughts reached a point h
now understood only too well. He remembered asking Col
why they'd had to leave so early, and Coll had gently put hin
off. Now, without the floating caused by all that brew, h
understood clearly why they'd had to leave. Those people i
the tavern had been afraid of them, and all because of wha
they'd done to stop that roughhousing. At one point in hi
life Clarion would have gloried in being feared by others, a
condition he'd considered far superior to being laughed at by
them. But now that he'd had the experience, he realized ho
childishly narrowminded he'd been. It wasn't satisfying to b
feared, it was depressing, and not only because their excel
lent carouse had been interrupted.

Clarion buried his face in the hand towel he'd taken from
its place beside the wash basin, trying to assimilate and mak
sense of the suddenly unpleasant situation he now foun
himself in. His life until today had been a lonely one, bu
he'd had hopes of seeing all that changed. He'd made up hi

mind to learn what he needed to in order to be like everyone else, but the cold truth was that he *wasn't* like everyone else and never would be. Those people last night were certainly low class drudges and meaningless nonentities, but they had one thing in common with the nobles he'd been raised among: neither group contained members even slightly familiar with those who were as much as Middle practitioners. Highs were completely beyond them, aside from rumor and gossip and endless suspicion.

"I can't imagine why I never noticed that before," Clarion mused, frowning down at the table. "Everyone *talks* about Middles and Highs and some even know where practicing Middles live and work, but they never turn up at parties even as novelties. Middles aren't quite good enough even if they're members of our class, and Highs are much too busy with truly important matters to be imposed upon. Or at least that was what everyone always said. . . ."

But now the likelier answer presented itself that his peers were just as frightened of Highs as the lowliest street sweeper. And the unpleasant fact was that he'd already done enough in passing that first test to guarantee that he'd never be allowed to attend a party again even if he were to return home today. They'd been parties where Mother had been invited that he'd simply been dragged to and been bored silly by, but even that would now be beyond him. He would be "one of *them*," which is never the same as "one of us."

So Clarion now had some serious thinking to do. Going back to the way things had been would have been impossible for him even under ordinary circumstances, but at least then he would have had the option. Now he had to find an altogether different life for himself, preferably one that involved his power level equals as well as his social equals. That meant staying with this tiresome testing program and doing his utmost best, which should eventually end him among those he belonged with—

As well as secure him that position he'd been thinking about, the one that would make him financially independent. He paused before the room's wardrobe, trying to decide whether to breakfast first or bathe first. He felt badly in need of a long soak, but it wasn't early and breakfast might soon be cleared away. Very well, food first, and then the soak followed by a leisurely shave. He'd never been allowed to come to table without first having shaved, but financial independence would mean personal freedom as well.

Yes, that was definitely the route to go, he decided as he chose just anything to wear. Independence and freedom. . . .

With so many people in the house I hadn't expected a quiet morning, but that was just what I got. No one was in the dining room when I went down to breakfast, but I learned that Beldara Lant had been there before me. The men had returned after the rest of us were already in bed, so no one expected them down for a while. Jovvi Hafford had apparently chosen to sleep late as well, so I ate alone except for my thoughts.

And what unexpectedly light thoughts they were, not to mention how odd they felt. After half a day of getting to know Jovvi, I'd grown closer to her than I was with my own sisters. I'd told her things I'd never told anyone else, and I was sure she'd done the same with me. That had to be what people called friendship, something I'd never expected to experience personally. I no longer felt all alone in the world, and the difference it made in my outlook was incredible.

I sat back for a moment with my cup of tea, considering that changed outlook. Before yesterday afternoon, I would have been frantic to realize that something wasn't quite right with the system I'd been counting on to free me from my parents' influence. Now it was just a vexing problem that needed to be investigated, but nothing to get frantic over. If I couldn't become a High I'd do something else, me and the person who was now my *friend*.

But I couldn't quite accept that something else being my becoming a courtesan. I laughed a little over the idea even as I felt my face warm, the mildest reactions I'd had yet to the suggestion. Even if what she'd said was true and there was pleasure to be had from men rather than pain, I couldn't see myself making that a career. Gimmis had always accused me of being exceptionally untalented in bed, and that was one opinion I'd never found reason to doubt—or particularly wanted to change.

So the idea of my becoming a courtesan was ludicrous. I'd certainly *cost* Jovvi more custom than I would bring in, but maybe she'd be able to use me as a lure of sorts. Men had

lways been attracted to my beauty, and it would be a
efinite kind of justice if for once I used the attraction for my
wn benefit rather than everyone else's. Yes, that was a real
ossibility. . . .

I finished breakfast while my thoughts wandered to im-
robable places, then went to the library and sat down to
ead. Second rest day was the time I'd begun to insist that no
ne intrude on my privacy, and the staff had finally learned
hat that included *their* problems. They were all quick
nough to make sure their own rest days were undisturbed,
ut mine had tended to be open to the world. Now that I'd
nanaged to get an entire day to myself, I felt reluctant to give
t up—although the change in circumstance had to be
onsidered. If everyone appeared for lunch I might have to
hare the afternoon, but the morning *was* going to be mine.

And I almost managed to keep that promise to myself. It
vas nearly an hour until lunchtime when a knock came at
he door, and then my steward Weeks appeared.

"Please excuse the intrusion, Dama, but visitors have
rrived," he announced in his stiff and distant way. "I at-
empted to suggest that you were unavailable, but they in-
isted."

"All right, I'll take care of it," I conceded with a sigh,
utting my book aside as I rose from the chair. Weeks was
eally very good about guarding my private time, so blaming
im for one failure wouldn't have been fair. Besides, it was
robably some of the people from the testing authority, here
o hand out more rules and requirements.

I stepped out into the hall expecting to see complete
trangers, and stopped short when only one of the three new
rrivals proved unknown. The other two were my parents,
nd the chills took me so quickly that I nearly shivered
vhere they could see it. My mother saw me and smiled that
loating smile of hers, the one I hated so much, and that
nade my father turn away from the man I didn't know to
ook at me the way he always did.

I suddenly remembered how much I'd loved my father as
 child, just the way all his friends and business associates
oved him. He was a fairly tall man with hair as blond as
nine, slightly overweight with a round and jolly face and
varm gray eyes. It was extremely rare to see him without a
mile, and his voice was never raised in anger. People had

always joked privately that they were amazed his marriage to an ice princess like my mother had turned out so well, but apparently even ice princesses weren't immune to his charm.

None of them knew—or would believe—that the marriage had turned out so well because my father was colder on the inside than even my mother could hope to be.

"Tamrissa, child, how good it is to see you again," my father said in his warm, friendly baritone, smiling lovingly at me. "Do come closer so that I may feast my eyes. I've let business keep me away far too long, but that's over with now. I promise we'll be seeing a lot more of each other from now on."

"You shouldn't make promises it won't be possible to keep, Father," I said after I swallowed, reluctantly moving to a place about six feet away from them. "You won't get this house away from me without a fight, and even if I lose then I won't return to your roof. I've already told that to Mother and now I say it to you: you'll never have the chance to sell me again."

"Oh, Tamrissa, your penchant for joking has never failed to amuse me," Father said with a delighted laugh, his eyes sparkling with enjoyment. "You know as well as I do that the proceeds from the sale of this house will go toward your new dowry, so nothing will be 'taken away' from you. And as far as returning to my roof goes, you're absolutely correct. You won't be coming back to your poor old parents, you'll be going to live with your husband."

"My husband is dead," I reminded him, terrified at the way his gentle conversation drained the anger out of me. Without the anger it would be impossible to fight him, and if I didn't fight. . . .

"Your first husband is dead, child," he corrected softly, with just the right amount of sadness and compassion. "And since you're much too young to spend the remainder of your life alone, I've done a father's duty and arranged your second marriage. This is Dom Odrin Hallasser, who will take you as his wife as soon as this testing nonsense is over and done with."

He'd glanced at the identification I wore on its chain before gesturing to the stranger, completely dismissing the possibility that I would be in the least successful with the testing. That might have been enough to bring back my anger—if I hadn't followed his gesture and looked at Odrin

Hallasser. The man was both taller and heavier than my father, with dark hair, a long, plain face, and sallow skin. His clothes were expensively designed for comfort as well as style, and his fleshy hands were covered with rings worth a fortune. He wet his thick lips as he stared at me, so lost to inspecting the merchandise that he made no effort to acknowledge the introduction. That was bad enough, but his eyes . . .

Those eyes were dead black in color, but there was nothing dead about the expression in them. Cold cruelty swam in their depths, along with a sickening anticipation even worse than what Gimmis had shown. The man couldn't wait to get his hands on me, and in addition he was at least fifteen years younger than Gimmis had been. This one was meant to keep me a good deal longer than two years, and the thought of that brought a shudder I couldn't suppress.

"I won't do it," I managed to get out, tearing my gaze away from the *thing* in human form trying to capture it and me. "You can't force me to marry, so I won't do it. Find another sacrifice for that . . . that . . ."

"What a silly child you are," Father said with an indulgent laugh, shaking his head in mock exasperation. "Of course you'll do it, just as you did the first time. It's all arranged, so there's no need to discuss it any further. And now you may tell your people that there will be three more for lunch, during which time you and Odrin may become acquainted. He and I have been discussing the possibility of a very large joint venture, but I shan't bore you with the details. And you needn't worry. The venture isn't scheduled to begin until *after* you return from your honeymoon."

So that was the price he'd sold me for: a business venture he couldn't afford to begin on his own, which meant it had to be very large indeed. And he'd even thrown in the price my house would bring. That told me how determined he was, which in turn spread ice all through my bloodstream. I'd never found it possible to stand up to him before, and fear was beginning to overwhelm my anger. What if he was right . . . what if I did find it impossible to refuse . . . ?

"Ah, Tamrissa, good morning," I suddenly heard, and then Jovvi was stopping beside me. "I don't mean to interrupt, but I've been thinking about the conversation we had yesterday. If you intend to sell this house I'll be glad to buy it from you, and I'm even willing to pay a bit above what

others might offer. This is exactly the kind of neighborhood
I've always wanted to live in, and you know you'll always be
welcome here—for as long as you care to stay."

"Who *is* this person?" my mother demanded, for all the
world sounding like someone who considered herself noble.
My father hadn't slipped so far that he actually frowned, but
his everpresent good humor evaporated to a large degree
before he regained control of himself.

"It really doesn't matter who the young lady is, my dear,"
he said to my mother with familiar self assurance. "The
courts aren't in the habit of allowing total strangers to outbid
their longtime supporters, so the house isn't likely to go to
her. And even if by some incredible chance it did, that would
hardly affect Tamrissa's marriage. Since it's all arranged, it
will go ahead exactly as planned."

"Are there different laws here in Gan Garee?" Jovvi asked
with a smile even sweeter than my father's. "Where I come
from, all the planning in the world can't change a refusal on
the bride's part. Without full agreement you can't have a
wedding—and I did hear you say no, didn't I, Tamrissa?"

"What she says or doesn't say is beside the point," my
father countered before I could speak, his manner now more
sleek and self-satisfied than open and friendly. "This marriage was arranged on her behalf, and Dom Hallasser would
be fully within his rights to sue both me and her if anything
should interfere. Again, I'm quite certain the courts would
insist on having the marriage gone through with rather than
allowing me to suffer for having acted out of concern for my
child."

"Odd that you should mention lawsuits," another voice
drawled as Jovvi and I exchanged a glance of frustrated
worry. My father *did* have a few members of the court on his
side . . . "Tamakins has already agreed to marry *me,* which
as a grown woman she's entitled to do. If you and your friend
try to press the matter, I'll have to sue both of *you* for
interferin' with my happiness. And daddy would certainly
stand behind me with every copper he has."

And then Vallant Ro was standing beside me to my right,
his arm coming to circle my shoulders. I had the strongest
urge to gape at him after what he'd said, but all that support
let me find something of my own to say.

"And on top of all that, you can forget about being allowed
to invite yourselves to lunch," I told my parents, delighted to

see the way my father fought to keep a snarl from his face. "Even if this house wasn't an official residence for the use of applicants *only,* you people would not be welcome here. Please leave now, and don't ever come back."

"If you're that upset, child, of course we'll leave," my father said soothingly, sparing Vallant Ro a glance that said he knew he'd been lied to. "But as far as never coming back—don't be foolish, my dear. Of course we'll be back, and then we'll get this misunderstanding straightened out once and for all."

He had to put a hand to his "friend's" arm to get his attention, and then all three of them left. The awful man hadn't stopped staring at me the entire time, and I couldn't keep from shivering again. My father had said that he refused to give up, and the thought of having to face him again made me sick to my stomach.

"You handled that very well," Jovvi said once the door was closed behind them, putting her arms around me. "And don't you worry. Now that they know they have more than just you to face, they won't be as anxious as he pretended to be to come back again. Aside from us, Dom Ro makes an admirably difficult opponent."

"Discouragin' them was what I had in mind," Vallant Ro said, having taken his arm away as soon as my "visitors" were out the door. "I've never liked seein' the helpless bein' taken advantage of, so if—'Tamakins'—needs my help again, it will be my pleasure to supply it."

"Helpless," I echoed, feeling even worse as I straightened away from Jovvi. "Everyone thinks I'm helpless, but I refuse to let all of you be right. I will be *strong,* and I won't give up no matter what they do. And for the sake of sanity, don't *ever* call me that nauseating name again!"

I left Jovvi and Dom Ro looking completely confused, and marched back into the library before leaning against the closed door and shutting my eyes. I'd meant to apologize to Dom Ro for what I'd called him and should have thanked him for helping, but instead I'd yelled at him and then had stalked off in insult. And all because he'd gotten even on his own by calling me helpless.

I took a deep breath and opened my eyes, then walked slowly to a chair and sat, feeling very tired. I hated the idea of being helpless, but the condition was so obvious that *two* new acquaintances had felt obliged to come to my rescue.

Maybe I'd been deluding myself into thinking I could win, in the tests as well as against my parents. Maybe I ought to just give it all up, pick a direction, and simply walk away. I'd heard it said that if you wander too far, you can never find your way home again.

Even if you actually have a home . . . or something to make you want to go back . . . instead of wanting to be dead. . . .

TWENTY-SIX

Vallant watched the girl Tamrissa disappear into the library, wishing he'd bitten his tongue. Of all the attractive and charming things it was possible to call a woman, "helpless" had to be at the top of the list.

"She wasn't really angry with *us*, you know," a gentle voice said from behind him. "She's horribly frightened of what those people want to do to her, and she thinks her courage failed. It didn't really, but I can't think of a way to tell her so that she's likely to believe."

"Not bein' a quitter is so important to her that even I can feel it," Vallant said, turning to look at Jovvi Hafford. "But she said she meant to be really strong from now on, so I guess I didn't put my foot in it as deep as I might have."

"She wasn't telling the truth," the beautiful woman said with a sigh, pain showing in her lovely eyes. "She was feeling despair rather than determination, and I can only hope she manages to pull out of it. That awful man . . . I'd kill myself before I'd let him touch me."

Vallant was shocked to see Jovvi shudder as she said that, a reaction he never would have expected from her. He'd met few women who seemed completely self-possessed and capable, but Jovvi Hafford certainly was one.

"Are you talkin' about the prospective bridegroom?" he asked, definitely disturbed. "I didn't get a very good look at him, because he's so unimpressive that he's easy to ignore. Aside from all those rings. I admit he seemed to be smitten with Tamrissa, but—"

"No, not smitten," Jovvi answered quickly and firmly. "He has . . . centered on her as an object he means to possess, an item of obsession that won't let him rest until he owns it. I've come across people like him before, and they never take no for an answer. Her father's a fool for thinking he can deal with someone like that, because the man will use anything including him to get what he wants."

"I think I knew someone like that once," Vallant said with a frown as a distant memory surfaced. "That man wanted my daddy's business, and set about tryin' to ruin it when Daddy refused to sell. I was young then and only startin' to ship out, and the man brought a bunch of paid bullies on board my ship one night. They were supposed to wreck the ship while he came after *me*, intendin' to kill me to pay Daddy back for refusin' his offer. He said as much before tryin' to throw me overboard near the place on deck where I slept."

"What stopped him?" Jovvi asked, her brows high. "He obviously didn't succeed in killing you, but I can't imagine what would have changed his mind."

"Dyin' stopped him," Vallant said, more disturbed than before but not because of the memory. "He and one of his bullies had Water magic and meant to use it to drown me, but they were both of ordinary strength. They were the ones who ended up overboard and drowned, and then I put out the fires and chased off the rest of his men. He had a bad reputation, so nobody official ever asked any questions about exactly how he'd died. . . . And you think this Hallasser is one like that?"

"I'd be willing to bet every copper I possess on it," Jovvi answered, her disturbed certainty adding even more weight to the contention. "He's determined to have Tamrissa no matter what he has to do to accomplish it."

"I'm goin' to talk to her," Vallant decided aloud, straightening a bit where he stood. "She won't want to hear anythin'

at all from me let alone somethin' like that, but she has to
know. I really do appreciate the help you gave her, and
I'll . . . talk to you later."

"It was my pleasure," Jovvi answered, now apparently
amused about something. "She and I have become friends,
so if either of you need me again, please don't hesitate to
ask."

Vallant nodded his thanks for the offer, then headed
directly for the library. If he hadn't been so distracted with
worry about Tamrissa, he would have wondered about
Jovvi's amusement. As it was, he reached the library door,
knocked once, then walked in without waiting for a response. Tamrissa was in a chair, her beautiful face looking
drawn and pale, and Vallant gave her no chance to order him
out.

"I know I'm intrudin', but don't let it disturb you," he said
quickly, closing the door again behind him. "There's somethin' you need to know, and then I'll get out of your way
again. But first I'd like to apologize for what I said. Somehow
it came out soundin' as if I was callin' you helpless, but I
really wasn't. It was the situation—"

"You came in here to apologize?" she interrupted, suddenly looking annoyed. "For the second time, when I haven't
done it even once? You seem to make a habit of apologizing
when you aren't guilty of anything, Dom Ro, but I suspect
you don't do it for everyone. Those who aren't helpless undoubtedly have to manage without."

"I was tryin' to say that that was a misunderstandin','"
Vallant replied, swallowing down a flash of his own annoyance as he moved a few steps closer to her chair. "That
bunch thought they could *make* you helpless, but they were
as wrong as it's possible to be. Even if Jovvi and I hadn't
come along to help, you still would have been able to handle
them."

"Only I wasn't handling them, and we both know it," she
said, the bitterness clear in her voice. "That means you're
lying in an effort to make me feel better, which would be
absurd if your reason wasn't so obvious. Helpless women
need to have their fears soothed, and men who consider
themselves gentlemen are honor bound to perform the task.
But now that it's been seen to, Dom Ro, I'd like you to go
away and leave me alone."

"I'm not in the habit of lyin'," Vallant said through his teeth, frustration adding itself to his increasing annoyance. "You're in a situation so bad I can't even imagine what it must feel like, to have your own parents care about nothin' but how they can use you. If it was me I probably *would* be helpless, but you're managin' just fine. Jovvi thinks so too, so why don't you ask *her*."

"Jovvi's a friend, so what else would she say?" the beautiful female mule responded with a gesture of dismissal, a stubborn glint now in those incredible violet eyes. "And for someone who's not in the habit of lying, you seem to do well at it. Or was it my imagination that you said you'd asked me to marry you? No wonder you have trouble with women. Being a Knight in Shining Aspect will do it every time."

"That wasn't a lie, it was moral support," Vallant stated, now thoroughly annoyed. "You listen to me, little lady, and you listen good. I don't have trouble with 'women,' I have trouble with beautiful females who have too much spirit for their good and mine. You could have agreed to whatever your father said, which you would have if you really were helpless. Instead you stood there defyin' his right to use you like a worthless piece of trade goods, and that took more courage than most *men* have. It's easy to stand up for yourself when the person givin' you grief is a stranger, but it's damned hard when they're somebody who's supposed to love you. You are *not* helpless, and I don't ever want to hear you say you are again."

By that time she sat there blinking at him wide-eyed, obviously unsure of how to react or what to say. Men usually jumped to agree with him when he used that tone on them, men often twice the size of the slender female who sat looking up at him without a word of the agreement he'd demanded. Briefly, Vallant wished he himself were female, so he'd be free to scream in frustration the way he so wanted to do. How was he supposed to get through such thickheaded resistance?

"Now see what you made me do," he grumbled after a moment of useless searching for the right thing to say. "I came in to apologize, and ended up yellin' at you instead. Just for that I ought to punish you by takin' a kiss."

He expected to see her laugh or get angry at that, the usual reaction that could be expected from a woman. Instead she went pale again, so quickly and completely that Vallant was shocked. And she'd begun to tremble! What in the name of the Five was wrong?

"No, please, I was only jokin'," he said as fast as possible, immediately crouching and reaching up to touch her hand. It was ice cold, and that look in her eyes—! "I'm not goin' to hurt you, I'd never hurt you. Are you all right?"

It took a long moment before she nodded, but Vallant still made no effort to straighten. Looming over someone you'd just frightened wasn't the way to reassure them, and he also reluctantly stopped touching her hand. She hadn't pulled it away from him, but it certainly seemed that she wanted to. It had to be the worst possible time to ask questions, but he simply had to know.

"What was it that frightened you so badly?" he put as gently as he knew how, watching her face. "I see now that it was a rotten joke, but do you dislike me *that* much? If so, I'll certainly leave at once—"

"No," she interrupted, clearly trying to pull herself together. "It wasn't really you at all. I—had an unpleasant marriage, and the ghost of it keeps haunting me. I don't want you to think you were responsible, not when you were just trying to help me. That would be very unfair."

Unfair. Vallant stared up at her without changing expression, but how he managed it he'd never know. If a thoughtless, offhand comment was able to terrorize her like that, it wasn't possible to really know what her marriage had been like. Unpleasant couldn't be anything like a proper description, but she'd pulled out of it just to reassure *him.* Vallant wished briefly but fervently that it was possible to get his hands on her former husband. If he had still been alive, he wouldn't have remained so for long.

"Tamrissa, I want you to hear me and believe what you hear," he said then, slowly but deliberately reaching for her hand and taking it gently between both of his. "There's nothin' in this world that will ever make me hurt you, and what's more I'll never let anybody else hurt you either. I mean to be there if your daddy comes back with that friend of his, and if I'm not you'd better make sure I'm called. Will you do that?"

"Certainly," she agreed after a short hesitation, her hand unmoving between his bigger ones, a spot of red on each of her fair cheeks. "If that's what you want, I'll be glad to see to it. May I have my hand back now?"

Vallant would have been much happier if he could have ignored that request, but it wasn't really possible. With great reluctance he released her hand then straightened, wondering in passing why she now looked so reserved. Well, whatever the reason, at least she wasn't terrified any longer. And it would have been heartless to return her to the state by telling her what Jovvi had said about Hallasser. That would have to wait for another time.

"Since it's nearly lunchtime, I think I'll go and freshen up," Vallant said when the silence grew too heavy. She sat staring down at her hands, obviously waiting for him to decide to leave. "I'll—see you in the dinin' room."

She nodded without looking up, so he had no choice but to leave the way he'd said he would. The hall was empty when he stepped back out into it and closed the door behind himself, so he crossed it to the stairs and went to his room.

There were any number of things disturbing Vallant's thoughts, but one of them kept returning while he washed his hands in the room's basin. She'd said she believed his determination to stand beside her, but something about the way she'd behaved led him to believe she hadn't been telling the truth. She *didn't* believe him, but why in the world would she doubt—

The answer came so suddenly that Vallant groaned, feeling like an idiot for not having seen it sooner. He'd told Tamrissa he would be there for her, but they'd already established that he would *not* be there, not at all. As far as she knew, he was determined to go home as soon as he could, so how could she expect him to be there for her? He'd let his emotions speak for him, making him both a fool and a liar.

But *had* he been lying? There was something about Tamrissa Domon that drew him more strongly than any other woman he had ever met, maybe even more strongly than the need to go home to the sea again. How he would get around his problem with closed-in spaces he had no idea, but suddenly he wanted to get around it. He *had* to stay to help her, but the matter still came down to whether his affliction would allow it. He'd given his solemn word, but would he be allowed to keep it?

Vallant took the hand towel and threw it as far as he could, then had to use the power to dry his hands. He seemed to have picked up the habit of acting thoughtlessly and then regretting it, but maybe things would change. Maybe somehow, in some way, he would find it possible not to be a liar after all. . . .

TWENTY-SEVEN

Lorand had come out to the gardens after breakfast, and even without bright sunshine he had enjoyed the serenity too much to go back inside. His mind kept replaying the events of last night, and he'd needed to be surrounded by vital living things in order to come to terms with what had happened. Everyone had been upset except for Clarion, who'd been too tipsy to think the thing through. And Drowd, who'd left the tavern—and them—at the first hint of trouble starting.

Which would have been considered nothing but prudence if Drowd had told them he was leaving rather than wordlessly sneaking away. Lorand crouched beside a flower bed composed of jonquils and peonies, an odd combination that nevertheless attracted him. All of the flowers and bushes and mosses and grasses seemed to have perked up only recently, as though something in the soil—or the atmosphere—had recently changed. He'd Encouraged the entire area in general when he'd first come out, and now could simply enjoy being near their happy eagerness to grow.

But the pleasure of that wasn't up to taking away *all* the unpleasantness of breakfast. Pagin Holter had been at the table when Lorand first walked in, but the little man had been so deep in his thoughts that Lorand had decided against disturbing him. Holter had worn a look of grieving since they'd left the tavern, his mind mourning the loss of something he couldn't speak of. Lorand knew he'd realized he could never go back to the places where he'd felt so at home, and he sympathized more fully than Holter would ever know.

A small amount of sunshine blossomed as the clouds briefly parted, then it disappeared again even more quickly than it had appeared. It took the beauty of the riotous garden colors with it, just as last night had taken the joy from Holter. He'd *had* to offer his help, just as the rest of them had had to agree to do the same, and it wasn't fair, although that was hardly a comfort. Even Mardimil had been affected, since he'd done little more than greet Lorand warmly before sitting down with his meal and sinking into his thoughts.

"But at least it did us a favor where Drowd is concerned," Lorand muttered, reaching out to the softness of a nearby daffodil. Drowd had appeared after Mardimil, and his air of amused condescension had returned as though it had never been gone. He'd talked languidly about nothing as he filled his plate, but once he'd sat down he'd tried to go back to his old tricks again.

"How nice it is to see you returned to us, Mardimil," he'd drawled while pouring himself a cup of tea. "The way you behaved last night, I was certain you'd decided to stay . . . 'under the weather' permanently."

"How would you know, Drowd?" Mardimil had returned with the same sort of drawl, surprising Lorand. "You ran away so fast, it's a wonder you had time to notice anything at all. And then to try to strand us there . . . I knew you were a liar, Drowd, but I hadn't realized you were that colossally stupid. Did you really think we didn't know simply because no one contradicted you on the spot?"

Drowd had gone flushed with an appalled look, and when he'd glanced at Lorand he must have seen confirmation of what had been said. For a moment he looked as if he would get up and leave, but then he turned his attention to his food and began eating. His favorite victim had suddenly turned into a predator, but he may have been hoping that after a while the unfortunate condition would pass. And that Mardimil had been wrong about everyone knowing what he'd done and tried to do.

"But it's too nice having him quiet," Lorand murmured to

another flower before straightening. "If the others don't do anything to make it happen, I'll have to try my own hand at it."

The attitude was more uncharitable than Lorand usually let himself be, but last night seemed to have changed him as much as it had the others. The values of the place he considered home no longer applied to him, not when the people there would turn from him in fear. And they would, he knew that with more certainty than almost anything else. How often had he heard the townspeople—and his own father—say something like, "He's as bad as one of them misbegotten Highs," or "He's about as welcome as a plague of Highs."

No, the people he'd grown up among would turn their backs if they learned he'd passed the first test for High, but so what? It wasn't as if he'd ever expected to go back there, so what they thought made no difference at all. They and their values could drop into a bottomless pit, and Lorand would do no more than say good riddance.

He turned away from the garden and toward the house, knowing it should be getting on toward lunchtime. It had only been a few hours since he'd finished breakfast and he hadn't done anything particularly strenuous, but when lunch was served he would be there to eat it. But then he saw Jovvi Hafford strolling out of the house with a smile of real amusement on her face, and all thought of food suddenly disappeared.

"Well, hello there," she said as soon as she saw him, her smile softening to one of greeting. "I hope you don't mind if I share this beautiful garden with you for a while. If you do, I won't mind waiting until later."

"I wouldn't mind even if I happened to be naked again," Lorand said at once, making her laugh that wonderful tinkling laugh. "I've been trying to find the chance to talk to you again, but life hasn't been willing to cooperate. Until now. What were you laughing about when you first came out?"

"Oh, just something silly," she answered as she reached him, then began to stroll with him deeper into the garden. "Dom Ro and I . . . intervened in a matter where Tamrissa Domon was being taken advantage of. Afterward he thanked me for helping her, as though he and she had something serious between them. He *says* he knows she hates him and he doesn't blame her, but that's not how he feels. He's really attracted to her, and would love to have her feel the same."

"But he won't talk about it, because he doesn't believe it can ever happen," Lorand said, more aware of her presence beside him than his ability made him aware of the world. "I can understand how he feels, and I sympathize. There are some things just too . . . impossible to discuss."

"You men are what's impossible," Jovvi said, pausing to look up at him with a smile. "You're so determined to grit your teeth and take whatever comes like *real* men, that you miss half the opportunities dancing past. Wouldn't it be much more pleasant if you joined in the dance, and left worrying about what's possible for some other, later time?"

"Join in the dance," Lorand echoed, his pulse beginning to beat faster as he looked down at her. Was she trying to say his advances would *not* be unwelcome? But what if he was wrong, an she ended up feeling insulted? What if—"To the Deep Caverns with it. Even if you end up hating me, at least I'll have joined in the dance for once."

And with that he took her in his arms and kissed her, something he'd wanted to do from the first moment he'd wiped the soap from his eyes. Her body felt soft and alive in his arms, her scent like the most marvelous flower ever grown, and her lips. . . . Silken didn't begin to describe them, especially when they immediately began to join in the kiss. His hand went to her glorious hair as her arms slid around his middle, and then Lorand was lost to an experience more intense than what he'd had above the tavern the night before.

It was quite a while before the kiss ended, and when it finally did Lorand had to keep an iron hold on his control. He wanted nothing so much as to lift her in his arms and carry her to his bed, but that, unfortunately, would have been rushing things more than most women cared for.

"If that's the way you hate, I hope you eventually get to loathe me," Lorand murmured after kissing her still-closed eyes. "And in case you were wondering, the dance was the best I ever attended."

"That's because you're a natural dancer," she returned with a laugh, opening those incredible blue-green eyes to look up at him. "I was hoping you were, and I haven't been disappointed. I find you very attractive, Lorand Coll, and I'm glad you find me the same."

"Did you somehow get the impression I was dead?" Lorand asked with a laugh of his own as he released her. Her hand made no effort to smooth her hair, which encouraged him even more. "Only a dead man would have trouble finding you attractive, but not as much as you might think. Do you have any plans for tonight that I might intrude in? After dinner, I mean, before going up to—"

Lorand stopped to keep from falling into that bottomless pit he'd been thinking about earlier, wondering in passing why his command of the language seemed to have deserted him completely. A man was considered crude if he mentioned his intentions straight out, a lesson he'd learned at an early age. The only kind of girl you behaved that way with was one you paid, another part of the same lesson. He would have to find a gracefully roundabout way to ask his question, but before the proper words showed up they were interrupted by the appearance of Clarion Mardimil.

"Ah, there you are, my dear," he said to Jovvi, nodding to Lorand as he came up to join them. "I've been looking for you, because I have something I'd like to ask you. Would you be so kind as to join me in my bed tonight? I promise to make the time one you'll never forget."

"Clarion, I need to have a word with you," Lorand said hastily, taking Mardimil's arm. "Let's step back a short way toward the house."

A glance at Jovvi showed Lorand that he was more embarrassed than she was, and what's more she seemed to be working hard to swallow amusement. He couldn't understand that, but confusion didn't keep him from pulling Mardimil out of hearing range for her.

"Really, Lorand, what's gotten into you?" Mardimil demanded with annoyance as he finally managed to free his arm. "You interrupted before the lady was able to give me her answer."

"If I'd waited, you probably wouldn't have enjoyed that answer," Lorand countered in a hiss, trying to get Mardimil to lower his voice. "I realize you know very little about women, Clarion, but surely you were taught *something* in the way of tact. The only time you walk straight up to a woman and make an announcement like that is if she's the sort you pay, and Dama Hafford doesn't happen to be that sort. Any other woman would have gotten terribly insulted, and it's simply your good fortune that she's kinder than that."

"You're saying it isn't done?" Mardimil asked, his frown now showing confusion. "I hadn't realized there was different protocol for different occasions and situations. Good grief, how complicated does this get?"

"More complicated than I can explain in one or two brief conversations," Lorand replied, feeling sorrier than ever for Mardimil. "Were you really taught nothing at all about . . . associating with women? It isn't necessary to sleep with them in order to learn how to behave in their company. Weren't you ever out alone with girls?"

"Alone?" Mardimil echoed, a distant look in his eyes. "No, not alone. I apologize for blundering so badly, Lorand, and would like to apologize to Dama Hafford as well."

Lorand would have preferred talking him out of that, but not being able to apologize would have made matters worse for the poor fool. Or poor victim, which was nearer the truth. He'd been taught nothing about how to associate with other people, as though his precious mother had simply decided he'd never need to know. What she expected her son to do after she was gone was a mystery, or possibly it was of no interest to her. As long as everything was done *her* way while she lived. . . .

"Jovvi, Clarion would like to apologize for what he said," Lorand began as soon as they'd retraced their steps. "He really didn't mean to insult you, it was just . . . a mistake."

"Yes, a mistake in choosing the proper parents," Mardimil said heavily, now the picture of depression. "I was trying to say how attractive I found you, and managed to disgrace myself instead. I humbly beg your pardon, and hope you will someday find it possible to forgive me."

"I forgive you right now," Jovvi told him quickly, interrupting the bow that would have preceded his hasty departure. "I know it wasn't your fault, Clarion, and I certainly don't blame you for giving me what was, in fine, the greatest compliment a woman can receive. Possibly, if you will allow it, I can return the gift with one of my own."

"What sort of gift?" Mardimil asked, sounding as confused as Lorand felt. "And what sort of gift did *I* give? I'm afraid I don't understand any of this, I really—"

"Hush," Jovvi interrupted softly again, putting a gentle hand to his arm. "I know how confused you feel, but I promise that one day you'll understand everything you care to. But about my gift. May I give it to you?"

"I would be most grateful for *anything* you cared to give, dear lady," Mardimil replied, sounding open and vulnerable and as defenseless as a child. Lorand ached for him, more than he had at any other time.

"Thank you," Jovvi said with one of her devastating smiles, her hand still on Mardimil's arm. "My gift is something that I promise will help you—if you decide to use it. If you don't, you won't be any worse off than you are right now. I would like to give you a different name: Rion. In my opinion it suits you far better than the one you have, even though it comes from the original. What do you think of it? Is it possible you may decide to use it?"

"Rion," Mardimil said, tasting the shortened name as if it were a new dish. "Rion instead of Clarion. I do believe I like it. Rion instead of Clarion. Thank you, dear lady, thank you very much indeed."

And then he bowed and walked away, repeating the name over and over with the same slow relish. Lorand watched until the man disappeared back into the house, and then he turned to Jovvi.

"I don't understand either," he admitted without hesitation. "Why did you do that, and what did you mean when you said he complimented you? He really did insult you, and I thought you were just being nice about it."

"Lorand, the poor man was floundering," she answered with a sigh. "I needed something to take his mind off how devastated he felt, and the idea of giving him a different name was pure inspiration. Clarion is the one who blundered so badly that he shamed himself, but Rion is shining and bright and entirely guiltless. It's a new beginning for him, which I'm sure you'll agree he desperately needs."

"More than you know," Lorand said with a nod. "And now that you mention it, giving him a new name was pure genius. I used to think Lorand was bad, but compared to Clarion it's better than gold. He must have been a laughingstock wherever he went."

"Which worked even more against his coming out into the world," Jovvi agreed. "And very frankly, his request surprised me. Only yesterday I had the distinct impression he had no idea what men do with women."

"Yesterday he did have no idea," Lorand admitted, trying not to blush. "We—ah—visited a tavern last night, and I adjusted the alcohol in his bloodstream to make his first—experience—less awkward. Apparently it was an overwhelming success, maybe too much so. And you haven't yet explained about the compliment business. Was that just more of the soothing you were trying to do?"

"Not at all," she said, now looking surprised. "I happen to know men well enough to have learned it *is* the greatest compliment they can give. Contrary to popular opinion, most men are quite meticulous about who they share intimacies with. Don't tell me *you're* not like that. Do you feel any woman will do, or do you have certain standards?"

"Of course I have standards," Lorand returned, trying not to feel that the conversation was getting out of hand. "But that's not a subject I'm used to discussing with ladies—even if they do seem to know more about it than I do. And while we're on the point, *how* do you know so much? You aren't—married?"

The possibility hadn't occurred to Lorand before, and not only because she wore no marriage band on her middle right finger. She didn't *act* married, but before Lorand could worry over the point, she laughed and shook her head.

"No, I'm certainly not married," she agreed with her usual amusement. "That would make my experience rather limited, which it doesn't happen to be. In Rincammon, my home city, I'm a fairly well-known courtesan. Some insist, if you will excuse the immodesty, the best known. Now, what were you saying earlier about my plans for this evening?"

She moved very close to Lorand again, and although his arms went around her automatically, his mind reeled so hard he nearly staggered. She was a *courtesan,* one of those women they refused to allow in Widdertown? Everyone had always insisted that the rest of the empire was evil for encouraging such goings-on, morally blighted the way *they* would never be.

But that didn't mean there were no liaisons in Widdertown, just none that were conducted out in the open. Someone had once suggested—before leaving the area only a year after having moved there—that there was more sneaking around in that supposedly morally rich town than in any of the ones they looked down on. No one had believed that, of course, but Lorand had wondered. And hadn't he decided that the values of his former home were no longer his?

Yes, yes he had. Lorand felt a rush of relief, only slightly tinged with lingering guilt. The old ways were no longer his, and there was no reason not to be charitable. He'd heard stories about how badly used all those girls were, and that none of them really wanted to do what they were doing. They were just never given a way out, but that could be changed in Jovvi's case.

"So you were a courtesan," he managed to say after only a brief hesitation, his smile trying to be warm. "That must have been terrible for you, but it's all over with now. After we get through all these tests, we should be free again to lead relatively normal lives. When that happens we can celebrate by planning our marriage."

"Marriage?" she echoed, raising her brows. "Why would I want to get married? And being the most famous courtesan in and around Rincammon wasn't terrible at all. Quite the opposite, in fact, not to mention enriching to the purse. If things don't work out with this High practitioner business, I mean to open my own residence here in Gan Garee. But that doesn't mean I can't have a . . . *special* patron, one who will never be required to pay. You aren't too shy to accept something like that, are you?"

"No, no, of course I'm not," Lorand got out, melting again to her smile while writhing inside. "We'll just have to talk about it."

"Talk will only take us so far," she responded with a laugh, putting her arms around him. "The rest will have to wait for tonight, but at least you can kiss me again."

Lorand couldn't have refused if his life had depended on it, but even as his lips took hers again his mind worked furiously. She was the most wonderful woman he'd ever met, but she was terribly confused about what was right. He would talk to her, and explain things gently, and eventually everything would work out. But in the meantime, he no longer had to worry about finding a roundabout way to entice her into his bed. . . .

Clarion—no, *Rion!*—walked into the dining room for dinner a bit early. He'd managed to miss lunch entirely, so taken had he been with the wonder of his new name, and now he was starving. Yes, starving, rather than quite hungry, the namby-pamby phrase Clarion would have used. Clarion had been a cripple too twisted even to see straight, but Rion was a man who simply had a few things yet to learn. It had surely been the Rion part of him which had become determined to learn, and now all of him was the same and under the proper name.

No one was at the table when Rion took his seat, which was disappointing even though expected. But the others were fairly prompt, so there shouldn't be too much of a wait. In the interim he took one of the fresh-baked rolls placed on the table by a servant, something else that poor fool Clarion never would have done. He'd been taught not to ruin his appetite by nibbling before a meal, and that no matter how hungry he was. Rion, however, was free to think for himself, not to mention satisfy part of his hunger with a roll.

Rion had been looking forward to the others arriving, but unfortunately the first to walk in was the liar Drowd. Rion gave the man a cool appraisal as he approached the table, making no effort to avoid the other's gaze. Drowd no longer disturbed him, not in any way at all.

"Well, how pleasant to avoid the boorishness of being first to arrive," Drowd murmured as he took his seat, his previous spitefulness apparently fully returned. "I see you do have your uses after all, Mardimil."

"I find it better to be useful even at something small, Drowd, than to be useless like you," Rion returned with an amused smile. "If I weren't so hungry, having you seated next to me would turn my stomach. Do us all a favor and just sit there quietly. You have nothing to say that any of us care to hear."

"My, my, look who thinks he's actually part of the group," Drowd returned, obviously struggling to keep to a languid drawl. "Your comment makes the situation laughable, Mardimil, because I happen to have something to say that would interest *you*. A short time before lunch I happened to be looking out a window over the gardens, and saw the most fascinating thing."

Rion gave the man silence for an answer, which would hopefully silence him as well. He must have witnessed the way Clarion had made a fool of himself, and now intended to use it for purposes of humiliation. But Clarion no longer existed, so Rion didn't care.

"I really had no idea Coll had it in him," Drowd continued in spite of the lack of a reply. "He was actually kissing that delightful Dama Hafford before you arrived, and did it again after he'd gotten rid of you. For a muck-footed farmer, he has a certain . . . élan. Another man probably wouldn't have been able to get rid of you quite that fast."

"Stop talking to me, liar," Rion growled without looking at Drowd, suddenly more than upset. Coll was his friend and would never treat him badly, but . . . he'd been *kissing* Jovvi? Both before and after his appearance? Could that be why *his* invitation to the lady was so inappropriate? Because Coll had meant to make the same invitation himself?

"Consider me a liar if you will, but you can't doubt the evidence of your own eyes," Drowd said, as if from a far distance. "Watch the two of them during the meal, and then *you* tell *me* how Coll feels. He wants the woman for himself, and had no trouble pushing a bumbling oaf like you aside. For a muck-foot, he's really quite facile."

Drowd fell silent then, but that didn't matter since Rion was no longer listening anyway. He now waited for the others with a different purpose, and when Coll escorted Jovvi into the room, a bolt of pain flashed through Rion. From the way Coll looked at Jovvi, there was no possible doubt. He wanted the woman and planned to have her, even though it was Rion she'd given that marvelous gift to. If not for Coll, *he* would be the one she smiled at so beautifully. . . .

Rion ate the food put in front of him, but the details of what it was blurred behind his thinking and planning. If Coll were put out of the way somehow, *he* would have a clear path to Jovvi. Disappointment in Coll let Rion do that planning, a painful disappointment he hadn't expected to experience. Muck-foot or not, Coll had started to be a friend, but friends weren't supposed to behave the way he had. Rion had never had a friend, but even he knew that much.

By the arrival of dessert, Rion had decided what he would do. Once Coll was asleep he would be easy to reach, and despite certain misgivings, Rion was determined to do that reaching. It would be—

"Excuse me," a voice said, cutting through thoughts and table conversation alike. "I have an announcement you all need to hear."

Rion looked up along with everyone else, to see Lady Eltrina Razas standing just inside the dining room doors.

The representative of the testing authority looked as cool and distant as ever, with a gleam of some kind of satisfaction in her eyes that Rion found vaguely familiar.

"Thank you," she said when everyone had given her their attention, then she held up a sheaf of papers. "I have here your first session assignments, which I will shortly distribute to you. Your new clothing was delivered today, I know, so be sure to dress in it and be ready bright and early tomorrow. Coaches will be here to take you where you must go, and I wasn't joking about how early it will be. For that reason you will all go to bed as soon after dinner as you may, so that you'll be well rested. Believe me, tomorrow you'll need every bit of strength you can gather."

With that she came forward to distribute the sheets of paper, leaving Rion, at least, undecided. Tomorrow they would all be tested again, so maybe he would do well to change his plans. It would be foolish to do away with Coll tonight—foolish and hard to force himself to actually do—when one of the tests tomorrow could well do the job for him. Yes, that was the ticket, he'd let the tests kill Coll for him, and do it himself only if Coll survived.

Feeling much happier, Rion accepted the sheet of paper handed to him and left the dining room—but not before taking a last, anticipatory look at the incredible Jovvi.

TWENTY-EIGHT

The following morning wasn't just early, it was also raining. I stood with everyone else in the entrance hall, waiting for the coaches to pull up closer to the front door. I hadn't expected to fall asleep quickly last night but I had, and strangely enough I hadn't even been bothered by bad dreams. I felt well rested and had eaten a good breakfast, and was more ready to face what came than I'd thought would be possible last night. Maybe the nice but useless offer I'd had had done more good than I'd realized. . . .

I looked over at Vallant Ro where he stood with the men, dressed exactly the way they were and almost indistinguishable from Lorand Coll and Clarion Mardimil. All three were tall and broad-shouldered and blond, but Vallant Ro wasn't really like them. He had no intentions of making the most of the opportunity he'd been given, and would be gone as soon as he was allowed to leave. That was what had made his offer to protect me so useless, but I hadn't had the heart to say so.

"They do look rather impressive, don't they?" Jovvi murmured from my right, amusement in her voice. "Lorand without those ill-fitting bags is even more attractive than usual, Rion looks positively handsome without one of his costumes, and Vallant looks more like the dashing sea captain than ever. Did you enjoy how concerned he was about you yesterday?"

"Who's Rion?" I asked, ignoring what she'd said about Vallant Ro. He was someone who would best be forgotten, even though some part of me insisted on remembering how gently those big hands of his had been holding mine. . . .

"It's Rion rather than Clarion now," Jovvi said with obvious approval. "I suggested the name change, but he was the one who embraced the idea wholeheartedly. It will hopefully take him out of the narrow confines of his previous life, and let him expand and grow as a person should. I take it you'd rather not talk about Vallant Ro."

"Not here, certainly," I answered with a sigh, very aware of the lack of privacy. "And especially not now, with the coaches pulling up."

She turned to look at the first coach, whose driver was climbing down from the box after tying off his reins. He wasn't one of the drivers we'd had previously, and he strode toward us, ignoring the rain which had turned his cape and hat sodden.

"First coach is for Domon, Hafford, Lant, and Mardimil," he announced briskly without coming inside. "The rest will take the second coach. Step lively, if you please."

Beldara Lant made a sound of annoyance, but whether it

was because she had to travel with Jovvi and me again, or because she'd been told to hurry, I didn't know. Two of my servants stood ready with very large rain-shields to escort us to the coach, so we four who had been named stepped lively. Beldara pushed forward to climb into the coach first, but neither Jovvi nor I cared. We let Clarion—no, Rion—help us in, then sat back for the ride.

This time we were taken to another part of the city, the one that lies across the Magross bridge in what's considered Noble territory. Most of it looks just like any other part of Gan Garee, but the only people living in the lower-class housing are those who work in the shops and businesses based there. The members of the patrol guard make it their business to know all of them by sight, since anyone they don't know is summarily ejected from the area. And it isn't even possible to claim to be there just to shop. The price of everything is double to nonresidents, and residency has to be proven.

Carriage and coach traffic was, of course, much heavier in that part of town. It would have been fractionally better if it hadn't been raining, but not enough to have made the trip any shorter. The very quiet trip, with Beldara and Rion lost in their individual thoughts, and Jovvi apparently as reluctant as I to break the silence. Logically we should all have been thinking about what lay ahead, but somehow I felt that that wasn't the case. Jovvi might have been considering the coming tests, but I was fairly certain the other two had different things on their minds.

We finally turned off the main thoroughfare into the approach drive of two large buildings which stood fairly close together. A stone awning arched across the forty or so feet between them, providing a shelter for the side doors which opened opposite one another over there. Our coach pulled up to the building on the right, and the second coach, filled with the rest of those at my house, stopped to the left. We four were guided out and into the right hand building, then up five or six steps, with our driver leading the way.

"Fire magic, Air magic, and Spirit magic sessions are held in this building," the man said, opening his rain cape against the unexpected warmth of the place. The floor was open all across its length, just like the building where I'd originally gone to register for the first test, but three separate areas

contained tables and chairs. All of them were empty of
people right now, and the driver pointed to large, draped
signs hanging behind the three areas of tables and chairs.

"You can see by the symbols which area is for which
aspect," he went on. "Go through the door behind your own
aspect, and you'll be told what to do next. The coach will be
back to pick you up again this afternoon."

With that he turned and left us, giving none of us a chance
to ask how *late* this afternoon. It was now barely past eight in
the morning, which would have made the answer somewhat
significant.

"Well, we might as well get on with it," Jovvi said, and I
gave up watching the departing back of our driver to see that
Beldara and Rion had already begun to walk toward their
respective doors. "Let's wish each other good luck, even if we
won't need it. We have skill and talent, which take the place
of a good deal of luck."

"You still won't find me turning down the luck," I said
with a smile before exchanging hugs with her. "And you'd
probably feel the same if you had Beldara sharing *your*
aspect."

"Not probably, definitely," she agreed, then grew serious.
"Be certain you watch your back where she's concerned. If
she can ruin things for you, she'll do it."

I nodded to show I already knew that, then parted from
Jovvi to follow after Beldara. The woman who shared my
aspect acted as if she were all alone in the building, but her
pace was faster than your average uncaring stroll. She
seemed to want to leave me far behind, but walking wasn't
the way she'd be able to do that. I increased my own pace a
little, and passed under the flame sign only a moment behind
her.

I was able to catch the door before it closed completely,
and walked into a fairly large room right behind Beldara.
There were four men standing around to the left of the door,
all of them wearing the same clothing and identification
cards that we did. The room itself was lamplit and separated
into sections by walls of what seemed to be transparent resin,
with a narrow hall running between the sections both left
and right. The area we stood in had been left unpartitioned,
and once Beldara and I were in it another man came from
one of the sections to the left.

"Well, how nice to see that the newcomers have finally made it," he said, looking us over with very little approval. He wore expensive trousers and coat in a bright green, a yellow silk shirt, and a very red ascot that didn't go with the rest at all. The way he moved said he considered himself quite important, and he obviously expected us to think the same.

"For those of you who don't already know, I am Forum, High rated Adept, and your examiner in Fire magic for the next few days," the man continued, flicking a finger under his red ascot. "Anyone wearing the color of our aspect like this is the same, so I would advise you newcomers to be on your best behavior. If you anger the wrong person, whatever promise you've shown will end a broken vow."

He looked around as he said that, apparently expecting something, but he didn't get it. One or two of the men shifted uneasily, but no one said a word.

"My goodness, you *are* becoming a promising group," he said with a laugh after a moment, his narrow face wearing a sarcastically patronizing look. "There's usually at least one among the newcomers who blurts out his horror at the idea of someone using their talent to harm someone else. That sort needs to be reminded that the laws aren't quite the same among *us* as they are everywhere else. But you already seem to know that, so let's get on with getting you started. Watch closely."

He took two paces back, and then a long rope of fire appeared in front of him. I say a rope, because that's what the section of fire most resembled. It burned as greedily as fire always does, but I could feel the way his talent held it firmly in the shape and state he wanted it in.

"Again for the newest newcomers, the first thing you will practice is achieving this exact shape," Adept Forum said, obviously not straining in the least. "What you want is an obedient length of hemp, and once you have it you must learn to divide it in two. When you have two obedient lengths, you'll then practice twining them about each other like so."

He'd separated his rope into two narrower ropes, with both of them still under perfect control. Then he began to wind the two lengths of fire around each other, but they weren't allowed to merge. They stayed individual lengths from top to bottom, which seemed to shock some of the others. Their gasps gave me the first hint that what was being done was considered unusual, since I'd been able to do the same for years. I didn't know whether or not to admit that, then decided to wait and see how things went.

"Please don't be overly impressed," Forum said then, his tone very dry. "You'll be expected to master that and more before you're allowed to compete with our more experienced applicants, and you must bear one very important point in mind: bonuses in gold are won only with a victory in a competition. If you don't manage to qualify for the competitions, you can't possibly win a bonus. Now follow me."

He led the way up the narrow hall to the right, and at the end of it put each of us in a separate area that was rather small, lit by a glaringly bright lamp, and which contained a single chair. The chair was a crude wooden thing that promised to be very uncomfortable, but I'd seen much better chairs in the areas closer to the door we'd come in by. That had to be another way to convince us to do the best we could, along with the threat of holding back the gold most of us needed to pay for food with. They were determined to find out what we were really capable of, but I'd decided to be determined about something too.

I sat down in the chair inside my little cubicle, but still had no trouble seeing the others through the transparent resin. Even the man in the cubicle opposite mine was behind resin, as the door to his cubicle wasn't lined up with my own. That had to be a precaution against someone losing control of the fire they'd summoned, which made a good deal of sense. Those who lose control also occasionally lose their heads, and I had no desire to need to defend myself.

But that only applied to someone's runaway fire. Where the people conducting those sessions were concerned, I meant to defend myself by hiding in a forest of other applicants. I would never be the first or the last to master some technique, at least until I'd had the chance to look around and maybe even speak to Jovvi. She and I had wondered what these people could be up to, and by remaining as invisible as possible we might find out. I'd have to qualify for the competitions and try to win there, of course, but that would come later. Right now what I needed was camouflage.

So I watched my fellow applicants out of the corners of my eyes, and when two of them had managed to gentle their pillars of flame, I did the same. It took the same two a bit longer to separate their ropes in half and keep them separate, but I followed along with quite a lot of shifting in my chair. And once things began to happen, I discovered I didn't have to hide my looking around. By then everyone was doing it, to see who was doing better and who worse.

About an hour after we started, four more people arrived. They were two men and two women, and their clothing and identification said they were also applicants. Adept Forum put them in another set of cubicles, ones with better chairs, and we soon discovered why. They all began with three strands of fire, and the patterns they wove were fairly intricate.

An hour later two more people came in, both men. When they took their places they began to form four-stranded patterns, and an hour beyond that brought a single woman who practiced with five strands. By then everyone in our original group had two separate strands, and winding them into a coil was the objective. I couldn't wait until we were beyond that point, because I wanted to try three strands. I'd never done that much on my own, and was looking forward to seeing how long it took me to master it.

About an hour after that, Adept Forum came through with a placard announcing lunchtime. I let my flames die out and got painfully to my feet, wondering if my back would ever be the same. Four hours of sitting in that chair had almost crippled me, and trying to stretch out the kinks hurt even more. I glanced around to see that the others were also on their feet, but Beldara was looking at me rather than trying to twist her body back into proper shape. Her face wore a look of spiteful triumph, and I didn't have to wonder why. She was the one I'd followed directly along after, which apparently had convinced her that she was my superior. Well, if it made her happy, let her think it. Only time would tell both of us the truth.

Our group had to wait until everyone else had left the room before we were free to go, but there were still plenty of empty tables where we could take our solitary meals. I'd hoped to be able to join Jovvi in either her area of mine, but the three aspects were being kept strictly separated. Most of our six stood or walked around their chosen table until servants appeared with trays of food and drink, but two of the men had collapsed into the more comfortable chairs as though they were exhausted. One of those two had only just managed a tentative coil before lunch was announced, and the other hadn't even gotten that far.

Tea was brought to everyone rather quickly, but food was another matter. The lone woman was served first and then the two men, and then there was a delay, as though only small amounts of food could be produced at one time. I poured a cup of tea and sat to drink it, at the same time beginning to rethink my position. It looked as if we were going to be arranged according to ability in everything, and the front of the line was quite some distance ahead.

Which brought back memory of the speculation Jovvi and I had indulged in. Not everyone testing could end up as a Seated High, or even qualify to try for the position, but everyone there was a *potential* High. One position for those who didn't quite make it was Adept examiner, obviously, but Adept Forum was someone who considered himself a good deal more important than he actually was. Important people don't spend their time with newcomers, showing them how to do beginning exercises.

So the position of Adept was one I had no interest in, for more reasons than simple prestige. I needed real power and standing to stay out of my father's reach, which at times stretched even to certain members of the nobility. That meant I couldn't afford to stay down near the bottom of the group, even if we *didn't* know what happened to everyone who showed strong ability. Not showing it would doom me as surely as anything the testing authority might do, since there was no doubt that marrying another man like Gimmis would break my mind. The first time Odrin Hallasser hurt me I would turn him to cinders, and then probably not even notice when they sent me to the Deep Caverns.

I took a long swallow of the tea to warm the chill from my insides, determined to keep any of that horror from happening. It was a shame that so few people knew those with more than ordinary ability, or fewer women would be savaged. No one tried to rob or attack a stranger, not when that stranger might be capable of anything, but those who were known were another story. If it was understood that even those supposedly known might show stronger ability under stress . . . Well, that was a dream. People knew what they knew, and facts weren't going to change their minds.

It was quite some time before food was brought to my group, and predictably enough I was the third to be served. Beldara luxuriated in that fact, all but preening herself and laughing aloud. Such spoiled-child behavior really irritated me, and I couldn't wait until the session started again.

Which didn't take long. When you're served last you have only a short time to eat, and I wasn't quite through when Adept Forum appeared to order us back to the room. I knew I should have anticipated that, so I was more annoyed with myself than with the testing authority when I reclaimed that awful chair in my cubicle. If I wanted to be free of harassment, I'd have to use ability to achieve it.

Which was not quite as easily done as decided. I opened myself to the power, formed two ropes of fire and coiled them about each other, then separated them again. That was to show I could do again what I'd done earlier, and was also something of a warm-up for my confidence. I *wanted* to handle three strands, but a lifetime of being doubted makes you sometimes think your critics might be right.

So I had to prove they weren't. Merging the two original strands and then separating them into three strands wasn't hard, but that was just the beginning. I had to open myself to more of the power to keep control of the three, and then had to concentrate on moving the strands while keeping them from merging back into a single pillar again. Fire must spread to live, and unifying with other parts of itself lets it spread more completely. I was in the midst of denying the very nature of fire, not an easy battle under any circumstance.

By the time I had a simple plait formed, the sweat on my forehead had begun to thicken. But I did have three strands of fire braided together, and only one of the others around me, a heavy man, had done the same. Beldara couldn't seem to keep two of her three strands from merging when she tried to weave them together, and the last three men couldn't seem to produce three strands. One of them was still having trouble handling two, and seemed about as far from achieving a coil as he'd been that morning. I wondered about that . . .

. . . and after a moment had a fairly good guess. The man's face was as covered with sweat as my own, but it was the sweat of fear rather than of effort. He seemed to be afraid to open himself to enough of the power to get the job done, a handicap I'd heard about once. It usually affected those who'd seen someone burn themselves out trying to accommodate more power than they could handle, and getting past the problem took more determination than most people had. Happily, though, that was something I didn't have to worry about; I'll take being burned out over being married off again any time.

Most of the afternoon had gone by while I fought with the three strands, and the woman and two men who had arrived last had already left. But Adept Forum hadn't come by to release us, so I started all over again with the three strands. Doing it a second time proved easier, and by then Beldara had tamed her three strands and had plaited them half way. She'd also sweated with the effort, but the heavy man who'd managed his plait along with my first sat cool and serene. He hadn't tried it a second time, only maintained his first effort, and maintaining is a good deal easier than doing.

Just a few minutes later Adept Forum came through with a placard that said the session was over, so I let the strands go with a lot of relief. The more power you use the more your strength is drained, and the less strength you have, the less power you can handle. Exercising an ability is like someone without Air magic walking a tightrope: one miscalculation can send you falling through empty air, to end broken and dead on the very hard ground below. You tend not to think of that when you're well-rested, but when you're tired. . . .

Adept Forum gathered us in the area near the doors again, then looked around and said, "You will all be here tomorrow morning at the same time, to practice the same exercise. For those of you who have been at it quite a while, let me remind you that this week is your last chance. If you haven't qualified by week's end, you never will."

The exhausted-looking man who hadn't even managed to coil his strands paled even more, but he didn't say anything. Two of the other men showed determined expressions, but the last of them was very upset.

"How can you do that?" he demanded in an unsteady voice. "I'm just about out of silver, and if I can't compete for gold I'll starve! You have to give me more time!"

"More time is not mine to give," Adept Forum returned, the sympathy in his voice so exaggerated that there wasn't a chance of its being real. "The Trials will soon be upon us, and everyone's efforts will be going into that. There will *be* no more sessions, no more residence for those who haven't qualified, no more chances of any sort. You have until week's end, and that's all there is to it."

The man who'd protested seemed about to cry, but he didn't say anything else. Adept Forum waited to be certain of that, and then he looked at me.

"You, my dear, may ignore what I said to the others," he purred, now more sleek and ingratiating than sarcastic. "If you wish, you may report here an hour later than these others, and you'll no longer be seated among them. Achievement earns many rewards, and your work with three strands has earned you those."

"Why just her?" the heavy man who'd formed his plait along with mine demanded, his round, fleshy face no longer cool and calm. "I did the same thing she did, and at almost the same time!"

"You did indeed," Adept Forum granted, looking the heavy man up and down. "But after that accomplishment you simply basked in its light, making no effort to repeat the performance and gain greater facility. You're like the rest of those left here, content to be just a little better than those around you, and you'll certainly join them in being left behind. This lovely young lady will forge ahead to the competitions, and the rest of you will be obscured by her glow. You are now dismissed."

He turned then and walked away to the left, leaving me with the urge to commit physical mayhem. He'd singled me out deliberately as an object of hatred for the others, someone they would now want to best at any cost. He obviously hoped to provoke them into making more of an effort, and the glares they sent toward me before stalking out said they meant to try. But even if they succeeded they would still hate me, and if they didn't. . . .

I stretched my back gingerly as I followed them, forcing away consideration of possible spiteful retaliatory actions in order to think about what was really more important. What we hadn't been told earlier was that these would be *practice* sessions, and that after this week there would be no more of them. Those who had passed the initial test months ago would have had all this time to practice for the Trials, but all *we* would have was this single week. If I'd thought the testing authority had any sense of decency and fairness, this latest fact would have quickly changed my mind.

There appeared to be less than twenty people left in the large building, but the others were all heading for the front doors rather than the side one I'd come in by, so I did the same. It would be nice if it had stopped raining, but it would be nicer yet if I could rid myself of the sinking feeling in the pit of my stomach. Adept Forum had said the people left in my session were those who would never qualify, and they'd obviously been trying for a good deal longer than a week. What if I turned out to be just like them, and couldn't qualify either? What would become of me then?

I discovered I'd stopped in the middle of the floor, one hand to my middle to hold back the sickness, so I hurried on toward the doors. I needed very badly to be home, to help me come to grips with the stark truth: in less than a week and in one way or another, my future would be settled forever.

Twenty-nine

The new Rion Mardimil thought he would take the opportunity of being in the same carriage with Jovvi to speak to her, but once they were all settled in place he changed his mind. What he most wanted to say to her would be awkward in front of two other women, especially when one of them was Tamrissa Domon. She attracted Rion almost as much as Jovvi did, but in a slightly different way. He wasn't certain why that was, but for the moment was unprepared to delve into the question. To go literally overnight from being all but unaware of women to pursuing two of them would have been far too much.

So Rion endured the silent carriage ride, accompanied the

ladies into the building they were brought to, then went in the direction of the banner with the symbol of Air magic on it. The door beyond the banner led into an odd sort of room, large but separated into individual cubicles, all to the left and right of the area just inside the door. In that area stood two women and a man, and a moment after Rion joined them another woman, without the identification the rest of them wore, appeared from the left. "Now that our newest addition has arrived, you may all take your cubicles," the woman said, her tone and manner almost as haughty as that of Lady Eltrina, the testing authority representative. "Go and begin your practice, and I'll see to him individually."

The others nodded and obediently moved off toward the right, making Rion frown. He was the only newcomer, and all the others were ahead of him? The thought of that was an uncomfortable one, but he wasn't given time to consider the point.

"I'm Adept Aminto, in charge of applicants in Air magic," the woman said almost immediately, her pretty face still showing disapproval. "You'd best be courteous to those who wear white ascots like mine, as they are also adepts in our aspect. I'll show you to a cubicle now and demonstrate what must be done, and then leave you to it."

"Just a moment," Rion said, stopping her before she might turn away. "I have one small matter I'd like to see to before we begin. This identification card which was given me has an error which must be corrected. My given name is Rion, not Clarion, so your records and the card have to be changed."

"Oh, bother," the woman grumbled, stepping closer to peer at the card hanging against his chest. "How did they manage to do *that*? Well, no matter, I'll simply have to deal with it later. For now, just follow me."

This time Rion made no effort to stop her, but merely followed as she'd directed. She moved up the hall to the right in the same direction the others had taken, hesitated when she'd nearly reached the end, then went on to enter the cubicle next to one of the women and opposite the man. Her manner seemed to be reluctant now, and when she turned to look at Rion she appeared apologetic.

"I'm sorry, but I really do have to put you in here today," she said, confirming Rion's impression. "You'll find the chair horrible to sit in, but as soon as you've mastered at least two of the basic exercises I'll be able to move you to a better cubicle."

"You're certain then that I'll master them," Rion said, trying not to show his surprise and confusion. "Since we've never met before, what makes you so certain?"

"How could anyone look at you and have any doubt?" she answered at once, then blushed and seemed ready to bite her tongue. "I mean, you do appear extremely competent. . . . Please sit down, and I'll demonstrate the first exercise."

Rion went to the wooden chair and sat, finding it just as uncomfortable as she'd said it would be. But he was too amused to be bothered, as he'd figured out why Adept Aminto had said what she had. The woman was attracted to him, he could feel it in each of her movements and words, and that was something which had never happened to him before. It made him feel odd, but definitely good-odd.

"The manipulation of air is too difficult to see, so we've provided these ribbons to make the exercises more visual," Aminto said as soon as Rion was settled, picking up two silk ribbons of different colors from a small table which held five ribbons. "What you'll do is surround them with columns—thin columns—of thickened air, and then you'll coil them about each other. But make sure the columns remain separate, otherwise the ribbons will show that they've merged."

As she spoke she used the power to do as she'd described, coiling the two colorful ribbons around as though they twined up an invisible pole. But then the ribbons suddenly rushed toward one another, and stuck together as though glued.

"You see?" she asked, glancing at Rion. "Only by maintaining two separate columns will you be able to keep the ribbons apart. Would you like to try it now?"

"In a moment," Rion said, suspecting he would have little trouble performing the trick. "Tell me first why these others seem to have failed at so simple a task. Haven't they been here for a while after having passed the initial test?"

"Yes, of course they passed the test, and they *have* been here for a time, but—" Aminto paused, as though searching for the proper words, but then she shrugged. "They did what they had to in order to save their lives, but beyond that they're useless," she stated bluntly. "They're the sort who have to be pushed into doing anything at all, because for one reason or another they can't turn their potential into reality by themselves. They're losers and will stay losers, because they refuse to take charge of their own lives."

She looked at Rion warily, as though afraid of what his reaction would be, then seemed relieved when he simply nodded. It was the only thing he *could* do, after all, when he understood the point so personally. He was really the same person he'd always been, but it had taken the government to force him out of his rut, and a name change to make him feel like a man. A *different* man, one who made things happen rather than one who struggled to cope when things happened by themselves. He didn't understand why "Clarion" hadn't done what "Rion" seemed to find so effortless, but he refused to argue with the results—or go back to being a "loser."

When it was clear that Rion had nothing more to say, Aminto left him alone to practice. He thickened the air around the red and yellow ribbons Aminto had returned to the table, then lifted them up and began to twine them about each other. He'd done the same thing any number of times with blades of grass when he was younger, but he took his time "learning" how to do it. What he'd already learned was not to rush into anything, at least until he'd had a look around.

Less than an hour later two more men appeared, each taking a cubicle closer to the doors. They began their practice using three ribbons, braiding them together— *almost* together—into a plait. After doing that, one of the two tried to bring a fourth ribbon into play. For a moment it looked as if he would succeed, but then all four ribbons flew together. He'd obviously lost control of the columns of air, and Rion wondered why. Were four columns that much more difficult to handle?

Rather than investigate the question immediately, Rion decided to be circumspect and work his way up to it. Caution was a concept he was unfamiliar with except where his magic was concerned, but he'd certainly had to be cautious with *it* to keep Mother from lecturing him after finding him playing with it. So he took his time coiling two ribbons, did it a few more times as though feeling the need to practice, then finally added a third ribbon. Keeping three columns of air distinct and separate took more power than he normally used, not to mention concentration. If one failed to pay attention, the columns merged into one and so did the ribbons.

By the time Rion had reached the point of plaiting the ribbons easily, two more men had arrived, one at a time. The first began to work with four ribbons and the second with five, but Rion was almost able to *feel* their efforts. What they did wasn't done easily, nor with very much confidence. It was as if they expected failure at any moment, and strove only to hold it off rather than continue on to improve their grip.

This made very little sense to Rion, but he wasn't given the time to think about it for long. Aminto appeared with a placard announcing lunchtime—and a private nod and smile for Rion—so he put the ribbons aside and left his cubicle. The others were all heading out the door, but the man who'd had the cubicle opposite Rion's fell into step with him.

"Congratulations on your progress," the man said wryly, glancing tiredly at Rion. "I'm Mern Follil, and if you're willing to share your secret, I'm willing to listen."

"Rion Mardimil," Rion supplied, completing introductions. "But what do you mean by 'secret?' If you have more than a Middle's ability with magic, you should be able to do the same."

"They say I'm a potential High, but I can't seem to pick up the knack," Follil confessed with a sigh, leading the way out of the room and toward the tables and chairs where most of the others were already seated. "And it *is* a knack, so I'd be grateful for any advice you'd care to give."

The man wasn't quite as tall as Rion and was thin with red hair and blue eyes, but Rion felt the urge to stare as though the other had two heads. What Follil had said was meaningless, but he didn't have the time to correct him.

"I'm afraid we're going to have to continue this discussion at another time," Rion said as Follil stopped at an empty table large enough for two. "I noticed an office of my bank only a block away from here, and I really must run over there to arrange a withdrawal. It's preposterous to walk around without a penny, I know, but—"

"You can't mean you don't know?" Follil said with a short laugh that had no amusement in it. "You're an applicant, so your bank won't be permitted to give you a single copper. You'll have to beg funds from the testing authority like the rest of us, or else go hungry. Until you qualify to compete, that is, but you still have a long way to go. There's double the difference in handling four strands rather than three than there is between three strands and two. When it comes to five strands you can triple the difference from four, so you might as well sit down to lunch and recoup your strength."

Follil pulled out a chair and took his own advice, but Rion hesitated. The man had sounded certain about what would happen at Rion's bank, but Follil was obviously not a member of Rion's class. Best would be to check on the matter personally, although a terrible suspicion had begun to grow in Rion's insides.

"Thanks for the advice, Follil, but I need some exercise anyway," Rion said, fighting to sound casual. "If I run over to my bank for nothing, at least I'll have gotten the exercise. See you later."

Follil raised his eyes to the ceiling and shook his head with a sigh, and that annoyed Rion as he strode toward the building's front door. A man who thought there was a "knack" to using the ability he'd been born with had no right to look down at *him*. It was almost too bad that he'd decided to see what he could learn from these people, and was therefore going out of his way to be polite. Under normal circumstances he would have told the man exactly what he thought of him.

Outside it was still raining, so Rion used a shield made of air to keep himself dry while he jogged to the bank. He also tucked his identification inside his shirt in case Follil was partially right, but he might as well not have bothered. The office's manager came out to bow and scrape, but his roundabout apology came to the same thing a rude rebuff would have: the testing authority had cut him off from all his funds, and the suggestion of a loan was quite impossible.

Rion jogged back to the testing building, needing the effort to help cool his temper. Those people had turned him into a pauper, and the only way to change that was to compete and earn one of their bonuses. Rion intended to do just that, but the idea of having no choice in the matter threatened to make him furious. He wasn't a loser who needed to be forced to perform, so how dare they do that to him?

Food was only just being brought out when Rion reached the tables, so he sat down and let himself be served. Only the tea was really palatable, but Rion forced himself to stuff down the fuel he'd need for the afternoon's efforts. He was just finishing up when Follil appeared and sat at the table without waiting for an invitation.

"Was I right?" the red-haired man asked airily, then waved a hand. "Of course I was right, otherwise you would hardly have come back in such a temper. But you can get even with them, you know, simply by teaching me that knack. In turn I'll teach it to the ladies, and then all of us can go forward and begin to compete. When we win they'll be forced to pay us gold and they'll hate that, so let's get started now."

The man looked at him with such pathetic eagerness and thinly veiled greed that Rion regretted having eaten the awful food. Barefaced stupidity tended to turn his stomach, and he was in no mood to respond with anything but the truth.

"Are *you* the fool, Follil, or do you take *me* for one?" Rion demanded, keeping his voice low only with effort. "There's no trick involved here, or what you keep calling a knack. You simply open to the power, pay attention to what you're doing, then accomplish what you set out to do. If you don't understand that, how did you survive the test?"

"I don't remember what I did during the test," the man responded sullenly. "I was too frightened to notice when I discovered the knack, so I lost it again. You didn't lose it, but you're not about to share it with anyone, are you? You're just like the others, refusing to give a fellow human being a hand, so to the Deep Caverns with you! I'll find it again myself, and when I do I'll see that you never win so much as a copper in the competitions!"

And with that he stood up and stalked off, leaving Rion to sit and shake his head. The man just didn't want to hear the truth, not when he needed a "trick" to help him do what he should have been able to do without one. Having lost that special knack was his excuse for not trying his absolute best, but Rion couldn't understand why anyone would do that. Wasn't life bad enough that no excuse was needed to make the effort to change it for the better? It was certainly easier to use the excuse and stay a loser, but why would anyone want to?

Those questions were apparently too profound to be answered quickly, as Rion was called back to the practice room with the others before any explanations came to him. He was prepared to return to the cubicle and that abominable chair, but Aminto stopped him before he reached them.

"You've earned a better cubicle just as I knew you would," she purred, putting her hand to his arm before pointing to a cubicle nearer the door. "You can use that one now, which you'll enjoy a good deal more. And tonight you'll be expected to go straight back to your residence, but perhaps tomorrow night . . . if you continue to improve . . . you can join me for dinner. We'll see. . . ."

She touched his arm again as though directing him into the new cubicle, but her palm slid over his biceps and triceps in a way that was more annoying than interesting. He hadn't invited her to touch him, so what right did she have to do it anyway? Such behavior was outrageous, and apparently it wasn't one of those things considered acceptable that Rion didn't know about. Aminto hadn't let the others see what she was doing, and once having done it she glided away to wherever she waited while they practiced.

Rion had to deliberately calm himself as he entered the cubicle, but sitting in the new chair helped. It was padded to a certain degree and angled a bit rather than rigidly straight, and that made sitting in it a good deal less uncomfortable. Not actually comfortable, but definitely less uncomfortable. Ah well, he was there to practice, after all, not to nap, but maybe once he'd mastered *four* ribbons. . . .

Visions of another step upward—or, rather, a better chair—put Rion's attention back into practicing. He plaited three ribbons again just to warm up, then tried his hand with four. His first try turned into a disaster, and the four ribbons, clinging to one another, fell to the floor when he released them. Managing four columns of air *was* harder than managing three, a lot harder than he'd thought it would be. Maybe Follil was right about those increasing degrees of difficulty . . .

"No," Rion said aloud, straightening in the chair. "Follil is a loser but I am not, so I refuse to believe an excuse. Four columns *are* harder to handle, but not impossibly hard."

And with that he set about trying to understand why he'd failed. After experimenting for a short while the answer suddenly came, but not an answer designed to bring soothing and satisfaction. It had occurred to Rion that he wasn't using enough power to handle four separate objects, but hadn't opened himself to more because he was already using more than he ever had before. There *was* such a thing as natural limits to what one did with one's aspect, and too often those who tried to pass the limits experienced all sorts of gruesome happenings.

But just what was *his* limit? Rion didn't know, and the truth of the matter was that the only way to find out was to press on until he was stopped. That was far from the best way of doing things, and sudden insight suggested that this was the problem which had stopped Follil and the others. Those two men who had achieved handling four and five strands respectively . . . no wonder they'd only been trying to hold their own rather than working for a surer grip. Doing the second would have required more power, and they surely feared they were already pressing their limits.

Rion took a deep breath as he studied his hands, wishing he could scoff at those fears as he once would have. Now he was in the midst of understanding them only too well, as he had no desire to die after having only just begun to live. As little as it was, he nevertheless had something to lose—but if he refused to take the risk, would he win? They would most likely release him eventually to return to the life he'd left, which was exactly what he'd wanted. But could he do that now, after everything he'd experienced? It had been hard enough then, which meant that now it would be impossible.

So he would be released to *not* go home, which would leave him where? Even if Mother continued to pay his allowance, how far would that rather modest amount go? And what would he do if the allowance was stopped, which was much more likely? Beg in the streets? Look for a woman like Aminto who had power and gold enough to support him as well as herself? Something told him he'd be better off choosing the streets and begging. . . .

But all that added up to a decision on his part. He took another deep breath, this time one of determination rather than depression, enjoying the sense of freedom which now filled him. Simply living would quickly become worse than a clean, swift death, so what did he have to lose by pressing his limits? If he lived it had to be on *his* terms, which meant winning a place for himself that couldn't be taken away at someone's whim. He was a member of the nobility, after all, so who had a better chance of being victorious?

Turning his attention to the ribbons again, Rion opened himself to enough more power to handle four separate columns of air. That brought him the hint of a tingle he'd never felt before, but the tingle faded quickly and didn't return so he wasn't distracted. Handling four columns and keeping them separate took concentration, but that too became easier with practice. Not easy, at least not at first, but certainly easier every time he did it from scratch.

By the time Rion had formed the third complicated arrangement using four ribbons and was no longer straining, Aminto came by with a placard announcing the end of the session. Instead of simply dropping the ribbons, Rion put them neatly back on the table where they belonged before he left the cubicle. Follil and the two women stood near the door with Aminto, and when Rion joined them Aminto smiled at him.

"For you, Dom Mardimil, another identification card with your name corrected, and our apologies for the error," she said, handing him the new card and chain arrangement which he'd forgotten he'd asked for. "I'll take the incorrect one, if you please."

Rion had been looking around for a place to throw away the card with his former name, but hadn't found one. Giving the thing to Aminto let him be rid of it, and then he put on the new identification with a good deal of pleasure.

"I'm also delighted to be able to inform you that you may choose to come here two hours later tomorrow morning," she continued, that purr still in her voice. "Your accomplishments have earned you that, as well as a new and even better cubicle. A pity these others will never earn the same. Good evening to you now, and I'll see you again tomorrow."

She turned left and walked away from them then, but not before showing Rion the gleam in her eyes at mention of the next day. She apparently looked forward to something that would never happen if *he* had any say in the matter, but there was no need to mention that. He would also save correcting her use of "dom" rather than "lord" to him, specifically if she tried to press him. Some men might accept that sort of treatment, but Rion had no intentions of being one of them.

Follil and the women glared at him before leaving the room with noses in the air, and that amused Rion as he followed. He had quite a lot of practice at being snubbed or ignored, and by people who were much better at it than these three fools. And it seemed to have stopped raining, which was delightful news. They would be able to await their coaches out front in the fresh air, rather than crowded together inside by the side door.

Rion felt considerably drained, but stepping outside and taking a deep breath of rain-freshened air restored him a bit. He stood in the midst of a number of others, and it suddenly occurred to him that he ought to be looking for the ladies he'd arrived with. So he turned to do just that—and promptly found himself being bounced off of. Someone had bumped into him, a rather small and soft someone.

"Oh, I'm terribly sorry!" a lovely—and somehow familiar—voice exclaimed. "I should have been watching where I was—Oh, goodness."

Rion looked down to see the lady he'd chosen in the tavern two nights earlier, the beautiful girl with dark hair and large green eyes. She wore considerably more clothing now, quite attractive and tasteful clothing, in fact, but her lovely face was flushed with embarrassment.

"Please excuse me, sir," she said hurriedly, a worried look also in her eyes. "We've never met, of course, and I didn't mean to imply that we had. I'll just—"

"But of course we've met," Rion interrupted, wondering why the pretty little thing seemed so nervous. "I find myself guilty of the unforgivable sin of not recalling your name, but I certainly remember all the rest—and with a great deal of fondness. I'm Rion Mardimil."

"And I'm Naran Whist," she replied with an even deeper blush, then lowered her voice to add, "Are you sure you don't mind talking to me? Most gentlemen find it embarrassing, so I've learned not to 'recognize' anyone. Even when they look as marvelous as you do in those clothes . . ."

Her voice trailed off in a way that made Rion grin as her gaze moved over him. Now *here* was appreciation from a lady that a man could enjoy getting.

"Not only don't I mind, I'm delighted we've run into each other again," he said, taking her slender and graceful hand to bend over. "It pains me that circumstances are such that I'm unable to invite you to supper, but I expect that to change very shortly. May I call on you when they do?"

"Oh, that would be wonderful," she said adoringly, her fingers to the place on her hand where his lips had touched. "I've never been invited to supper . . . But I really must ask you to excuse me now. I have a—an appointment here, and I'm already a bit late. It was so nice to see you again . . ."

"Wait," Rion said as she began to leave. "Where can I find you when the supper becomes possible? At the tavern?"

"Oh, no, that was really my first time there, and I haven't gone back," she said with a small laugh. "The memory of our time together was too wonderful to ruin. I live in Seeleem Street, Wishfon White. First is Wishfon Blue, then Wishfon Green, then Wishfon White."

"I'll find it," Rion called after her as she fled into the building with a final wave. He really did hate to see her go, and that was very strange. He'd lain with the girl, but other than that knew nothing about her. Why, then, was he even now wishing he hadn't had to let her go?

The question was so absorbing that the ladies found him instead of him finding them. Their coach was just behind the one now being boarded, so when it pulled up he helped them inside and climbed in himself. All three of them looked just as tired as he felt, and when the carriage began to move, Tamrissa sighed deeply.

"On the way home at last," she said with weary satisfaction. "And if we ladies don't get to use the bath house first, I vow to poison every gentleman in the residence."

"Anything but that," Rion pleaded with a grin while Jovvi laughed. "Lunch was poisoning enough for one day, so for my part I willingly grant you ladies first use. And since the others surely know what's good for them, I'm certain they'll agree."

"Good," Tamrissa said, her bloodthirsty satisfaction unusual but seeming perfectly natural. "I'm really too tired to bother with poison, but I will if I have to. On important worldly matters, one must always stand firm."

Rion joined Jovvi's second laugh, but noticed that Beldara was back to ignoring the world. This time the red-haired woman's silence seemed more sullen and seething than previously, but Rion was too uninterested to wonder why. He had much better things to think about, like Naran Whist and when he would be able to see her again. He'd have to get to those competitions as quickly as possible, and then he'd have to win. . . .

They were nearly to the house before Rion remembered that Jovvi was there, and what his plans had been concerning her. He still found her incredibly, deliciously attractive, but something small had changed inside him. No longer was he willing to harm Coll in order to have Jovvi to himself, which came as a great relief. He liked Coll and valued the man's advice, and now that would not have to end. Perhaps he would mention Naran to Coll, but then again, perhaps not. . . .

THIRTY

Jovvi took a wrap with her to the bath house rather than a change of clothing, and was pleased to find Tamrissa doing the same. They would have to dress again for dinner, and her weary body felt that that was quite soon enough.

"No sign of Beldara," Tamrissa remarked as they moved up the walk toward the bath house. "Either she's already inside, or she's decided against joining us. And if she's already here, I'm certain she'll leave as soon as *I* walk in."

"You outdid her, then," Jovvi said with an approving nod. "I was afraid you might be foolish enough to let *her* do better just for the sake of peace."

"In a manner of speaking I did just that until lunchtime, and then I realized how foolish I was being," Tamrissa answered, reaching for the door pull. "What was *your* session like?"

"Difficult in more ways than one," Jovvi replied, rubbing

ᴇr back with one hand as she walked in to find the bath ʜouse empty—as she'd known it would be. "That first chair ᴡas impossible, and the second one was almost as bad. They ɢenerated fields of pitching emotions for us, and we had to ʙalance tiny spheres in the field. You have to use both ꜱtrength and finesse to balance the emotional field, and once ʏou get it settled with two spheres, they add a third. It goes ᴀll the way up to five spheres, with each balance-point ᴅifferent, but I don't know what happens after that."

"After that, I think, are the competitions," Tamrissa said ꜱlowly, also slowing in the midst of undressing. "Jovvi . . . I ᴋept my progress down to a minimum at first because of ᴡhat we discussed, you know, not knowing what happened ᴛo all those people who passed the test. I still don't know if I ᴅid the right thing by passing so many of the others, but we ᴡere told that this is the last week of sessions. Anyone who ᴅoesn't qualify by week's end won't have another chance to ᴅo it."

"We weren't told that," Jovvi said with a frown, also pausing for a moment. "What did they say would happen to those who don't qualify?"

"Nothing specific, except for being thrown out of their residence penniless," Tamrissa said, and Jovvi was able to feel the girl's surge of fear at the thought. "That would be horrible for me, but you shouldn't mind it much. It would let you continue on with the plans you've made."

"Would it?" Jovvi asked, finally able to discuss the thoughts she'd had on the subject. "It occurred to me that I've never met anyone who'd been through testing for High, and didn't even know someone who had. The only Middles I've ever met weren't strong enough to qualify for testing, so they don't count. Have *you* ever met a former applicant, or know someone who met one?"

"No," Tamrissa admitted, and again Jovvi felt a thrill of fear flash through the other woman. "That could mean there are just very few of them, or else—or else no one who fails to qualify really is turned loose. Do you think they're . . . killed?"

"I have no idea," Jovvi admitted frankly, a faint chill touching her as well. "But we have to remember that death isn't the worst thing that can be done to you. That's why I worked as hard as I could, on the theory that a slim chance is better than none. We also don't know what happens to successful applicants who don't win a place as High, but whatever it is won't happen as soon as the result of failing to qualify."

Tamrissa silently nodded her reluctant agreement with that, and then they finished undressing in a matching silence. Jovvi led the way into the water, submerged completely to rid herself of the leavings of sweat, then headed for a corner and a headrest where she might soak a little.

"We can't stay in here *too* long, but I'm in no state to just wash and get out," Jovvi said when Tamrissa came up from her own submersion. "And I've been thinking that we ought to tell the others about what we've been discussing. They should have the chance to decide which they'd rather risk, success or failure."

"That assumes they all have the choice," Tamrissa pointed out, gliding to another head rest near Jovvi's. "Judging by all the people in my session who haven't gotten anywhere—or who are afraid to try—some of the others here will fall into the same category. Or will choose to fall into it, without even considering anything else."

"You sound as if you mean someone in particular," Jovvi commented, turning her head a bit to look at the girl. "Who's so blindly determined to fail that they'll take the chance of being killed or worse?"

"Vallant Ro," Tamrissa grudged after a moment's hesitation, her voice low and her gaze on the warm, rippling water around them. "He's never wanted to be here, and made that perfectly plain right from the beginning. I . . . mean to apologize for calling him a quitter and a coward, but I'm afraid that's just what he is. Getting back to the marvelous life he left is all that concerns him."

"No wonder he was so convinced you hate him," Jovvi murmured, uncertain whether Tamrissa heard her. The girl's misery was so strong that Jovvi could feel it without the least effort, including the other emotions mixed in. That faint jealousy tinged with bitterness, for instance. . . . It was obviously aimed at the fact that Vallant Ro did have a life he wanted to go back to, the sort of "marvelous" life that Tamrissa had never had herself. It's a terrible thing to have to admit that your parents care nothing about you, and tends to make you believe that everyone else is just the same.

"And then there's Eskin Drowd and Beldara Lant," Tamrissa said after taking a deep breath. "Beldara wants to succeed with every fiber of her being, but I don't think she's had much practice in delicate manipulation. She probably put on lavish shows for her townful of admirers, throwing giant gouts of flame all around. If you never have to keep your doings small and inconspicuous, you can easily miss the possibility that you might someday need to."

"And Drowd almost certainly lacks the self-confidence needed to stretch himself," Jovvi agreed. "If he didn't have rather strong feelings of inferiority, he would hardly spend so much time telling people how important he is—and how inferior *they* are. Or trying to make trouble among those around him. I'll bet anything you care to name that he didn't do at all well."

"And is now blaming everyone else for it," Tamrissa said with a nod. "Clarion—Rion, that is, seemed enormously pleased during the ride home, and that leaves Lorand Coll and Pagin Holter. I wonder how those two did."

"Both of them want to win, so I'm sure they did very well," Jovvi answered, smiling a bit at the thought of Lorand. "We can ask them later to be certain, but I'm not worried. I just wish we were absolutely sure *we're* doing the right thing."

"As things stand, there's nothing else we *can* do," Tamrissa pointed out with a sigh. "And I think I'll finish washing and then go back to my apartment. I could use a nap before dinner."

Jovvi agreed with the idea of a nap, so she reached for her own jar of soap and finished washing. Once they were out of the bath and toweled off, Tamrissa used her talent to dry most of the residual dampness from the two of them. Delicate manipulation, she'd called it, and delicate it was. The flames had been almost invisible, but had done an efficient job. They all seemed to be in better condition than they'd been after the test, but that had to be because they'd expended all their strength during the test in order to stay alive.

They left the bath house together carrying their well-worn session outfits, but as soon as they reached the sitting area just inside the main house Tamrissa uttered a low squeak and then disappeared at a run. The poor thing was obviously embarrassed over being in nothing but a wrap, because all the men were in the sitting area, clearly waiting for their turn in the bath house.

Jovvi paused to smile at them and wave a hand to show that the bath was all theirs, and Eskin Drowd was the first to respond. He stalked past Jovvi without acknowledging her existence, which led her to believe that the man had done as badly as she'd suspected he would. Rion smiled and nodded as he passed her, but Pagin Holter just nodded. There was a . . . coldness inside the small man that hadn't been there before, but before Jovvi could wonder about it she saw Lorand.

"What's wrong?" she asked softly when he stopped beside her, raising one hand to his drawn and exhausted-looking face. "You look as if you went through the test again."

"I also feel like it," he admitted, his voice almost as pale as his face. "I'll tell you about it later, if you like, but right now I really need that bath."

She nodded to show she understood and then stepped aside, and he continued on out to the bath house in what could only be described as a determined plodding. Jovvi was more than a little worried about what might have happened, but she'd have to wait until later to find out about it. Forcing patience on herself she turned away from the garden door— only to find that all the men hadn't left. Vallant Ro still remained in the sitting area, because he'd fallen asleep. Apparently Lorand wasn't the only one who'd had a hard time.

Jovvi considered letting him sleep, but the man was sprawled in a chair that was more decorative than comfortable and would certainly wake up feeling as if he'd gone through torture. A nice warm bath would do a lot more for him, so she walked over and put a hand to his shoulder. It actually took two shakes before he woke, and then he looked at her blurrily.

"The others have already gone to the bath house," she said, speaking slowly and clearly to give him the chance to wake up all the way. "I can see that you're really tired, but you'll be better off washing the sweat away and then stretching out in bed."

"I'd be best off just cuttin' my throat and gettin' it over with all at once rather than in pieces," he muttered, running a hand over his face. "Another day like today, and I'll probably do it."

"Didn't you do well?" Jovvi asked, automatically soothing his jagged emotions. This wasn't a reaction she'd expected, not from someone who supposedly *wanted* to fail.

"Actually, I did wonderfully," he said, sitting forward to rest his arms on his thighs. "I was so badly in need of somethin' to take my mind off that room, that I got all the way up to usin' four strands of water. I was about to try for the fifth when they told us it was time to leave, and I couldn't keep myself from runnin' out. Now I have to go back tomorrow, and I don't know if I can."

"Something about the session room bothers you?" Jovvi asked, finding it impossible to resolve the muddle of his emotions. There was quite a lot of fear present but not an ordinary fear, and Jovvi had never seen anything like it. "Tell me what the something is."

"It's . . . not important," he said, the short hesitation before answering overridden by strong resolve. "All that matters is that I have to go back tomorrow, and the next day, and probably all the days after that until they let me go. But I'll never last that long, so I don't see any point in—"

"Vallant, that isn't true," Jovvi interrupted quickly to head off the incipient panic she was able to feel in him. "The time won't stretch on that long, because this is the last week anyone can qualify for the competitions. As soon as you're able to handle five parts of your aspect with control, they move you out of the sessions and over to the competitions."

"You know, I believe you're right," he said with a frown, having begun to argue before thinking better of it. "I wasn't able to pay attention to much in that place, but I did notice that the woman usin' five strands of water in her weavin' wasn't doin' it easily. I could feel her struggle all the way to where they'd put me, and it hadn't changed even by the end of the day. That has to be why she's still there, because she doesn't have full control. But where do they send you once you've gotten the control? Someplace better—or someplace worse?"

"Tamrissa and I have been trying to figure that out," Jovvi said, hoping to distract him from the agitation that threatened to descend on him again. "She and I agree that we've never met anyone who'd gone through testing only to be sent home again, and we never knew anyone who'd personally met someone like that. Have you?"

"Now that you mention it, I can't think of anyone at all," he answered, his frown lightening as his gaze sharpened. "And I ran into a lot more people than most, visitin' different ports as I do. So what have you and Dama Domon decided it means?"

"We're not certain, but we don't think it means anything good," Jovvi said, faintly amused that he'd decided against calling Tamrissa by name. "We've all proven ourselves to be potential Highs, don't forget, and just because someone can't use his or her potential today, that doesn't mean they won't manage to use it tomorrow. If you were in charge of this thing, would you simply let them walk off and then forget about them?"

"Yes, but we're not dealin' with someone like me," Vallant responded, now disturbed in an entirely different way. "They would hardly go to so much trouble to get us here, and then let us walk away again. I hadn't thought of that, so I'm glad you mentioned it. Did you and Dama Domon come up with any particular plan of action?"

"We decided to move forward as far and as fast as possible," Jovvi told him, enjoying how quickly he'd managed to pull himself together. "It also isn't clear what happens to those who qualify but don't get Seated, but continuing on gives us a longer time to find out—and the chance to come up with a plan to protect ourselves. If you like, you're welcome to join us in that."

"It seems as though I might have to," he allowed, looking less than pleased with the prospect. "To keep breathin', if for no other reason. Well, I'd better get to that bath now. Thank you for your concern, lovely lady, and for takin' the trouble to show it."

He rose to kiss her hand, then took his clean clothing and left the sitting area. Jovvi very much enjoyed the way he said thank you, and smiled all the way back to her room. If Lorand hadn't been there, Vallant would have made a substitute almost as good. Jovvi decided she'd have to find a way to get Tamrissa and Vallant much closer together. The poor girl could use a little pleasure in her life, and the poor man felt so awful thinking he was hated. But Tamrissa *didn't* hate him, and all Jovvi had to do was let them both know that. . . .

THIRTY-ONE

Vallant forced himself to banish the thought of sitting down again, and plodded along to the bath house. He was the one who needed a bath the most, but all the others had gone in ahead of him. They probably hadn't noticed that he'd fallen asleep, so it was a good thing Jovvi had. If not for her, he probably would have missed dinner as well as the bath.

Walking into the bath house showed the other men already in the water, but there wasn't much in the way of conversation going on. Coll and Mardimil were closest to the entrance steps, while Holter and Drowd had retreated to the two farther corners of the bath. Both of them seemed to be taking pains to show that they had no interest in socializing, something Vallant already knew about Holter.

While beginning to get out of his clothes, Vallant tried again to understand the change that had come over the small groom. Holter had been silent that morning on the way to the sessions building, but not thinking-silent. He gave the impression of being through with thinking, of having made up his mind about something. He'd worked his strands of water in the proper order, taking a little longer than Vallant but getting just as far. Fatalistic might be the best word to describe the man, that and bitter. Holter had obviously been hurt when his friends had drawn away from him in fear, but the decision he'd come to because of that wasn't quite as clear.

Once his clothes were in a heap, Vallant moved slowly down the steps into the water. Thinking about Holter and the change in the man let Vallant forget what he himself had gone through, but not completely and not for long. The room where his session had been held was totally without win-

dows, and if there had been doors on the cubicles it would
have taken a platoon of guardsmen to get him into one. It
had been hard enough without that, fighting to keep from
giving in to panic, fighting not to run, fighting to make
himself understand and believe that no one stood between
him and getting out. Walking in quietly and sitting down in
the chair was one of the hardest things he'd ever done, but at
least no one had been between him and the way out. If there
had been. . . .

That *if* had haunted him a good deal more in the room, so
he'd diverted himself by concentrating on the exercises
they'd wanted him to do. Vallant ducked under the water as
he remembered the trouble he'd had at first, then how he'd
found it easier as his talent and ability adapted. He'd *had* to
go on as far as possible, otherwise his mind would have
returned to thoughts of suffocation, being trapped, needing
to escape. . . .

"Glad to see you made it, Ro," Coll said quietly after
Vallant wiped the water from his eyes. "When I realized you
were missing, I also realized you might have fallen asleep. I'd
just decided to cut my bath short and go back when you
walked in."

"Dama Hafford woke me, so we both owe her thanks,"
Vallant said, nodding to Mardimil as the other man moved
over to join them. "She also told me a few things that ought
to be passed on, things she and Dama Domon have been
discussin'. Were either of you told that this is the last week
anyone will be able to qualify for the competitions?"

"That wasn't mentioned in my session," Mardimil said
with raised brows. "Not that it makes much of a difference,
since I'd already decided to qualify as soon as possible. I'm
almost there right now, so another day or so ought to see it
done."

"It wasn't mentioned in my session either, and in my case
it makes a big difference," Coll said, sounding as if he
grudged every word. "I . . . can't seem to get beyond handling more than three strands of earth, and I really tried. I
can't remember ever trying so hard in my entire life, but it
just wasn't any good. I'd been thinking that I'd have the time
to work it out somehow, but now. . . ."

Coll's voice trailed off as he stared down at the water, and
Vallant couldn't think of anything to say that would do any
good. Coll was the one who had wanted to be there while
Vallant and Mardimil hadn't, and now Coll was the only one

in danger of failing to qualify. It wasn't ironic, it was damned unfair, but life had a bad habit of being just that way.

"You know, I've been thinking about something," Mardimil mused aloud, and Vallant looked up to see that he spoke to Coll. "This fool came over to me at lunchtime, and asked me to share the 'secret knack' I'd discovered that let me handle the ribbons in strands of air. When I told him there wasn't any secret, he stalked off after calling me a liar. At the time I thought I spoke the truth to him, but now . . . You *do* realize that the more you must handle with your ability, the more power you have to use? That sounds elementary and juvenile, I know, but—"

Mardimil's words ended abruptly, and Vallant could understand why. The man *had* just been stating the obvious, but the way Coll now stared at him . . . an admission of pleasure-murder along with the intention to repeat the act with Coll as the victim might have deserved that kind of stare, but not many other things.

"So that *is* your problem," Mardimil said gently to Coll, putting a hand to his shoulder. "I could feel that in some of the people around me, the fear of opening themselves to enough power to do the exercise properly. I hesitated myself at first, but then I realized I had very little to lose if I lost control of whatever power I drew in. I'm all through with being pitiful and useless, and I'd rather be dead than fail to earn myself a place in this world."

"And that could be exactly what failure does earn," Vallant put in, lowering his voice a bit. "The ladies had been speculatin', and I had to admit I'd never met anyone who'd gone through the testin' and then been sent home. Have either of *you* met or heard of anyone like that?"

"No," Coll answered while Mardimil frowned and shook his head. "I was hoping something would come along to distract me from that 'solution' to my problem, but this isn't only just as bad, it's worse. Are you saying that anyone who doesn't qualify is killed?"

"That or made to disappear in some way," Vallant agreed with a shrug. "It makes a twisted kind of sense if you stop to realize how much they go through to get all potential Highs sent here. They obviously want us all accounted for, so they're hardly likely to turn us loose now."

"But then what do they do with the ones who lose the challenge to their Seated Highs?" Coll asked, looking as confused as Vallant felt. "Applicants are brought to Gan Garee for the entire year from all over the empire. There's one Seated High and two alternate Seateds for each aspect, a total of fifteen against *how* many hundreds applying? So what happens to the ones who don't make it?"

"I've never heard anyone ask that question," Mardimil said, looking just as disturbed. "Mother and I even attended a challenge once, and the defeated challenger was carried away to be looked after by a physician. But no one ever mentioned what happened to the man afterward, and no one even suggested they'd like to find out. The man wasn't killed, but he did become . . . erased."

"Apparently the ladies have considered that point as well," Vallant said, wishing more than ever that he might sit down. "I was told that they're aware of the danger ahead, but movin' in that direction anyway will buy them the chance to think of a way around the thin ice. They feel that if they don't keep movin', they're likely to fall through the ice sooner rather than later."

"They have a very good point," Coll said, then made a wry face. "And I feel like a child left behind by the grownups. The 'ladies' thought about all these things, but we great strapping men had to have it shown to us. I can't say I've been delighted to hear it, but I'd rather know about it than continue to stumble along blindly. It's information I'll need —assuming I can find a way around my problem."

It should have been comforting to Vallant to know that he wasn't the only one who had a problem with the sessions, but in that particular situation it was more depressing. His own problem had forced him to go forward, while Coll's could end up costing the man his life. Vallant sat down right where he was, needing the feel of warmly soothing water on his exhausted body.

"I wonder if I should speak to Drowd," Coll said, following Vallant's example and sitting, with Mardimil rejoining them a moment later. "My problem has limited me to three strands, but he's still struggling with two. The only people in our group who are still down that low are three women, and Drowd was livid when he couldn't manage to leave them behind."

"Drowd doesn't deserve anything better," Mardimil said with grim satisfaction. "The man is a liar and a cheat, and he takes great pleasure in starting trouble among those around him. It's said that a man can't complain if he gets what he gives, and what Drowd gives is a complete lack of concern over the well-being of others."

"Not to mention the fact that he'll probably get worse rather than better if he learns the truth," Vallant added, seeing Coll's look of indecision. "An immediate life-threat forces a man to react without thinkin', but a time limit focuses him on the time instead of the problem. If he's goin' to pull out of it, he's more likely to do it if he's left alone."

Coll nodded his agreement, then said, "What about Holter? He's a decent-enough sort, and maybe he can make use of the warning."

"Holter doesn't need it," Vallant said, beginning to feel overwhelmingly sleepy again. "He's movin' ahead as fast as I am, and there's a chance that knowin' what we do would harm him rather than help. He hasn't been the same since his friends turned their backs on him, and I'd hate to see him suddenly stop tryin'. But I think *I'm* goin' to stop tryin'—stayin' awake, that is. The sooner I'm out of here and stretched out on my bed, the sooner I can let my eyes close. I'll see you later at dinner."

"I think I'll do the same," Coll agreed, starting his own struggle to get back to his feet. "I'm almost as wiped out as I was after the test, but at least I don't have to be out of here quite as early tomorrow as today. Managing three strands buys you an entire extra hour."

"Managing four buys you two extra hours, but I've decided against taking them," Mardimil said, remaining seated. "I noticed that those who take them seem to be stuck in place, and that's the last thing I want happening. With the bank refusing to release any of my funds—thanks to our friends of the testing authority—I need to get to the competitions and do some winning."

Vallant frowned at mention of the bank, since he'd forgotten all about his own intention to make a withdrawal. He'd spent the allotted lunch time standing out in the rain, drinking in the feeling of having no walls of any kind around him. That was the only thing which had sustained him during the afternoon hours, so it couldn't be considered a waste of time.

But as he reached for a soap jar, he realized he wasn't surprised to hear that he couldn't touch any of his own money. The authority wanted applicants doing their best in the competitions, so they had to have a way to coerce people into making the effort. Vallant wondered briefly why Mardimil seemed so doggedly determined to get his hands on victory gold; it wasn't as if they were being forced to do without something vital, but then he dismissed the question. Mardimil's reasons were his own, and Vallant had enough to think about.

Like the sudden worry he felt over Tamrissa Domon. She was stuck in the middle of that mess with them, and even her father wasn't likely to be able to get her out of it again. He'd promised to take care of her and not let anyone hurt her ever again, but how he would keep that promise in their current situation was something he had no idea about. Between that and his problem with closed-in spaces, he'd be lucky to keep *himself* in one piece and sane. By rights she should have laughed in his face when he spoke about protecting her, instead of gently dismissing the boast with polite thanks. . . .

Vallant paused a moment in his washing, self-disgust filling him like torrential rains filled a dry streambed. Had he gotten so used to moaning and complaining that it was making him forget how to be a man? He'd had to fight twice as hard for a captaincy of one of his daddy's ships, simply because he was his daddy's son. He'd had to prove beyond all possible doubt that he deserved the job, since he and his daddy wanted no one to think that *anyone* could hold a position with their family's firm without earning it. And the ragging he'd had to put up with before he did get a ship of his own. . . .

So what was it that was now making him give up on all fronts without even a token fight? As soon as he saved his life by passing that test, he should have admitted to himself that going home again would be impossible. He was neither stupid nor innocent, and had known—without admitting it!—even before he left that he would never see Port Entril again. And the way he'd been behaving with Tamrissa . . . He'd never met a woman who drew him so strongly, so what did he do about it? He apologized for living and stayed out of her way.

At that point Vallant realized he was almost scrubbing his skin off, and eased up a bit. He deserved a good hiding for the way he'd been acting, but that was about to change. He *would* get through those sessions and competitions no matter what he had to do to accomplish it, and he would find a way o keep his word to Tamrissa. But first he had to make her understand that his wasn't a passing interest, and she'd better get used to the idea.

He'd take care of every bit of that—as soon as he finished taking his nap.

THIRTY-TWO

Lorand expected to sleep until he was called down to dinner, but something woke him and didn't let him fall asleep again. Something. The thought of that evasion made him sneer at himself, but there wasn't much force behind the sneer. Looking down on other people's shortcomings was easy, but a man's own fear hit too close for that.

And it *was* fear. Lorand sat up and ran his hands through his hair, refusing to let himself call it ordinary sensible precaution. That sensible precaution had almost gotten him killed during the test, and now it was keeping him from doing what he'd come to Gan Garee for in the first place. So admit it, man, and face the truth: you're *afraid* to open yourself to any more of the power than is absolutely necessary.

"Damn!" Lorand muttered, really becoming disgusted with himself. That "absolutely necessary" phrase was another evasion, brought forward to make himself think that the use of any additional power was *un*necessary. He seemed ready to do anything to keep from having to admit that it was all over if he didn't get a grip on himself. If only he didn't have the picture of that little girl in his mind from so long ago, of her sitting unmoving in the rain, mindless from being burned out—

Lorand got to his feet quickly, but the surge of nausea

quieted down to the point where he could control it. All day today he kept seeing *himself* like that, unliving rather than dead, no one on hand to ease him by ending it completely. It was stupid to think even for a moment that no one would see to him if he did burn himself out, but part of him insisted that he wasn't "home." At "home" his father would have taken care of the matter even after the words they'd had, but he'd never be able to go "home" again.

Lorand sighed and began to dress, wondering just how much had to happen before he actually got it through his head that he would never, under any conceivable circumstance, return to the place he'd once considered home. Intellectually he knew all about it, but emotionally he was a child crying in the woods, frightened at being lost and screaming for his parents to come and find him. His mind knew well enough that he would have to find his own way out of the woods, but those child-level emotions. . . .

Being alone with his thoughts was just making things worse, so he wandered downstairs to see if his luck had changed and Jovvi was also up and around. He'd promised to tell her about the problem he was having, but even more than that he wanted to discuss the idea of marriage. She seemed to think there was nothing wrong with the life she'd been leading, and he had to make her see the truth. As much as he wanted to take her in his arms, he couldn't get over the feeling that it was wrong.

At first the house seemed deserted, but then Tamrissa and her companion Warla came out of the library. They seemed to be discussing something about the house, which Warla must have been in charge of. Lorand had caught glimpses of Warla during the last couple of days, but the girl had always been hurrying to or from somewhere, or in the midst of speaking to the servants. Lorand was about to leave them to the privacy they probably wanted, but Tamrissa saw him and smiled.

"Dom Coll, how nice to see another of us up and about," she said, almost echoing Lorand's thoughts. "If you'll give me a moment, we can share a cup of tea and chat until dinner is ready."

Lorand smiled and bowed his agreement, feeling courtly in his freshly cleaned new outfit. The pants and shirt were what he'd worn all day, but he'd gotten into the habit at home of coaxing his clothes to shed all dirt and even stains.

Cotton was the easiest fabric to work with since it responded as quickly after being drawn, spun, woven, cut, dyed and sewn, as it did in boll form. He felt less of a backwater hick in the new clothes, so he'd become determined to take very good care of them.

Tamrissa and Warla finished discussing whatever it was they'd been talking about, and Warla curtsied to them both before starting off on the run again, while Tamrissa began to walk toward him. Neither one of them took more than two or three steps, however, before someone knocked at the front door. Tamrissa stopped short with dread and fear flashing briefly across her face, but Warla veered toward the door with the obvious intention of answering it. Remembering what Jovvi had told him about the trouble Tamrissa had been having with her parents, Lorand moved quickly to stand by her side. He was ready to handle anything—except for what the situation turned out to be.

"It's someone asking for *you,* Dom Coll," Warla said, turning at the door to look at him. "Shall I ask him in?"

Him? Lorand thought even as he nodded his agreement. I don't know anyone in Gan Garee, but maybe it's Master Lugal, come to see how I'm doing. Guild men don't usually leave the area where they live and work, but maybe—

Lorand's mind stopped dead then, because his caller had shuffled through the door. Dirty and rumpled, unshaven and obviously hung over, uncomfortable and looking completely out of place, it was still, without any doubt—

"Hat," Lorand whispered, then he shouted, "Hat!" and ran to meet his lifelong friend, dragging him into a hug before pounding on his back. "Hat, you miserable excuse for a friend! I thought you were dead! Why didn't you let me know you were still alive to complain about things?"

"Because I didn't know where you were," Hat answered hoarsely, strangely stiff and standoffish, and then he forced a laugh. "They made the stupidest mistake during that test, you know. They miscalculated the amount of earth to drop on me, and because of that I passed out. When I woke up I was out of that room, but I was also being told to go home. Just a Middle, they said, you're nothing but a Middle. Go home and get a job you can handle."

Hat's familiar features had twisted into something ugly, a perfect match to what Lorand's insides felt like. Hat had been so determined to pass the test, to prove to the world that he was somebody. Being a working Middle wouldn't have made him a somebody with a big enough S, so he'd decided not to believe the testing people.

"But they were wrong, of course, because I'm much better than just a stinking Middle," Hat continued, swiping at his nose with one hand. "They gave me a coach ticket to get rid of me, to hide the fact that they'd made a mistake, but I'm no hayseed to be gotten rid of *that* easily. I'm staying right here in Gan Garee, where I can *prove* how wrong they were."

Hat's eyes were almost blazing now, but Lorand couldn't think of anything to say. How do you tell your best friend that his dreams had died so he might as well forget them? It would hurt Hat less to have a knife plunged into his chest, but Lorand wouldn't have been able to do that either. Maybe if he told Hat the true situation . . .

"I think I'd better tell you right now how lucky you really are," Lorand began, incredibly relieved that he'd thought of a way to help Hat. "This isn't anything like what we imagined it would be, and you're lucky to be out from under. You see—"

"Lucky?" Hat barked, that ugly look back on his face. "You're trying to tell me I'm lucky to have been cheated of what's mine? Look at those clothes you've got on, and look at this house! I've been sleeping in *alleyways,* you fool, and I haven't eaten since yesterday morning! Everybody in this city is a thief, stealing everything I had and then going after my blood! It wasn't as if I expected those dice games to be fair, but I *couldn't* have lost as much in them as they said! They cheated me when all I wanted was a good-enough stake to keep me alive until I proved the testing people were wrong! Even the silver I got from turning in the coach ticket is gone, so you've got to help me! I saw you in that carriage this morning and knew your driver from the neighborhood I've been sleeping in, and that's how I found you. Now you've got to help me, you've got to!"

"Hat, take it easy," Lorand tried to soothe, jumping into the tirade at the first opportunity. Hat was completely out of control, and the sight was painfully pitiable.

"Don't tell me to take it easy!" Hat tried to shout, but the hoarseness his voice had become refused to let it happen. "I just want to hear you say you'll help me! You owe it to me, Lor, you know you do. If you hadn't been there when I went to take the test, they wouldn't have stolen my place from me!

I figured out that they must have a quota, only one High applicant accepted at a time, and they took you because you're taller and better-looking. So you owe me plenty, and you'd better start paying up!"

"What kind of help do you want, Hat?" Lorand asked, trying to stay quiet and reasonable. "Would you like to join us for dinner? I'm sure there's enough for one more, and I can help you clean up while—"

"Excuse me, Dom Coll, but that won't be possible," Warla interrupted in little more than a whisper. Both women were still there, wearing expressions of pity, but Warla forced herself to go on. "Lady Eltrina was painfully clear on what we can and cannot do, and feeding or sheltering someone who hasn't been assigned here are two things we're forbidden. I might be able to put together some bread and cheese to be taken away, but—"

"You can keep your stinking bread and cheese!" Hat tried to shout at her, making the poor little thing flinch back. "I'll buy *real* food when he hands over all the silver he has left, which is probably more than he started with. You hear me, Lor? You run and get that silver, and then you can start thinking of the words you'll use when you tell your fancy friends that you're giving up your place to *me*. It should have been mine anyway, so they'll find they're getting a true bargain. Now—"

"Hat, stop it!" Lorand snapped, finally admitting that reason and patience would do nothing against Hat's delusions. "I have no silver left at all, and the idea that I can give up my place to you is ridiculous. I know how disappointed you are that you didn't pass the test, but telling yourself fairy tales won't change anything. There isn't any 'quota,' and I didn't steal your place. I know what Master Lugal told you before we left, so why are you doing this?"

"I wouldn't have believed it," Hat said slowly, staring at him as though he were lower than grub slime. "You're in with them, my best friend is hand in glove with the garbage who stole my place! Is that the deal you made with them, Lor? They'd give you new clothes and a great place to live, and you'd help them keep their mistake quiet? Have I finally gotten to the truth?"

"You'll have to make up your mind, Dom," Tamrissa put in, stepping closer to stand beside Lorand. "Either they made a mistake, or they had a quota. If you're going to lie to yourself, you ought to keep the lies straight. But you know as well as we do that Dom Coll had nothing to do with your failure to pass the test. You managed that all on your own, and now I'd like you to leave my house the same way."

"You're all trying to confuse me, but it won't work," Hat said, shaking his head, and Lorand finally noticed that the man was more drunk than hung over. He would have removed the alcohol if he could have, but even Middle strength in their shared aspect was enough to let Hat keep himself from being touched in that way.

"No, trying to confuse me won't work because I know the truth," Hat continued, and then his expression crumpled. "But you *have* to give me the silver, Lor, they said they'll kill me if I don't get it! They cheated me and robbed me, and now they're threatening to kill me! If you don't give it to me, there's no place else to get it!"

"Maybe *he* doesn't know any better than that, but I do," Tamrissa put in again while Lorand stood wrapped in sudden guilt. Hat needed money, but he didn't have any to give! "If you're a certified Middle in Earth magic, you can get a job just by asking for it. There are always streets that need to be recobbled, lawns that need to have weeds Discouraged, pets and working animals that need to be coaxed and—"

"No!" Hat interrupted as sharply as his hoarseness allowed. "That's scut work, and I refuse to do scut work! I'm a High, not some crummy Middle, so why should I lower myself? Lor will give me the silver, and then I'll—"

"Hat, I don't have it!" Lorand interrupted in turn, now more disgusted than pitying. "They made sure we don't have money, so we have to do everything their way. Is that what you're jealous of, not being in a position where other people have the say over your entire life? What happened to the common sense you used to have?"

"You won't do it?" Hat said, obviously hearing nothing but what he wanted to. "You won't part with some lousy silver even to save my life? Something told me it would be that way, but I refused to believe it until it happened. Now I *have* to believe it, but there's something for you to believe as well: I'll get even for this if it's the last thing I ever do. Enjoy your silver and your clothes and your fancy house, because you won't have them for as long as you think."

"Hat, don't do this," Lorand began, but the other man was

lurching toward the door and then out into the night. Warla closed the door gently behind him before hurrying away, and Tamrissa put a commiserating hand to his arm.

"In spite of everything you're probably still worrying about him, but you shouldn't," she said in a gentle voice. "He lied about everything including his life being in danger, that I can assure you. We once had a servant who came by with the same story concerning a gambling debt, but my husband refused to give him an advance on his wages. I fully expected the man to be killed, but his creditors just had him beaten up. Not badly enough to keep him from working, but badly enough for him to hurt while he did. The point, I was told, was that dead men can't pay up on what they owe."

"I wonder if that applies to men who *refuse* to work," Lorand said, sending her a brief smile of thanks. "But in any event, I appreciate the help you tried to give. Maybe if he hadn't been drunk, what you said might have done some good."

"I doubt it," Tamrissa replied, wrinkling her nose. "I can understand being horribly disappointed, but I can't understand passing up a chance to make things even a little better. He found it easier to blame *you* for his troubles than to do something about them, which means he doesn't deserve the least amount of sympathy. But at least we learned something: if you can't pass the test, they don't really let you die."

"We don't know that for certain," Lorand warned her, using the new topic to get the bad taste of his former friend out of his mouth. "He said he was told he was a Middle, which means he wasn't a legitimate candidate for High. If actual potential Highs are also saved and sent home, we either ought to know of some, or this city should be crawling with them."

"Well, I don't know any, and the city isn't crawling with them," she answered with a sigh. "That brings us back to where we were, but you may not know yet where that is. Jovvi and I have been discussing some things, and we've come up with certain guesses and decisions."

"Yes, I know," Lorand replied, following her gesture as she began to lead the way back to the library. "Dama Hafford mentioned the matter to Dom Ro, and he passed it on to Dom Mardimil and me in the bath house. We decided not to say anything to Dom Drowd and Dom Holter, because the speculation could well do them more harm than good."

"Please make yourself comfortable in that chair, and I'll pour the tea," she said with another smile and gesture after closing the door. "And I agree completely about not telling Dom Drowd, but not because of any worries over him. The man is positively poisonous, and doesn't deserve to have any of us help him."

"Rion—Dom Mardimil—feels the same way," Lorand admitted, taking the chair she'd pointed out. "I can't say I like the man myself, but that doesn't mean I'll enjoy seeing him dead or worse. Which will happen if all our speculations turn out to be true."

"It's hard to see how they won't," she said, coming over with his tea before taking another cup to her own chair. "I really hope we turn out to be wrong, but either way we'll have to wait and see. But now you and I will have to find something else to talk about. I invited you in here to give us privacy when I told you about our guesswork, and it will look strange to any of the servants in Lady Eltrina's pay if we end the talk too soon."

"Is this what they mean by intrigue?" Lorand asked with faint amusement. "If it is, I don't like it nearly as much as I thought I would as a boy. But there *is* something we can talk about, if you don't mind my asking for some advice. And if you and Dama Hafford are as close as you seem to be."

"Aha!" she said with a grin, leaning forward in her chair. "I think I'm going to enjoy this topic a good deal more than the other one. I don't mind in the least giving any advice I can, Jovvi and I are becoming fast friends, and please call me Tamrissa."

"With pleasure, Tamrissa," Lorand responded with a laugh that hopefully wasn't too self-conscious. "And I'm Lorand, or, if you prefer, Lor. And now I wish I knew where to begin. The subject is a delicate one, and not the sort of thing I'd ordinarily discuss with a lady. Now that I think about it, I'm sure I've made a mistake bringing it up in the first place. Maybe we could talk instead about—"

"Lorand, don't you dare!" she interrupted, looking as if she were close to tears. "No one has *ever* asked for my advice before, and if you don't give me a chance I'll—I'll—never forgive you. Do you want me to never forgive you?"

"No, I don't believe I could live under a burden like that," Lorand surrendered with a sigh, silently cursing his big mouth. If he hadn't blurted out the most pressing thing on his mind—! Well, done was done, so he'd better make the best of it.

"Good," Tamrissa said with her smile returned, settling back with her teacup. "Now tell me all about it."

"Let me see if I can find the proper way to put it," Lorand temporized, thinking frantically. How was he supposed to describe Jovvi's profession to an innocent and sheltered young lady? But with that as the core of his problem, he *had* to describe it. Why couldn't he have just kept his mouth shut or simply discussed the weather?

"It's taking you a very long time to find the proper way to put it," Tamrissa ventured after what really was a long, awkward silence. "Couldn't you just put it—improperly?"

"I suppose I might as well," Lorand agreed with another sigh, all his thinking having given him very little. "Let me begin by saying that I hold Jovvi in the highest regard, and I feel honored that she seems to return my feelings to a small degree. I've . . . even broached the subject of marriage—assuming we all get through this testing business in one piece—but that was something she *didn't* find interest in. Apparently her former profession . . . biased her against marriage, and has become something of a—stumbling block between us. You see, she was a—ah—that is, a—"

"A courtesan," Tamrissa supplied without a blink. "Yes, I know, she told me. What about it?"

"What about it?" Lorand echoed, unsure of whether to be relieved or shocked, and then he understood. "Oh, I see, you know the word, but don't know what it means. Now, how can I explain it without offending you . . . ?"

"Lorand, I'm not a child," she said with the slightest trace of annoyance in her tone. "I know what a courtesan is and does, and just like most young girls, I used to dream about being one. On some level I still consider the life unbelievably romantic, even if my late husband made the thought of associating with men more than just a little distasteful. But that's my problem rather than yours. What part of all that did you need advice about?"

"Romantic?" Lorand said, finding it almost impossible to get beyond that word through his shock. "It isn't romantic, it's . . . wrong. And what did you mean by that dreaming comment? Most young girls do *not* dream about becoming courtesans."

"I'd say I'm in a better position to know about that than you are," she returned, now looking at him oddly. "Unless, of course, you've actually asked thousands of young girls, and had a way of knowing you were answered truthfully. Did you?"

"Of course not," he said, trying to ignore the blush he felt on his face. "I just happen to know what I know, the same thing everyone in my neighborhood district knew. No decent girl would ever dream of becoming a courtesan."

"What has decency got to do with being a courtesan?" Tamrissa asked, beginning to look as confused as he felt. "A standard of decency is applied to things that would harm others, but what harm does a courtesan do? Her task is to provide pleasure, and the more popular she is, the more of it she provides. What's indecent about that?"

"It . . . just isn't right," Lorand insisted, trying again to put his point of view into words. "A courtesan's main purpose is to . . . lure men into coming to her, into wanting to be with *her* rather than with his family. How do you think such a man's wife feels? Isn't *she* being harmed?"

"Personally, I would have danced with glee if my husband had ignored me in favor of a courtesan, and then I would have felt terribly sorry for the poor girl." Tamrissa's words were on the dry side, but there was no doubt she meant them. "But that's just me, so let's examine the silliness you just offered from a more objective stance. Are you saying men are so weak-willed and pliable that they would leave women they loved to spend time with the first courtesan who crooked a finger at them? Would *you* do that?"

"No, of course not," Lorand conceded, feeling his frown. "But I happen to be a man of principle. Some men are not, which brings their wives endless grief."

"Are you saying now that courtesans are responsible for those men being scoundrels?" Tamrissa asked, her head to one side. "I've learned that scoundrels don't simply change because there's no easy opportunity for them to take advantage of. In the absence of courtesans, they go prowling among unsuspecting single women and the wives of their friends. You've found it otherwise?"

Lorand immediately thought of the rakes in Widdertown, and the long lists of conquests they were always boasting about. The lack of courtesans in the area hadn't stopped any of *them*. . . .

"And then there's that matter of love," Tamrissa went on, having grown thoughtful. "It's difficult for me to picture what that must be like, to be so close to someone else that they matter more than anything else in the entire world, including yourself. I read that once, a long time ago, and still don't really understand it. But even more, I don't understand why someone who feels like that would find a courtesan at all attractive. The only possibility I can think of is that they don't feel like that at all, and only claim to."

Once again Lorand's memories of home returned, this time centering around community picnics and gatherings. How many of the husbands had stood around staring at and daydreaming about all the prettier girls and women? How many of the wives had stood whispering and laughing together while inspecting the most handsome young men? But all those married people had claimed to be very happy and very much in love. . . .

"And then there are the women who, like your friend who visited earlier, enjoy blaming others for their own shortcomings. One of the men in my husband's circle of acquaintances was married to a woman who never had a kind thing to say about or to him, not to mention sweet or loving things. Nothing he ever did pleased or satisfied her, and it was actually painful to be around them at a party. And yet when he began to see a courtesan on a regular basis, she was shocked and outraged. What right did she have to feel like that, when she was the one who drove him away?"

"Possibly she was disappointed that he failed to live up to the vows he'd taken," Lorand suggested, unable to meet the direct gaze she now regarded him with. "If you commit yourself to something, you're honor bound to stay with it no matter how difficult it becomes."

"I think we're discussing peoples' lives, not building a house," she objected gently, the words softer than her stare. "And sometimes other people or the circumstance of the time commit you to things without consulting your preferences. Staying in an unbearable situation doesn't make you honorable, it makes you a masochist. And what about people who hide what they're really like until they have you trapped? Why do you have to be honorable when they lied about what you were getting into? And—"

"Please, enough," Lorand interrupted, holding up a hand. "Your points are well taken, but that doesn't change the fact that the whole idea of courtesans is . . . immoral. Just because everyone else might be doing wrong, that doesn't make what they do right."

"Weren't you ever taught that morality is a purely local thing?" she now asked, studying him with a curiosity that suggested he was some odd and foreign artifact. "Our school made a point of teaching us that, because so many different parts of the empire are represented in this city. They explained that if any group in a small place wants or doesn't want a particular thing, they announce it as moral or immoral. Very few people have the nerve to stand up and speak against something 'moral' or for something 'immoral,' so the group gets its way without having to come forward with reasonable or logical arguments for or against the thing. Isn't that what your people did, calling courtesans bad and immoral without listing any real reasons for believing that?"

Lorand almost stated the reasons he'd been given, but then he remembered they'd already discussed and dismissed them. Scoundrels would be scoundrels with or without courtesans, no man turns his back on true love, and some women drive their husbands to other arms than theirs. It was something else entirely bothering Lorand, and he was finally forced to admit it.

"All right, it isn't some nebulous objection about her profession," he blurted, saying it fast before he lost his nerve. "It's the fact that she shared herself with other men, and intends to keep on doing it. How am I supposed to live with *that?* I really love her, and I don't want to share her with anyone. If that's being selfish then I'm selfish, and I don't *want* to get past the feeling. It's too important to me, too . . ."

"Personal," Tamrissa finished with a sigh when his words simply trailed off. "Again, I don't have any idea how that feels, but I'd like to understand it. Do you mean that if Jovvi had been married and widowed seven or eight times, you'd still feel the same? I met a woman once who was betrothed to six brothers, one after the other, and none of them lived more than a year. There was something in their blood that was killing them off one after the other, but the two merchant families were determined to have an alliance. There were ten brothers all together, and the last I heard, number seven was lasting longer than any of the others. But that gets away from my question. If that were Jovvi and the last brother died and ended the chance of alliance, would you refuse to marry her even though you loved her?"

"Why, I don't know," Lorand admitted, considering the question with surprise. There had been a family like that on a farm near Widdertown, where every one of their boy children suffered from uncontrollable bleeding. The smallest scratch had turned fatal for three of them, and the family physician had said the others would probably go the same way. The family had put themselves into debt to travel to Gan Garee and consult a High practitioner in Earth magic, but the man hadn't been able to find anything in the way of a germ that didn't belong. They might as well have stayed with their family physician who, like many other physicians, was an ordinary practitioner of Earth magic.

"Actually I do know, and the answer is no, I wouldn't refuse to marry her," Lorand corrected himself after thinking for a moment. "But that's just the point. I *want* to marry her, but she wants a—a—permanent liaison while she continues to be a courtesan. That's the part I'm really having trouble with."

"So it isn't what she did, but what she intends to do," Tamrissa said with a nod after sipping her tea. "I feel silly asking this, but I'm really trying to understand . . . If Jovvi was a cook in a fashionable dining parlor, would it bother you to eat the meals she prepared at home because she also cooked elsewhere? Would you want her to stop cooking for everyone but you?"

"That *is* a silly question," Lorand responded with a small laugh. "Of course I wouldn't want her to stop cooking for others. But there's a big difference between cooking and doing what *she* does, don't you think? It simply isn't the same thing."

"Why not?" Tamrissa asked, her head to the side again. "What does that big difference consist of?"

"You must be joking," Lorand said with a different laugh, one of disbelief. "There's a big difference between cooking and—and—lying with other men. There's nothing intimate about cooking, nothing . . . personal and direct. And what about children? How could I know that any child she had would be mine?"

"You would find it impossible to love a child of hers even if you weren't its father?" she asked, brows raised high, then gestured a dismissal of the question. "No, never mind, that question isn't relevant. What *is* relevant is the fact that women have known how to keep from conceiving for some time now. The preparation called closum is made from two of those minerals I forget the names of, but it's available from every streetcorner practitioner of Earth magic even if your family physician won't hear of giving it to you. I looked into the matter before I found out that Gimmis was sterile, and I'm surprised that *you* don't know about it. Or do you?"

Lorand did, and had even produced some closum once for a girl at school who'd been a close friend. She'd fallen in love with one of the older boys, but hadn't wanted to limit her options by becoming pregnant. . . . Lorand nodded reluctantly in answer to her question, but couldn't find any words.

"So if there *were* any children you'd know who their father was," Tamrissa said once it was clear he had nothing to add. "That leaves the rest of your objection, which comes down to sharing intimacy. I hate to keep asking, but could you explain that? I know what the word means to me, but not how others look at it."

"Intimacy means sharing your bodies in pleasure," Lorand said, disturbance over what Tamrissa's life must have been like breaking through his self-absorption. The girl was downright solemn when she admitted not knowing about certain things, and Lorand ached for her. If her husband had still been alive. . . . "And it's supposed to be pleasurable, Tamrissa, for both of the people involved. It's a sharing of love, of the deepest feelings two people can have for each other, and it means everything if you do it with the right person. If you do it just for coin, or for passing pleasure, the real thing is somehow—tarnished."

"I think that's the best way I've ever heard it described," she said with a shy smile that illuminated the beauty of her face. "Thank you for telling me that, Lorand, it was very kind of you. What did Jovvi say when you told her the same thing? Doesn't she see it like that?"

"I don't know, because I haven't told her," Lorand said, the words coming out like a revelation. "I just let the whole thing bother me, and never tried to discuss it with her. But if I'd tried sooner, I would have gotten bogged down in all sorts of things that don't really matter—like right versus wrong, and moral versus immoral. It's how she and I feel about things that really matters, and I owe it all to you that I've finally realized it. Tamrissa, you do a mighty fine job for someone who's never given advice before."

"But that wasn't advice," she protested with a laugh as her cheeks colored. "Advice is when you tell people what to do, not when you cause them to make up their own minds—isn't it?"

"I suppose it is, but in that case what *you* do is better," Lorand assured her with a grin. "At least *I* like it better, so it's settled. Now, what else can we talk about until dinner is ready? How about the weather?"

She really laughed at that, and Lorand joined her with pleasure. Tamrissa could be sharp-tongued at times, but less of the time than most women and she was really sweet. If he hadn't met Jovvi first . . . But he *had* met Jovvi first, and now he could hardly wait to get her alone to talk to her. How they both felt made a very big difference . . .

If *anything* made a difference with the threat of death or worse skulking around in the shadows. And if he somehow managed to get around his other personal problem before he ran out of time. . . .

THIRTY-THREE

Rion was dressed again in his new clothing when he went downstairs for the meal. Rather than use the second outfit which was meant for the next day, he'd soaked the worn shirt and trousers in his bedchamber's wash basin, gently squeezed them out, and then used Air magic to dry them. Everyone had responded to the clothing so well that he meant to wear it as often as possible until he was able to replace it with more of the same style but in better fabrics.

He was definitely hungry again when he went downstairs, but this time he wasn't the first to show up at the table. As he reached the bottom of the stairs just behind Vallant Ro, Lorand Coll and Tamrissa Domon came out of the library together, laughing. All four of them ended up walking into the dining room as a loose group, where Pagin Holter and Beldara Lant were already seated. Then Jovvi Hafford arrived, followed a moment later by Eskin Drowd, and dinner was underway.

There was a small amount of conversation during the meal, principally among Tamrissa, Jovvi, and Coll. Rion was included from time to time as well, and he felt that his responses were a good deal more satisfactory than the ones made by Ro. It was as if Ro had other things on his mind besides idle conversation, but Rion couldn't imagine what that might be.

At meal's end, Tamrissa invited everyone to join her for a short while in the library, where a lovely brandy was waiting to be sampled. Holter refused politely and left the room, while Beldara Lant simply walked out without the least response. The others ignored those two and left the dining room amid companionable chatter, and Rion was about to join them when Drowd put a hand to his arm to gain his attention.

"I see you haven't yet managed to find a way to protect your own interests," Drowd drawled insultingly with a smirk. "Coll continues to take most of the attention of the lovely Jovvi, leaving you no more than crumbs outside the window. It was rather unlikely that you were man enough to repay Coll for thrusting you out of his path to the lady, but I did think you at least had it in you to try."

"Did you really," Rion said, studying the man thoughtfully. "You expected me to do something to Coll, and because I didn't I'm unfit to be called a man by you. Is that because you're so very deeply concerned over my welfare, or because Coll outperformed you today—as you suspected he would. Come, come, Drowd, don't be shy about telling the truth. You might find it a fascinating experience for once."

"Coll did not outperform me," Drowd growled, his face now dark with anger. "He simply got the hang of the exercise sooner, but he clearly reached his limit. Tomorrow *I* will be the one to do better, and the following days will see the same. The bucolic hayseed doesn't live who can outdo Eskin Drowd."

"And to be sure of that, you'd like me to do away with Coll for you," Rion said, taking pains to show his disbelief clearly. "I certainly do hate to disappoint you, but I'm afraid my interest in the delightful Jovvi isn't quite as deep as you believed. There *are* other lovely women in the world, and I may have found one. But the others are waiting, so if you will excuse me. . . ."

Rion's bow was pure sarcasm, a fact Drowd saw quite clearly as Rion walked away from him. The man obviously fought against becoming livid, so Rion happily left him to it in private. The others greeted his appearance in the library with smiles, a glass was pressed into his hand, and his opinion on the vintage was actually sought. Rion tasted the brandy then declared it the best he'd ever had, but that wasn't the vintner's doing. The warmth of the group that actually welcomed his presence meant enormously more, but he kept that part to himself to save everyone concerned the embarrassment.

They had only been together for a short time, when a servant appeared to say there was a visitor at the door. Both Tamrissa and Coll immediately lost their amusement for some reason, but it wasn't either of them the servant turned to. It was Rion the man clearly meant to address, but before he was able to add details to the first of his message, the visitor brushed past him into the room. For one heart-stopping moment Rion had hoped it might be his lovely, dark-haired Naran Whist, but instead it turned out to be—

"Clarion, my poor darling, I'm appalled!" Mother announced in ringing tones as she swept past the helpless servant. "To think that you've been forced to live in such squalor these past days! And what have they done with your lovely clothes after giving you *those* rags? This entire situation is completely intolerable, and I'm taking you home with me at once!"

Rion's mind skidded to a halt in shock and mortification. It was hardly the first time Mother had burst in on him when he was with people who might have become friends, but at those other times he'd barely begun to know the people involved. When they'd drawn back from him in offense or ridicule, he'd been able to tell himself they were simply not worth knowing. That wasn't the case with the people he now stood among, but he was helpless to stop what was happening.

"And see the outrage they've committed with that ridiculous sign!" Mother went on, pointing to his chest. "They've written your name wrong, as though you were just anybody and of no consequence whatsoever! Well, we'll see about that soon enough. You are my darling Clarion, and before I'm done every one of them will know it!"

Rion winced, knowing she wasn't joking. She would show up at the sessions building and make such a row that everyone in the building would hear about it. She would force them to replace his identification card just to silence her, and he didn't want it replaced. His new name meant too much to him, and the threat of its loss was enough to help him find his voice again.

"No, Mother, the name isn't a mistake," he said almost at once, his insides twisting with the realization that he was attempting to disagree with her. "I told them to change it to this, and I—I—mean to keep it. I've decided that it suits me better."

"Suits you better than the name *I* chose for you?" Mother said, her eyes beginning to widen in a way Rion was much too familiar with. Whenever he found something to get stubborn about, Mother had never argued. She'd merely shown her frailty and utter dismay, and Rion had always ended up giving in.

"But my darling, Clarion is the name *I* chose for you," she said, appearing close to tears. "I spent all the months I carried you in my body, searching for the perfect name, and at last I found it. I can't begin to tell you how joyous I felt, but if my joy and happiness mean nothing to you, by all means, pervert the name as you wish. I've always loved you too much to deny you anything. . . ."

Her words trailed off as tragedy peered out of her eyes, and Rion knew he was lost. He'd never been able to stand up to the suggestion that he was harming her, and probably never would. Even if he knew, deep inside, that she wasn't being harmed at all. He parted his lips to admit defeat, but a small, gentle hand placed suddenly on his left arm kept the words from being spoken.

"You can't mean it took you *that* long to find the most

ridiculous and demeaning name possible," Jovvi said to her with a smile. "Surely a woman of your talent and ability was able to accomplish the thing much sooner than that."

Mother actually began to preen at what seemed to be a compliment, but then she actually heard everything Jovvi had said and immediately went stiff.

"Clarion, who *is* this person?" she demanded, looking daggers at Jovvi. "Tell her to remove her hand from your arm at once, and to apologize to me immediately! Even though you stand about while I'm being abused, I refuse to accept such treatment from a commoner!"

"Is she a commoner because she won't let you get away with treating a grown man like a half-wit boy?" another voice put in, and then Tamrissa stood beside him to his right. "And if you think *she* abused you, that's only because you haven't dealt with *me* yet. I never thought I'd meet anyone worse than my own mother, but you've surpassed her. To come bursting in here and embarrass your son nearly to death, and then to claim to *love* him? It's yourself that you love, and at least my mother never made any attempt to deny that."

"How dare you!" Mother whispered in a fury, her skin going pale and then red and then pale again. "Have you absolutely no idea who I am, that you would dare to even *think* such things in my presence? Clarion, fetch your possessions at once! You're leaving with me this instant!"

"You seem to have difficulty with your hearing," Jovvi said, causing Mother's head—and glare—to snap around in her direction. "His name is now Rion, not something designed to make everyone snicker at him behind their hands. It did the job of keeping him completely under your thumb because he had no one else to turn to, but now he's finally broken free of you. Why don't you accept that gracefully instead of trying to make a scene?"

"And you can forget about his going with you," Tamrissa added as Mother's face turned an even deeper red. "The law insists that he stay right here, and I'd guess that you've lost to the law once already. If you hadn't, he never would have come here in the first place. If you had even the least amount of ordinary manners I'd invite you to join us for a while, but as you were so obviously raised in a barn, you can flounce out just the way you came in."

"Ohhh!" Mother exclaimed, obviously completely mortified. No one had ever dared to say such things to her before, although Clarion had sometimes had the impression her "friends" would have enjoyed doing exactly that. Her social position was such that no one could afford to offend her by failing to invite her to a party or gathering, but many of them had seemed to wish they could.

"Clarion, I insist that you say something!" Mother ordered in a strangled voice, so livid that it was a wonder she didn't burst. "Tell these harlots that you haven't a copper of your own, and then let me hear that you mean to accompany me! I refuse to stay in this disgusting place one moment longer than necessary!"

Rion had been feeling painful guilt over what Jovvi and Tamrissa had said to the mother he'd been so close to for so long, but her last speech changed that. Suggesting that the only reason the two women had defended him was because they thought he had money hurt, the sort of pain she'd always given unthinkingly. For her he was only there to jump to her beck and call; he wasn't someone she truly cared about, and it was time he admitted that to himself.

"My name is now Rion, Mother, and you'd do well to remember that," he said after a short hesitation, his tone as firm as he was able to make it. "It was vile of you to suggest that these ladies came to my aid only because they had hopes of being paid, but this is hardly the first time you've been vile to me. With that in view, you'd better do as they said and go."

Disbelieving fury flashed briefly in her light eyes, and then her entire demeanor changed in the way she was so good at accomplishing.

"Oh, my poor darling, they've gotten you all confused, haven't they?" she whispered, tears now glinting in those eyes. "They've deliberately poisoned your mind against me, the tragedy I've always tried to protect you from. But please don't fret, I understand that it isn't your fault, and there's no question but that I forgive you. And you needn't worry that I'll abandon you while you remain in their clutches. I'm not without influence in this empire, and my letter may have been ignored but my person won't be. I'll free you, dear, and then we'll be back together again forever."

Rion felt a chill grip him at that, but he stood silently while Mother came close to kiss his cheek, then watched as she turned and left. Tamrissa stepped to the door as the servant hurried in Mother's wake, and after a moment Tamrissa closed the library door and turned back to them.

"She's gone, thank goodness," Tamrissa announced, one hand to her middle. "She makes my insides turn over, and I don't know how I managed to speak to her like that. As soon as she was out of here she stopped floating and started stalking, and Eskin Drowd was nearly run down. You were very brave to stand up for yourself, Rion, but at least it's over with now."

"Unfortunately, it's not," Rion disagreed after emptying his brandy glass in a single gulp. "I've seen her like that before, and she's only just begun. She'll start to visit everyone she can think of, and eventually they'll get so tired of her nagging that they'll give her anything she wants just to get rid of her. I used to admire that behavior, but now it's my life she's after. . . ."

A life he'd only just begun to live. The idea of being dragged back to the terrible isolation and unhappiness he'd been chained to before was enough to make him weep, right then and there in front of them all. He had no doubt that they would understand and sympathize, but he couldn't bear to give them what would also be an unconscionable embarrassment.

"I think you'd do well to remember that you're not a child any more, Mardimil," Ro said, breaking a silence that had grown almost awkward. "She can rant and rave as much as she likes, but she can't *force* you to go back to her. As long as you say no and stick to it, there's nothin' she can do."

"And the testing authority isn't about to just let her walk you away," Coll pointed out, obviously trying to change the atmosphere from depressed to enthusiastic. "We're right in the middle of things, remember, and if you qualify for the competition they certainly won't let you leave. But what we speculated about hasn't changed, so maybe you would be better off if she—"

"No!" Rion interrupted harshly, then held up a hand in apology. "No, I would *not* be better off even if we were certain about what lies ahead. I would rather be dead than return to what was, so I have to thank each and every one of you for the help you've given me. But now, if you don't mind, I believe it's time for me to retire."

No one tried to dissuade him, but Tamrissa patted his arm and Jovvi kissed his cheek before they allowed him to leave.

The hall was empty and he crossed it quickly, taking the stairs two at a time to let him reach his room sooner. For some reason he abruptly remembered his original intention to complain about that room, a place that had grown more welcoming than his apartments in Mother's various houses had ever been. How could he have seen it as stiflingly small rather than cozy, garish rather than lively, inferior rather than wonderfully warm . . . ?

Even as his mind asked those questions, the answer became obvious. He'd thought those things because he'd still been looking at the world through Mother's eyes, the only way he'd ever been permitted to look at anything. It wasn't possible to consider going back to that, to consider giving up the small amount of progress he'd made toward becoming a real person. If any of Mother's "friends" tried to insist, he'd have to remind them that he was just as noble as she was . . .

Yes, that was it. Rion smiled where he'd stopped in the middle of the room, and then began to get undressed. He'd forgotten briefly that he *was* a noble, and no one forced nobles to do anything they didn't care to. He'd make certain he qualified for that competition thing, and then he'd remind anyone who became involved that he was no commoner to be told where to go and how to live. Yes, that would work—

—hopefully against any and all trouble that Mother would certainly manage to generate. . . .

THIRTY-FOUR

Vallant actually found it a relief to reach the sessions building on this second morning. After what he'd gone through yesterday—and undoubtedly would again today—

he should have felt anything *but* relief, and yet that wasn't so. He'd spent so much of last night and all of this morning's drive thinking about Tamrissa, that anything pulling him away from his thoughts had to be considered a good thing.

Holter, Coll, and Drowd were in the coach with him again, and the first coach also carried its original complement. Apparently everyone had decided to start as early as they had yesterday, and that no matter what level they'd achieved. Vallant wanted the torture over and behind him as quickly as possible, but others, like Drowd, needed the extra practice time. The man looked positively grim this morning, and if stares could have killed, Coll would have been an unmoving body on the ground.

This time, with the sun shining brightly, the coach stopped at the front of the building. Drowd was out as soon as all motion had ceased, and Coll wasn't far behind him. Vallant waited until Holter stepped down before getting out himself, but he couldn't keep from pausing at the top of the steps. The others had already gone inside, all of them including Coll . . .

And that brought it all back, the breast-beating he'd done ever since he'd seen Tamrissa and Coll the night before, laughing as they came out of the library together. That could have been caused by almost anything, but then he'd noticed during the meal that they called each other by their given names. Apparently Coll had moved ahead while Vallant had hesitated and wasted time, and now Vallant's opportunity with Tamrissa was lost for good.

But he'd spent the entire ride thinking, and now it was time to decide that he *hadn't* lost out. It wasn't like him to simply give up without a fight, but this being stuffed into tiny, airless spaces was playing havoc with his usual self-confidence. He *had* to take care of that first, but as soon as he got back to the residence he intended to go looking for Tamrissa. He'd find out if he really had no chance with her, and if that *didn't* happen to be the case. . . .

Having made up his mind brought Vallant almost to the point of whistling, but he wasn't quite that confident about going back into the session room. He *was* able to square his shoulders and enter the building as if doing it were easy, and actually crossed the floor without hesitation. The hesitation appeared when it came time to walk into the room itself, but Vallant forced himself to bear in mind that the sooner he got to it, the sooner it would be over. Swallowing from a dry mouth proved rather difficult, but remembering that no one would be between him and the door finally let him go inside.

The same Adept was there, and the man smiled coldly before leading Vallant to a cubicle only a few steps from the door. Holter was already inside the one opposite, his four strands of water already beginning to form. Vallant had to clench his teeth and his fists before he was able to enter the cubicle, but thinking about forming those four strands before trying five let him do it. It wasn't actually necessary for him to start with four strands again, not when he already knew how much power was needed to control them, but it would give him a chance to get the same control over himself before going on.

Vallant noticed vaguely that the lamplight was softer and the chair much more comfortable in this new cubicle, two benefits that made very little difference to his state of mind. What he had to concentrate on was forming strands of water and then weaving them together, three patterns each for the four and five strands. He'd gotten all three patterns for the four strands, but went through them again anyway to see if he'd forgotten anything important.

But not only hadn't he forgotten anything, forming the patterns was so easy it was as though he'd done it all his life. Vallant frowned at that, not understanding why it had happened. It was true that he'd found using his talent easy over the years, but he'd never needed to do anything this complex. Maybe weaving five strands would prove more of a strain, the same strain he could feel in the stranger who wove water to his right.

Vallant opened himself to more of the power than he'd ever tried to control before, the silent roaring of its arrival echoing in his head. He also experienced a surge of strength and vitality, making him feel like a seven-foot giant of good health, but that feeling couldn't be relied on, he'd learned. The more power you took in the faster it drained your physical strength, and that no matter how good you felt before you fell over from exhaustion. The best thing to do was to get on with it, do what was necessary—and then get out.

So he gathered enough moisture from the air to form a fifth strand, and began to weave them together into the first of the three patterns. Vallant knew there were buckets of water standing around in that room, replacing what was taken from the air. They'd been cautioned not to take the water directly from the buckets—easier by far than taking it from the air—because the water in the buckets was only there to keep the air breathable. With so many people stripping moisture from the air, it would soon have felt like a desert to their lungs and skin.

The distraction of those thoughts should have slowed Vallant's progress with the weaving, but to his surprise it didn't. The weaving formed one turn and knot after the other until the entire length of the five strands was used. But that was the easiest of the three patterns to do, so it remained to be seen what would happen with the others. They also required more concentration, but once they'd been formed the first time, Vallant was able to go through all three of them again with very little effort.

A movement out of the corner of his eye took Vallant's attention, and he turned his head to see Holter getting up to leave his cubicle. Vallant remembered glimpses that showed Holter going through the three patterns as well, and now the man seemed ready to leave. In Vallant's opinion that was an excellent idea, so he banished the five strands back to the air they'd come from, then forced himself to follow Holter *slowly*.

The Adept in charge waited for them near the door leading out, *near* the door and happily not in front of it. Vallant wanted nothing more than to just keep going, but the Adept obviously waited to tell them something. If Vallant let himself run out the way he so badly needed to, he'd just end up having to come back. Keeping control of the panic another couple of minutes was a much smarter idea, and the sweat running down his face could simply be ignored.

"Congratulations, gentlemen, and welcome to your new standing in life," the Adept said, sounding for the first time as though he addressed equals—or near equals. "You've managed to qualify for the competitions just as quickly as you're supposed to, so tomorrow you won't be returning here. Just relax and enjoy yourselves through the rest of today, for tomorrow the true enjoyment begins."

Something about his smile disturbed Vallant, but Holter was heading for the door after nodding, so Vallant lost no time following. The large open floor of the building's interior brought a small amount of relief, but what Vallant needed was the true outdoors. For that reason he lengthened his stride to reach the front door more quickly, stepped outside into the sunshine, then moved to one side to lean against the wall and close his eyes. He had no idea how long they'd have to wait before the coach returned for them, but he'd be fine as long as he could do his waiting right here.

"You okay?" a voice asked after a moment, a disturbed voice that nevertheless sounded reluctant to speak. "You need help t'go back in an' sit down?"

"Anythin' but that," Vallant muttered, opening his eyes to see a frowning Holter staring at him. "I . . . don't like bein' indoors, especially not on pretty days like this one. I'll be just fine, but since you brought up the question, I'll give it back to you. Are *you* all right?"

Holter stiffened, as though on the verge of withdrawing back into himself again, then he moved his gaze from Vallant's face and shook his head.

"No, I ain't okay," he stated, the words almost flat. "My friends don't wanna know me no more, like I ain't the same man who drank an' laughed with 'em an' done 'em all them favors. I ain't good enough fer 'em anymore, but that's whut *they* think. I mean t' prove I'm *better,* an' then we'll see who looks down on who. An I'll do 'er, too, no matter how rough doin' 'er is. . . ."

He let his voice trail off before walking a few feet away, the bitterness in him so sharp that Vallant could almost taste it. He tried to imagine how *he* would feel if all his friends had drawn away in fear and loathing, but quickly dismissed the question. The pain of it would have been almost unbearable, even though Vallant had those in the residence he might talk to and associate with. How much worse was it for Holter, who'd felt out of place right from the beginning?

That was another question Vallant preferred not to get into, especially since it didn't seem possible to do anything about it. The little man had been invited to join them in the library for brandy last night, and he'd refused. It isn't possible to ease the pain of someone who doesn't want to be eased, someone who's decided to use the pain as a goad on the way to success. Obviously that's what Holter was doing, and the man didn't seem prepared to let himself be diverted.

They had to wait almost half an hour, but finally the coach arrived to take them back to the residence. Other people had come out to wait with them, but no one who was a member of their residence. As the coach moved through the crowded streets, Vallant tried to wonder how the others were doing. He really did care, but thoughts of a single one of the others kept crowding out everyone else. Today he would find out exactly where he stood with Tamrissa, who would hopefully be home as early as he was. After that . . . after that . . . well, they'd have to see, but he'd made up his mind that there *would* be an after that!

Lorand left the coach right after Drowd, still upset about the night before. He'd meant to speak to Jovvi right after the small party, telling her how he saw things and then asking how *she* saw them. It would have been the perfect time, if Mardimil's mother hadn't shown up. The woman had probably bribed someone to tell her where Mardimil was, and then she'd sailed in and tried to take over Mardimil's life again. Once he'd left for his room, Jovvi and Tamrissa had been furious, which ended the possibility of any sort of calm exchange of ideas.

Sighing as he walked across the floor, Lorand had to admit that he had more pressing problems to concern him than a missed opportunity for conversation. He knew what he had to do in order to qualify for those competitions, and couldn't honestly say he hadn't known sooner. When Mardimil had put the answer into words he could no longer ignore he'd almost run, something the others had undoubtedly seen. But having to face the need to open himself to even more of the power that could kill so easily . . .

Lorand pushed that thought away, along with the picture of that little girl from so many years earlier. Deep inside, the whole thing still made him tremble and probably always would. What he had to keep firmly in mind now was that Jovvi would certainly move ahead to the competitions, and he couldn't stand the thought of not being there with her— and for her. If she needed him and he wasn't there, he'd never forgive himself even if he lived.

Which wasn't all that likely to happen. He eyed the door he approached, the one Drowd had already gone through, trying to remember if he'd *ever* heard someone boast about almost having made it to the High competitions. He hadn't realized sooner that he *should* have known someone like that—unless those who came close never went home again. Middles were a different story, but then there was no competition involved with being declared a Middle.

So Lorand had to accept the fact that his life was probably at stake again, and refusing to use the necessary power wasn't likely to save him. Not to mention get him any of the gold he needed, for others as well as himself. Hat . . . Hat had been his friend for a very long time, and couldn't be blamed for what he'd said while drunk. The disappointment had been devastating for him, but he'd always been a lot stronger than he looked. He'd pull out of the depression and disappointment and then begin a new life—with the help of the gold Lorand would lend him.

But first Lorand had to win the gold, and in order to do that he had to qualify for the competitions. He stopped just inside the door of the session room, fighting not to sweat as he waited for Toblis, the Adept, to come back from placing Drowd in a cubicle. Drowd was back where they'd both been yesterday, and when Toblis took Lorand to a different cubicle, Drowd tried to kill him with a glare again. The academician obviously found it intolerable that a mere farmer was able to outdo him.

Well, that was just too bad about Drowd. Lorand sat down in the chair that was better than the one he'd had yesterday, and prepared himself to start all over from the beginning. If he was ever going to do what was necessary, he had to do it *now,* before he lost his nerve again. He just had to remember that he risked nothing in trying to use more power, not even his life.

Weaving two and three strands of earth from the containers provided in each cubicle turned out to be much easier than it had been yesterday, encouraging Lorand to go straight to four strands. He held his breath when it came time to take in more of the power, but it still seemed to be well under his control. That helped him to relax even more, which let him go through all three of the required patterns twice by the time lunch was announced.

Lorand had noticed in passing that Drowd had managed to reach three strands, and the man fought to braid them a second time when the lunch placard was brought through. Lorand expected the struggling academician to at least finish what he was doing, but instead Drowd dropped the earth and led the others out to the tables. Lorand could see that the man's lips were tight with fury, as though it were all Lorand's fault that Drowd had never learned to finish a job before indulging his own needs and wants.

Lunch was less of a help than Lorand had hoped it would be, except for the fact that he was put in yet another cubicle when they all went back. Drowd still wasn't moved, and when the academician demanded to know why, Toblis explained in that distant manner of his. Drowd certainly had reached the three strand level, but he hadn't reached the point of completing the braiding easily. Only when that happened would he be ready to move up to four strands, and only when he moved up would he qualify for a more comfortable cubicle. And then, of course, he added the icing.

"You really ought to try applying yourself like Coll there," Toblis drawled, gesturing toward Lorand without looking at him. "At this rate, you'll be eating his—dust—for the rest of your life."

Toblis turned then and walked away, chuckling at his little joke. Drowd wasn't chuckling, though, since it's difficult to laugh when you're livid. This time he'd just about been *told* that all his troubles were Lorand's fault, exactly as he'd suspected all along.

Lorand turned away from the man's murderous glare, walked to his new, very comfortable chair, and sat. This new cubicle was very much of a lure to relaxation, a place where he'd be very comfortable while he pretended to try for control over five strands. That was what he had to do next, open to enough more of the power to control five strands of weaving, but the thought of that made Lorand sweat even more than he had before lunch. He was still ahead of Drowd, after all, so he had plenty of time before he would really need to move ahead. . . .

It took quite a lot for Lorand to get out of that chair and sit down on the floor, where he would be a good deal less comfortable. Fear let you use anything to distract yourself from doing what caused the fear, even if you *didn't* have as much time as you wanted to believe. This was the last week anyone would be able to qualify, and there was nothing to say that the testing authority people actually would wait until week's end before ridding themselves of those who clearly would never make it. If he really did intend to qualify, it had to be right now without any excuse or argument.

Taking a deep breath did nothing to loosen the knot of fear inside Lorand, but he refused to let that stop him. It was either qualify or die, so he really did have nothing to lose. He held tight to that statement and fought to believe it as he opened himself to more of the power, nearly missing the surge of strength that came with it. It was almost as if the greater amount of power brought the strength necessary for its control along with it, but that was absurd. Beyond a certain point the power killed, it didn't *help*.

Nevertheless, Lorand should now be able to handle five strands of earth. He moved them out of the container one at a time, making sure he had complete control over one before adding the next. The power roared inside him, demanding that he *do* and *accomplish* faster and with more assurance, making him dizzy as he fought to control it. That control became easier once he had all five strands and began to weave with them, but he did have to concentrate more than ever before.

For a while Lorand seemed to move in a dream, aware of nothing but the three patterns he had to produce. Distantly he realized he was bathed in sweat, but only when Toblis appeared outside his cubicle to beckon with one finger did Lorand raise an arm to blot his face on his sleeve. It took some effort to release the power and stand, but by the time he reached the place near the door where Toblis waited he was on the way back to feeling normal again.

"Congratulations, Coll, on managing to qualify," Toblis said, now sounding distantly amused. "I was certain you would, but didn't think you'd go so far as to produce the patterns four times rather than twice. But I suppose it's one way to be certain that you won't be here tomorrow for your—friend—to glare at."

"Where will I be tomorrow instead?" Lorand asked, turning to see that Drowd still struggled with braiding three strands. It *would* be nice to be away from the man tomorrow; too bad the same thing couldn't be accomplished tonight.

"Tomorrow you'll be introduced to what the competitions are all about," Toblis answered, then waggled his fingers. "Run along back to your residence now, and get as much rest as you can. I promise you'll need it."

Toblis walked away from him then, so Lorand left the session room and headed for the front of the building. Only half of the afternoon was gone, but hopefully he'd be able to get the coach to take him back to the residence now rather than later. He needed badly to use the bath house, and then he would find Jovvi and get to that conversation he meant to have. Tomorrow would bring new situations and new problems, so he'd be smart to take care of the old ones before the new ones arrived.

Even if he *was* already dreading what he'd need all that rest for. . . .

THIRTY-FIVE

My stomach tried to do flip-flops when I walked into the session room, but I managed to quiet it with less effort than it usually took. Yesterday I'd been terribly afraid of coming back here to try again, afraid that I'd fail and lose everything. Now . . . now I seemed to have more assurance, borrowed in part from Jovvi and, surprisingly, Rion Mardimil.

Rion had been distracted during the drive this morning, which was only to be expected after what he'd gone through with his mother last night. Once we were out of the coach Beldara Lant took off without a backward glance, but apparently Rion heard Jovvi trying to assure me that I could do anything I cared to. He hesitated in the midst of walking away, then turned back to come over and take my hand.

"Dearest lady, you mustn't entertain a lie which detracts from your golden strength," he said softly and gently, looking down into my eyes. "Anyone able to face Mother the way you did last night is clearly much stronger than I am, and I expect to have no trouble at all in qualifying. If you use the same protectiveness for your own benefit, your difficulties will be even less than mine. Please tell me you will."

I couldn't help blushing as I nodded with a smile, noticing

for the first time how really handsome Rion was. Jovvi
agreed with him enthusiastically, and the two of them
walked me almost to the door of the session room. I knew
they would be disappointed if I failed, so I had to succeed for
their benefit as well as my own. I'd never had anyone care
about me before, even in passing as their concern probably
was, and I just couldn't let them down.

So I followed Adept Forum to my cubicle with more
determination than ever before. Beldara already sat in her
original cubicle among the four men we'd been with yesterday, but this time I ignored her as thoroughly as she'd been
ignoring me. I had things to do, the first of which was to run
through the braiding exercise again. Starting with three
strands warmed me up, so to speak, and then I was ready to
try four.

It had been unexpectedly easy to work with three strands,
and opening to more power let me do almost the same with
four. There were three separate exercises to go through that
weren't as difficult as they looked, and when I finished them
the second time I opened myself to the power again to try
five strands. I was well on the way to finishing the first five-
strand exercise, when a double scream, the second following
swiftly on the heels of the first, almost made me lose control
of the fire in my talent's grasp. I quickly anchored the strands
in place, then hurried to the door of my cubicle to see what
had happened.

"All right, now, let's settle down," Adept Forum said as he
came through, heading for the cubicles in back. "This does
happen from time to time, tragedy though it is. It's not likely
to happen to the rest of you, or it would have done so
already. Settle down, I say, and let the men do their job."

The men he referred to were right behind him, six men
who went past the point where he stopped. They entered the
two cubicles involved, two men in one and four in the other.
Those who had come out of their cubicles moved back to
give the men room, but that number didn't include Beldara
Lant. She still sat in her chair with an expression of scorn
and superiority on her face, unlike the two remaining male
applicants left in the area. They both looked ill, and they
returned to their chairs to sit slumped in dejection and fear.

"Yes, I know exactly what happened," Adept Forum said
to one of the men in my own area who had obviously gone

over to him to ask the question. "That fool sitting there staring at a world he'll never come in contact with again is burned out, and he did it to himself. In all this time he hasn't even been able to coil two strands, but he obviously decided to change that. I felt him open himself wide enough for a herd of horses to pass through, showing he had no sense of judgment at all. You do have to walk before you can run, but what he tried was to fly."

Adept Forum and the other man had to step into an empty cubicle to let the two men leading the burned out one to go by, and I couldn't stop staring until it was no longer possible to see the slack face above the stumbling body. A small shiver passed through me at the sight, but nothing I couldn't cope with. The man was now beyond anyone's ability to hurt him, a condition I considered quite comforting. The other one, though . . . the smell was definitely beginning to turn my stomach.

"As you can see, the first man's scream caused that second fool to lose control," Adept Forum went on once he and the other man were back in the hall. "The power was freed to do as it willed, and what it willed was to burn him to cinders. It will take hours to clear away the results, so just go back to whatever you were doing."

The man he spoke to glanced at the horrible mess the four men were trying to clean up, then he took his pale face and trembling hands back to his own cubicle. The stench of burned flesh was trying hard to make me ill, but beyond that I felt strangely untouched. Both men were free of having to worry about what the world would do to them next, a luxury I didn't share. The thought of failure brought me greater fear than the possibility of death, and that was what I still had to fight against.

After returning to my chair I finished the first pattern with five strands, then did the other two. Running through all three for the second time was easier yet, and then Adept Forum was gesturing to me through the cubicle's clear resin wall. I rose and followed him out, not to the area near the door but through the door to the open floor of the building.

"Ah, that's much better," Adept Forum said once the door was closed behind us. "That smell was beginning to give me a headache. But now on to more pleasant matters. You're due congratulations, my dear, both for qualifying and for

surprising me. I surely expected you to be too deeply upset
by the incidents to finish qualifying today. I'm sure you'll be
delighted to know that you needn't return here tomorrow."

"You're right, I am," I responded, really detesting the man
and his manner. "Where do I go instead?"

"To the competitions, of course, something your driver
will know," he answered, interest flickering through his eyes
as he examined me. "I expect you'll enjoy yourself rather
more than most, which pleases me. Perhaps we'll meet again,
my lovely."

His bow was as sarcastic and condescending as the rest of
his attitude, but I ignored it as I turned and walked away. It
was almost lunchtime, and I had no intentions of taking the
meal there. I wanted to be home, and I only had to find our
coach to make it happen.

Stepping outside felt wonderful, as though I'd been released from some invisible shackle, and a pleasant surprise
was waiting. Jovvi and Rion stood together to one side, and
when they saw me they waved me over.

"Tamrissa, you did it!" Jovvi enthused once I was close
enough, then her smile dissolved as she studied me. "I mean,
you did do it, didn't you? You're out of there early, but you
look a bit on the pale side. Is everything all right?"

"For me it is, at least so far," I responded, hurrying to
reassure the both of them. "And I don't doubt that I look
pale. One of our people exercised very bad judgment, and
managed to burn himself out. His scream distracted another
man, making him lose control of the power. That one ended
burned *up* instead of out, but I swear the Adept was glad it
happened. That smell will eventually drive everyone out of
the room, either by making them qualify or making them
give up."

"What about Beldara?" Jovvi asked, her hand to my arm
and the words very quiet. Rion also looked disturbed, but no
more than I felt. "She wasn't the one who . . . exercised bad
judgment, was she?"

"No, she just sneered, then went back to what she'd been
practicing," I replied with a headshake. "She seems to be
finally getting the idea of what she's been doing wrong, so she
ought to qualify in another day or so herself. If she does, I
doubt if any of the others will manage it along with her."

"I know precisely what you mean," Rion said with a nod.
"None of those others in my session room will ever qualify,

not if they try for the rest of their lives. They *should* be able to do it, but for one reason or another they don't. I was told that those with true potential always qualify by the second day, at the very latest, by the third. That leads me to believe the sessions won't go to week's end, even if they claim it will."

"I got the same impression," Jovvi said, then waved a hand beyond the steps. "There's our coach at last, so let's not waste any time getting to it. We're supposed to relax and enjoy ourselves today, and that's what I mean to do. I get the impression that tomorrow will be harder than anything we've faced so far."

"I'd consider that an understatement," I said as I joined her and Rion in heading for the coach. "All those people who tested and passed and qualified before us have been practicing and competing for who knows how long, and they're the ones we'll be going up against. In order to get anywhere at all, our names would have to be written in the Prophecies. If we're ever going to need a plan of action, this is the time."

"I don't care how good they are," Rion said after helping Jovvi and me into the coach and then following. "I need the gold that winning a competition will bring, so I intend to win. Plan or no plan, I *will* succeed."

"I wish I had your confidence," I told him with a smile, speaking nothing but the truth. "It would be nice to believe that I'll turn out to be the strongest one competing in my aspect, but that's not very likely to be the case."

"Why not?" Jovvi asked, turning in her seat to my right to look at me. "*Someone* has to be the strongest, so why can't it be us? We're not competing against each other, after all, so why can't all of us be best? I think we *can* be, so that's what I'm going to expect."

"And I," Rion agreed with a merry grin, just about the first I'd seen him show. "The idea is marvelous, and I agree with it completely. We're all the best, and when we win positions as Highs, we'll have parties and invite only each other."

"That would make for very small parties," Jovvi said with a laugh. "I think we ought to invite everyone who ever gave us trouble, and dare them to try it again. Then we could watch their feeble efforts and laugh."

"Yes!" I agreed, finally letting myself share the enjoyment

of the silliness. "And if they try to give *too* much trouble, I can singe their bottoms to make them jump. Then we'd have no need to hire dancers and acrobats."

They both laughed aloud at that, then tried to find other things we would do to those we disliked once we became Highs. Daydreaming is supposed to be a useless waste of time, but those who say that are wrong. On the one hand, making the dreams come true justifies the time spent. If it doesn't involve something that's likely to come true, simply enjoying the faint possibility justifies it on the other. As long as you don't try to live your life in those dreams, there's a lot more good in them than bad.

Before we knew it we were back at my house, so we went inside intending to see about lunch. We actually made it about halfway across the hall before Warla appeared and stopped us.

"Excuse me, Tamrissa, but I've been waiting for you to return," she said, looking faintly upset. "There are people here to see Dama Hafford, and I've put them in the sitting room. They arrived more than an hour ago . . ."

"And have been cooling their heels and fuming all this time," Jovvi said with surprise when Warla let the words trail off. "I can't imagine who it can be, so let's go and find out."

Our good mood still clung to us, so Rion and I agreed at once to go with her. Warla led the way to the sitting room, and that location showed her opinion of the visitors more than anything else. If she'd approved of them, she would have put them in the larger and much more comfortable library. I wondered who they could be—until we followed Warla in to see a woman and two men. The woman was no longer young but still very beautiful, the men were the sort I would have been much happier not meeting, and all three together took the merry smile from Jovvi's face.

"Why, Allestine, what a pleasant surprise," Jovvi said at once, a neutral smile replacing her previous one. "And you've brought Ark and Bar with you. What brings you from Rincammon all the way to Gan Garee?"

"Business, child, rather important business," the woman Allestine replied with a smile of her own that I didn't like at all. She also remained seated in the room's only comfortable chair, while the two men had risen to stand to either side of her. That she would play noble receiving lowly callers in *my* house annoyed me, almost as much as her slow examination of my face and body disturbed me.

"You may remember the trouble I had with that tiresome girl Eldra," the woman continued, moving most of her attention back to Jovvi. "After you left I informed her that it was time she joined the staff of the residence more fully and began to repay some of the gold I've spent on her, and the silly chit disappeared. At first I though she would be hiding in or around the residence, but finally came to the conclusion that she'd decided to make her way to you. If you'll tell me where she is, I'll put her under my protection again."

"I have no idea where she is, because I haven't seen her," Jovvi replied with a frown, now looking concerned. "But how would Eldra have gotten here? She hasn't any silver or gold, so she'd have to travel on foot. A trip like that would take forever, with no means to get food or shelter along the way. Are you certain she's trying to reach Gan Garee?"

"I'm certain she's trying to reach *you*," the woman answered, her smile as sleek as her manner and words. "I have no idea how she'll accomplish it, but I have every faith that she will. With that in view, I think it would be best if you gathered your things now and prepared to return with me. These people here in Gan Garee are easily bribable, which means I don't expect to have any trouble in getting them to release you. And until I find the proper people to approach, I'll just stay here in this house."

"Guess again," I said, the words popping out when I felt the surge of panic in Jovvi. It wasn't unusual for *me* to be afraid, but there was something . . . criminal in doing the same to her.

"I beg your pardon?" the woman said to me, her pleasantness having turned the least bit hardened and calculating. "You weren't addressing *me,* I'm sure . . . but we really must get to know one another, dear. You and my darling Jovvi seem to have grown close, so it shouldn't be difficult to convince you to come with us and visit Rincammon. I'm certain you'll love it, so much so that you'll most likely decide to remain permanently. You'll—"

"That's enough," I interrupted, now closer to outrage than I'd been in quite a while. "You and my parents must have been born under the same rock, and you make me just as sick as they do. To begin with, this is an official residence of the testing authority, so deciding to move in won't do you the least good. In the second place, your search for someone to bribe will be a long one, since both Jovvi and I have just qualified for the competitions for High practitioners. In the third place, I have no intentions at all of getting to know you, nor do I intend to let you take me over and own me. With all that in view, you can leave now."

"Throwing temper tantrums isn't at all becoming in a beautiful young lady," the woman said, the look in her eyes hard above a brittle and uncompromising smile. "You'll certainly learn better once you've been with me for a while, just as Jovvi and the others have. I've no idea what this— qualifying—is, but it undoubtedly means nothing at all. And with *that* in view, you may now find rooms for me and my . . . associates. We've had a long and exhausting trip, and their tempers are unfortunately a lot shorter than they should be."

Her words and the spitefulness added to her smile seemed to be a signal for the two big men. They began to step toward us, an inhumanly uncaring expression in the eyes of each. My heart had been pounding a little and my hands trembling from the speech I'd made, but seeing those two men start for us sent a flash of terror through me. Rion's presence meant nothing to them, and it was clear that they would hurt him badly if he tried to interfere with whatever they meant to do. Which could well be the hurting of Jovvi and me . . .

And that was when something . . . clicked inside my head. It was a very small happening, not even really a sound, more like a change of direction of sorts. I'd sworn not to let myself be hurt again, but even more I couldn't bear the thought of letting my friends be hurt along with me. I'd never had friends before, I'd never been allowed to have them. Now that I'd gotten past the restriction, I'd never go back to the old way again.

So instead of retreating from the men who had just begun to advance on us, I borrowed part of the qualifying process I'd just gone through and called five wide strands of fire into being between us. The heat of it made the men stop short and then flinch back, and the woman seated like nobility went pale.

"Even common footpads know better than to try their tricks with a stranger," I said, feeling oddly remote as I made certain that my fire burned nothing in the room. That was actually harder than weaving with the flames, a distant fact that flickered through my awareness and then was gone. "I can see you're not as bright as common footpads, so let this be a lesson to you. And in case you were wondering, *this* is what that qualifying nonsense is all about. Now get out."

"You . . . you can't use that . . . that . . . obscenity against us," the woman tried in a trembling voice once I'd let the flames die, her eyes certainly wider than she would have liked. "It happens to be against the law, which I'm sure you know. If I report this incident you'll be sent to the Deep Caverns, so—"

"Really, Allestine, I considered you much more worldly than that," Jovvi interrupted as ice began to form in my blood. The Deep Caverns . . . ! "I was told that the laws don't apply to those of us who have qualified to compete as High practitioners, something that should be perfectly clear to a practical woman like you. We're of more potential value than people who have barged in where they don't belong, so if anyone is charged it won't be us. And now I think you'd better take Tamrissa's advice and go."

The woman was furious as well as frightened, but she did seem to understand that she had no choice. She gathered herself together and then stood, glared at us for a moment, then began to lead her ruffians out of the room. I was delighted that the trouble seemed to be over—until the two ruffians reached me. One grabbed my arms while the other folded a fist with the clear intention of hitting me, and terror froze me where I stood. They were going to knock me unconscious to keep me from using my talent against them, and they were about to succeed—

—when they both choked at once, then began to claw at their throats. As soon as I was free I rushed over to where Jovvi and Rion stood, for the first time noticing the terrible expression Rion wore.

"Men who attack women aren't men at all," he said, looking at Allestine, who had gone white again. Her ruffians continued to claw at their throats and began to turn very red, no more than grunts coming from them. "And women who tell men like that to attack are even worse, lower than the lowliest peasant. If anything like this ever happens again, you'll join them in searching fruitlessly for enough air to fill your lungs. Do you understand me?"

The woman nodded jerkily, her eyes wide again as she tried not to watch her ruffians suffocating, and then Rion stopped whatever he was doing and let them have air to breathe again. They were both down on hands and knees by then, and as soon as air was available they began to drag it in in great gasps. But they only took an instant to do that before beginning to struggle to their feet. Their expressions said they would leave the house *now* even if they had to crawl, and their employer apparently felt the same way. As soon as they were erect she headed for the front door which Warla already held open for them, and a moment later they were gone.

"Oh, you two were wonderful!" Jovvi exclaimed, looking back and forth between Rion and me. "Allestine is the most poisonous woman I've ever met, especially when she uses those two conscienceless curs to get her way. This is probably the first time in years that she hasn't gotten exactly what she wanted."

"I apologize for simply standing here and watching until it was almost too late," Rion said, finally allowing that terrible expression to disappear. "It never occurred to me that those two animals would dare to try to harm a lady. When it became obvious they meant to do no other thing, my outrage seemed to grow a life of its own—along with a purpose. I've never heard of anyone doing something like that before, but I'd judge it to have been rather effective."

"It certainly was," Jovvi said with a laugh, giving him a hug before turning to me. "And so was what Tamrissa said and did. What you told Allestine infuriated her, Tamma, something I could see even if you couldn't. I noticed her deciding she wanted you in the residence as soon as she saw you, and no girl she's ever decided on has managed to refuse her successfully. You were marvelous to come to our rescue like that, and I couldn't be more proud of you."

"Even though I was terrified almost the entire time?" I asked as she hugged me, not quite up to pretending otherwise. "I'm actually very much of a coward, Jovvi, and there's nothing in that for anyone to be proud of."

"Why have you suddenly forgotten the truth?" Jovvi asked, stepping back to study me while Rion made a sound of polite ridicule. "Isn't it true that in order for bravery to exist, there has to be fear when you act? Without fear there's nothing to be brave about, nothing to make the act different from any other. Cowardice is when you let the fear get the better of you to the point of keeping you from acting, so how can you be guilty of it? You did what was necessary, and proved your bravery in no uncertain terms."

"Something which many ladies would have found beyond them," Rion said, sober and obviously sincere. "There are any number in Mother's circle who would have allowed themselves to be imposed upon even without two animals threatening them, simply because they see themselves as helpless. I've begun to learn that one is helpless only if one believes it so, and you and Jovvi, my dear, happily see it otherwise. The two of you are so marvelous, in fact, that should either of you wish someone to lie with tonight and give you pleasure, the honor would most definitely be mine."

I could feel my cheeks warming behind my smile as I shook my head, a curious sense of regret behind the refusal. Most men wanted me simply because of what I looked like, but here was one who claimed to admire my bravery instead. Despite what they'd said I knew it was more stubbornness than bravery, but it still felt strangely good to be wanted for the facet of my character that my parents most deplored.

"Oh, Rion, you've become quite dangerous to ladies in a very short time," Jovvi exclaimed with a laugh, obviously teasing. "I actually find myself tempted to accept your offer, which would not have been the case only a few days ago. You should be congratulated on learning far more quickly than most other men."

"Breeding always tells, of course," Rion responded with that very handsome grin, then he offered his arm. "If I may escort you into lunch, we can continue our discussion on the way. For instance, just how attractive do you find me, and what may I do to increase the allure to a point where you'll no longer be able to resist?"

Jovvi shook her head at him with mock impatience, but still took his arm with an amused smile. They left the sitting room still exchanging comments which made them both laugh, and I watched for a moment with my own smile before beginning to follow. Jovvi's ease in handling herself with men was something I really admired, and maybe one day I'd also be able to—

"Hello," Vallant Ro said as he just about materialized in front of me. "I'm glad to see you're back early. I hope that means you're through with qualifyin'."

"Yes, all three of us are," I agreed, gesturing toward Rion and Jovvi, who were continuing on toward the dining room. "We got back a little while ago, and—But you're back as well. Does that mean you've also qualified?"

"Yep," he answered with a grin, actually looking proud. "Holter and I were first back, and both of us qualified at just about the same time. I don't know about him, but I owe my success to you. If you hadn't given me a good talkin' to, I probably never would have seen what I was doin' wrong."

"Were you doing something wrong?" I asked, feeling my cheeks heat again as I looked away from his very handsome smile. He smelled so good, as if he'd only just come back from the bath house, and the nearness of his big, hard body brought waves of warmth very much like my flames.

"What I was doin' wrong was believin' I could ever go back to my life the way it was," he replied, the words sad but not depressed and miserable. "It was the stubborn dream of a boy desperately lonely for the haven of his home and family, not the realization of a man that the time had come to make his own way in the world. But I understand that now, and wanted to thank you for helpin' me see it right. Most women just wouldn't have bothered."

He took my hand then and raised it to his lips, but his light, compelling gaze never left my face. I both saw and felt the slow, deliberate kiss reach my hand, and a shiver raced through me. But not a shiver of fear, at least not entirely.

"I . . . really did nothing at all," I managed to get out, both wanting and not wanting to pull my hand back. "You were the one who—accomplished it all, and—and—so all congratulations should be yours."

"I would much prefer to share them with you," he murmured after finally ending that kiss. "But only if you don't mind. You're much too marvelous to be made to do anythin' you don't care to, especially now that your protector is goin' to be around for good. What kind of protector would I be, if I was the one you needed protectin' from?"

His grin made me laugh, bringing back my previous good mood with a rush. He was going to *be* here, just like the rest of us, and now *wanted* to be here as well. I hadn't thought it would happen, hadn't even hoped because hope never works, but now . . .

"May I have the honor of escortin' you in to lunch?" he

asked, offering his arm the way Rion had with Jovvi. "I'm starvin' and you're probably the same, but maybe later we can walk in the garden. It would be a real nice place to share thanks and congratulations."

"Yes, I'd like that," I said, hesitating only a heartbeat before taking his arm and joining him in walking toward the dining room. The beauty of the garden was usually ruined for me by awful memories, so perhaps it was time to reclaim it with some pleasant ones. That word, pleasant, so close to its other form, pleasure. Everyone said that was what was supposed to come from a man and a woman being together, not pain but pleasure. For the first time I found myself believing it might be true and real, as true and real as the strong, solid arm my hand rested on.

Maybe . . . later . . . I'd find out. . . .

THIRTY-SIX

Jovvi enjoyed Rion's attentiveness during lunch, but she couldn't help noticing that Lorand hadn't gotten back yet. Vallant Ro sat in his place next to Tamrissa, speaking to her in a low voice that occasionally rose a bit in shared laughter. Tamma's cheeks seemed to have turned a permanent pink, but she obviously enjoyed the attention Vallant paid her. Jovvi was happy for her, but—

But Lorand's absence was becoming more upsetting. Pagin Holter sat to Jovvi's left, polite but so tightly withdrawn that she couldn't even consider trying to reach through to him. He had no intentions of sharing his disturbance with anyone at all, and he ate quickly before leaving with no more than a nod. Rion, on the other hand, was in a light and expansive mood, reveling in the memory of having come to the rescue of two women. His offer to her had been sincere and interesting as well as flattering, but not difficult to deflect. Rion was definitely becoming a very charming man, but he still lacked the experience to make refusing him difficult.

And none of that was able to distract her from the fact of Lorand's continued absence. Was he having trouble qualifying for the competitions? Well, that was a silly thought, of *course* he was having trouble. Jovvi helped herself to a cherry tart and took a bite of it, but couldn't keep her mind from asking the much more pointed question she'd been trying to avoid: he was certainly having trouble, but would he be able to overcome it?

The answer to that lay out of reach, invisible along the path of the unsolidified future. Jovvi finished the tart and then her tea, spoke lightly to Rion for another minute or two, then excused herself. She needed to be alone for a while, to balance the worry that threatened to ruin her entire equilibrium. And it was so silly! It wasn't as if she and Lorand were going to build a life together or anything. So why did the worry over him even distract her from the near disaster of Allestine's visit?

Jovvi didn't know, but as she climbed the stairs to her room she thought again of how close she'd come to being right back under Allestine's hand. And with Tamrissa to keep her company! She wouldn't have minded having Tamma in her own residence here in Gan Garee, but wouldn't have wished even Beldara Lant the burden of having to work for Allestine. As long as you were obedient and popular with the clients, Allestine was all sweetness and smiles. But just try to balk her on something. . . .

As Jovvi entered her room, she wondered if Eldra really had run away from the residence. She wouldn't put it past Allestine to use the story as an excuse to let her come to Gan Garee herself, most especially if she'd noticed that Jovvi had taken most of her favorite outfits. That was probably the silliest thing she'd done, but there was no helping it now. Allestine was here and would be back, just as soon as she got over her fright, but—

But where was Lorand? Jovvi discovered that she now stood with her hand on the door after closing it behind her, only two steps into the room. Obviously she was very badly in need of restoring her balance and equilibrium, when she wasn't even sitting down to worry. She had to find a comfortable place quickly and do what was necessary, so she started for the bed—

—and nearly tripped over something invisible halfway there! Running into whatever-it-was hadn't been painful, but it *had* almost sent her sprawling. Jovvi spent a moment trying to see what it was, then gave up using her eyes and instead used her hands. Bending down and groping found her the invisible obstruction, and she ran her fingers over it.

"Neither warm nor cold, and soft but not really yielding," she muttered, at the same time distantly wondering where it could have come from. It hadn't been here this morning, when she'd gone down for breakfast before leaving for the session. It was rounded and about mid-thigh height on her, and stood directly in her path to or from her bed and the door. It also had no odor, and was very smooth to the touch.

Moving around the thing to the left brought Jovvi's hands into contact with an opening, which turned out to be a hole in the circular object. As soon as she realized that the hole was large enough for her to climb into, Jovvi went from mystified to delighted. As a child she'd had a favorite hiding place where she'd gone for refuge anytime life began to be too much for her, an old, discarded barrel that no one had ever claimed for a more practical use. Now here was almost the same exact shape, and just when she needed it so badly. But who could have done this for her, and how had they known?

And then it came to her what the invisible barrel must be made of, which told her who had produced it. It could hardly be anything but solidified air, and that meant the gift was from Rion. But how had he known she needed a refuge, and how had he found out about her childhood one? Those two questions didn't have answers at all, but Jovvi was still grateful for the gift. Without wasting another moment, she bent and crawled inside.

By the time she came out again, her equilibrium was as restored as it was going to get. Possibly it was the fact that she could see out of her refuge through its invisible walls that had kept it from being wholly effective, or maybe she'd just been trying too hard. Jovvi wasn't sure, but at least the time she'd spent curled up had done *some* good. She no longer felt like being cooped up in that room, which was always a step in the right direction.

Taking a book to keep her company, Jovvi went downstairs and out the back door with the intention of sitting in the garden and reading. She'd gone no more than three steps up the path, though, when she saw Tamma and Vallant strolling through the garden. Tamma held to the big man's arm with more confidence than she'd shown yet, and the blush seemed to have finally faded from her cheeks. The two seemed delightfully involved with each other, and Jovvi didn't have the heart to intrude and ruin the time for them.

So she turned back to the house with a sigh, resigned to finding an indoors place to read. Maybe the library, she mused as she retraced her steps to the front hall, with the door open enough so that new arrivals could be heard— Jovvi stopped short in both her thinking and her walking, since the sound she now heard *was* the front door opening. Telling herself it could be anyone—like the other missing members of the residence—let Jovvi walk rather than run the rest of the way, but it wasn't just anyone. It was Lorand who had just come in, and his face looked tired but not in the least defeated.

"You qualified, didn't you," Jovvi said, bringing his immediate attention to where she stood. "It wasn't easy, but you did it."

"I certainly did," he answered, matching her smile as he took three steps in her direction. "I just threw caution to the winds, and it was no harder than jumping blind off the top of a cliff. I'll be glad to tell you all about it—as soon as I pay a visit to the bath house. If I come any closer to you before then, I'll probably knock you over."

He'd stopped after coming only those three steps nearer, and Jovvi couldn't help laughing gently.

"I'm not quite as delicate as all that, but visiting the bath house is a good idea. Just be careful not to disturb Tamrissa and Vallant, who are currently walking in the garden. Try to get to the bath house without them seeing you, and put the 'occupied' sign on the door."

"I'll do just that, and I'll also be back before you know it," he promised, already edging toward the stairs. "Just don't disappear anywhere, because I want to talk to you. You don't mind not disappearing, do you?"

The afterthought was very sweet, and Jovvi shook her head as she drifted toward the stairs herself. Once he had his answer, Lorand grinned, waved a silly little wave, then turned and went up the stairs two at a time. Jovvi waited only until he was completely out of sight, then she raised her skirts and went up the stairs at her own best pace. There was no real reason to wait for Lorand—when she could join him in the bath house.

Jovvi broke records getting out of her clothes and into a wrap, and didn't even really notice that the invisible barrel was gone. She hurried downstairs and out to the back at top speed, then crept along the path to keep Tamma and Vallant from noticing her. Personally she didn't care *who* saw her, but Lorand was still sensitive about things like this. She'd have to work on him—*after* she showed him exactly what he was missing.

The "occupied" sign was on the door the way it was supposed to be, so she opened the door slowly and quietly and slipped inside. The warmth of the air quickly surrounded her, and she saw that she didn't have to worry about Lorand noticing her at once. He was already in the bath and scrubbing his long dark-blond hair with soap, and obviously hadn't heard her entering. She smiled at that as she moved to where he'd left his clothes, then slipped out of her wrap and slippers. He'd know she was there soon enough, and in the right way.

Moving down the steps into the bath had to be done slowly, and Jovvi kept her eyes on Lorand as the water lapped higher and higher against her body. His broad, muscular form glistened with the same water, suds from his hair marking him here and there with sliding foam. As he finished scrubbing and began to rinse the soap away, Jovvi paused in her approach. For some reason she suddenly felt very shy, as if she'd never shared a bath with a man before. She had, of course, many times, but only once before with *this* man and he hadn't enjoyed the experience. Would the same thing happen again? Or worse, would he be angry? Had she made a terrible mistake doing this?

And that's the way Lorand first saw her when he wiped his eyes, standing and staring at him wide-eyed, too terrified to approach any nearer. She couldn't bear the thought that he would turn his back and walk away from her, determined never to associate with her again. He was just an attractive man she happened to like, no one of any real importance in her life, but if he decided he never wanted to speak to her again. . . .

"Jovvi, what's wrong?" he asked at once, deep disturbance in his eyes as he began to move toward her. "Are you here because something terrible has happened? Tell me what it is."

"No, nothing has happened," she reassured him at once, then couldn't hold back the truth. "I . . . simply decided to surprise you by joining you in here, then suddenly realized you might be . . . offended. I'm sorry, Lorand, and I really didn't intend to embarrass you. I'll leave at once. . . ."

She turned to do just that, unable to look at him any longer. If the anger and outrage came she didn't want to see it, not when simply knowing about it would be bad enough. She managed to take two small, slow steps through the water, and then his hand was on her arm, turning her back to him.

"I'm not offended and I'm not embarrassed," he said slowly and clearly, looking down at her with his beautiful brown eyes. "Surprised and delighted would be a more accurate description of how I feel, especially since I've already washed. Now there's no danger of knocking you over."

His grin tried to coax a smile from her, and what it brought out was a rather silly specimen of one. Jovvi knew her smile was foolish, but the relief she felt was out of all proportion to the incident. She felt as if her life had just been saved, as if she'd been given water on the verge of dying of thirst, as though she'd been pulled back from the edge of a precipice. And then his arms reached out and pulled her even closer, making it all a thousand times better.

"Why . . . why don't you try to knock me over in a different way?" she suggested hesitantly in a whisper. "It's the oddest thing, but I feel as if I've . . . never done anything like this before."

"That's because you haven't," he murmured in answer, his dark eyes bright with desire as his big hand stroked her hair. "Not with me, at least, and that's going to make all the difference."

That sounded nothing at all like the Lorand she thought she knew, but then his lips came to hers and all coherent thinking was immediately beyond her. The surge of power passing between them almost did knock her over, and she had to circle his body with her arms in order to stay on her feet. Not that she minded touching him like that, with her entire body as well as her arms. Without knowing it she'd ached to be held by him like that, and now, at last, it was happening.

But that wasn't the only thing happening. Jovvi had once had a Middle practitioner in Water magic as a patron, and being in the man's arms had been more pleasurable than being with an ordinary patron. That time, though, was nothing compared to sharing Lorand's kiss and feeling their bodies touch. The power flowed back and forth between them as though they stood in an electrical storm, lightning flaring through their flesh without burning them to nothing.

Although she *was* being burned, and Jovvi moaned with the feel of something so intense that it almost reached the threshold of pain. Lorand's lips were consuming hers, his hands now moving over her back and bottom with long, deeply felt caresses, her own hands moving over his body in the same way. But as incredible as the feelings were they also seemed to be building toward something, a something that would take a horribly long time to reach.

And then Jovvi felt herself lifted off her feet and put down gently on something soft, which had to be one of the lounging pads on the bath's wooden verge. She hadn't realized they'd left the bath, but didn't really care. Lorand was all she cared about, that and his kiss and caresses. He now knelt above her where she lay, his lips still hungrily clinging to hers. One of his hands now stroked her breast, the other exploring the full length and area of her thigh.

But then she became aware of something else, something impossible. She knew exactly where Lorand kissed and touched her, but all at once she was also being kissed and caressed *inside* her body! That was the only way to describe the searing touches of indescribable ecstasy, as though she were being kissed all over beneath her skin. She writhed beneath Lorand and tried to escape his kiss in order to ask what was happening, but he refused to release her. His own moaning joined hers, but his lips continued to hold hers captive.

And an eternity of time passed like that. Jovvi was frantic after the first few minutes, clawing at the bands of steel that were Lorand's arms, writhing against the warm, soft stone that was his body, whimpering as the tide of flames lapped higher and higher until she was all but drowned. She'd never felt that way before without attaining immediate release, but this time there was no relief. On and on it went, building and growing without end—

—until suddenly, exquisitely, Lorand was beginning to enter her. She raised her body to meet and welcome him, feeling as though she'd been waiting for nothing else. So large and hard he was, the most perfect of men, and as he fit himself within her she felt her talent reach to him without her conscious effort. Balance was the ruling aspect of her life, but where it was possible to bring balance to raging emotions, so was it possible to remove the balance in the most desirable way. Lorand groaned as he felt a rush of wild perfection turned just far enough to be out of his reach, but not so far that he couldn't eventually make contact. All he had to do was begin the most natural act between men and women, the most wonderful ever conceived of.

And that was exactly what he did. His stroking was so deep and hard that Jovvi thought she would die of the pleasure. Her body worked to match his movement completely on its own, as her mind was too busy reveling in ecstasy to direct it. On and on it went, the perfect blending of man and woman, and when release came it was long moments in the ending. Jovvi shuddered in incredible delight and clung to Lorand, and he held her so tightly that she never wanted to be released again.

When it was finally and completely ended, Lorand pulled over another lounging pad and lay down beside her. They were both breathing heavily and covered in the fine sweat of their lovemaking, and when she managed to turn to him he leaned close and kissed her nose.

"Somehow I knew it would be like that," he said, reaching out with one hand to brush her hair back. "It's now perfectly clear why you were the most popular courtesan in Rincammon. There can't be another woman like you in the entire empire."

"And there can't be another man like *you*," she said with another of those smiles she considered so foolish, reaching out herself to touch his chest. "I've never experienced anything like that, and I wish you would tell me what you did. I know it sounds silly, but it was almost as if you were inside me in more ways than one."

"I was," he answered with a grin, putting his own hand

over hers on his chest. "I've never even thought of using my talent in that way before, but I *needed* to be inside you in as many ways as possible. Physicians and surgeons are practitioners of Earth magic, you know, so you shouldn't be surprised. How do you think surgeons operate? By cutting people open?"

"Of course not, silly," she responded with a laugh. "Any surgeon who had to cut people open would have very few patients. And you're right, I *should* have realized that that was what you were doing. I suppose I got sidetracked into thinking that Earth magic just covered soil and growing things and metal and animals. Probably because you mentioned weaving strands of earth during your session. I wonder why they didn't use something else."

"Probably because facility with one part of the aspect can be translated into facility with the others," he suggested with a shrug. "But with the testing authority involved, there's no way of knowing for certain. Those people are—a waste of time to talk about, especially when there are more important things to discuss."

"That's right, you did say you wanted to talk about something," Jovvi remembered aloud, loving the sensation of his flesh against her hand. "We'd probably have more fun doing something else again, but you've had a hard enough day. We can talk for a time while you regather your strength."

"I like your enthusiasm," he said with a laugh, "but I admire your understanding even more. I agree that there are better things we might be doing with our time, but this is something that has to be said. Our futures are very uncertain right now, but there's always the chance that we'll somehow get through whatever is ahead and then find that normal lives are possible. If that does happen, I want you to know how I feel."

"I think I already know, because I feel the same way," Jovvi said, once again nearly overwhelmed with shyness. "I've . . . never known anyone like you, Lorand, and I can't bear the thought of losing you."

"Yes, you do know how I feel," he said, smiling softly as he tightened his hold on her hand just a little. "That means we have nothing to discuss after all. If we get out of this mess with whole skins, we can be married right away."

"Married?" Jovvi echoed, trying to understand what he could possibly be talking about. "I can't marry you, Lorand, not when I'll have a brand-new business to establish. After a while I'll have enough other courtesans in the residence that I should be able to retire, but that won't happen right away. I'll find it easier than Allestine does because I won't keep my people all but enslaved, but it's not something you do in days or weeks. I'll have to—"

"Jovvi, listen to me," Lorand interrupted, the smile gone from his face. "Once we're married *I'll* provide for us, including any children we might have. That means you don't have to do a thing but be there with me. All this talk about establishing a residence is just—just—"

"Unnecessary nonsense?" she finished tonelessly, working her hand free of him. "And how unnecessary would it be if something happened to you, and I was left alone—or with children? My mother found a way to survive after my father died, by selling my brothers and sister and me. Until then we came close to starving, and sometimes I wished we'd died along with Daddy. I won't put any children of mine through something like that, and I won't go through it again myself. I intend to find safety and security in any way I have to, and I'm more sorry than you know that you can't understand what I mean."

"Unfortunately I do understand," he replied as she began to get to her feet. "I've seen women left alone in Widder-town, and what they had to do to survive was pitiful. But there's something *you* have to understand as well: I can't bear the thought of sharing you with other men. Call it selfishness if you like, but giving strangers what you give me when we share love—the very thought of it tarnishes what we have together, ruining the uniqueness of it for me. Isn't there anything else you can do to satisfy your need for security?"

"What?" she asked very simply, meeting his gaze again. "If you can think of something that will do just as well, I'll gladly choose that instead. If you can't. . . ."

She let the words trial off, but he still nodded to show he knew what she meant. Their happiness had disappeared like fog exposed to the morning sun, and there didn't seem to be a way to get it back.

"Let's both think about it," he said with a sigh after a moment. "It's not as if we need the answer immediately, after all, not when we haven't gotten even a single look at the competitions. If one or both of us win seats as Highs, there won't be a problem any longer."

"No, you're right, there won't be," she said, forcing a smile and taking his offered hand after he rose. "But right now we'd better wash and get out of here. Others might be waiting to come in, and it would be rude to make them wait any longer than necessary."

He gave her a sound of neutral agreement, and they went back into the bath together. But not together, not really, not the way they'd been at first. They both had needs and wants they were chained to, and it was highly unlikely that their differences would ever be resolved. Jovvi felt like crying her heart out, but that wouldn't have stopped the pain. As she let the warm water flow over her, she decided to save her tears for when she and Lorand had to part for good.

When that day came she would need more than tears to help, but she already knew she'd never get it. . . .

THIRTY-SEVEN

Rion stood by the window in his room, staring out at the pretty little garden. And it *was* a little garden, at least by the standards he'd been raised by. Nothing but the best, Mother would always say, for me and for my lovely boy. Don't worry, darling, I'll always be there to make certain you get nothing else.

Remembering how pleased he'd been to hear that, Rion could have cried. Back then he'd had no idea he was being cursed rather than blessed, chained rather than freed. Mother had always made a point of keeping her deliberately given word, and in that nothing had changed. There'd been a letter waiting for him when he'd returned to his room after lunch, written in her secretary's flowing, familiar script.

"My darling boy," the letter had begun, just as though he were still ten years old. "I knew allowing you to come to Gan Garee without me would end badly, and so it has. Those trollops living in that so-called residence with you have obviously taken advantage of your sweet-natured innocence, but I refuse to abandon you in your hour of need. I've demanded an audience with the Blending, and this time I won't allow them to sway me. One way or another I'll soon have you out of there, and back with me where you belong.

"As far as other things go, I must tell you frankly that I'm deeply disappointed. I sent word to Gan Garee ahead of you, to Dom Hoclan, my business manager. He arranged to have men keep watch over you, to protect you in case of trouble, and to discover what bad influences you might be exposed to. He was also supposed to keep you from those bad influences, but mistook my intention and merely had his men keep watch. When I received his report this morning, I immediately took to my bed.

"My darling, how could you betray me so by indulging in the rutting practiced by animals and peasants? I realize you certainly had no idea how filthy and disgusting the thing you were made to do really was, but surely you should have known that what has my approval you have already been permitted to indulge in? That this very obvious truth failed to stop you I attribute to your being in the company of those nauseating peasants, and as soon as I have your word that it will never happen again, we'll speak no more of it.

"In the interim, I ordered Dom Hoclan to have the sickening female who desecrated you arrested by the guard and thrown out of the city. As soon as she's found your honor will be avenged, and no one need ever know. The pain in my heart will remain, of course, but once you've returned to me and enough years have passed, the pain will surely do the same.

"Be brave, my love, it won't be long, you have my word on that. Until then, I remain, your adoring mother."

His adoring mother. Rion shuddered at that phrase as it rang over and over in his head. She'd decided to have Naran Whist arrested and thrown out of the city so Rion's "honor" would be avenged, and that without knowing how much he burned to see the girl again. If she ever found out, Naran's life would be worth less than a copper, and all because she'd generously turned a sheltered boy into a man. The boy's mother didn't want him to become a man, and all her considerable power and influence would be bent toward returning him to his place under her thumb.

A wave of illness made Rion close his eyes for a moment, and when he opened them once more he was able to see Tamrissa and Ro again. The two had been walking in the garden since before Rion had come to the window, and something told him they had used a private part of the garden to share a kiss. He had very little experience in judging the matter, but he still had that definite feeling. And just a few moments ago, he'd seen Jovvi hurrying to the bath house in a wrap. Ordinarily that would have meant nothing, but Coll had gone into the bath house a short while before her, and now the "occupied" sign hung very conspicuously on the door.

Rion turned away from the window, frustration and anger rising dangerously within him. His mother's minions would interfere with the woman he most wanted to associate with, and the only two other females he found the least interest in had refused his company before accepting that of other men. Was he so pitiful, then, that no decent relationship with a woman was possible for him? Was he doomed to be nothing more than "mother's darling boy" for the rest of his days? He couldn't bear that thought, he simply couldn't, it was so damnably unfair!

Anger turned so quickly to fury and rage that Rion would have been shocked if he hadn't been so deeply caught up. Instead he snarled and lashed out with a fist as he'd been taught to do in his exercises. The motion was intended for the releasing of tension and pressures, a deliberate spilling of excess energy that might otherwise overwhelm him. He lashed out with his other fist even as he took another step— and the blow landed on something soft and yielding which was also invisible.

For a brief moment Rion was startled, but then his wildly lunging thoughts found the answer. The exercise set he'd learned to form from solidified air as a boy; his mind had realized he needed it very badly now, and had formed the set without his being aware of it. Another blow in the same place showed Rion that the set really was there, so he began to use it as it was meant to be used.

Pummeling the wide cushion until his breath came in gasps was the first step, and then he moved to the left, where the knobby pole was positioned. Grabbing the invisible pole and strangling and shaking it was immensely satisfying, and brought him to the point of being able to move to the right, again beyond the cushion. Separate sections of solidified air lay there, and he took one in each fist and began to raise and lower them. Their weight had been increased rather dramatically, so lifting them over and over was no easy thing.

After the weights came the ladder, which he climbed up and down so many times that his leg muscles cringed at the thought of continuing on. His arms already felt that way, so he was finally able to leave the set and go to collapse on his bed. The fury and rage had been completely burned out of him, leaving his mind free to try rational thought again. But the anger wasn't gone, far from it, and likely would never be gone again. Unless and until he found a way out of the madness his mother was determined to drag him back into.

Rage tried to surface again, but this time it was easily brought under control. Rage accomplished nothing but destruction, and only constructive thought had a chance of freeing him. Rion understood that, but where was he supposed to begin? With an answering letter to Mother, telling her he now knew the truth? She claimed to love him above all other things in life, but actually it was herself she loved. Keeping him a pitiful child had been for her benefit, certainly not for his.

The thought of writing a letter like that brought a faint smile to Rion's lips, but he knew how useless the effort would be. After reading it Mother would take to her bed in a "faint," and when she arose again she would be even more determined to reclaim him. It would be the "bad influences" which had caused him to reject her great and selfless love, and she would give her word again to save him from the evil and return him to her side.

But that was something which would never happen. Rion had lost himself to rage because of the fear that she might succeed in regaining possession of him, not realizing just how impossible she would find that. He would sooner live on the street, in filth and squalor and begging coppers, than go back to the nightmare of his previous life. That firm decision freed him more surely than all the letters and protests in the universe, sending his previous fear to a place from which it could never return.

"Sorry, Mother, but your darling baby has finally begun to grow up," Rion murmured, his smile now a good deal more serene. "And if I find Naran before your people do, she'll be just as safe from you. Yes, she isn't at the tavern any longer, so I should have a chance to do just that. But I'd better remember about those people watching me. . . ."

For the first time since he got his mother's letter, Rion was grateful she'd sent it. He added a silent thank-you to what he'd just said, then began to make serious plans. And tried not to remember what Jovvi and Tamrissa so obviously thought of him. . . .

Vallant finally went back to his room to get ready for dinner, keeping himself from whistling only with the greatest of efforts. He'd spent all afternoon walking in the garden with Tamrissa, and she'd even agreed they might do the same again this evening. She might decide against it at the last moment, but not because she was uninterested in him. She was just so shy where men were concerned, when she wasn't telling them off, that is. . . .

He laughed lightly as he closed the door behind himself, feeling as if he walked on air. She was just as interested in him as he was in her, he knew it more surely than he'd ever known anything in his life. In his old life, that was. If he had to lose that, he seemed to have gained what would turn out to be incredibly more.

Giving in to the urge to whistle a few notes, Vallant started across his room to the bed, intending to lie down for a short while. He certainly had the time, and he certainly had what to daydream about. He grinned as he walked, intending to take full advantage of the daydreaming, and then suddenly, unexpectedly, he ran into something that tripped him. He fell forward, expecting to sprawl full length on the floor, but it didn't happen. He sprawled on something soft and springy instead, a good three feet *off* the floor.

Vallant blinked as he looked down at the carpeting he hadn't fallen onto, trying to figure out what was going on. He lay on something invisible, but it wasn't meant to harm him or it would have done so already. So what could it possibly—

"Of course!" he said aloud with a laugh, absolutely delighted. "It's an invisible cloud, supplied to let me float as much as I like."

The idea was perfect, and Vallant knew he'd have to thank Mardimil for it. His cloud had to be made of solidified air, and there was only one practitioner of Air magic in the house. Mardimil must have seen him and decided to do a bit of gentle teasing, but that was perfectly all right. Vallant didn't mind being teased like *this,* not when it fit his mood so perfectly.

He turned over and stretched out, finding the cloud to be even more comfortable than his bed would have been. It was something he would have loved to show to and share with Tamrissa, just as he wanted to share everything with her. For the daughter of one wealthy merchant and the widow of another, she'd had so very little in her life.

"But that applies only to pleasure," he muttered, a darkness descending over his happiness. "When it comes to pain she's had enough for ten people, but her father still isn't satisfied. He'll use her to get what he wants until she's all used up—unless somebody stops him. Somebody like me, for instance, who'll never let her be hurt again."

Vallant made that promise out loud once more, but this time for himself rather than for Tamrissa. He'd never met a woman he felt so complete with, and the more he spoke to her the more certain of it he became. It was as though she'd been given to him in compensation for having lost his family, but he had to remember she hadn't really been *given.* He'd have to work harder to win her than he'd ever worked in his life, because she still couldn't quite trust men.

He sighed then, remembering how she'd tried to wish her beauty away. She felt it had brought her nothing but grief, and she honestly believed that being plain or downright ugly would have saved her from what she'd gone through. It was possible she was right so Vallant hadn't argued, but something told him she was mistaken at least in part. What lay inside her, what made her the woman she was, was every bit as attractive as her face and body. Vallant felt the pull of her essence, and suspected a good number of other men would and did feel the same. That man Hallasser, for instance. . . .

Vallant felt every trace of humanity leave him at thought of the man Tamrissa's father was now trying to give her to.

According to Jovvi, Hallasser would be worse than Tamrissa's first husband, but that would happen only if he got his hands on her. If it ever actually came down to that, Vallant knew he would unhesitatingly pull every drop of water out of the man's body. Hallasser would die a shriveled dust-corpse, and Vallant would spend not an instant in regret. And then it would be Tamrissa's father's turn. . . .

Thoughts of that sort were usually accompanied by rage, but the matter was too important for rage. Vallant lay very still on the cloud, wearing a faint smile at the cold calm inside him, grimly satisfied with his thoughts. No matter what the cost, he *would* protect the woman he had begun to fall so deeply in love with. The woman he wanted so badly to *make* love to, but that would have to wait. She wasn't yet ready to accept him in that way, and he was prepared to wait as long as necessary until she was.

But in the meanwhile he could daydream, which he did until it was time to go down to dinner. To see her again, and be near her again. . . .

THIRTY-EIGHT

By the time I reached my room, I was almost sorry I'd insisted on leaving Vallant for a while. Being with him had been wonderful, so unexpectedly filled with . . . *fun.* I still found it hard to believe that such a thing was possible, to *enjoy* being in the company of a man. Even the boys I'd known at school had been more hungry than humorous, more intent on conquest than on comfortable exchange. But Vallant was so marvelous, so unique. . . .

I just about danced inside my sitting room, closed the door

to the hall, then did dance around a little. I'd never before felt the way I did right now, and the experience was pure delight. It made me want to dance, and sing, and fly—!

I stopped short in the middle of the room when I banged into something, but couldn't see what the something might have been. That part of the room was empty of everything but carpeting, but I hadn't imagined brushing against something. So I put out a hand and felt around, and sure enough a moment of groping at last put my fingers on the thing.

Whatever it was. I blinked over the fact that it was invisible, then used two hands to explore its dimensions. Again it took a moment to make sense of what I felt, and then I was more confused than ever. Unless I was mistaken, the thing felt like a swing, the kind of net garden swing I'd used only once as a child, at the house of one of my father's business associates. The associate's children were allowed to use the swing anytime they pleased, but my sisters and I weren't permitted any activity which might damage us or leave a scar. . . .

At first I tried to imagine how an invisible swing could have gotten into my sitting room, but then the answer became obvious. Rion had supplied it by solidifying air, and it didn't matter whether he'd done it on his own or Vallant had asked him to do it. I now had what fit my mood perfectly, and no one was there to say I couldn't use it.

I moved around carefully until I was able to lower myself into the swing, muffling giggles over the thought of a net swing without any netting. But the thing was comfortable and felt really solid, so I held to its sides and began to swing. Pushing against the floor with my feet let me swing for quite a number of minutes before I had to push again, so I was able to let my mind drift off into pleasant memories.

Like the way Vallant had told me about his family, not to brag but to share the idea of what a real family was like. His mother had an odd sense of humor and enjoyed occasionally teasing her sons, which usually made them laugh. His father was a big man with a very strict sense of honor, but he'd always shared that sense with his sons rather than imposing it on them. They all loved each other very much, and I was finally able to understand why Vallant hadn't wanted to be parted from them.

I'd told him very little about me in comparison, but he hadn't pressed for details he seemed to know I didn't care to discuss. Instead he'd called me Tamakins, insisting that the awful nickname suited me perfectly. I'd tried to retaliate with Valsi-Walsi, but the sound of that had been so ridiculous I hadn't been able to say it without laughing. At first he'd pretended to cringe at the name, but it wasn't long before he couldn't keep from laughing either.

And then, not long before we'd come in, he'd put a finger under my chin to raise my face, and then he'd kissed me. It had been such a gentle kiss, and such a short one, but my lips still tingled with the feel of it. I'd expected him to ask for more, dreading what would happen when I was forced to refuse, but he never did. He simply kissed me gently for a moment too quickly over, and then we'd resumed strolling. With my hand held firmly to his arm, just as he'd insisted. . . .

I thought about all that for a timeless time, then stopped thinking and just let the sensation of pleasant memories wash over me. Things had been fairly pleasant when I was a small child, but since then there'd been nothing to compare with what was really a simple walk in a garden. And I'd agreed to think about doing it again, later, after dinner. In the dark rather than the light, with paper lanterns brightening only certain portions of the path. . . .

I expected the idea of that to make me blush, but all it did was cause me to laugh and swing higher. Everyone kept insisting that associations between men and women were supposed to be pleasant, and I suddenly found myself ready to investigate the claim personally. Or almost ready. There were still so many ugly memories that needed more burying first. . . .

I swung long and high, but after a while I remembered that I was supposed to be getting ready for dinner. I could have stayed in the skirt and blouse if I'd wanted to, the way most of the men had stayed in their uniform trousers and shirts. But instead I found myself leaving the swing and hurrying to my wardrobe, to pull out the best dress I had. I wanted to look really marvelous for Vallant, to make him glad he'd asked me to walk with him again. I could see his platinum hair and pale-blue-eyed handsomeness clearly in my mind's eye, and couldn't wait until I saw them again right in front of me.

The dress of melon silk trimmed with lots of white lace took a short while to get into, and that after washing some in the basin. Once dressed I ran the brush through my hair quickly, then hurried out of the suite. I was certain I would be very late, and only hoped Vallant hadn't decided to wait for me before going in himself. Walking in late is bad enough; walking in late with a man beside me . . . I'd probably never live long enough to stop blushing.

Happily, Vallant hadn't waited, and I was surprised to see that I wasn't the last to get there. Two other chairs remained empty at the table, and as soon as I was seated I found out why. I was in the midst of exchanging a smile with Vallant, who had returned to his original seat, when Warla appeared to stop beside me on the right.

"Please excuse the intrusion, ladies and gentlemen, but I've been instructed to tell you something," she began in her usual, hesitant way. "This afternoon some people came, and they packed up Dom Drowd's and Dama Lant's belongings and took them away. They . . . said to tell you not to expect those two back, even if they manage to qualify before week's end. If they do they'll be put in another residence, and if they don't they'll be . . . released to return to their ordinary lives. That means dinner will be served immediately."

She curtsied and left then, and a moment later the servants began to bring out our meal. No one said a word until the servants were gone again, and then Jovvi sighed.

"I won't pretend I liked them, but this upsets me," she said softly, apparently speaking the thoughts of most of us. "Some of us were told everyone has until week's end to qualify, but for some reason I don't believe it. Unless I'm mistaken, they have no more than two days left."

"If that," Vallant agreed, looking as serious as everyone else. "I'd put my money on tomorrow bein' their last real chance, with the day after used to . . . clean up the leftovers. If the testin' people actually waited till week's end, half of those left would stay in their residences, already havin' given up."

"You're probably right," Lorand agreed as well from my left, a dark shadow heavy in his expression. "First they'll take care of the leftovers, and then—what? When will it get to be our turn?"

"Probably not until we fail in the competitions," Rion said, sounding more distant than he usually did. "But first we have to fail, which I, personally, have no intentions of doing. Success will bring more than gold, so we'd all do well to concentrate on nothing else."

Jovvi and Pagin Holter nodded in abstraction, but Vallant and Lorand looked as uncertain as I felt. I fully intended to do my absolute best, of course, but the ghost of what-if-that's-not-good-enough? continued to haunt me. I had no idea what the competitions would consist of, but that damned uncertainty I was cursed with kept whispering doubts and fears.

The meal was a very silent one, with each of us wrapped mostly in our thoughts. Once I looked up and happened to meet Vallant's gaze, and he tried to smile at me reassuringly. I tried to return his smile in the same way, but neither one of us succeeded. But we did try, and that in itself made me feel a bit better.

When everyone had finished eating, we moved our silent group out into the front hall. Pagin Holter disappeared the way he usually did, followed this time by Rion. I thought it strange that he would walk off so abruptly, but then Vallant came over to me and everyone else was forgotten.

"I hope you've been thinkin' about that stroll I suggested earlier," he said with a slightly better smile. "After that announcement, we need it more than ever."

I returned his smile and was about to answer, when a knock came at the door. One of the servants was there to see if we wanted anything—or possibly to listen in on our conversations—and he went to the door and opened it. Standing just outside was my father, the person I least wanted to see in the entire world.

"Well, good evening, my dear," he said, coming inside only a single step before stopping to smile at me. "I thought you would all be finished with dinner by this time, and I'm pleased to see I was right."

"What do you want?" I asked, fighting to keep my trembling from showing. "I thought I told you not to come back. I won't be sold again, and especially not to that—that—"

"Actually, child, I'm here to look after my daughter's best interests," he interrupted smoothly. "That—gentleman—beside you announced to all of us that you and he were engaged, but I'm afraid that may not be true. If what I suspect is so, the man has betrayed you by not mentioning that he's already engaged to another woman entirely."

I barely had time to remember that Vallant *had* said we were promised to each other on my parents' last visit, when my father abruptly stepped aside. Behind him was a very beautiful woman with thick auburn hair and dark, sultry eyes, and when she saw Vallant she smiled dazzlingly and hurried inside.

"Vallant, my love, how wonderful that I've actually found you!" she exclaimed, rushing into his arms. "Daddy was terribly disappointed that I didn't insist you marry me before you left, and so he sent me here with enough gold to arrange everythin' now. He and Momma are only a few days behind me, so they'll certainly be here for the ceremony."

"By a happy coincidence, the young lady's father and I are business associates," my father purred while I stood there with my mind clanging in shock. "She came to me asking for assistance in finding her intended, and you may imagine my surprise when her description seemed to match the young man involved with my daughter. You really must—"

"Get out," I interrupted his gloating in a choked voice, hating him more than I'd ever thought was possible. "Get out of my house and don't you dare come back!"

I turned and ran for the stairs then, shaking off the hand Vallant tried to put on my arm despite the woman crawling all over him. He undoubtedly had a perfectly reasonable explanation why he'd neglected to mention that he was promised to another woman, but I didn't want to hear it. He'd managed to hurt me more than Gimmis had ever accomplished, and I was on the verge of losing control of myself. If I'd stayed there even a moment longer, flames would have leaped out to consume everyone in reach.

But when I reached my bedchamber with two doors closed firmly behind me, the only thing that came was tears. I sat on the floor in my beautiful silk and lace dress, sobbing hopelessly, wishing I were dead. For a very short while I'd let myself believe there really was such a thing as pleasure, but it was a lie. The world and life contained nothing but pain, and I'd never let myself forget that again. Or ever let anyone come close. Not ever . . . not again . . . not when it hurt so much to be wrong. . . .

Vallant tried to call out Tamrissa's name to stop her, to tell her it wasn't true, but Mirra chose that moment to throw her arms around his neck and smother the words with a kiss. She hung on like a leech with the strength of a pit bull, and by the time Vallant had freed himself, Tamrissa was gone.

"Why, Val, darlin', whatever is makin' you treat me in so ungentlemanly a way?" Mirra pouted after catching her balance. She'd nearly fallen from the shove he'd given her, and he thought it was a shame that she hadn't. "I know you're glad to see me, darlin', just as glad as I am to see you. Why don't we go to your room to . . . discuss the weddin'. . . ."

She grinned at that and tried to close with him again, but Vallant put a hand on her chest and shoved again. This time she stumbled back into the man who'd brought her, hopefully crushing his foot at the very least.

"My daddy taught me to be a gentleman with ladies, which means you don't qualify, Mirra," he growled over her screech of outrage. "You know well enough that we weren't engaged, just talkin' about it, and even that ended before I left. Now, I believe I heard the lady of this house order the slimy cur who brought you to leave, and I want you gone along with him."

"How dare you, sir!" Tamrissa's father hissed as Mirra went into that full pout she had so much practice with. "Such denigration is actionable, which you'll find out when I have you hauled into court!"

"Sellin' a daughter to a sadist and then tryin' it again means you deserve every filthy name a man can put lips to," Vallant countered, his growl becoming more pronounced. "You go right ahead and sue me, and then the whole city can know what you are. But right now, get out and take—*her*— with you."

"You'll be sorry you said that, darlin'," Mirra hissed while Tamrissa's father went pale with fury, her words obviously referring to the disgust she'd heard in Vallant's tone. "You're the one I want and the one I mean to get, but you'll be real sorry you spoke to me like that. Just wait and see if you're not."

Her head came up with a sniff and then she turned and flounced out, followed by Tamrissa's father after the man gave Vallant a small bow. He'd recovered control of himself so quickly that Vallant frowned, wondering what the man could be up to now. He was far from beaten, there was no doubt of that, but something much more important clamored for Vallant's attention. As soon as the door was closed he turned toward the stairs, but Jovvi's hand was on his arm before he could take even a single step.

"Wait," she said, the intensity in her tone halting him more successfully than chains would have. "She won't speak to you now, and even more importantly won't listen. She's all locked up inside again, and needs time to get over the disappointment."

"But there's nothin' for her to be disappointed about," Vallant protested with a chill touching his insides. "Mirra was lyin', and she's got to understand that."

"She won't believe it," Jovvi said, sympathy pouring from her like water. "I could feel that clearly, and even understand why to a small extent. Believing things leaves you open to being hurt, and she can't take any more pain. It's easier for her to simply refuse to believe, but give her some time. She got around the problem once, so there's no reason why she can't do it again."

"I'm willin' to give her all the time she needs, but we still don't know how much the testin' authority means to give *us*." Vallant knew his voice had gone lifeless, which fit the situation perfectly. "The longer I know that girl the more deeply in love I fall, but now she won't even talk to me. And I don't even know how long I have to change her mind. What if it's not long enough . . . ?"

Vallant let the words trail off, but no one added anything in the way of encouragement. Only Jovvi and Coll were left in the hall with him, and they seemed to have problems of their own. The careful distance between them seemed deliberate, and the pain he felt in them seemed more than a mirroring of his. Maybe he ought to say something to them. . . .

But words of compassion refused to come, so he simply went upstairs to his room and lay down on the bed. Everything had been going so beautifully, and now . . . now they were dirt and ashes. He'd managed to bring her around once so maybe he could do it again, but how long would it take? He would have willingly spent years, but they might turn out to have no more than weeks. Or days.

"Damn Mirra, damn that travesty of a father, and damn me for handlin' this so badly," Vallant whispered into the lonely silence of the room. "But most of all, damn that testin' authority. Damn . . . damn . . . damn . . . !"

THIRTY-NINE

Lorand joined the other men in climbing into the first coach, leaving the second for the ladies. Everyone was unusually quiet this morning, except for the one time Ro spoke to Tamrissa in the dining room during breakfast. Tamrissa had apparently taken lessons from the now-absent Beldara Lant, her attitude telling everyone that she was entirely alone in the room.

"I can see you don't want to talk to me, but this you're goin' to hear," Ro had said once Tamrissa was seated with a plate of food in front of her. "Mirra was lyin', and so was your father when he said I betrayed you. I did nothin' wrong, and if you insist on believin' their lies, you're helpin' them win."

Unless Tamrissa had stopped up her ears she must have heard him, but not even a flicker in her eyes had supported that. She just went on eating quietly and calmly, ignoring Ro along with the rest of the world. Mardimil and Holter had looked faintly puzzled, but neither had asked any questions.

As the coach pulled away from the residence, Lorand's thoughts returned for the thousandth time to what had gone on between Jovvi and him yesterday afternoon. The lovemaking had been as marvelous as he'd expected it to be, but nothing had gone right after that. He'd explained his point of view to Jovvi—and then she'd explained hers. He hadn't expected her to be so desperate for security, and he hadn't been able to argue her point of view. If he'd been wealthy it would have been a different story, but as it was. . . .

Lorand took a deep breath and let it out slowly, staring at the landscape going past without seeing it. He *wasn't* a wealthy man, so it was impossible to argue with Jovvi. He hadn't realized that her mother had actually *sold* her children, and the idea had disturbed him so much that he'd retreated to his room to rid himself of it in peace. He remembered wishing he were still back at the farm, where he'd had a small, secret room among the bales of hay in the barn.

Whenever his father had spent part of the day talking about the future he intended his sons to have, Lorand would take the first opportunity to go to his private place and make his own plans. He'd decided early that he would not spend his life working for his father to save him the cost of hiring a Middle to help with the harder jobs. In his private place he'd repeated his vow over and over, until he'd grown big enough to make his own plans come true.

Lorand remembered thinking about that as he began to cross the room, and then the craziest thing had happened. He'd tripped on and fallen over absolutely nothing, and ended up lying on top of the nothing. Feeling around finally gave him an idea about what it was, but that was even crazier. It felt just like the bales of hay which had contained his secret place, all the way down to the opening he would crawl through. The whole thing was a lot smoother, but more importantly it was also invisible.

It had taken awhile for Lorand's battered thoughts to realize what it was, which was solidified air. For some reason Mardimil must have provided the thing, and Lorand had been too relieved to have his favorite place back to wonder how Mardimil had known. He'd simply crawled inside, and spent some time telling himself everything *wasn't* lost. He'd come to Gan Garee to earn a High practitioner's position, and if somehow he actually managed to do it, all his problems would be solved.

He'd meant to thank Mardimil at dinner for his help, but Warla had made that announcement about Drowd and Beldara Lant and he'd forgotten all about it. Later Mardimil had disappeared and then there'd been that to-do with Ro and the woman and Tamrissa, and now it was really too late. Even if Mardimil hadn't looked distracted and withdrawn this morning, any thanks would seem like an afterthought about something trivial.

And besides all that, Lorand was too worried about what was ahead of them to spend time trying to thank someone gracefully. They'd gone in a different direction this morning, and now the coach was crossing a small bridge which seemed to lead out of the city proper. The road they traveled wasn't a wide one, and there were open fields on both sides of it. But not planted and tended fields. They'd been lying fallow for quite some time, and had gone mostly to grass.

A couple of miles up the road the coach began to slow, and then they turned off onto another road of the same size. But on this one it was possible to see structures in the distance, ones that didn't seem to be buildings. It wasn't yet possible to see what they were instead, but waiting until the coach moved closer didn't help much. Walls of smoky resin blocked easy sight of the things, leaving only hand-painted metal symbols of the various aspects to differentiate one section from another.

And those sections stretched out for quite a distance to both the left and right of the road. Their coach turned left, and a short way down it stopped in front of the symbol for Air magic. That made Mardimil the first to get out, which the man did without hesitation or comment. There was an opening in the resin wall behind the sign, and Mardimil disappeared through it as the coach began to move again.

Next out were Holter and Ro, both of them leaving the coach in the same preoccupied way. *We've become a group of strangers,* Lorand thought as he watched them go, *more so than when we first met. I'd wonder where all this was leading, but I don't think I want to know.*

The idea was unsettling, but before he could fall too deeply into considering it, it was his turn to leave the coach. He stepped out onto a resin walk near the sign of Earth magic, then went through the opening in the wall with almost no hesitation. The coach kept on going, undoubtedly to the area to the left of this new road up ahead, where other coaches stood. There were also two ordinary buildings over there, one much larger than the other. A stable for the horses, then, and a posting house for the drivers. . . .

And then Lorand was beyond the wall, and all other thoughts left him. What had looked like structures from a distance weren't; thin, transparent resin rested on poles of the same material, acting as a flat-topped roof over almost every foot of the vast area. Some parts were sectioned off with walls, making both larger and smaller areas, and some of the walls were smoky rather than clear. There also seemed to be chairs in some of the areas, multiple chairs in one of them along with tables. Most of the areas had something other than furniture, though, and Lorand was so intent on figuring out what the something was that he almost missed the man walking up to him.

"Fascinating, isn't it?" the man asked with a friendly smile. He was a bit short of his middle years, a slightly rounded man not quite Lorand's size with a round face, brown hair, and mild brown eyes. "I'm Hestir, the Adept assigned to show you around. As you'll probably be the last newcomer, my job is almost over."

The man didn't seem terribly upset about that, and his easy manner led Lorand into deciding to take a chance.

"But I thought the others had until week's end to qualify," he protested mildly, as though only faintly curious. "Most of those in my sessions seemed rather determined, so I expected to see them arrive only a short while after me."

"Those in your session have been determined since they first arrived," Hestir responded with a dismissive laugh. "We've learned over the years that those who don't qualify by the third session at the latest usually don't ever manage it. There was one once, about nine years ago, who finally forced himself into qualifying at the last moment. Nothing came of it, though, since he couldn't quite get himself together for the competitions. But enough idle chatter, something I'm quite marvelous at. We'll start the tour over there."

"Over there" was an area to the extreme left, a large one with comfortable chairs surrounding a core of tables and chairs obviously meant to be used for meals or snacks. There were a few people moving around some of the areas, but this one was empty.

"When the others arrive, some of them will stop here for another cup of tea before beginning practice," Hestir said, the words more conversational than lecturing. "Behind that wall is a cooking area and a place for the servants, as those of us in this section take our lunch here. If you want a servant and there aren't any about, just ring that bell and one will come out from behind the wall."

Hestir had pointed to a small cowbell hanging from one of the posts by a rope, another length of rope available to ring it with. Lorand nodded as though ringing for a servant was the most usual and unimportant thing in his life, and Hestir smiled.

"Now, over here is our very first practice area," he said, leading the way to a series of smallish sections surrounded by smoky resin. "It's what you'll use to begin with, before you start the first of the competitions, but please don't confuse it with a warmup area. Those are arranged around the sections devoted to interactive competition, between that and the individual competition area."

"There are different kinds of competitions?" Lorand asked, surprised enough to stop where he was. "For some reason I thought there would be only one."

"A common enough mistake, and one I made myself in the beginning," Hestir said with a chuckle, stopping with him. "It takes a moment to realize that there are different parts to our aspect, more parts, in fact, than with any of the others. We must prove our strength in *all* of those parts, as well as in the two methods every aspect uses. The first method is, of course, competing with another applicant to show strength and speed. The first to complete the assigned chore is the winner."

"Like in a foot race," Lorand said with a thoughtful nod. "That must be the individual competition you mentioned. But that has to mean the interactive competitions pit us directly against each other. Don't you lose a large number of applicants that way?"

"Only the hopelessly incompetent ones," Hestir replied, obviously amused by that thought as well. "One of the things you must learn is how to shield yourself from the products of your own aspect. Any fool off the street can attack with his aspect, the strength of the attack depending upon the fool's own strength. But to defend with your ability—Ah, that takes imagination and a sense for planning as well as strength. Let's take a look at the first practice area now, shall we?"

Lorand nodded even as he tried to swallow against the roiling feeling in his middle. He'd wanted to ask about where the positive parts of his aspect came in, the ones you didn't use for something like attack or defense against attack. But asking something like that would have made him look naive, which could end up being a very bad mistake among these people. Predators think of the naive as prey, and even the round, overly pleasant Hestir was more wolf than sheep.

"Oh, goodness, the morning sun is in that uncomfortable part of the sky again," Hestir exclaimed when they stepped into the first area. The sun was between two stands of trees visible in the distance, and glaring as only an early-morning sun on a soon-to-be warm day can. With nothing but empty air to block the sight of it, even squinting didn't help much.

"I think we need to do something about that," Hestir said in a way that made Lorand instantly suspicious. "Now let me see, what can that something be? Well, how about this."

Hestir had been looking at a mound of clumped-together soil, the only thing to be seen in the area. The next moment the mound—*exploded!*—throwing a fine mist of soil into the air. The sun's glare was blocked out, of course, at least until the mist began to settle down again.

"Please note that the dispersal was contained, and didn't go beyond this area," Hestir said while Lorand stared, at the same time working automatically to keep the dust out of the volume of air he currently breathed. "That's the first thing you must practice, control of the material you touch with your ability. If even one grain of soil ends up outside this area, you haven't yet perfected your control."

Lorand nodded again, realizing that Hestir was telling him about doing two things at once. Well, he'd done more than two things at once during that test, but he'd never actually *exploded* anything. . . .

"We'll have to let the dust settle before you can try it yourself," Hestir said, chuckling at his little joke. "During that time I'll show you the other areas. Come along now."

Lorand was about to ask why they didn't simply gather the soil back into its original mound, then dismissed the question. Hestir was undoubtedly too important to spend his time and talent on a menial chore like that, especially when there were other areas to be shown. So Lorand simply followed the other man, then stopped beside him in the second area. Instead of soil, this place held a small mound of iron ingots. Each ingot was about two inches square, and Hestir pointed to one lying a couple of feet away from the mound.

"I'm going to do the same thing to that ingot that I did to the soil, but not as spectacularly," he said. "Watch and see what I mean."

It was still necessary to squint against the sun's glare, but that didn't stop Lorand from seeing the way the ingot began to come apart. It crumbled into small chunks from one end to the other, uneven chunks that rocked a bit before lying still.

"And that's all there is to it," Hestir said, this time pretending nonchalance. Lorand had been able to feel his effort, which hadn't been minimal. "Do you think you can manage that?"

"I guess I'll have to try it and see," Lorand replied, working now to sound self-effacing. He wasn't about to mention that a bent nail was useless on a farm, but did rather well as a prop for a boy to impress the girls with. He'd be able to take that ingot apart a lot faster and more thoroughly than Hestir had—but not while the man watched. There was no sense in making accidental enemies, not in a place like that.

"Good man, that's the spirit," Hestir enthused, his broad smile back. "A willingness to try means everything, and is usually the difference between success and failure. Let's go on to the next area."

The third area contained a small-meshed cage filled with rats, well-fed rats by the look of them. Lorand didn't have the usual farm-bred hatred of rats, nor did he fear them as some people did. He understood that their depredations were the result of their will to survive, and had never tried to hurt them unless his own survival—or his family's—had been at stake.

"Now, here we're looking for something else entirely," Hestir said, just saving Lorand from making a fool of himself by refusing to take apart the rats. "Once again it's a matter of control dominating strength, as the rats aren't to be harmed. Here's what you have to learn to do."

Lorand felt Hestir begin to exert himself again, and then the rats began to move away from the center of the cage. They didn't go willingly or easily, but at last there was a cleared space in the middle. After a moment there was movement among the rats to the right, and then a single rat came slowly and reluctantly into the cleared space. It stood alone only for a brief moment, and then all the rats were running around freely again.

"So you see," Hestir said, breathing somewhat heavily. "First the entire group must be induced to clear the center of the cage, and then one rat must be returned to stand alone. This, in a manner of speaking, is like Encouragement, but considerably more specific."

"Yes, a lot more specific," Lorand agreed, considering the

matter. "I have experience with Encouragement, of course . . . but what is something like *this* for? How can it possibly be useful to a High practitioner?"

"That's something you'll find out if and when you become a High practitioner," Hestir said easily, dismissing the idea. "We lesser mortals don't need to be told, we only need to learn what we're instructed to. And remember, the rats aren't to be harmed."

When Lorand shrugged and nodded, Hestir smiled again and clapped him on the shoulder.

"Good man," he said, clearly approving. "Now, once you've mastered these three exercises, there will be more of a different sort for you to work at. I'll show you one or two of those, and then you'll begin at the beginning. The ones beyond here are simply variations of the first three, so please don't spend your time worrying about any hidden surprises."

"What I will be spending my time on is wondering how long it will take to reach the competitions," Lorand said, working to put the sort of upper class pettishness you sometimes heard from Mardimil in his own voice. "It's rather tiring, but all our funds have been depleted and we'll soon need to pay for our food or starve. That was told us right at the beginning, and the next payment time draws uncomfortably near."

"Oh, that's not something to worry about immediately," Hestir said with a deprecating gesture. "You'll be given a silver din for each of the first three areas you master, and two for each of the areas after those. By that time you'll have reached the competitions, and will be ready to win yourself some gold. So let's continue on, and then you'll be able to begin."

This time Lorand followed with a bit more eagerness, more than ready to begin. The only one of the first three areas he expected to have to practice was the first, and even that shouldn't take much time to master. Depending on what the next areas held, he could well be at the competitions before he knew it! If he had stacks of gold to offer Jovvi even before the matter of a High position became immediate, he might have a chance to change her mind.

"I won't demonstrate these next exercises," Hestir said, drawing Lorand from his thoughts. "They're either too messy for anything less than serious practice, or would require a replacement for some part or parts of what you must work with. This first, as you can see, is a large kettle of thick black liquid that doesn't smell very nice at all."

"It looks a bit like axle grease and even smells like it, but it's not as thick," Lorand observed, studying the large kettle where it stood in the center of the area. "What am I supposed to do with it?"

"The same thing I did with the soil, dear boy," Hestir replied with a wave of his hand. "This liquid comes from the earth, and therefore falls under our aspect. It's considerably more difficult to scatter liquid, but practice will soon see you doing it. Now, in this next area is a simple arrangement of wooden wheels, but there's a section of metal on the inside holding it all together. Can you feel the metal?"

"Yes," Lorand answered with a frown. "But the metal is steel, not iron. You aren't going to tell me I have to take steel apart?"

"Nothing less, dear boy," Hestir confirmed with a grin. "And how clever of you to tell that it's steel. Many of the applicants coming through aren't able to discriminate that clearly. I expect you'll do very well indeed here, and I'll have been the first to realize that. Oh, and when you're ready to go beyond the first three areas, be sure to ask for the presence of an Adept before you begin. Each mastery must be verified by one of us, and if we're not there to see it you'll just have to do it all over again. Let's pause for a cup of tea, and then I'll leave you to it."

Lorand let himself be bustled out of the area and back toward where they'd started from, his elation of a moment before now gone beneath depression. The first three areas would be very little trouble for him, but the next ones would hardly be the same. Scattering that liquid *would* come under his aspect rather than under Water, since there wasn't any water in it. But handling something like that. . . . And steel. Were they serious about expecting him to be able to pick apart steel as easily as he did iron?

Hestir chattered on about nothing important as they walked toward the eating area, but Lorand wasn't fooled. The round, smaller man was trying to distract him from the fact that the Adept hadn't demonstrated those last two exercises because he couldn't. Hestir worked for the testing authority and was allowed to call himself an Adept, but in reality he wasn't very powerful. He must have qualified for the competitions in his day just as Lorand had in the last two, but he hadn't gone much beyond that.

So the question was, just how far would *he* go? How many of all the people who came here actually made it into the competitions? And there weren't that many Adepts. If you didn't make it and they had all the Adepts they needed, what then? What became of all those potential Highs who simply reached their limit?

And if you needed so much talent just to reach the competitions, what would it be like to challenge a Seated High . . . ?

FORTY

Jovvi let herself be helped into the coach after Tamrissa, feeling disturbed over more than just her own personal problems. She and Lorand were leagues apart in how they viewed the necessities of life, but it would be a while before their differences actually drove them apart completely. Tamma and Vallant were another story, however, and their pain was so strong Jovvi could have woven with it.

So once the coach began to move she said, "He wasn't lying, you know. I was there last night when he reminded that woman to her face that they'd never been engaged, and that their relationship had ended before he left for Gan Garee. He also called your father some rather interesting names, then threw them both out. Your father threatened to take him to court, and he told him to go ahead and do it."

Jovvi felt a faint sense of pleasure in Tamma over that, but not so much that it changed anything.

"Whether or not he was lying doesn't matter," Tamma

replied after a moment, looking out the window rather than at Jovvi. "He never said a word about that woman, which let my father use her against me. I can't afford to give my father any more routes into my mind than he already has, so Dom Ro can find some other woman to charm. I'm sure the one last night was only a single representative of the hundreds he's gone through."

"You're blaming him for being a healthy man?" Jovvi asked with a frown. "He never told you he'd grown up in a barrel, and you had no right to think that he had. He really cares about you, Tamma, and wants your trust more than almost anything."

"How can I trust someone who makes me more vulnerable so easily?" she asked, her gaze still firmly out the window. "He has no idea what I'm up against, and no real idea what I'll have to face if I lose. If someone makes you weaker rather than stronger, you're a fool to let them anywhere close. Besides, there are more important things to think about now, including whether or not we'll survive. We don't *all* have to, you know."

That suggestion chilled Jovvi so thoroughly that she let the subject drop. It wasn't as if she hadn't realized it herself at some level, she simply hadn't let herself think about it. Now she had to, and the thought made her strangely ill. How had Lorand gone from being an ordinary, interesting man to someone whose survival was vitally important? Even if they never found a way to be together, she couldn't bear the idea that he might not survive. There had to be a way, for all of them, and what *she* had to do was find it.

The decision in favor of action rather than sitting around waiting for something to happen made Jovvi feel better. She looked out her window to see that they seemed to be heading out of the city, across a bridge into an area that ought to be filled with the estates of the rich. Anywhere else it would be, but Gan Garee apparently had another use for the area. Odd that there weren't estates and mansions anyway . . .

Or maybe not so odd. When they turned onto a side road after the men's coach in a relatively short while, Jovvi thought she understood. Either the testing authority had been permitted to claim the entire area for its own uses, or anyone with enough power and gold to build in the area knew better than to do it. They had to be close to where the competitions were being held, and no one with any sense would want something like that outside their back door. Accidents could happen even with her aspect, and some mistakes can never be repaired.

When they reached a road running parallel with a resin wall, the men's coach turned left and theirs turned right. Tamrissa was the first to get out when the coach stopped beside a metal sign painted with the standard Fire magic symbol, but she didn't simply leave. After a brief hesitation she put her hand over Jovvi's and squeezed gently and reassuringly, and then she got out of the coach. She hadn't met Jovvi's gaze, but she *had* wished her luck.

Jovvi managed to return the squeeze before Tamma was gone, and then the coach continued on. It went quite a long distance, actually, before stopping beside a sign with the Spirit magic symbol. Jovvi discovered how reluctant she was to leave the coach when it came time to do it, but that didn't stop her any more than it ever had. She'd learned that simple problems could sometimes be run away from, but the rest had to be faced and defeated before it was safe to turn and walk away.

Jovvi closed the coach door behind her and headed for the opening in the resin wall, preferring not to picture deputies of the testing authority pursuing her. And they *would* come in pursuit, that was absolutely sure in a world of uncertainties. They went to a lot of trouble and expense gathering in all potential Highs, so there was no chance at all that they would shrug and forget about any who tried to escape them. They had to be avoided in a different way, most likely through the exercise of aspect power.

But the question still remained: how much power would be considered too much, and how little too little? The entire situation screamed out a need for careful balance, but as Jovvi looked around at what lay behind the resin wall, she felt the frustration of not knowing where the balance point lay. That was the key to all balance, knowing where the balance point was; without knowing, stabbing around in the dark after a hidden enemy would be just as productive. Pure luck might bring you success, but relying on luck was notoriously unreliable . . .

"Good morning, my dear," a smooth, pleasant voice said, taking Jovvi's attention. "I'm delighted to see that another of us has made it."

Jovvi examined the woman smiling at her even as she automatically returned the smile. The person greeting her was perhaps ten years away from middle age, but the woman radiated a sense of balance that suggested centuries of practice and exercise. She was tall, handsome rather than pretty, and had shining brown hair and soft brown eyes. Her dress was on the plain and businesslike side, a dark rose trimmed with gray, but was obviously expensive.

"I'm Genovir, the Adept who will be showing you around," the woman continued, putting out a friendly arm to draw Jovvi closer. "We'll have a cup of tea while I describe what you need to know, and then I'll get you started. Let's take that table over there."

There were quite a few tables with chairs standing just beyond the entrance area, and the one Genovir pointed to stood on the far side of the arrangement to the right. Jovvi let the friendly arm guide her into joining the woman, who paused to ring a bell hanging on a post before going to the table and sitting. Even before Jovvi was settled, a servant came out from behind a wall to the right, took Genovir's order for tea, then the man disappeared back behind the wall.

"Our servants are extremely efficient and quite pleasant," Genovir said when the man was gone, giving Jovvi another smile. "We generally all lunch in this area as well as take tea during times of rest, and you need only ring that bell when you want service. Some even take tea before they begin, as we're doing now."

"There aren't many people around, and none at the other tables," Jovvi observed just as mildly. "Is everyone already at practice then?"

"Oh, dear me, no," Genovir replied with a pleasant laugh. "Most of the applicants haven't arrived yet, it's much too early. We're here because this is your first visit, and you need someone to tell you what's expected. Tomorrow you may return early or with everyone else, just as you choose."

"I see," Jovvi said, then waited for the returning servant to set down a teapot and cups, pour for each of them, and then bow and leave again. "My goodness, they *are* efficient," she added.

"Once you reach this level you're entitled to a bit of pampering," Genovir responded, almost taking the compliment personally. "And once you've gone through hours of practice—or a competition—you'll appreciate it even more. Our range may not be as varied as some of the other aspects, but it can be more intense."

Jovvi nodded and sipped her tea after adding sugar, then let her gaze wander over everything in sight. A canopy was suspended from poles high above their heads, ready to ward off the heat of a noon sun when it arrived. Beyond the area of tables where they sat was a wide lawn of lovely grass, interrupted only by four stone paths. Each path led to an odd-looking round structure of resin, two of them small, two large. The small ones were to the left and the large to the right, and Genovir noticed Jovvi's curiosity.

"The small buildings are practice areas, the large, competition areas," she supplied after sipping at her own tea. "The small resin building to the left is where you'll begin, at first taking up where you left off at the sessions. The only difference here is, you'll be facing the people whose emotions you must balance, rather than having them behind walls and out of sight somewhere."

"The way they were during the sessions and even at the test," Jovvi said, knowing she showed a small frown. "But why am I suddenly going to be facing them? I can affect them just as easily through a wall."

"Not through a resin wall, and that's the only sort we have here," Genovir responded, still projecting nothing but kindliness and patience. "In addition to that, you have to become accustomed to working with the people around you. We're all of us raised not to interfere with those who are closest to us, sometimes even in matters of self-protection. You've reached the level where that changes, and you must become accustomed to the idea."

She gave Jovvi a moment to think that over, a moment Jovvi gladly took. She'd used her talent both to defend herself and to further her career, but at all other times she'd followed the restrictions and hadn't gone beyond soothing an occasional someone in great distress. She'd been taught, along with every other child, that using her ability to affect other people was both disgusting and absolutely forbidden, and it was going to take some effort to get beyond that.

"You'll have six people to work with, and they'll begin by shaking fists at you and simply being angry," Genovir continued after the pause. "That will give you a sense of being endangered, which should help to get you past ingrained reluctance. And they'll all be standing together, which will make balancing their emotions easier. Once you've mastered that they'll separate into two groups, which you'll find is just a bit harder to handle. After that there will be three groups, and finally all six will stand individually around you. When you can meet and master *that* situation, you'll be ready to move on to the next small building."

"What's done there?" Jovvi asked, mostly to keep from thinking about having six people all around her who had to be balanced into harmlessness and serenity. That would be much harder than what she'd already done, but somehow she'd have to manage.

"The second small building is where you'll practice reversing what you did in the first," came the answer, the words so smooth and matter-of-fact that Jovvi was instantly on guard against showing the wrong reaction. "The people you'll be working with will just stand there, and it will be up to you to change serenity into anger, and perhaps into some of the other emotions. We *can* do both with our talent, you know. Unbalancing is merely the opposite side of the coin."

"So it is," Jovvi agreed with a faint smile, inwardly more than a little disturbed. Whatever were these people after . . . ? "And when I complete that part of the practice, then comes the competition? How does that work?"

"My, aren't we eager," Genovir said with a smile that was just a shade too pleasant. "I certainly do hope our ability is able to match our ambition. But of course it will, so you must be told that the first competitions are time, strength, and speed tests where you are, in effect, competing with yourself. When you prove your mastery over your current peers, you then step forward to face those who have risen to the heights before you. So you see the whole thing is quite simple."

"Simple to discuss, yes," Jovvi said, making certain her tone was wry. "Accomplishing it will be another matter entirely, but I have cause to be concerned about the gold they told us could be won during the competitions. In just a short while I'll need to pay for my food again, and I don't yet have the full amount."

"Ah, yes, I'd forgotten about that," the woman said, and

now her smile was considerably more relaxed. "The pressure of needing to earn your supper. Well, you need not fear an empty belly quite yet, as you'll earn a silver din for each section of the first building that you master, and two silver for every section of the second. Does that ease your mind?"

"Yes, thank you, it certainly does," Jovvi replied, making certain she sounded gratefully relieved. "Hopefully I'll have enough time to earn what I need for week's end, and after that I can work toward future times. Yes, that should do quite nicely, and I appreciate your putting my mind at rest."

"That's one of the things I'm here for, my dear," Genovir replied, superiority fairly oozing out of her. The impression of total balance was a false facade, Jovvi could see now, erected to hide a rather shallow personality. And as easy as it was to get through the facade, the woman couldn't be terribly strong. And yet she called herself an Adept, which was supposed to be a position only just below that of High practitioner.

Jovvi sipped her tea in silence, trying to make sense of what now lay before her. The practicing she would soon do had a purpose, she couldn't be more certain of that. But the nature of the purpose was hidden behind requirements without explanation—and statements apparently designed to raise thoughtless protest.

Like their short discussion about the second practice building. Jovvi had the very strong conviction that she was supposed to have protested the idea of creating unbalance; that would have shown she felt concern over others, the strength of her protest indicating just how strong that concern actually was. They could have been looking for a sense of humanity, but if that was so then why had Genovir seemed so pleased when Jovvi hadn't displayed one? And Genovir *had* been pleased, Jovvi had felt that clearly, but the emotion hadn't seemed personal.

So Genovir probably wasn't making an estimate of Jovvi for purely personal use. She was supposed to look for certain qualities, but ambition wasn't one of them. The thought of that hadn't set well with the Adept, but that part of it *might* have been personal. The woman was guarding herself in an effort to keep from being read, but not particularly well. There was a good chance she would soon relax, and then Jovvi would be able to get a better idea of what was going on.

But in the meanwhile Jovvi would have to watch what she said and did. The day was growing brighter and more pleasant, an external outlook that didn't quite match Jovvi's inner one. She still had to find out how strong was considered too strong, and how weak too weak. Playing that balance was the only thing that would let her move forward in relative safety—until she reached the end of whatever line it was that she walked.

"Are we ready to begin now?" Genovir asked with the pleasant patience that was beginning to grate on Jovvi. They'd both finished their cups of tea, and apparently having a second cup wasn't part of the grand plan.

"Oh, yes, I'm quite ready to begin," Jovvi answered, then stood as Genovir did. She had to remember to be eager about some things, not so eager about others. And she had to remember that she was supposed to be nearly penniless. Her cache of gold was quite safe where she'd hidden it, but it had to be forgotten about. That meant she had to earn at least one more silver din before week's end, but would that be considered adequate progress? Assuming she found herself able to move ahead rather quickly, just how quickly should that be allowed to happen?

Jovvi sighed as she followed Genovir onto the path leading to the first of the small, round resin buildings. The next days weren't likely to be pleasant, not in the least. . . .

FORTY-ONE

Rion left the coach without a backward glance, still too wrapped up in his plans and feelings to be able to concern himself with those around him. Especially when things didn't seem to be going well for the others. Tamrissa and Vallant Ro appeared to have had some kind of falling out, and there was a definite . . . distance between Jovvi and Lorand Coll. Perhaps the ladies now regretted having given their attentions to other men rather than him, but that possibility had to be shelved for the moment along with the rest.

This time there were no guardsmen to bother with, so Rion walked through the opening in the resin wall. Beyond lay an open area which wasn't terribly large, then an expanse of ordinary tables and chairs, and then a stretch of lawn broken only by stone paths. Two small, round resin buildings stood beyond the lawn to the left, and two similar but larger buildings stood to the right. There was nothing to say what any of the buildings were for, and that annoyed Rion.

"Good morning," a voice said, and Rion turned to see a man approaching him. The man was dressed plainly but rather well in blue trousers, a pale green shirt, and a light gray vest, but the expensive clothing would have looked better on a thinner man. This one obviously enjoyed indulging himself at the expense of his waistline, and even through sleeves his arms looked fleshy rather than muscular. A half beard circled his mouth and matched the brown of his hair, all of that ordinariness working to camouflage the sharp look in his dark brown eyes.

"I'm Padril, the Adept assigned to assist you," the man said, stopping to give Rion a quick inspection with those eyes. "I see they were right, and your name *is* incorrect on your identification card. I'll arrange for a proper one immediately, and—"

"No," Rion interrupted, outrage suddenly beginning to grow in him. "My correct name is just as you see it on *this* card, and it's not to be changed to anything else. You may tell whomever else is involved that that decision is final."

"They're certain to find that pronouncement confusing," Padril said, now looking at Rion with curiosity. "Apparently someone made quite a fuss over the mistake, and insisted that it be corrected at once. Now you tell me there *is* no mistake, and nothing's to be changed. I'm afraid explanations will be demanded before the matter can be resolved."

"As far as I'm concerned the matter is already resolved," Rion answered, his tone quite chill. "You may tell those people that I'm a grown man, and therefore completely capable of deciding what my name will be. If someone appears and disputes the correctness of that name, they need only refer the someone to me. No one's word is to be taken in this matter above mine."

"I doubt they'll be pleased, but I'll certainly pass on what you've said," Padril assured him, faint amusement behind the words. "Now that we've settled *that* misunderstanding, let's take a cup of tea and discuss what you're here for."

The man gestured toward one of the tables, then led the way over to it. Rion followed, watched as Padril paused to ring a bell hanging on a post before taking a seat, then took his own seat. By then a servant was coming toward them from behind a wall to the left, already carrying a tray with a pot and cups.

"I requested the tea just before you arrived," Padril explained while they were being given cups and then having the cups filled. "We take lunch and refreshment at these tables, and ringing a bell will bring you immediate service. It goes a bit more slowly at lunchtime, when most of us are here at the same time, but the wait never stretches beyond reason."

Rion nodded and sipped at the hot tea until the servant had left, then he gestured to the buildings.

"That, I take it, is where the goings-on go on," he said, trying to lighten his mood. "Do any of the buildings relate to one another, or do they all have separate purposes?"

"The two small ones are for practice, the two large ones for competitions," Padril replied without hesitation. "There are also two sorts of competitions for each segment, which I'll explain about shortly. You're not fond of idle chitchat, I take it. Most newcomers avoid the topic of what's to be required of them until their Adept guide insists on discussing it, but you've brought it up yourself. I would guess that this name thing has really upset you."

"You find it beyond reason that I'm merely eager to get on with things?" Rion countered, leaning back just a little in his chair. "An applicant's ultimate aim is supposed to be the achievement of a High position, and I've never heard of the position being awarded to someone shy and retiring. But perhaps I'm mistaken, and the reticent *are* the ones who achieve the glory."

"No, you aren't mistaken," Padril admitted with a chuckle. "The positions do indeed go to those most able to take and defend them. But my own position requires that I be certain the applicant under my wing is able to do his or her best, and in your case I'm not certain at all. Are you unaware of the fact that inner turmoil can and does interfere with the full use of your talent?"

"Truthfully, I've never heard that," Rion said, and the words *were* the truth. He'd never heard anyone discuss the subject, but his own observations didn't match the conclusion. A week earlier he would have said so without hesitation, but now some newly-awakened sense of caution made him keep the matter to himself.

"The connection between personal distress and a lessening of ability is quite well documented," Padril assured him with a sincere expression both on his face and in his eyes. "You must dismiss all other concerns when you engage in operating at this level, leaving your mind clear to concentrate on what's before you. If you tell me about the problem troubling you, it will not only make you feel considerably better, I'll then be better able to act on your behalf. If I can, I'd like to see to it that you're not troubled again."

Rion hesitated, uncomfortable with the thought of unburdening himself to a stranger, but there was no real harm in doing it. Padril would most likely find himself helpless before Mother's determination, but possibly one of the man's superiors would not be the same.

"If you can keep me from being troubled again, you'll undoubtedly be set on the Fivefold Throne all by yourself," Rion finally allowed with a wry smile. "I've recently decided to . . . exert my independence as an adult, and my mother dislikes the idea intensely. She's been insisting that I retain the name she gave me, but I find only the last part of it acceptable. I even had the identification card changed, and don't intend to allow it to be changed back again. But Mother does wield a good deal of power, so the battle won't be easily or quickly over with. If I were you, I'd seriously consider staying well out of the affair."

"It sounds as though that would certainly be the wisest course," Padril agreed, equally wry. "Mothers can sometimes be so unreasonable where their children are concerned. And when they have power as well . . . The temptation to withdraw is certainly there, but I'm afraid

I'll have to ignore it. Your potential value to the empire is a good deal greater than your mother's, so we have no choice but to support your stance rather than hers. Does knowing that ease your mind at all?"

"Actually, it does," Rion admitted, surprised to discover that he wasn't lying. "If you can keep Mother from distracting me, I should be able to give you a showing that will make you glad you did. And since that *is* supposed to be what I'm here for, things would work out quite well."

"Having something to point to before my superiors would help a good deal," Padril admitted in turn, now studying Rion thoughtfully. "Suppose I describe what will be expected of you, and then you give me an estimate of how quickly you think you can accomplish each thing."

"Go ahead," Rion agreed, now even more eager to get down to details. If these people could be gotten *actively* on his side, his problem with Mother might be solved rather more easily than he'd imagined.

"As I mentioned, there are two buildings for practice," Padril said with a nod for Rion's agreement. "In the first you will have six other people besides yourself, and you'll need to practice keeping them and yourself supplied with air to breathe while the room is being filled with smoke or some such that would make breathing difficult. At first the six will be together, but then they'll separate, first into two groups, then three, then they'll stand individually. How long do you think it will take you to accomplish all that?"

"Not long once I get the hang of working with more than three groups," Rion answered honestly, remembering the test he'd survived. "Learning comes rather easily to members of my class, after all, so I anticipate very little trouble."

"Good," Padril enthused, leaning forward just a bit with a warm smile on his face. "And for each milestone you master, you'll earn another silver din. But the achievements in the second building bring two silver dins each, and that's the place most applicants have the most trouble. Someone like you, though . . ."

"Won't have any trouble at all," Rion finished happily when the other man's voice trailed off. "What's involved that so many people have difficulty with it?"

"In a manner of speaking it's just the reverse of the first building," Padril said, still obviously approving. "You'll need to *take away* the air from about the six people, first with them standing in a group, to the end where they stand individually. It's really quite simple, so I don't understand why so many have trouble with it."

"They must have been members of the lower classes," Rion commented, already elated over what would soon be a major success. "And you need have no fear at all, since I've already practiced that little trick with two people and had no trouble at all. Six will simply take a bit more concentration and effort."

"Marvelous," Padril breathed, leaning back again with shining eyes. "You've already practiced what many of those sharing our aspect are unable to manage at all. You certainly will be worth an enormous amount to the empire, and I feel privileged to be the one who will assist you. When you reach the competitions—But I haven't described the competitions yet, have I? What a fool I am, to be so easily distracted by magnificence."

"And that's where the gold is paid," Rion said after joining Padril's self-laughter. "We must certainly *not* forget about the competitions."

"Oh, you'll undoubtedly soon be swimming in gold," Padril said with another laugh, then leaned forward again. "The first competitions are merely time trials, you and the others of your level working to see who can do the most the fastest. You'll certainly win there rather easily, and then you'll face others of your new level in true competition. Each of you will try to take the other's air while keeping your own, and at each stage more people will be added to 'your' side. When you win *there,* the gold will really begin to flow."

"I can hardly wait," Rion said, leaning back in his chair while visions of true independence flowed lazily through his mind. His power and importance would exceed Mother's rather than simply equaling what she wielded, and his happiness would thereafter be assured. No one would dare to tell him what to do or when and how to do it, and his protection of the sweet and lovely Naran would be personal and constant.

"I'm glad you were first to mention waiting," Padril said, bringing him back to the currently-real world. "I, too, can hardly wait to see what you'll accomplish, so what say we finish our tea and get you started, eh? The sooner begun, the sooner on to greater things."

"Yes, you're absolutely right," Rion agreed with a grin, then he finished his tea in a single swallow and stood. "First we begin, and then on to greater things."

Padril actually left his tea and simply rose, the man's entire countenance and demeanor showing how pleased and satisfied he was. It felt odd to have a stranger show such deep emotions where *he* was concerned, but Padril obviously knew a man of quality when he saw one. And soon he would see one accomplishing marvels. . . .

Rion followed Padril toward the first building, happier and more at ease than he'd ever felt in his life.

FORTY-TWO

I left the coach before Jovvi, and my relief at not having to worry about any more conversation with her just about balanced my nervousness about what lay ahead. I'd worried about that—during the few, brief periods when I hadn't been thinking about Vallant Ro.

As I walked toward the opening in the resin wall, I tried to understand why Jovvi would defend the man. During the time he and I had spent together, he'd just about sworn that I was the only woman he'd ever found any real interest in. I'd let myself forget that other people couldn't be trusted, and I'd started to believe him—and then that woman had arrived. I'd suddenly realized that he must have told *her* the same exact things, and that I'd been a fool to even consider believing him. And what hurt the most was that Vallant Ro had put me in a position where my father could embarrass and humiliate me. Again.

Just inside the smoky resin wall was an open area, with

tables and chairs arranged to the left and cubicles of some
sort about fifty feet ahead. To the right of the cubicles and
another fifty feet beyond them stood a round building made
of milky-white resin. The arrangement looked ordinary
rather than threatening, and even the cubicles were mostly
open and larger than what we'd used during the sessions.

I stopped a short way past the entrance wall and stood
looking around, wondering where I was supposed to go next.
There wasn't another living soul in sight—until a woman
came out from behind a wall to the left, beyond the tables
and chairs. She wore a yellow skirt and white lace blouse,
seemed to be close to her middle years, and strutted rather
than walked. As she came closer I could see that her face was
mostly unlined, but wore an expression of . . . assured arrogance, I suppose you could call it. Her brown hair and eyes
were unremarkable, but her attitude said that could only
matter to someone else, not to her.

"Good afternoon," she said rather dryly, stopping about
five feet away to look me up and down. "It's about time you
got here."

"I got here when the coach did, whose arrival I had no
control over," I answered immediately, trying to ignore how
fast my heart had begun to beat. "And this is the morning,
not the afternoon, but don't bother correcting yourself.
Whichever, it isn't particularly good."

"So you're not as much of a little priss as you look," she
said with something of a shrug, her tone lightening just a bit.
"That will make you easier to live with, but don't expect us
to ever be bosom friends. I don't like your sort, and I'm only
associating with you because I've been assigned to do it. I'm
Soonen, your Adept guide, and you'd better remember what
I say because I don't intend to repeat myself."

"Say it clearly the first time, and you won't have to," I
countered, really disliking the woman. "And what do you
mean by my 'sort.' What sort is that?"

"The sweet and pretty little girl sort," she returned,
looking me over a second time. "Your kind never gets anywhere, because it's so much easier to stand there acting
helpless until some male fool rushes over to take care of
things for you. And don't tell me that that's the way you were
raised to behave. It's not a reason, it's an excuse."

"So what's *your* excuse for judging people according to

your own prejudices?" I came back, beginning to be too angry to be nervous any longer. "I *was* raised to be helpless and do as I was told, but that never quite agreed with me. For that reason I now do as *I* like, and don't wait for *anyone* to do things for me. If I can't do them for myself, I practice until I *can* do them. You—"

"Okay, enough," Soonen interrupted, raising both hands palms toward me. "You talk a good game, but that doesn't mean you can actually do anything. We'll get this tour routine over with, and then you can put your power where your mouth is."

Fuming is too calm a word to describe how I felt, but I still lapsed into silence. I did want her to finish up what she described as a "tour," and then maybe she would leave. If she didn't and accidentally got singed at some point, it wouldn't be *my* fault.

"These tables are where we take our lunch and any refreshment we might want," Soonen continued, waving a hand without looking toward the objects she discussed. "There are bells on the posts scattered through the area, and when you want service you just ring one of them. Now come this way."

She turned and walked toward the cubicles, heading for the one on the far left. There was at least twenty feet between the last of the tables and the cubicles, and when I followed Soonen to the first of them I found out why.

"This is where you'll practice," she said, now gesturing to the small rooms which had no ceilings. Some of the others farther down the line also had no back wall, but this one had clear resin closing it in. "The exercises aren't anything like what you've already done, because by now you ought to be able to handle your flames without any trouble. Now you have to learn to handle them along with other things."

She turned away from me and walked into the cubicle, then stepped down hard on the end of a long lever. The lever was attached to a wide box, whose lid flew open to allow a shower of dirt to be thrown up into the air. The cloud of dirt spread out even before the lid closed again, but it never got the chance to settle down onto the floor of the cubicle. There were suddenly flames all through the cloud, and when they disappeared there wasn't a speck of dirt left.

"Burning dirt isn't easy, but if even one grain falls to the floor you haven't mastered the ability," Soonen said, turning again to look at me with malicious amusement. "There's a technique to doing it, but that's something you'll have to discover yourself. I'm not allowed to tell you what it is."

That might or might not have been the truth, but I wouldn't have begged her help even if I'd needed it. That seemed to be what she was after, wanting me to humiliate myself in order to be told what I had to know. The only flaw in her plan was that I'd already seen what she'd done, having touched her flames automatically with my talent to get a closer view, so to speak, of what was going on. Visually it didn't seem like it, but she'd woven her base fires the way we'd learned to do during the sessions.

"Now, in this second practice area you'll find something different," Soonen went on, walking into the next cubicle. "And if you thought burning dirt was hard, wait until you try this."

This time the lever she stepped on ran up the righthand wall and was attached to a metal tank of some sort suspended above the cubicle. Stepping on the lever opened small holes in the metal tank, which immediately began to leak a fine mist of water. Soonen released the lever and then reached out with her flames again, but this time with a different pattern of weaving. Burned water usually turns to steam, but once her fire had swept through the shower of droplets there was nothing left whatsoever.

"And that's the way it has to be done," Soonen said, looking at me with even more smugness. "Producing any steam at all is a failure at mastery, since any fool can produce steam. Now come in here."

She moved from the second cubicle to the third, which had a pile of wood in the middle of the floor. Each piece in the pile, about a foot in length, was carved into a different shape, and all the shapes and pieces were jumbled together.

"Can you see that long oval in the middle of the pile, the one with a splotch of orange paint?" Soonen asked, pointing toward a piece that was almost completely buried in the midst of the others. "Well, the object here is to burn that piece to nothing but ash—without touching any of the other pieces. The smallest singe mark anywhere else will be considered a failure, but you'll just practice until you get it right—won't you?"

"Yes, I will," I returned through my teeth, her ridicule

immediately grating on my temper. "But why don't you really show me how good you are, and do the exercise rather than talk about it? You did the others, after all, so why not this one?"

"It so happens I'm not in the mood to go after another marked piece of wood," she answered with the same smile, only her eyes showing an instant of raging hatred. "If I destroyed this one I'd then have to bury its replacement in the pile, and I'm not in the mood to dirty my hands either. Let's move on to the next rooms."

She brushed past me in a very firm way, closing the subject of her doing the exercise in a flat and final manner. But her back had stiffened quite a lot, showing she suspected that I knew the truth—which I did. This marvelous and high-level Adept who thought so little of me *couldn't* do the exercise, not the way it was supposed to be done. I'd thought I'd felt her straining with the first two exercises, but decided I was imagining things—until she simply described the third.

"These following rooms are variations on the third, with progressively more delicate—and flammable—materials," Soonen said, pointing into the next cubicle without looking at me this time. "Here you'll find wedges of leather, then strips of cloth, and finally a pile of feathers. Mastery there will require you to burn one single feather of a particular color at a time until ten are done, with your examiner pointing out which feathers to burn when."

"And will you be my examiner?" I asked, mostly to keep from showing how appalled I felt. Ten *feathers*, one at a time? How was anyone supposed to do *that*?

"No, I'm not an examiner," Soonen answered, an edge of bitterness to her tone. "Our aspect has twice or more the number of women than it has of men, but the examiners are still all male. Not stronger or better, just male. How are you supposed to prove what you can do if none of them will give you the chance?"

I almost told her that waiting for someone else to give you a chance was the same as refusing to try because you weren't sure you could do something. I was hardly the possessor of the world's greatest amount of self-confidence, and trying even when you aren't sure is horribly difficult. But it has to be something *you* do, something you make up your mind to try even if you're sure you'll fail. No one can decide on that for you, just as no one can give you a chance. You must find your own chances, or live your life without them.

"You don't have to worry about the last set of exercises until you master these first ones," Soonen continued, now sounding a shade angrier than she had. "They're a repetition of the first set, with the addition of an Adept, in this case me, trying to burn your delicate little toes while you perform each exercise. You must learn to defend yourself while doing something else with your talent, and this is the best way to make an applicant understand the need."

"Best for whom?" I couldn't help asking, noticing at the same time that her mood had improved. Anticipating all that fun must have done it, fun that I had to fight to keep from shivering over.

"Why worry about something you probably won't ever have to face?" Soonen asked, disparagement heavy in her voice and manner. "You're too pretty to actually accomplish anything, and the men will be able to carry you only so far. After that you'll be off the hook, and then you'll be able to relax."

"Does that mean you've decided not to discuss the competitions?" I countered, now fighting to keep from losing my temper completely. "It's always possible that some fluke will occur and I'll master these exercises in spite of your expert opinion to the contrary, so why not humor me and tell me what I'll need to know."

"You *won't* need to know it, but I'll tell you anyway," she said with a sound of derision, the look in her eyes dismissive. "The first of the competitions is you against your level-peers, just like in a foot race. Strength, speed, and ability are what you need to win, but what you win is the interesting part. The prize is the chance to face someone a good deal stronger, this time one against one rather than everyone against the competition itself. The more advanced competitors can kill you, and worse, you might even break a fingernail."

"What about the gold?" I choked out, more furious than I could ever remember being. "We were told we'd be able to win gold, but no one said it would take so long to reach a position where it's possible. What are we supposed to meet our obligations with in the meanwhile?"

"Oh, didn't I mention that?" she asked, laughing at me silently. "I suppose it slipped my mind with everything else we discussed. Every time you master one of the first segments, you'll earn a silver din. If you move on to the second set it will be two silver dins a segment, but you can most likely forget about that. You won't get even as far as the third segment in the first set."

"Why not?" I demanded with matching ridicule and my fists on my hips as I looked up at her. "Just because *you* didn't? What makes you think I'm as backward as you are?"

"We'll see who the backward one is," she growled, now showing all her hatred in her eyes. "You won't get anywhere at all, and when that happens I'll laugh."

"And if it doesn't happen, you'll burn," I said in my own growl, then realized how close I was getting to losing control. I couldn't let that happen, especially not in that place, but with that woman around it wouldn't be possible to calm down. "But at the moment I can use a cup of tea, so why don't you run along back to wherever you came from. If I need you I'll ring a bell."

She began to snarl something, changed her mind, then simply stalked off looking like a thunderstorm about to happen. I had the definite impression she'd wanted me to start the exercises immediately, before I'd regained control of myself. If I'd died pulling in more power than was wise because my judgment had become impaired, she would have been able to cross me off her list of those who might do better than her if left to their own devices.

Well, that wasn't going to happen. I walked back to the area containing tables and chairs, rang one of the bells, then sat at a table. I would have my cup of tea and regain control over myself, and then I would start the first of those exercises. I didn't yet need the silver din I would earn with each mastery, but by next week's end I would. I'd be much happier having the silver *before* I needed it, and that's why I was eager to start. To earn the silver, not to prove something to that stupid woman. . . .

The servant who appeared actually brought a cup of tea with him, expecting me to sip it while I waited for whatever else I wanted. He seemed disappointed when I said that the tea would do fine, and he returned behind the wall a good deal more slowly than he'd come out. Once he was gone I forgot about him, concentrating instead on regaining full control of myself. Men didn't interest me, neither servants nor applicants in Water magic, *especially* applicants in Water magic. I'd decided not to listen to any of them ever again, and I'd stick to that.

I had no need of anyone to protect me, and I meant to prove it. There might have been a faint tremor in my hand when I lifted the teacup, but that didn't matter. I'd show *all* of them that I needed no one other than myself, I *would* . . . I *would* . . . I *would* . . . !

FORTY-THREE

Vallant spent most of the coach ride sunk deep in agitated thought. He'd fully expected Tamrissa to show *something* in the way of reaction when he told her the truth, even if that happened to be accusing him of lying. That he could have coped with, but her absolute refusal to hear him had been the most frustrating experience of his life. How do you cope with being turned invisible by the woman you've discovered you don't want to get along without?

If someone knew the answer to that, it wasn't Vallant. When the coach finally stopped beside a metal representation of the Water symbol, he still hadn't thought of anything. But Holter was leaving the coach, so he had no choice but to do the same. Mardimil had already left without Vallant's noticing, and he himself was outside with the coach beginning to move before he realized he hadn't said anything to Coll. It wouldn't have hurt to wish the other man good luck, and then he might have even gotten the wish returned. . . .

But the opening in the milky-white resin wall didn't seem to lead *into* anything but more outside, so Vallant followed Holter with only the smallest hesitation. Just beyond the wall was an open space, with tables and chairs arranged to the right. Straight ahead about fifty feet away was a line of odd-looking cubicles, and unless Vallant was mistaken there were no back walls or ceilings to them. That came as an incredible relief, even with the presence of a large, round, white resin building visible a short distance beyond the cubicle. It might be possible to avoid going into that building, at least for a time.

"One fer each a us," Holter murmured, and Vallant looked around to see what he meant. Two men were coming toward them from behind the wall beyond the tables and chairs, and Holter's commenting on their approach probably showed how nervous the small man was. Vallant didn't blame him, especially since the two approaching were a mismatched set.

They were both dressed rather well, but the smaller and heavier of the two looked as if he were wearing someone else's clothes. Discomfort over clothing not yet gotten used to often produced that rumpled, ill-fitting look, and the lopsided grin the man wore did nothing to improve the image.

The second, thinner man wore a faint smile as well as showing greater self-confidence, but he also gave the impression of holding himself away from his companion. As if to avoid contamination, Vallant thought, which meant he was too late by years. His smile showed he'd already been contaminated by the assumption that he was better than the crude sort of man ever could be, which made Vallant sigh.

"Copper to gold I know which of those is meant for me," he murmured, loud enough for no one but Holter to hear him. "I'd also be willin' to trade him for the one who's yours. Would you like to trade?"

Holter glanced at him with the first true amusement Vallant had seen him show in days, but a firm headshake accompanied the amusement. Holter wasn't stupid, which meant Vallant was stuck with the thinner man. Vallant sighed again, which made Holter chuckle, and then the thinner man had reached Vallant while the other drew Holter aside.

"Good morning and welcome," the man said, his voice deep and melodious and somehow out of place. "I'm Wimand, the Adept assigned to show you around. Your companion will be seen to separately by Podon, as we've learned that group introductions to our precincts are most often less than successful. We'll sit and have the tea I've already ordered, and I'll tell you what we're all about."

"My friend doesn't seem to be havin' tea," Vallant observed as he followed Wimand to the table the other man had gestured toward. "He and Podon are goin' straight to that first cubicle on the left, and Podon is tellin' him somethin'."

"He's telling him about what each of the practice rooms is used for," Wimand replied as he sat, his smile completely unperturbed. "Those of the common class usually have very little patience, so we routinely let them go through the tour first. I promise you it won't make any difference, and in a short while you and he will be taking turns using the rooms—for as long as he can keep up, that is."

"What makes you think he won't keep up?" Vallant asked as he watched a servant approach with a tea service. "Holter and I were in the same session, and he's had no trouble keepin' up until now."

"It's rather sad, but it *is* a fact of life," Wimand replied, letting the servant pour tea for them and leave before continuing. "Yes, it's very sad, but lower class applicants never get very far beyond this point. Success depends on strength, and strength very often depends on self-assurance. They know they're not as good as we are, you see, and that knowledge defeats them every time. But let's discuss the things *you* must know, like what Podon is about to demonstrate."

Vallant turned to look at the other Adept without comment, but not because he had nothing to say. He simply knew how useless it was to argue with a man's prejudice, especially one that involved self esteem. Those who spent time talking about how inferior others were, were actually saying how afraid they were that *they* were inferior. Finding something different that couldn't be denied—like having been born into a lower class—let these people feel superior without their ever having to do anything to prove the contention.

"That first exercise room and the one next to it have the same purpose, but use different methods," Wimand explained. "Your task will be to create spheres of water around first one group of objects and then two groups, and then more all the way up to six separate groups. The first room has a large vat of water for you to work with, but in the second you'll need to draw your moisture from the air."

The man Podon was in the midst of demonstrating the thing to Holter, and Vallant could see that six head-sized globes of water had been created around six round forms of resin standing on movable pedestals. The exercise wasn't particularly easy, but it would certainly be easier than drawing the necessary water from the air.

"The next set of rooms contains oblong boxes of the sort bread is often kept in," Wimand went on after sipping at his tea. "In each of the two rooms you'll be able to see the boxes, and you'll need to put a globe of water inside each of the boxes. You'll begin with doing one box at a time, then two at a time, and then move all the way up to six. As with the first set of rooms, one will have a vat of water, and one won't."

"How will I be able to tell if I've positioned the water properly?" Vallant asked, watching Holter and his Adept guide move on to the second set of cubicles. "Seein' it leak from the bottom of the box won't tell me if half the globe ended up on the far side, and only *seems* to be comin' out from the inside."

"If you see any leaking before pulling the release cord, you haven't done it properly," Wimand explained, gesturing to the two who now stood staring at an oblong box. "The inside of each box is made to funnel the water into a holding dish with a false bottom, and pulling the release cord springs the bottom. But the funneling into the dish will happen only if you position the globe properly, otherwise you'll get leakage from the sides. Again, only one of the rooms contains a vat of water."

"Why do you have those duplicate arrangements?" Vallant asked, the oddity finally taking his notice. "Anyone able to do the exercises by taking moisture from the air should be able to do it with a supply of ready water even more easily. I can understand startin' with the two different methods, but why keep on with them?"

"For the most part it's a question of flexibility," Wimand responded smoothly, giving Vallant the strange impression that the explanation was . . . prepared. "We've discovered that having applicants practice in only a single way makes them forget there *is* another way, which I'm sure you'll agree is rather limiting. The rest of the reason is that taking so much moisture from the air is far from easy, and most applicants do better when they begin with ready water. Ah, see? That's what the box does when the sphere is properly placed."

Vallant turned back to see that Podon had pulled on a rope, and water was obediently pouring out of the box and into a bucket. He wondered just how large the proper area inside the box really was, but didn't ask. Once he began to practice, he'd certainly find out.

"The third set of rooms is naturally the hardest," Wimand commented with a small chuckle. "If you watch, you'll notice that Podon will explain to your companion about it, but won't demonstrate. That's because he can't, of course, not without using more power and concentration and effort than he cares to show in front of an applicant. This exercise is the one he never quite got the hang of."

"What's so complicated about it?" Vallant asked, making no mention of the fact that Wimand hadn't yet done *any* of it. He talked a good game, but sitting back and smirking at someone else's efforts isn't the same as bettering those efforts.

"The fact that the boxes are hidden behind curtains makes the exercise harder," Wimand replied, surreptitiously watching Vallant closely. "You must use your power to locate the things before you can put spheres of water in them, and the box sizes get progressively smaller behind the curtains. Anyone who reaches the point of being able to fill the smallest size using nothing but air moisture *deserves* to move on to the competitions."

"Ah, the competitions," Vallant said, turning his head to look directly at the so-called Adept. "That's what I've been lookin' forward to hearin' about, since that's where the chance to win gold lies. What's involved there, and how long will I have to starve before I get a chance to try it?"

"Oh, you won't starve while you're practicing," Wimand assured him with a chuckle. "You'll be paid a silver din for each exercise you master using ready water, and two dins for the exercises using air moisture. That should keep you for a short while at least, and then you should be up to the competitions."

"They're held out here, where the practicin' is done?"

Vallant asked casually, as if the answer were completely unimportant. "There's certainly enough room for everyone to watch whatever goes on."

"What goes on first is a general competition, where applicants show what they're capable of," Wimand said after reaching over to pour more tea in his cup. "Strength, use of ability, and amount of time elapsed are the deciding factors in choosing a winner, and those you strive against are your skill-level peers. The winner, however, goes on to face someone from the next level up, and that contest is you against your opponent directly. And there may be enough room out here to hold the competitions, but we prefer to be a bit—more formal. They're all held over there, in that round white building."

"I thought that was probably what it was for," Vallant commented as casually as possible while his insides turned over. "But I haven't even begun the exercises yet, so the buildin' won't concern me for some time. And speakin' about the exercises, when can I get started?"

"As you can see, your companion has returned to the first room," Wimand said, annoyance in his tone as he gestured. "Podon was to have gotten him to take tea now so that you might begin first, but the man appears to be unusually obstinate. I can speak to him myself if you like, and possibly point out the merits of sitting with his feet up until after lunchtime."

"No, don't bother," Vallant told him with a wave of his hand. "I don't mind beginnin' after lunch, and by then Holter should be glad to take a breather. I suppose he and I will just have to take turns for the rest of the time we're here."

"Only until the man reaches his limit," Wimand reminded him with a smirking smile as he stirred in his chair. "I know that won't take very long at all, so your patience will soon be rewarded. Right now we could use another pot of tea, and perhaps a few sweet cakes to keep it company."

The Adept rose and went to a nearby post to shake a rope attached to a bell, and by the time he'd returned to his seat a servant was already on his way over to them. The tea and cakes were ordered and then Wimand began to chat about nothing of importance, which let Vallant listen with half an ear while his mind worked on other things.

The most pressing thing was the realization that in order to compete, he would have to enter a building without windows and stay in it for an indeterminate time. On most scales the building was fairly large, but on his own private scale it was tiny and airless and would be suffocatingly confining. He'd want out of it even before he walked inside, so how was he supposed to compete? Compete and win, that is. Competing and losing would be all too simple.

Vallant smiled and nodded to whatever Wimand happened to be saying, privately wishing it were possible for him to hide somewhere. He *had* to compete and win if he wanted to keep up with Tamrissa, as the girl would find *some* way to win even if she had to half-kill herself to do it. Vallant had no doubts about that, any more than he doubted his own ability. If the competitions were held outside, nothing would keep *him* from winning either.

But they weren't held outside, and he had to sip from his teacup to hide the bleakness that touched him at that thought. First Tamrissa refused to acknowledge him, then he was saddled with a prejudiced fool as a mentor, and now this devastating news about the competitions. On some level he'd known it would probably be that way, but he hadn't wanted to think about it. No competitions meant no advancement, which would put him in the same class as the fool Wimand.

That thought held only for an instant, and then Vallant had to work to keep himself from stiffening. Wimand and the other Adepts worked with applicants, but after this week's end there would *be* no more applicants this year. That would put the current Adepts out of work, so the testing authority wasn't likely to take on any others. What, then, would happen to those applicants who didn't advance? The question had been asked before, but suddenly it had become a good deal more imminent.

". . . and you really must try the fish here for lunch one day," Wimand was saying while he examined the sweet cakes which had been brought. "It's absolutely marvelous, but that's only to be expected. Successful applicants will certainly become very important men, and no one would wish to get on the bad side of a very important man."

Vallant agreed with a smirk to match Wimand's, but privately he seethed. The applicants would *not* all become very important men, some would become very important women. Wimand's prejudices weren't just class oriented, obviously, and Vallant felt as though the fool had deliberately insulted his Tamrissa. She would reach the *exact* place she wanted to be, and anyone who tried to get in her way would have *him* to deal with!

It took something of an effort for Vallant to calm himself, and in some odd way it didn't work completely. A small part of him had become fired up by the anger, and that part had made a decision. Somehow, some way, he was going to qualify for those competitions, enter them, and win. And after that he would have a talk with Tamrissa, one she would *not* be able to ignore. And maybe that talk ought to come first, while he was in the midst of accomplishing the rest. He didn't need the distraction of their not getting along; what he needed was her.

Having made that decision caused Vallant to sit a bit straighter, and even to smile to himself. The prospect of forcing a potential High in Fire magic to listen to him wasn't one he should be looking forward to, but insanity had obviously claimed him. He couldn't wait to get Tamrissa alone to try his best, and if he ended up singed . . . or even burned to ashes . . . wouldn't that be better than having to live his life without her?

Vallant smiled again, knowing there was no question about it.

FORTY-FOUR

Lady Eltrina Razas walked into the room beside Lord Ollon Kapmar, enjoying the way the others jumped to their feet at sight of him. Ollon was one of the most powerful men in the entire empire, and he was never handicapped by sentiment. He always did what was necessary without hesitation, no matter who it was he had to do it to. It was said he'd once had the woman he was sleeping with removed, simply because she hadn't handled some matter as well as she should have. That made sleeping with the man even more deliciously exciting for Eltrina, although there was really no risk at all for *her*. She had always handled matters perfectly, and also always would.

"You may be seated," Ollon said to the others once he and Eltrina were in their chairs, hers the first one to his right. There were still more than a dozen liaisons present, although by meeting's end that number would be lessened as more files were closed out. Looking at Ollon's strong handsomeness, the man still broad-shouldered and vital despite the gray in his blond hair to match the gray in his eyes, Eltrina wondered how most of the others could be eager about no longer needing to report to him.

"It always pleases me to reach the final week of categorization," Ollon told them after leaning back in his chair, letting his cold gray gaze touch each of them in turn. "There will be no further applicants arriving until after the beginning of the new year, and then this process will start all over again. Some of you will find it possible to pursue other interests until then, and I do believe I'm beginning to envy you. Twenty-six years of seeing this through to its ever-surprising end has grown rather nervewracking in my old age."

Eltrina joined the others in giving him the polite laughter his joke had called for, a variation of the same joke they said he made every year. This was the first time she'd heard it personally, but she'd certainly chuckled over it secondhand before. An ever-surprising ending to the sorting out indeed.

"We'll begin with those of you who have closed out the residences you've been responsible for," Ollon said once the laughter had ended. "You may submit your final reports and then leave."

Four people, three men and a woman, rose to come forward clutching their reports. One by one they handed over the paperwork, told Ollon it had been a pleasure working with him, and then they'd made good their escape. For supposed members of noble families, their craven behavior annoyed Eltrina no end. But at least the girl was gone, which was quite a relief. Among the remaining ten there were only three women, and Eltrina was now the most attractive of them.

"This year our efforts have a double purpose," Ollon said once the four had left and closed the door behind them. "In most respects it will be business as usual, but I caution you again to keep in mind that this is a twenty-fifth year. There must be an absolute minimum of five challenging common Blendings to match the five put forward by our noble brothers, so you mustn't waste anyone capable of being put into one. Begin thinking now about which of your charges will be saved, and which will be fed to our Seated Highs."

"Sir," one of the younger men said, raising a questioning hand. Eltrina recognized him from parties and such, but couldn't remember his name. "I still have three residences filled with advanced applicants, but I'm told that most of them won't even make the competitions, much less win in them. Two or three of them have the proper temperament to make adequate Adepts, but the rest I'd expected to send to my father. I happened to see him last week's end when he came home for a brief visit, and he mentioned that he needs them."

"I'm aware of your father's needs, Lord Kogrin," Ollon replied, frowning at the situation rather than at the man he spoke to. "He took the opportunity to visit me as well, but there's only so much I'm able to do for him. A twenty-fifth year finds us short in many areas, and we can do nothing other than cope. For instance, we have more than enough Adepts right now. Use the best you have as members of a Blending and substitute the ones you would have used as Adepts to challenge the Seated Highs. The Highs have been cautioned to destroy only the very strongest of their challengers, leaving the rest alive to help fill our other needs. Does that sound workable to you?"

Young Kogrin nodded and settled back in his chair already sunk in thought, obviously having no idea how ridiculous he was being. This was Ollon's *second* twenty-fifth year, which meant his suggestions had little need of being approved by a child. Everything would work out just as it was supposed to, adding another marvelous triumph to Ollon's record.

"All of you have written reports, I know, but I'll need an oral summary for my own preliminary report," Ollon continued after sipping at the cup of tea which servants had provided before the meeting began. "I have an appointment with one of the Advisors this afternoon, after which he means to leave for a few days of personal enjoyment. By the time he returns everything will have been settled, and I'd very much like to tell him then that nothing but small details need be added to my report. Lady Eltrina, you may begin."

"Of course, Lord Ollon," Eltrina replied with her best smile, privately laughing at the others. They would now be terrified of giving Ollon incorrect information, but she had nothing of the same to worry about. "I still have four residences under my wing, and I've already begun to rearrange them with an eye toward this being a twenty-fifth year. I expect to have at least one full Blending to offer for the Grand Competition, possibly two."

A murmur went through those seated at the beautifully polished oval table of gray wood, a sound of surprised dismay which widened Eltrina's smile only on the inside. Some of those present had fairly powerful relatives, and it simply wouldn't do to flaunt her superiority.

"Most of those in my residences have already completed their sessions, of course," Eltrina went on as though unaware of the reaction she'd caused. "Six of the remaining ones might well qualify today, and I've put them in a single residence together. If they do qualify, they'll already be settled in and will simply go on to the practice sessions. If they don't, their disposition will be the same as any of the others who haven't managed to qualify."

"What if some qualify and some don't?" Lemmis Admen asked in the nasal whine she used for a voice. The woman was horse-sized in both face and body, had the frizziest hair Eltrina had ever seen, and considering the clothing she usually wore, was probably colorblind. If Lemmis had been the least bit intelligent she would have kept her mouth closed unless it was absolutely necessary to speak, but what she said usually showed how little intelligence the horsy thing had.

"I mean, it *is* possible some of the six will qualify and some won't," Lemmis whined defensively when Ollon moved his gaze to her. "I don't intend to rearrange my residences until after today, when I'll know for certain which will be which. You never do know for certain until it happens, you know."

"And yet, with the help of the sessions Adepts, it's possible to make educated estimates," Eltrina replied smoothly once

Lemmis ran down. "Most of the six are expected to qualify, so no more than one or two will need to be moved again. All of my residences now contain at least one of each of the aspects, which was the main reason I took the opportunity to move people around. After the dust of final decision settles, I'll know just what I have in the way of possible Blending members, and what I'll need from the rest of you to round them out."

This time there was more of a muttering to be heard from the others, low vocal resentment that she had managed to get a jump on them. If she was properly organized while they were not, she would end up above them all.

"Has anyone else arranged the same thing in their residences?" Ollon asked, looking around at them blandly. "No? Well then, the organization of the next phase indicates itself. We'll use the lady Eltrina's established base, and supply her requirements before any other dispositions are made. You'll also show her the compositions of your various residences, and she'll choose one to house a full Blending. When she does, the residence will be added to the four already . . . under her wing."

Ollon smiled when he said that, which kept the others at the table quiet despite their displeasure. Eltrina had managed to become his second in command, and it was no longer possible for any of them to stop her.

"Now Lady Eltrina will tell us about the possible Blending she mentioned a moment ago," Ollon continued, moving his smile to her. "Are they all quite marvelous and strong, with an excellent chance of winning the Fivefold Throne?"

"What else?" Eltrina responded with a laugh, one which some of the others joined in. "They *do* happen to be strong, and all six in the residence have passed the first step in qualifying for the competitions. The one duplicate aspect is Water, and I haven't yet decided which of the two to include in the Blending. One of them is a low-class peasant who doesn't fit in with the other four at all and knows it, but the second has quarreled with the female representing the Fire aspect."

"And you'll certainly choose the one most likely to make the most trouble," Ollon said with an approving nod. "Tell us about all six, and why you consider them such excellent candidates for membership in a challenging Blending."

Eltrina glowed, only a short step from preening herself. Ollon was letting *her* tell the others what to look for, intimating that she knew and they didn't. If there hadn't been people present who were close to her husband, she might have kissed Ollon.

"These people are suitable only for being in the same Blending," she explained, looking around at the others with a half smile. "Each of them is quite strong in his or her aspect, and we certainly wouldn't want them where their strength could be fully utilized. The first Water candidate I mentioned, the low class one, is bitter because he's been rejected by his former cronies and just doesn't feel comfortable with his new acquaintances. He'll keep a certain amount of himself back from any Blending, causing it to be considerably less than an effective whole."

"And the other one?" Ollon prompted after nodding his approval. "Is his argument with the Fire female the only strike against him? If so, I would certainly assign him elsewhere. Arguments have been known to be made up."

"That's the beauty of it," Eltrina told him with an amused laugh. "It doesn't matter whether he makes up with the female or not, because he has a personal problem that may well cost him any victories in the competitions. It was noticed after his test that he was desperate to get out of the testing building, so he was watched during the sessions. He was terrified every moment of the time he spent in the sessions room, and couldn't wait to get outside again. He can't bear to be enclosed, so how deeply into a Blending do you believe he'll be able to go?"

Her only answer was matching laughter, sharing the delicious joke. No one with a disability like that could *ever* become a full member of a Blending, and that no matter how strong he was.

"Now, the female with Fire magic is another story," Eltrina went on after the laughter had quieted. "She's attempting to avoid another forced marriage by pretending to be strong and fearless, but only her Fire talent is strong. She herself is a fearful little thing who came close to attacking someone with her ability, showing how uncertain she is and how lacking in adequate control. The leading aspect of any Blending is always the Fire talent, who has to be the strongest and steadiest of the lot. This particular leading aspect will surely panic, and lead the others into wasting their strength before any real danger approaches."

Ollon nodded and smiled while the others murmured or chuckled, so she took a sip of tea and continued.

"The Earth magic member is a backwoods clod who seems to be terrified of burning himself out. He's managed to qualify so far, but his fear makes him hesitate in a way that will ruin the balance of the others. The Air magic member is that ridiculous son of Hallina Mardimil, the one she always bores everyone with when she drags him to parties. Until now he's been incapable of thinking or doing anything for himself, but she's finally pushed him into rebellion. He's in the process of declaring himself a grown man, and has even discovered the difference between boys and girls. Between that and the persistence Hallina will show trying to get him back under her thumb, he probably won't even notice what else is happening about him."

The laughter was much more raucous and ridiculing this time, as Hallina had inflicted her doltish offspring on all of them at one party or another. It served her right that she was now having trouble recovering him, as he never would have been assessed strong enough for testing if she'd excluded him the way she should have.

"You haven't yet mentioned the last member of your Blending," Ollon prompted, obviously as amused as everyone else. "Does he or she have a similar personal problem?"

"No, Lord Ollon, the young lady doesn't," Eltrina replied, smiling only to herself as she avoided his trap. "Even those tiresome neutral judges would notice if *every* member of a challenging Blending had personal problems, so the Spirit magic member is the one who seems to be completely well adjusted. She's the one who will represent the group in public, and the others *look* perfectly normal. It's the balance I think every challenging Blending should have."

"And so they shall," Ollon agreed, sending her a personal smile before giving his attention again to the others. "Make sure Lady Eltrina is fully informed about every applicant in your residences, most especially in the matter of the sorts of problems she's mentioned. All five of the challenging Blendings must *look* capable, but we certainly don't want them to be anything but handicapped. Do any of you have questions for Lady Eltrina or myself? No? Then let me ask a question you've heard before, but one which is still supremely important. Have any of you seen even a hint that one of your people may be one of those mentioned in the Prophecies?"

A muttering ran through the group as they exchanged bothered glances, and the resulting headshakes looked tentative and unsure. Ollon had just asked the question they'd all been worrying about, but personally Eltrina had decided that the fuss was really covering nothing real. She had no idea who had decided that the Prophecies were true, but they must have been senile or stupidly innocent to believe in them. None of *her* people could possibly have fit the requirements, so her headshake was firm and positive when Ollon looked at her.

"That's something of a relief," he said when he had denials from all of them. "We expected to begin seeing people matching the first Prophecies by now, and the fact that we haven't is beginning to change the minds of some of us. Not everyone believes that the Prophecies will come true, but those who do are more powerful than those who don't, so we'll certainly continue to watch. And each of you is to report anything at all that might support an appearance. Is that clear?"

This time the nods were much firmer, more like the one Eltrina had already given. They were afraid of those who supported the idea, and would be happiest when the time was past and no one was able to claim they'd missed a vital clue.

"Very well then, let's get on with what we're here for," Ollon said, turning his attention to one attendee in particular. "Lord Miklas, would you do us the courtesy of being next with your verbal report?"

The tiresome Miklas began to drone out his report, but Eltrina had no need to listen. The man would end his speech by summarizing everything he'd said with the brevity he should have used in the first place, and Eltrina would be able to listen then. In the meantime she leaned back in her chair with her teacup between the fingers of both hands, and simply enjoyed the heady flavor of success.

Yes, success at last. Eltrina breathed deeply with the pleasure of the thought, knowing she'd finally found her proper footing. One day soon she would have Ollon's position, and when that happened she'd also have the power to rid herself of the tedious bore she'd been forced to marry. Then she would be free to do as she pleased, but first she had to prove her brilliance by making all of Ollon's plans go as he wanted them to. Just that, with her as his fully-acknowledged second in command, and then it would be time for a terrible accident to befall poor Ollon. . . .

Eltrina smiled to herself as Miklas droned on, then she made a deliberate effort to listen to the man. She intended to know everything necessary, so that nothing would ruin her plans and Ollon's. *Nothing* would go wrong, not with all the preparations she'd made, and then, after the unfortunate demise of all those challenging Blendings, she'd have her reward. She'd earned it, she deserved it, and soon she would have it. . . .

Those of you reading this in what we consider the future must now be wondering just when I'm writing this account. The others didn't want me to say, but how can you decide how to take it without knowing that piece of information? I don't think you can, so I'll tell you—in a way. I don't want you to picture me sitting in the Palace of the five, grandly writing our history after we won the day. We've done only a little winning, and the most important battle is still ahead of us. Before the day of facing that comes, we wanted to put down everything that's happened until now.

Because chances are good that we won't survive. The Prophecies say that we're needed to win, not that we will win. There's a big difference there, and every day that passes brings us a better understanding of that difference. Thinking about it is enough to make some of us ill, so that same some of us try not to think about it. Great lot of good it does. . . .

But I still haven't come really close to what the five of us consider present day, so I'd better continue with this. The opposing five we ultimately came up against were already together and getting ready for us, but happily we didn't know that. We had other problems, big and small, and the first thing to happen was. . . .